I0769270
Charmed,
I'm sure.

Cover by Chelsea Chira with Sterling Dawn Art & Design

Illustrations by Jessica Hoffa via Canva

Editing by Samantha Swart (www.samanthareadsspicy.com)

First edition 2025

ISBN E-Book:

ISBN Paperback:

Contents

To everyone who felt like they never fit in.
The ones that like their hair as colorful as their language and wield
sarcasm like a weapon.
Magnolia is for you.

Author's Note

Hey, hi, hello!

The Witches of Bellevue series came to me late one night while I was still writing my very first book. I had the names of my characters, the location it would take place, the plot lines for the first two books figured out in a matter of days, and the first chapter written shortly thereafter.

Charmed, I'm Sure started as a passion project, one that I would flit back and forth to when I needed a break from my fantasy series, and quickly became my heart's work.

I wrote this book while moving states. While struggling through solo-parenting while my husband was deployed, the death of my Poppie, and my Mom's cancer diagnosis.

I poured so much of myself, my friends, and my experiences from growing up in Louisiana into this book—and the series as a whole.

It is by far my favorite thing that I have written, and I hope that it brings you joy.

So, without further ado, welcome to Bellevue. Or as we say in Louisiana, Bienvenue én Bellevue.

Xoxo,

Jessica

Glossary and Pronunciation Guide

Andouille: *aan-doo-ee*; a spicy pork sausage seasoned with garlic, used especially in Cajun cooking.

Bayou: *bi-you*; a marshy outlet of a lake or river in the South

Beau: *bow*; old way of saying 'boyfriend', also means 'handsome' in French

Beignets: *ben-yay-z*; a square of fried dough eaten hot, sprinkled with confectioners' sugar.

Belle Amour: *bell uh-moor*; beautiful love

Boudin: *boo-dan*; a spicy, rice-and-pork sausage that is a staple in Louisiana

Buggy: shopping cart

Cher: *sha*; means "dear" or "sweetheart"

Chile: ch-i-ll; child

Daiquiri: *da-kr-ee*; a slushie-style cocktail made with rum, lime juice, sweetener, and ice, blended together. These can be found throughout Louisiana and come in many varieties.

Geaux: *go*; a Southern way of spelling 'go', especially in context with the LSU Tigers

Git: means "go"

Gumbo: a spicy chicken or seafood dish thickened typically with okra or rice.

Houma: *ho-muh*; a city in Southern Louisiana

Laizzes les bon temp rouler: *lay-say le bon tom roo-lay*; means "let the good times roll" and is a common phrase used throughout the South, especially during Mardi Gras

Pain au Chocolat*: pan oh sho-co-lah;* bread with chocolate

Rougarou: *roo-ga-roo*; a Cajun legend similar to a werewolf that lives in the bayous of Louisiana

Roux: *roo*; a cooked mixture of flour and fat (butter, oil, etc)

Sauce Piquante: *sauce pee-kah-nt*; refers to a spicy, tomato-based sauce, often used as a gravy or sauce for meats

Zydeco: *zai-da-ko*; popular music of southern Louisiana that combines tunes of French origin with elements of Caribbean music and the blues and that features guitar, washboard, and accordion.

Prologue

22 years ago...

IT WAS AN UNUSUALLY cold day in January when all of Louisiana was hit with a freak snowstorm. Cities all around the state shut down because—well, it's the South. We don't get snow very often. It's like hurricanes hitting New York City—rare. Unfortunately, that didn't stop my parents from having to go to work.

They both worked at a local hospital, and since most people can't even drive in the rain, icy roads made for treacherous journeys. Sometime after midnight, they were on their way home when a car in the opposite lane hit a patch of black ice and hydroplaned. My dad swerved, trying to avoid a collision, but the other car slammed into them, throwing them through a bridge railing and into the river below. They didn't make it home that night...or any night after.

I was eight, my sister Madison was six, and little Meredith was only three.

The only family we had left was outside New Orleans, so we packed up and moved from Baton Rouge to Bellevue.

Bellevue, a tiny town with one stoplight, giant oak trees, and even bigger gossips. Known for its strawberry and crawfish festivals, gumbo competitions, and the "witch" who lived in Bellevue Manor. That so-called witch just happened to be my Aunt Evangeline. And it wasn't until my sisters and I moved in with her that I learned the quotations my mom always put around the word were unnecessary.

Aunt Evie was young and fun. With hair flowing down to her waist and dyed the color of a firetruck, she looked a lot like Jean Grey from X-Men—just with bell-bottom jeans, cut-off band tees, and an amethyst pendant dangling from her neck.

She took us in without batting an eyelash, going from footloose and fancy-free to Auntie-mommy with two kids in school and one who had just gotten the hang of using the "big potty."

But from the moment I walked into that house, my life changed.

Her house was full of plants and books, love, and *magic*.

I felt it the moment I stepped through the large teal door of Belle-vue Manor, a tingling sensation brushing against my skin, like it was saying, "Hello, nice to meet you at last."

It felt like coming home, even though I had never been there before.

Madison had felt it, too. She'd tugged on my hand, her eyes wide as she turned to me. "Mags, do you feel that?"

Aunt Evie let out a low laugh behind us when I nodded. Squatting down to our level, she pulled Meredith between her legs and grabbed both mine and Maddie's hands. "My sister," she began, clearing her throat as she blinked back tears, "was an amazing woman. And though she wasn't ready for you to know about this part of our family just yet, fate and the Mother had other plans. You have magic, little ones. Beautiful, blessed magic. And this home, and all within it, is our legacy. *Your* legacy. Welcome home, little witchlings."

As the last word fell from her lips, flecks of light, like fireflies, danced around our heads, forming tiny crowns.

And despite myself—despite the fact that I had just lost my parents and the only home I had ever known—I smiled. Madison joined me, and even little Meredith giggled.

Home. We were home.

1
Dear Maria, count me out.

Magnolia

Present Day...

OH, FUCK ME.

Sophie Larson was practically skipping toward me as I slipped the key into the door of *CharCutie*, dragging some poor soul behind her. The sun was bright behind their heads as they made their way down the sidewalk, so I couldn't see his face, but good gravy, that man was tall. Towering a good foot over Sophie's head with a seemingly good head of hair and well-toned legs that went on for days, there was no way he didn't have a face to match. But it was the tightness in his broad shoulders that pulled my focus. Poor guy looked more anxious than a long-tailed cat in a room full of rocking chairs, probably desperate to be rescued from little Miss Shrill.

"Maggie!" The excitement in her voice grated against my nerves like nails on a chalkboard as she hollered my name again.

Groaning, I finished unlocking the door and turned toward her, a manufactured smile plastered on my face. I couldn't stand the woman. She was the head cheerleader in high school and had made it her sole mission in life to make me feel the size of an ant—something that hadn't changed after high school either.

I silently thanked the Mother as a cloud rolled in front of the bright sun, then promptly retracted it and cursed her instead as my lady boner shriveled up and died. Taylor mother-fucking Hallows. The bane of my existence in high school and my sworn enemy—not that he knew that. I was pretty sure he didn't remember me or the torment he and his cronies put me through during their final year at Bellevue High.

"Maggie, you remember Taylor Hallows from Bellevue High, don't you?" Sophie beamed at him like he was the fat, prized pig that had won the blue ribbon at the fair. Pig? Yes. Fat? Pretty sure his body had never heard the word.

Squinting, I canted my head to the right, pretending to give a shit. "Can't say that I do."

As the words left my lips, Taylor's gaze lazily perused down my body before settling back on my face. A small smirk tugged at his lips as he extended his hand. "Taylor Hallows, pleasure to meet you."

My eyes flicked from his face to his outstretched hand, then back again, before I slipped mine into his. "Magnolia Bellevue, the pleasure is all yours."

His smirk grew a fraction, but he didn't release my hand. "I believe you mean, 'the pleasure is all mine,' Ms. Bellevue."

He practically purred the words, and it took a great deal of effort not to roll my eyes. Instead, a sickly sweet, Southern-belle, bless your heart smile spread across my face as I stared him straight in the eyes. "That's what I said, Mr. Hallows. The pleasure is all *yours*."

Sliding my hand from his, I pulled open the door to my little shop and stepped inside, leaving Sophie standing there with her mouth gaping open like a big-mouth bass, and Taylor looking like he was still trying to figure out what had just happened.

The cool air of *CharCutie* kissed my cheeks—thank god for air conditioning, since Louisiana still hadn't gotten the memo that it was supposed to be fall. I flipped the switch by the door, sending the fluorescents flickering to life. After pulling my phone from my back pocket and connecting it to the sound system, I scrolled through my Spotify playlists, deciding what kind of vibe I wanted today. I listened to a little bit of everything, from Kelsea Ballerini and Luke Combs to Queen and ELO, or Paramore and MCR. After the encounter I'd just had outside, it was definitely a Paramore kind of day. The Mother—or maybe it was just irony—had a sense of humor, as *Ignorance* by Paramore filtered through the speakers.

It was early, and with the blinds still down on the front windows, I sent tendrils of magic throughout the space, flipping the switches in the display cases and turning on the large neon sign that read Cheese! which hung on a wall of fake greenery in the "photo-op corner" at the front. I had just finished starting up the POS system when Jaelyn, my best friend and only employee, walked in from the back. *CharCutie* was technically owned by me and my sisters, but they let me run it however I wanted, and they pitched in when I needed help... or when they were bored.

"Morning, bestie!" she trilled as she plopped her slouchy bag on the counter.

"Morning, sunshine." My tone was light, but there was an edge to it that she could've picked up all the way in Georgia.

Jaelyn narrowed her caramel-colored eyes, tilting her head slightly before her expression shifted, her lips pursing as she nodded. "Rough morning? Or is this just the vibe for today?" she asked, gesturing to my outfit.

Like my music, my outfits reflected my mood. Today it was black cutoff shorts—despite the fact that it was October—a cropped tee that read Caffeinated, but dead inside, and my Jadon Dr. Martens.

"It's just today's vibe."

Her dark brows shot up to her hairline, her expression saying she wasn't buying anything I was selling.

"Okay, fine. It started as a vibe... then slowly became a mood."

"Oh?" she asked, pulling her phone from her bag. "What happened? It's not even ten a.m."

Rolling my eyes, I huffed my way into the back of the shop, Jae following to help with opening duties. "I ran into Taylor forking Hallows this morning. Well, more like had his unwelcome presence thrust upon me by none other than Sophie Larson herself."

When the swish of her maxi skirt stilled behind me, I turned, finding her rooted to the spot, her eyes the size of a cheese wheel. "I'm sorry... you ran into *who*? What in the fuck is that douche canoe doing back in town? I thought he left to go do... fuck if I know. I just know he wasn't here anymore."

I couldn't help the laugh that bubbled up my throat at Jaelyn's outburst. She'd been there for me through the thick of Taylor's torment in high school. Whether it was them knocking my books out of my hands, the endless jokes about my clothes, or his cronies following me around making Chewbacca noises because I didn't shave my arms, Jae had been there through it all. She even tried to convince me to get Aunt Evie to hex him after his group "accidentally" spilled coffee all over my pale blue dress before an awards ceremony, staining it muddy brown. It was meant as a joke, but since my aunt was the town "witch," I knew she actually could... and I'd even considered it for a brief moment.

"I don't know why he's here, or why Sophie felt the need to let me know, but seeing his smug mug was not how I intended to start my day," I said, pulling out a stack of orders for the day.

CharCutie was my baby. After going to community college in Baton Rouge for two years and realizing college wasn't for me, I traded the campus for a kitchen, enrolling in the Louisiana Culinary Institute. Sixteen months later, I graduated with an Associate's in Baking and Pastry, moved back to Bellevue, and started *CharCutie* from Aunt Evie's kitchen. Meshing my love for aesthetics, culinary pairings, and bite-sized foods, I created a charcuterie board business.

Like most small businesses, the first year was slow, but it ever so gradually picked up—especially after I added dessert boards to the lineup. Who knew swirls of buttercream, chocolate, pastries, and fruit would be what put me on the map? Three years later, with help from my sisters, I opened my own brick-and-mortar shop, taking orders daily for personal and party-sized platters.

After splitting the orders between morning and afternoon pickups, I started pulling ingredients from the walk-in cooler while Jae assembled the boxes.

An easy quiet settled around us as *Dog Days Are Over* by Florence + the Machine filled the speakers. Soon enough, we were both singing along, albeit horribly off-key, and dancing around the kitchen. Was it the most efficient way to prepare orders? Probably not. But it was fun and lifted my mood instantly.

That was, until the bell chimed over the door, and I turned to find none other than Taylor Hallows standing in my shop.

·))●((·

Taylor

The bell over the door of *CharCutie* chimed as I pushed it open. Sophie had explained that it was a charcuterie board shop as well as a bakery, and I had to admit the "cutie" part of the name threw me for a loop. But standing inside, it made sense. It looked like a 1950s diner, with black-and-white checkered tiles on the floor. Every wall was bright pink and covered in vintage signs—except for the one behind the counter, which was robin's-egg blue and filled with black-and-white photos of Bellevue throughout the years. There was also a greenery wall with a neon sign that read Cheese!

Cute.

I was just about to take a step toward the glittery teal vinyl booths that lined the far wall when Magnolia turned. The smile on her face faltered before she pulled it back into place and stepped out of the kitchen, her hands tucked securely in her back pockets.

"We're not open yet."

God, this woman. I'm pretty sure she intended for the smile on her face to look friendly, but the bite in her tone said otherwise.

"You should probably keep the door locked then, huh?" I smiled. She bristled.

Her eyes narrowed as she took me in, and I had to keep from laughing when *I'd Do Anything* by Simple Plan came over the speakers. At least I knew she had good taste in music, unlike most of this town.

A smile tugged at her lips, but it was so sickly sweet it made my teeth hurt. "Is there something I can do for you... sorry, what was your name again?"

I angled my head to the side in question, taking her in bit by bit. Magnolia Bellevue. She hadn't changed much since her freshman year of high school. Still rocking the grunge-goth look, except now, her hair was anything but natural, and she seemed to be covered in tattoos. Pink and blue strands were piled into a messy bun on top of her head, looking like pulled-apart cotton candy. Intricate lines of ink cascaded down her arms and along one of her thighs.

I'd seen her around town for years leading up to high school. She was cute in her own way, confident—you had to be when people threw words like "witch" at your family—and I'd always admired that. I even hoped she'd remember me, but now, I wasn't so sure I should've wished for that.

High school had been rough for me until senior year when puberty slapped me upside the head with a two-by-four. I went from dorky kid to hot jock and felt like I was trapped in that movie, *Can't Buy Me Love*—only I didn't pay the popular girl to date me; I just happened to pack on some muscle and get contacts the summer before senior year. The problem was, I was still me. Still the nerd who loved comic books and Star Wars. Still excelled in academics. My looks were the only thing that changed, but with that, so did the crowd that wanted to be around me.

Unfortunately, that crowd also took a liking to picking on Magnolia. And though I never directly did anything to her, like an idiot, I did nothing to stop it either. I'd been in her shoes, and having just stepped out of them, I did everything I could not to climb back in.

The sound of snapping pulled me out of my thoughts, and it was then I noticed she had crossed the room, and it was her making the noise.

"Helloooo, anyone in there?" she asked, her head cocked and brows raised.

"Sorry," I said, rubbing the back of my neck. God, I'm an idiot.

"Did you forget your name in the last—" she glanced at her wrist, where she most certainly did *not* have a watch, "what, forty-five minutes?"

My brows shot up before a smirk tugged at my lips. "Why is that so hard to believe? You certainly seemed to."

A look of clear indignation crossed her face, her cheeks turning pink as her eyes widened and lips pursed. Inhaling through her nose, she plastered that fake smile back on. "Is there something I can help you with?"

"Actually, yes, I'd like to place an order. I hear you do dessert boards?"

Magnolia nodded, rolling her eyes as she made her way behind the counter, grabbing what looked like an order form from a rack against the wall. Did I need a charcuterie board, let alone a dessert one? Absolutely not. But I was enjoying ruffling her feathers.

Grabbing a pen from the cup on the counter, she clicked it open, and the sound echoed through the room. Her overly sweet smile returned as she turned to me. "Name?"

"Taylor Hallows, but you knew that."

"Did I?" Her brows furrowed slightly, but there was also a small smirk on her lips she was trying to hide. "What size were you looking for? Personal or party? And if it's a party, how large is the gathering?"

"Uhhh... personal?" I meant it as a statement, but it definitely came out as a question. Who knew there were so many options for putting food on a board?

Magnolia continued to run through the form, asking about preferences, allergies, when I needed it, etc. When she finished, she finally looked up to meet my gaze. "Anything else I can do for you?"

Before I could answer, someone walked into the main space, her hands full of trays of pastries. "Need any help out here, Mags?" she asked, her eyes flicking between *Mags* and me.

"No, we're just about done here," Magnolia said, before turning back to me. "If there's nothing else—"

"There is." Her eyes narrowed infinitesimally at my interruption. "Go out with me."

Something like a laugh mixed with a scoff escaped before she could stop it, and her hand flew to cover her mouth. "I'm sorry... *what?*"

"Go out with me."

"You're joking, right? Weren't you just with Sophie?"

"I ran into her while walking through town," I said with a shrug.

"You don't even know me."

"Hence me asking you out. To get to know you."

"Well, first off, you didn't ask. It was more of a demand. Secondly, Mr. Hallows—"

"Taylor."

She blew out an exasperated breath. "Fine. *Taylor*, no."

"No?"

"That's what I said. You do know what 'no' means, right? And that it's a complete sentence?" Her tone was cocky, like it was the highlight of her day to turn me down. And maybe it was, but I smiled anyway. She was no longer the meek, quiet girl who walked the halls of Bellevue High. No. Magnolia Bellevue had grown claws since the last time I saw her, and she kept them sharp.

Pushing up from where I'd leaned against the counter, I turned toward her companion, who was desperately trying to focus on her task despite overhearing everything. Her eyes were wide as she carefully placed confections in the glass case next to the counter. "Those look good."

The woman flicked her eyes up to mine, offering a terse smile as she nodded.

"They are, but unfortunately, we aren't open yet, so you'll have to come back once we are." Magnolia's voice drew my attention back to where she stood at the register, tapping away at the screen. "Your total is $50 plus tax, which brings it to $54.50. We take a fifty percent deposit upfront, and you pay the rest when you pick it up."

When she looked up at me, her expression dared me to argue with her prices. Fifty dollars for a board of deconstructed cake and fruit? Ridiculous. Did I pull out my debit card anyway? Yes. Yes, I did.

After she handed me my receipt, I headed toward the door. No need to stay and embarrass myself any further. I cast a glance back toward the counter as I pulled the door open, but Magnolia was already back in the kitchen, dancing along to *Dear Maria, Count Me In* by All Time Low, the volume rising as the door closed behind me.

2

The Firefly

Magnolia

PULLING UP THE GRAVEL driveway that led to Bellevue Manor never got old. It was lined with towering oak trees on either side, their branches so dense they wove together to form a canopy over the ground. Even this close to Halloween, the trees were lush, thanks to a spell Aunt Evie had cast over the flora.

I put my sunshine-yellow Xterra in park, hopped out, and sent a wisp of magic toward the carved pumpkins lining the steps. The tiny tealights inside flickered to life, illuminating the intricate designs and standing out against the growing darkness.

"Aunt Evie? Maddie? Anyone home?" I called as I stepped through the door, a rush of magic tickling my skin as the house welcomed me home.

As I pressed the door closed behind me, the soft jingle of bells announced the family familiars' approach. "Hey, guys! Meowfoy, you're looking dapper today in your jack-o-lantern bow tie. Very festive. And, Hermeownie, did you get brushed today? Your coat is extra shiny." Both cats trilled in response, bumping against my shins, each caress laced with meaning. *I'm hungry, feed me.* Every press of their heads was a link to their minds, their thoughts filtering through my consciousness as though they were speaking aloud.

"Evie's in the greenhouse tending the lavender plants. Mama Jo called—she needs more for Samhain, and she's out with the influx of tourists," Hermeownie, our orange Maine Coon, informed me through our connection.

"Maddie's in the study working on her latest novel. Asked not to be disturbed," added Meowfoy, our snow-white Maine Coon.

Stooping down, I scooped Meowfoy into my arms and rested my forehead against his fuzzy head. "Has she at least eaten today?"

He purred, but through our mental link, told me she hadn't.

"Well, alrighty then," I said, setting the familiar back on the floor. "Time to pry her out of her world and bring her back into this one. But first, I need to talk to Aunt Evie."

Behind the manor were beautiful gardens and a small pond, home to a few fish whose species I could never remember. Beyond that stood Aunt Evie's greenhouse, brimming with lavender, chamomile, and rosemary. Though our small coven used it, most of the herbs were sent to Mama Jo in New Orleans.

I pushed open the door to the glasshouse and spotted Aunt Evie kneeling in the dirt, clipping sprigs of lavender and placing them in her wicker basket.

"Close the door; you're letting the bugs in," she chided without turning around.

Chuckling under my breath, I stepped fully inside and sealed the door behind me. "You and I both know that's not true."

She shrugged, placing her shears in the basket before turning my way. "What's up, Magpie?"

Leave it to my aunt to combine my name with my love of baking and come up with a bird as a nickname. "Nothing much. Hermeownie told me you were cutting sprigs for Mama Jo. Did you need me to make a run down there for you?"

Mama Jo ran *Crescent Witchery* in New Orleans, a tiny occult shop in the French Quarter that catered to tourists and natural witches alike. We supplied most of the herbs she used for her smudge sticks and teas.

"Would you? I don't want to put you out."

I knelt beside her, picking up her shears. Lavender was my favorite scent—its magical properties for happiness and healing were just an added bonus. "I don't mind at all, as long as you don't mind me hanging out for a day or two to spend Halloween with Jae on Bourbon Street?"

Jae had asked me earlier if I wanted to go with her. We used to go all the time, but now we could only make it when Halloween fell on a Friday or the weekend.

Aunt Evie sighed, shaking her head as a small laugh slipped out. "Magpie, you're thirty years old. You don't need to ask me if you can party in New Orleans."

A huge grin spread across my face, but it quickly fell when she pinned me with her *mom look*.

"But you need to find a safe place to stay. You know the veil is thinner on All Hallows' Eve. I don't need you accidentally—or intentionally—stumbling upon something wicked. You catch my drift... pick up what I'm putting down... smell what I'm cooking..."

I couldn't help the laughter that bubbled up. "Yes, yes, I got it. Geez, stop with the cheesy metaphors."

"Good. Now go drag your sister away from her computer before she gets square eyes."

"Aunt Evie... you know that's not a real thing, right? You told us that when we sat too close to the TV as kids, but come on."

She shrugged. "Same difference. You knew what I meant. Now scoot." She wiggled her fingers at me, waiting for her shears.

After handing them over, I pressed a kiss to her cheek and left her to her pruning, heading inside to find my sister.

→)❯●❮(←

Maddie hated when anyone disrupted her writing. She always claimed she couldn't get back into the same groove, ruining the process. I, of course, called bullshit, since I interrupted her all the time, and her books were still amazeballs.

She might have grumbled some—okay, a lot—but I knew that, despite the complaints, she'd pull herself away from whatever fictional world she was building when I needed her. And tonight was one of those nights. So, after I promised to leave her alone for the rest of the weekend—and bribed her with homemade cinnamon rolls—she threw on a sweater and jeans, tossed her chestnut locks into a high pony, and slapped on a smile.

Neon signs advertising beer flickered against the blacked-out windows of *The Firefly*, the only bar in town. Its owner just so happened to be one of my favorite people... even if he barely tolerated me.

As soon as we walked through the door, Jordan Davis's *Almost Maybes* hit the speakers. A smile spread across my face as I sidled up to the bar. "Raayyyy," I sing-songed, dragging out his name.

He rolled his eyes, wiping down the bar in front of where Maddie and I sat. "What do y'all want?"

"Hey now, Ray, no need to be sassy," Jae said, stepping up behind us.

"Oh great, the whole gang's here tonight. I still don't understand why y'all insist on calling me 'Ray.' You know that's not my name."

Maddie snickered beside me, hiding her grin behind her hand.

"Your name is Trey... Ray could be a nickname for that," Jae said, leaning against the bar with a cheesy smile.

"It's not." Ray's tone was flat, his expression unchanged as he stared us down.

I shrugged, pulling out my debit card and punch card, setting them on the bar. "Ever seen *Princess and the Frog*?"

The blank look on his face gave me my answer.

"Well, there's this little firefly in the movie, and his name is Ray. So, tomato, potato. You own this bar; you're Ray now. Can I get a large 190-Octane, please?" I flashed him my best Southern Belle smile, but he just rolled his eyes and snatched my cards off the counter.

"And y'all?" he asked, nodding toward Maddie and Jae.

"I'm DD tonight. Mags had a bad day at work," Maddie replied.

"A large strawberry, please!" Jae chimed in, bouncing on her toes.

After Ray returned with our daiquiris, he handed me my cards, and we headed to our usual table near the dance floor. It was still early for a Friday night, which meant we had time to let the liquid courage kick in before the line dancing started. We knew the dances, but that didn't mean it wasn't intimidating to get up in front of everyone else and do them.

We'd been there a few hours, dancing along to songs we knew, but when *Thick as Thieves* by Lauren Alaina and Lainey Wilson came on, Jae squealed and jumped up. "Come on, Mags! Maddie!" she whined, grabbing our wrists and pulling us toward the dance floor, where rows of people were already lining up.

I groaned, rolling my eyes as I reluctantly followed her out past the rail that framed the floor, Maddie dragging her feet behind me. It didn't take long for us to fall into step with the rest of the group. Every heel clicked in sync on the wooden floor, whoops of excitement filling the air as we spun and added our own flares.

I was having the time of my life—until *he* walked in.

Until sapphire eyes behind tortoiseshell glasses locked onto mine. For the third time in one day, Taylor Hallows was invading my space.

Taylor

As soon as I walked through the door, I spotted her cotton candy hair in waves down her back, standing out like a beacon among the mundane. But I forced my feet toward the bar and ordered a drink. She was smiling, and I'd be damned if it wasn't brighter than the moon on a clear night. The moment the dance spun her to face me, though, that smile vanished, replaced by a mask of pure annoyance.

It seemed there was more to Ms. Bellevue than I had originally thought. She'd traded her cutoffs and snarky tee for dark, high-rise bell-bottom jeans and an ivory off-the-shoulder sweater that let her tattoos peek over the neckline. A complete contrast to the dark grunge look from earlier. A softer side. Despite that, her hardened glare burned its way into my soul.

Deciding that looking like an idiot twice in one day wouldn't kill me, I pushed away from the bar and crossed the crowded space to the dance floor.

"Maggie," I greeted when I stood in front of her. Crystalline blue eyes, with sunbursts of gold, locked onto me as her friends stood behind her in solidarity, arms crossed and lips pressed into thin lines.

Magnolia rolled her eyes and huffed. "It's Mags or Magnolia, never Maggie."

"But Sophie—"

"Sophie's a two-bit nobody who needs to mind her own damn business," chimed in the friend from the shop earlier.

"And you are...?" I asked, raising a brow.

"Jaelyn Jackson. We went to school together... but you probably don't remember me, since you and your cronies were too busy being asshats and bullies." Jaelyn's eyes narrowed, and if looks could kill, I would've been ash and dust. It seemed I had my work cut out for me with more than just Magnolia.

Smiling, I turned my attention to the other woman. "I suppose you hate me as well?"

She tilted her head, lips pursed in contemplation. "Hate's a strong word, Mr. Hallows. I'd prefer 'loathe,' 'despise,' or 'wouldn't blink if you happened to disappear.'" Her smile curved like the Cheshire cat's, sending a chill down my spine. I rubbed the back of my neck to shake off the feeling.

A nervous laugh escaped as my eyes flicked between the women. "So, uh, might I have the name of the person probably planning my demise?"

"Madison Bellevue."

"Ah. Makes sense."

An uncomfortable silence fell over our small group, but Magnolia's gaze flicked up toward the ceiling as a new song started playing. A smug smile spread across her face as her eyes returned to me. "Fitting, don't ya think?"

"What is?" I asked.

"The song," she gestured toward the speakers. "It's called *My Bar* by Priscilla Block."

I couldn't help the grin tugging at my lips. That was the second time today she'd sassed me into silence.

Magnolia: two

Me: zero.

As people paired off and began two-stepping around us, two men I didn't recognize swooped in to ask Madison and Jaelyn to dance. They agreed, but only after Mags said she could handle me on her own. The way she said it, with eyes lit with fire and a wicked grin on her lips, had my blood heating. I was in deep shit.

She turned on her heel to leave, but she didn't get more than a few steps before I was in front of her again. I smiled sheepishly when my brain caught up with what my feet had done. "Dance with me?"

"Why would I do that?"

"Why wouldn't you?" I flashed my best smile, but she only quirked her brow as if to say *you're joking, right?*

"Aww, bless your heart—"

My heart dropped. Not bless your heart. I'd almost prefer her telling me to fuck off. Bless your heart was worse. So much worse.

"You and your cronies made my life a living hell. Why would I give you the time of day?"

"Ah-ha, so you do remember me."

"Excuse me?"

"This morning, when Sophie introduced us, you said you didn't remember me. Clearly, you do." Magnolia crossed her arms over her chest, shaking her head as her eyes rolled. "It's just a dance, Magnolia. We're already on the floor. Humor me." I extended my hand and waited.

Her eyes narrowed, and just as she opened her mouth to respond, a large man came up behind her and wrapped his arm around her shoulders. "Everything alright here, Mags?"

Something like shock crossed her face before she leaned into the embrace. "Yeah, Ray. Everything's fine. Taylor here was just leaving."

"Taylor?" Ray asked, not moving from Magnolia's side.

"Taylor Hallows," I offered, extending my hand.

Ray simply looked me up and down, sucking on his teeth. "Right. Well, let me know if you need anything, or if pretty boy here gives you any trouble, alright?"

Pretty boy? Good lord, did everyone in this town hate me?

"Don't worry. He won't."

Ray nodded and returned to the bar.

"So, about that dance," I said, extending my hand again before she could walk away.

Magnolia narrowed her eyes and stepped forward, holding a finger in front of my face. "One dance. One. And then you leave me be. Got it?"

A full-fledged smile spread across my face—the kind that made your cheeks hurt if you held it too long. "Deal."

She slipped her hand into mine, and I wrapped my arm around her back, making sure to keep it loose. It had been a while since I two-stepped, but I still knew my stuff.

Guiding her across the floor was easy as we let the previous song play out. But when it shifted to *Lovin' On You* by Luke Combs, a grin spread across my face. The faster pace of the tune gave me just what I needed to twirl her, and after the second spin, even she couldn't suppress the smile tugging at her lips.

We moved together like a well-oiled machine. She followed my every lead, never missing a beat, gliding with me like water across a smooth surface.

"Done this before?" she asked after I spun her back into my hold.

"Maybe once or twice." I winked, and her eyes crinkled at the corners as if she was fighting back a laugh.

As the song came to an end, her icy exterior seemed to have thawed, and I was about to ask for another dance. But before I could, Kyle slipped in behind her and wrapped his hands around her waist.

Kyle LeBlanc, the guy who used to be my best friend, was now nothing more than a parasite who peaked in high school and never learned to take no for an answer. Not that he ever had to, with his daddy being the mayor of Bellevue.

"Damn, Maggie. When did you turn into such a fine piece of ass? Why don't you give Taylor here a break and let me take you for a spin?" Kyle flashed me a grin over her shoulder that said he wanted more than to dance, and the possessive way he held her made my stomach churn.

Magnolia's face pinched in rage, but she took a deep breath, then plastered a fake smile on her face as she turned in Kyle's embrace. "Kyle," she said through clenched teeth, resting her hands on his shoulders, "back. The. Fuck. Off." Each word was clear, and then she moved so fast, I barely registered she'd kneed him in the balls.

Kyle dropped his hands, clutching himself as he doubled over. "You'll pay for that, bitch," he spat as Magnolia turned back to me.

Her eyes scanned down my body before settling on my face. "Seems he's not the only one who hasn't changed." A look of disgust crossed her features as she shook her head and sidestepped around me. Jaelyn and Madison, who'd seen the whole thing, weren't far behind her.

Fuck.

By the time I pulled my head out of my ass and turned around, she was gone. Whipping back toward Kyle, I shoved his shoulder. "What the fuck, dude?!"

"What's your problem? She's a freak."

Grabbing Kyle by his tacky-as-hell shirt—I mean, really, who still wore Ed Hardy?—I pulled him upright. "You need to grow the fuck up, Ky. This isn't high school anymore; you can't just walk all over people." I shoved him away and turned to leave, but his voice stopped me.

"You didn't seem to have a problem with it back then."

I sighed, turning to face him again. "You're right. I didn't say anything in high school. But I should have. And unlike you, I've learned from my mistakes. Grow up."

As I walked away, Kyle placed a hand on my shoulder. "You're going to regret walking away from me, Hallows."

Shrugging him off, I headed to the bar to pay my tab and left.

The heat from inside the bar faded as I stepped outside, Louisiana's weather finally cooling to welcome fall. The crisp air stung my cheeks as I walked to my blacked-out Bronco, the wind biting through my thin button-up. As I opened the door, my phone pinged in my pocket, and I groaned. Only one person would be texting me this late on a Friday.

Settling into the driver's seat, I pulled out my phone and opened my texts.

DAD

I need you to come in. We're swamped and short-staffed.

TAYLOR

It's my night off, and I was at the Firefly.

DAD

Did you drink?

Fuck me. I let my head fall back against the headrest, pinching my eyes shut as I contemplated lying. I hadn't had anything stronger than Dr. Pepper since I drove, but... My phone pinged again, ending my window of excuse-making.

DAD

I'll take that hesitation as a no. I'll see you in fifteen.

Groaning, I fired off one last text before tossing my phone onto the passenger seat.

TAYLOR

Be right there.

3

Libated minds make for liberated ideas

Magnolia

A WEEK HAD PASSED since the incident at the bar and, thankfully, had remained Taylor free. I hadn't bumped into him in town. I hadn't seen him enter the shop, but Jae said he'd dropped by to pick up his order while I was out. It was good. A welcome reprieve after seeing him three times in one day. So why did I expect to see him standing there every time the bell over the door chimed? And why was it that I was slightly disappointed when he wasn't?

Hormones. That had to be it. It was *that time* in my cycle. The one that makes you all boy and sex crazy because your baby box is insisting that you give it an inhabitant. That was the only explanation for why my sex-deprived brain was latching onto the man who waltzed back into town like he hadn't made my life a living nightmare throughout high school. It had absolutely nothing to do with the fact that assholes like him never got hit with the ugly stick. It had nothing to do with his chiseled jaw or the stubble that looked to be just past the prickly stage that hurt when you kissed someone, but like it would be soft beneath my fingers instead. Certainly had nothing to do with those deep blue eyes that seemed to sink into my soul...

Son of a bitch, Mags. Pull yourself together.

I shook my head and took a deep breath. I needed to focus. The first "Meat-Cute" mixer was tonight, and I needed it to go off without a hitch.

It had been a random idea I'd had during a girls' night with Jae, my aunt, and my sisters. We were all complaining about how hard it was to meet new people in this tiny town we called home, and well...libated minds make for liberated ideas, I guess. I'd thrown out the idea of hosting a mixer for singles. A safe space where people could mingle, meet others, and potentially find someone they connected with. We'd talked for hours about the logistics, but the conversation that had us all almost peeing in our pants was the one over the name.

"Just call it the *CharCutie Mixer*," Maddie suggested as she took a sip from her White Russian daiquiri.

"Ughhh, that's boring," Jae chimed in from her position on the couch, hanging upside down.

Names like *Singles Mingle* and *Flirty Fridays* had been tossed around as well, but Aunt Evie's idea won. "How about *Meat-Cute*... ya know... because meet-cutes are in romantic comedies... but spell it M-E-A-T because you sell charcuterie boards. Get it? Y'all get it, right?"

Silence had descended as we all looked at one another before peals of laughter filled the house once more. We all fell in love with the idea after that, and when it didn't go away once the alcohol wore off, I decided to give it a shot.

The plan was to set it up like speed dating—only I'd never been speed dating, so I was winging it. We'd give each person a card with three slots to write down the names of the people they clicked with throughout the night. Then, the girls and I would play matchmaker, and anyone who matched would get the other person's information.

It was a completely private event. Everyone attending had to sign up and pay a cover charge to help offset the cost of food and drinks that *CharCutie* was supplying. And it had blown up like gangbusters. We'd actually had to turn off the sign-up form because we were creeping on max capacity for my space. And it wasn't just people from Bellevue or the surrounding towns. People had signed up from Baton Rouge and New Orleans, too.

As I scrolled through the guest list one more time, making sure we weren't over capacity, my to-do list ran through my mind like a hamster on one of those little wheels. It was simple, really. All I had to do was make a bunch of charcuterie boards—both savory and sweet—clean the entire shop, set up the high-top tables, make sure that the wine and alcohol in the cooler were actually *in* the cooler, double-check that my liquor license was displayed... *and on and on and on.*

My list was never-ending and seemed to grow by the minute. *Why* had I decided that this was a good idea? I was an introverted extrovert. I was happy and free with people I knew but put me in a room full of strangers, and my social battery depleted faster than a hot knife could slice through butter.

The sound of the back door opening pulled me from my mental spiral, and I turned toward the kitchen as Jae poked her head out. "Hey, boss lady, where do you want these tables set up? The guys from the rental place offered to carry them in for us."

Oh, blessed Mother, thank you.

"Umm, just have the guys bring them in here. Once we figure everything out, we can shimmy them into place."

"You got it, boss!" she hollered, giving me a mock salute before turning back toward the exit.

I took a few deep breaths and pulled my crystal locket from beneath my shirt. The simple silver cage held a small rose quartz stone. It was meant to relieve stress and anxiety, and as I clutched it in my palm, it did just that. The negative energy surrounding my mental space seeped away as positive energy flowed in.

It hadn't taken long for the guys to set up the high-top tables; they'd even stuck around to move them into place for us. Although I'm pretty sure it had more to do with Jae's sultry smile than the tip I'd slipped into each of their palms before they left.

Jae took off shortly after they did, and I sighed in relief as I looked around my little shop. The tables were all covered in white tablecloths, with small pink rose arrangements gracing each center. I'd already spelled the lights to dim, giving the space a more intimate feel. My Spotify "Party Playlist" was cued up and ready to go, and even with nerves prickling against my skin, I was excited.

Glancing down at my phone to check the time, I blew out a relieved breath. Four-thirty. The event was set to start at six, so I had just enough time to get home and change before I had to be back to set out the charcuterie boards and drinks. Taking one last look around, a small smile pulled across my lips.

Perfect. It was perfect.

+)) ● ((+

It was absolutely, one hundred percent, *not* perfect.

"How in the hell did he even get in?!" I whisper-yelled at Maddie, who was helping me put together another dessert board in the kitchen. The Meat-Cute was going off without a hitch. People were laughing and taking pictures in front of the photo wall. My phone had been blowing up nonstop with all of the tags on Instagram, and I couldn't share them fast enough. I'd even booked *CharCutie* to cater at least three parties in November and one in December. It was amazing, and I couldn't have asked for it to go any better... at least until Taylor waltzed in. I hadn't seen him in a week. *Why* was he always around at inconvenient times?

"I don't know, Mags. I didn't see his name on the list the last time I checked, but it must be there if Mer let him in."

Meredith, my baby sister and bouncer for the night. She was five-foot-five-inches of unicorns and sparkles most days, with gorgeous blonde hair that many women would pay an arm and a leg for at the salon and killer blue eyes that brought men to their knees. But if someone got on her bad side? They would have been better off poking a hornet's nest.

Unfortunately, between her classes at the university in Baton Rouge and her job, she could only come home a few times a month. And I had been beyond grateful to see her little baby-blue VW Beetle in the driveway when I'd gone home earlier.

"What? Like, I'd miss seeing all of the cute guys and gals coming here tonight? In your dreams, Mags," she'd said as she hugged me hello.

"What do you want to do about it?" Maddie's voice cut through my thoughts, pulling me back into the present.

Groaning, I looked back over my shoulder. There wasn't much I *could* do if he'd actually paid to be here. "Nothing, I guess. Plus, he's here now. Throwing him out would cause a scene."

Maddie nodded, but a small smile tugged at one corner of her lips.

"What?" I asked, my eyes narrowing as her lips curled inward.

"Nothing... just that, well... at least now we know he's single."

"*Madison!*" I admonished through a whisper, tossing a strawberry top I'd just cut off at her.

She chuckled and used a wisp of her magic to deflect it into the trash can at her side. "I'm just *saying* it's a good tidbit of information to hold on to, that's all. I mean, Mags. You have to admit. He's not bad to look at."

Her eyes flicked up behind me, and though everything in me told me not to, I turned around.

Good god. It wasn't fair, really it wasn't. Taylor was a walking wet dream, and it pissed me off. He was in dark wash jeans that looked like they had been painted onto his body, hugging his thighs like they were holding on for dear life. The sleeves of his sky-blue button-down were rolled to his elbows, which did him far too many favors. It made his sapphire blue eyes take on a lighter, brighter hue... not that I noticed. And I never did understand why forearms were sexy, but his most definitely were... fine. They were fine. His dark chocolate hair was neatly mussed, and he was wearing his godforsaken glasses. Why were men in glasses hot?

Fuck. Me.

"Earth to Magnolia..." Maddie's voice trickled into my mind, and when I turned back toward her, I wanted to wipe the smug look off her face. "See something you like, sis?"

"Fuck off. So he's good-looking, so what?"

Maddie's face paled slightly as she curled her lips inward and glanced back toward her board.

"Wha—"

"Who's good-looking?" A deep timbre sounded behind me, cutting through my question and sending a chill down my spine.

Mother above—of course, he's standing behind me.

Grabbing my piping bag, I picked up where I'd left off and began swirling lines of ivory buttercream around the board. "Oh, loads of people," I said, not bothering to turn in his direction.

Maddie nodded emphatically, fighting the smile threatening to stretch across her face. "Mm-hmm... like Tom Hiddleston and Ryan Reynolds."

"Or Jensen Ackles and Jared Padalecki from *Supernatural*, they're pretty hot, too," I added. Aunt Evie and I were binge-watching it, and as much as I loved that show, I was beyond grateful that the supernatural part of *my* life was nothing like theirs.

"Oooh, what about Misha Collins? Isn't he the guy who plays Castiel?" Maddie said as she snickered and waggled her brows at me.

I mentioned it *one time*. One. That Taylor looked kind-a, *sort-a*—if you squinted and tilted your head just right—like Misha Collins, and she just *had* to bring it up in front of him.

"Oh?"

Taylor's voice was closer now, and the hair on the back of my neck stood on end. Piping bag still in hand, I turned toward him. "What do you mean, 'oh'?"

"Nothing. Just didn't realize you went for *older* guys, that's all."

His grin was far too smug, and my grip on the frosting bag was far too tight as it slowly started slipping through the tip. I placed the bag down on the counter before I ended up painting his face in buttercream and crossed my arms. "Is there a reason you're in my kitchen?"

Maddie snickered behind me, then slipped back into the mixer, having finished both of our boards. Taylor took a step closer, but I refused to give an inch. This was my space. My business. There was no way I was going to let him dominate it. It didn't matter that he was a good four or five inches taller than me, and I had to crane my neck to look him in the eyes.

"You're in here."

"Yes, well. It's *my* kitchen."

"So you've said… twice now."

The absolute gall of this man. Fisting my hand around my pendant, I took a deep breath. "Taylor, do I need to teach you manners like I taught Kyle?"

He flinched, actually flinched at my words, and a small part of me wanted to apologize. But then I remembered that he hadn't said anything, hadn't *done* anything—then or ever—and that small part died as quickly as it bloomed.

"Magnolia, about that—"

"Taylor, I don't want to hear it. I'm a big girl. I can handle myself." I patted his chest and skirted around him. I hadn't even reached the threshold before his hand wrapped around my wrist, pulling me to a stop. When I met his gaze, guilt filled those ocean blues.

"I know, I just wanted to say I'm sorry."

My brain slowed to a crawl at his words. *Sorry?* Did Taylor Hallows just apologize to *me*? That certainly wasn't on my Bingo card for this year. Not sure where to go from there, I forced my head to bob, pulled my hand from his grasp, and disappeared into the crowd.

I felt his eyes on me the rest of the night. Felt them burning holes into my back while I talked to the guys at the party. Felt them searing into me as I stood behind the counter or went into the kitchen. He stayed the whole time, but he didn't seem to really be interested in chatting with the women who were there. Which begged the question, *why?* Why was he there if it wasn't to meet someone? Was it just to bother me?

Shaking the notion free from my mind, I focused on the smiling faces in front of me. But I also couldn't help but notice when he slipped out the door.

4
Rougarou, is that you?
Taylor

WHAT THE FUCK WAS I thinking? That was the only thought circulating through my mind the morning after the mixer. I stood on my parent's back porch, a cup of black coffee in my hand, and watched the early morning light filter through the Spanish Moss on the trees.

I knew *why* I went. My mom had insisted on it, her eyes pleading as she laid on the thickest guilt trip known to man when we'd met for lunch. I took a long drag of my now tepid coffee and watched the mist dance along the grass, the dew shimmering in the growing sunlight as I replayed our conversation in my mind.

"I signed you up for a mixer in town tonight." The words were completely casual as the waitress walked away from our table after taking our drink orders.

"Mama—"

"Don't you 'mama' me. You're thirty-four. It's time you settled down." I rolled my eyes—something you should never do to a mother, let alone a Southern one—and she smacked me upside the head like she had when I was a teenager. "I'm not getting any younger, you know. I'd like to have some grandbabies before I'm eighty."

Never mind the fact that she was barely in her sixties, she acted like she was turning eighty tomorrow and would die the day after.

She also seemed to have selective memory since her daughter, my thirty-two-year-old sister, was getting married the next year.

"Ma, Addy is getting married soon. Why can't she give you grandkids?"

Her mouth popped open, hand flying to the pearls around her neck in stereotypical Southern woman fashion like I'd just cursed in church. "Adelaide will have babies when she's ready."

When I raised a brow at her words, she grasped my hand, her eyes turning all dewy and sentimental. "I just want you to be happy, Taylor."

"Laying it on kind of thick there, Ma."

"It's just because I love you. I signed you up for it. You're going." Just as the last syllable left her lips, our drinks arrived, and she switched subjects. "So, how's work?"

The sound of the French doors opening behind me pulled me from my reverie, and I listened to the shuffle of soft footfalls as the interloper sidled up beside me.

"Hey, TayTay," Addy said with a smile before taking a sip of her coffee.

She was the only person on the planet allowed to call me that. It started when she was a toddler, unable—or unwilling—to say Taylor, and it just... stuck.

"Morning, Addy. You're much too chipper for six a.m.," I grumbled.

"And you're much too morose. What's got you all Grumpy Gus this morning?"

After taking a sip of my coffee and grimacing at the cold liquid that should have been hot, I sighed. "Mom signed me up for the mixer down at *CharCutie* last night, and I went."

The squeal that came out of my sister's mouth was far too loud when the magic bean juice hadn't worked its... well... *magic* yet.

"Did you meet someone? Are you bringing them to the engagement party? Oh my gosh, what's her name?"

Rolling my eyes, I turned toward my sister and placed a hand over her mouth to keep her from rambling anymore. Her eyes popped wide before turning into a glare.

"If I remove my hand, will you stop?" I asked, raising a brow. Addy huffed into my palm but nodded. "Good." Begrudgingly, I did just that and placated her with answers.

Yes, I went.

There's no name to tell because I didn't meet anyone.

No, I'm not bringing anyone to the engagement party... because I didn't meet anyone.

No, I will not be going again.

She didn't need to know that the spitfire owner was the one who'd captured my attention. Didn't need to know that ruffling Magnolia Bellevue's feathers was the most fun I'd had in years. Because if she did, I'd never hear the end of it from her or our mom. It wouldn't matter that Magnolia seemed to try to light me on fire with her eyes anytime she saw me. If they knew that anyone had caught my eye, they'd be up my ass for details that didn't exist and planning my wedding before I even asked them on a date.

Addy looked at me skeptically, her eyes narrowing as if she could see through my carefully placed mask and read my mind. "I don't believe you for a second, but I'll let it slide."

Shit, maybe she could.

After a beat of silence, I looked down at my watch, the hands nearing the six-thirty mark. *Shit.* I had a shift in thirty minutes. "Addy, I love you, but I gotta head out before Dad has an aneurysm." I gave her a peck on the cheek, then turned for the door, her words following me as I entered the house.

"It's a beautiful day to save lives!"

Someone really needed to talk to her about her obsession with *Grey's Anatomy*... and the difference between an emergency room doctor and a neurosurgeon. A shiver took over my body at the realization that A) I knew the quote, and B) I knew it was said by Derek Shepherd *and* that he was a neurosurgeon.

I really need to find my own place.

+)‚)●((‚+

Work had been a cluster-fuck, and that was putting it mildly. Outside of the usual emergency room visits from people who couldn't get in to see their primary care doctors because it was the weekend—*colds, flu, strep, etcetera*—there were sprained ankles, psych holds, asthma attacks from the rapid drop in temperature, the list just went on and on. But that's all just a day in the life of an ER doctor.

What pushed it over the top were the hunting idiots.

It was basically hunting season—of some kind or another—all year round in Louisiana, but deer season was just ridiculous.

I stitched up not one, not two, but *three* hands that had been sliced open by a gutting knife because some drunk idiots decided that they couldn't wait until they'd sobered up before whipping out sharp objects.

I was exhausted and in desperate need of a shower by the time my twelve-hour shift ended at seven... fifty-two. Ever heard of a medical professional leaving on time? Yeah, me neither. But instead of heading back to my parent's house to do just that, I swung by the local grocery store near the hospital to grab some Blue Bell ice cream and beer.

Blue Bell was the best damn ice cream there was, no matter what anyone else said, and unfortunately for me, it was also damned near impossible to find outside of the South. Since I did my residency in the northeast, I hadn't had it in years. Couple that with the shit day I just had? I didn't care if I had to spend extra hours in the gym; I was going to eat the damn ice cream.

I'd just turned the corner in the frozen dessert aisle, buggy full of odds and ends that I'd remembered I needed and some that I didn't, when cotton candy-colored hair above bright baby blues pulled my attention from the row of freezers.

"You've *got* to be kidding me," Magnolia said, not quite under her breath.

"Fancy seeing you here." I smiled, inching my cart closer to where she was standing. God, she was beautiful. There was not a single speck of makeup on her face, allowing the dusting of freckles across her cheeks their moment to shine. Her hair was piled haphazardly on top of her head, little wispy pieces sticking out on all sides and falling into her face. And there were paint splotches covering her pale jean overalls and the black Chucks on her feet.

I knew I was staring, but I hadn't realized how *long* I'd been staring until she cleared her throat.

"Taylor? Can I help you with something?" She sounded as exhausted as I felt. I had no clue whether it was due to my mere existence or the day she'd had.

A nervous laugh slipped past my lips, and I tried—and failed—to cover it with a cough. *Why do I turn into a teenager around this woman?* Glancing toward the freezer, I thanked whatever benevolent being was watching me at that moment for a reason to have approached her. "Yeah, actually. You're in my way." *Shit. Should not have said it that way.*

"*Excuse me?*"

Yep, definitely fucked that up. "The freezer. You're in front of the one I need to get into."

Magnolia quirked a brow, shifting her gaze to the glass door, then back to me. "You're buying ice cream?"

"It would appear that way, yes."

"Let me guess, you're a natural vanilla bean kind of guy."

"What gave you that impression?"

Her eyes raked down my frame, and I swore I could see heat behind that gaze, but whatever it was had extinguished by the time they returned to my face. "I mean, look at you. There's no way you eat the super sugary stuff, like buttered pecan."

The chuckle that came out was darker than I had intended it to be, and evidently, my mouth ran away from my brain because there was no stopping what came out next. "Trust me, *cher*, there's nothing vanilla about me."

Should I have said that? Probably not. But watching her cheeks turn a delicious shade of pink as her mouth popped open in the tiniest little *o* before she subconsciously pulled her bottom lip between her teeth was beyond worth it.

I kept my eyes glued to hers as I gently maneuvered her buggy out of the way of the freezer door and pulled it open. The frigid air broke the spell, and Magnolia looked anywhere but at me while I reached in for my ice cream. Package secured, I turned back around and was met with a brow raised in skepticism and eyes that flicked from my gallon of frozen deliciousness to my face. "What?"

"Rocky Road, interesting."

"Well, it seems you took the last of the chocolate chip cookie dough, so this is a close second." I shrugged, placing my bounty in my cart.

"You like chocolate chip cookie dough?"

"It's ice cream and cookie dough. What's not to like?"

"Can't argue with that logic."

"I'm sorry. Did *the* Magnolia Bellevue just agree with me? Someone find a calendar and write that down."

"Fuck off. I am capable of being nice, ya' know," she said with a light laugh.

"I know. It's just nice to be the one it's directed at for once."

"Yeah, well." She shrugged as if that was all that needed to be said. And if I was being honest with myself, it was. She had no reason to be nice to me, and that was something I intended to change.

I had just opened my mouth to apologize again—for what happened at the bar, in high school, anything and everything—when her phone rang, *Tennessee Whiskey* by Chris Stapleton echoing through the aisle as she dug through her purse to find the device.

Her eyes flicked from the screen to mine before sliding the green dot over to answer the call. "Hey, give me a sec." Cradling the phone between her shoulder and ear, she grabbed her buggy and walked away, tossing a small wave in my direction as she passed.

+)❭●❬(+

"That's the last of them," Dad said as he joined me in the open doorway of the makeshift clinic. For as long as I could remember, my dad—and grandfather before him—would take the drive over to Houma, Louisiana, and open a small clinic one weekend a month. It wasn't anything grand, but it was a way to give back to the community that meant so much to our family. A way for people to get minor ailments tended to or get their vaccines up to date. It didn't matter if they had insurance or not; we took care of our own down here.

My grandfather grew up in Houma, and after he became a doctor, he moved to New Orleans and would make the trek over to his tiny hometown to help the community he considered family. When my dad was old enough, he'd been indoctrinated into the tradition, and while I'd spent almost every weekend of my childhood fishing on the bayou, I'd always found myself wandering into the clinic to lend a helping hand.

That's what we did down here: Helped our neighbors without expecting anything in return, boosted the community, and did what we could to keep our heritage alive. That sense of purpose and pride in what my family had accomplished is what brought me back to the Bayou State.

We stood there for a moment, both of us staring out over the crowd that had gathered for the annual Rougarou Festival with smiles on our faces. To anyone outside of this state, it would look like a hodgepodge of chaos, with the parade of Witches and Zombies, Zydeco music filling the streets, costume contests, and food vendors scattered about. But to me, it was a tradition that I loved to see kept alive and one that benefited the wetlands in the South.

The Rougarou itself was a bedtime nightmare told to little kids who didn't listen to their parents. With the head of a wolf and the body of a human, I guess you could call it Louisiana's werewolf. As a kid, I was petrified of the damn thing, my grandfather filling my mind with stories of it snatching me out of my bed while I slept if I didn't eat my collard greens—which I did, begrudgingly. As an adult... well, it was still kind of creepy, and I now avoided collards like the plague.

"Y'all have a good one!" our charge nurse, Jeanie, said as she passed us and headed out into the festival's crowded streets.

"Thanks, you too," Dad and I said in unison before he turned to me, "You staying or heading back home?"

"I think I'm going to head—" Pastel pink and blue waves drifted across my line of sight, cutting my words in half.

"Son?"

"Yeah, I think I'm going to stay for a bit. Grab a bite." I was halfway down the sidewalk that led to the street when I heard him holler behind me.

"No, I'm fine. I don't want anything. Thanks for asking."

"Okay, see you back at the house!"

Magnolia

Mother, have mercy. Weaving through the crowd at the Rougarou Festival was a serious pain in my ass. Especially since I had to drag a wagon full of supplies clear across the festival from where Aunt Evie had parked the damn car.

We came every year, setting up a joint booth of her tea blends, candles, herbal remedies, and my charcuterie boards and pastries. It was always a hit, so much so that we had to minimize the number of days that we attended, opting for only one of the three days. But that also meant taking multiple trips back and forth to the car to bring all of the supplies to the booth. This was trek number three and, thankfully, the last one.

"Are you sure we brought enough?" Aunt Evie asked when I finally made it to our aqua blue tent, her brow furrowing as she rearranged the table set up...again.

"Would you stop fidgeting? We do this every year, and every year, you move things around only for them to end up right back where they started."

"Ugh, fine. Did you get the last of it from the car?"

Nodding, I pulled the wagon into the booth and began handing her the boxes of extras to stash under the table. I'd barely gotten a chance to breathe since we got here, and as I took what seemed like my first full breath, piercing sapphire eyes above a cocky smirk locked onto mine.

"You know, if I didn't know any better, I'd think you were stalking me."

"And *do you* know better?" I asked, my brow raising as I crossed my arms over my chest.

Aunt Evie stifled a laugh, busying herself with adjusting the candles to make sure all of the labels were facing outward—they were—before injecting herself into the conversation. "Who's your friend, Magpie?"

Mother save me.

"Magpie?" Taylor questioned, his eyes sparkling like a kid in a candy store.

"Don't. You. Dare," I seethed, cutting him a sharp glare before shifting my attention to my meddlesome aunt. "He's not my friend."

"Oh, come on, *Magpie*. I thought we were best friends after we bonded over ice cream."

Red. Deep, burning depths of hell red was all that I saw.

"Taylor, I swear to God—"

"Taylor? As in Taylor *Hallows*?" Aunt Evie cut in.

"The one and the same. Nice to meet you." He extended his hand toward my aunt, and I watched as the once playful look on her face shifted to one of annoyance.

Should it have brought me an ounce of joy? No. But I was downright giddy, a haughty smile pulling at the corners of my mouth. "Aunt Evie, you remember Taylor, don't you?"

"Yep." She popped the *p* with so much force that I could have sworn it echoed through the crowded lane of booths. Taylor's eyes widened, a small flush coloring his cheeks as he palmed the back of his neck. *Was he embarrassed?* "Is there something we can do for you, Mr. Hallows, or are you just here to harass my niece some more?"

"I assure you, I have no intention of harassing Maggi—" If looks could kill, the one I just shot him for almost calling me *Maggie* would have incinerated him on the spot. Thankfully for him, he noticed and corrected himself. "*Magnolia.* I saw her when I was leaving the clinic and just wanted to say hey." His eyes dropped to our tablescape, and he picked up one of the clamshell containers. "Did you make these?"

"Of course I did. It's one of my best sellers."

"Pain au chocolat, right?"

"Yeah, but we just call them chocolate croissants... it's easier."

An awkward silence settled over our tiny tent as he continued to peruse the rest of the contents on the tables. He picked up each candle, gave it a sniff, and then set it back down. Releasing a heavy sigh, I rounded the table and asked, "Can I help?"

"Just can't decide on a scent."

"Where are you putting it?" I asked as I closed the distance between us, which ended up being a colossal mistake on my part. Taylor Hallows smelled *divine*—like a mahogany teakwood *Bath and Body Works* candle with the tiniest hint of vanilla. It really should be a crime to look as good as he does, smell like a goddamn man-candle, and be a complete... well, maybe not *complete*... asshole.

"Does it matter?" he asked, pulling me from the haze.

"What?"

"Does where I'm putting it matter? When it comes to scents, I mean."

"It can." My aunt's candles weren't just your regular, run-of-the-mill wax containers with wicks. Each had an intended purpose, and whether or not they were used that way wasn't any of our business. "*The Maiden* is lavender and chamomile scented and is for relaxing and bringing love and harmony to the space, so it would be best in an open area like a living room. Then you have *The Crone*, which is eucalyptus and rain. It's for clarity and protection from negative energies, so it could go anywhere. And finally, *The Mother*, which is her most popular. It's sandalwood and patchouli."

"What makes it so popular?" he asked, lifting the amber glass to his nose.

Had it been anyone else, anyone in the world who asked me that question, I wouldn't have flinched. Wouldn't have hesitated. Hell, I answered it a thousand times during this festival alone. But for some Mother-forsaken reason, saying *it's for inviting love into your life and should be in the bedroom* to Taylor Hallows was where my thirty-year-old brain turned into a pre-pubescent one, and my girlie bits decided to sneak into the party.

"It's for opening your heart and inviting love into your life. You should put it in the bedroom," Aunt Evie supplied, shooting me a quick, questioning glance when Taylor looked back at the table.

"I'll take it. Do you have a bag?"

"Which one?" Aunt Evie asked when my voice still hadn't made its grand reappearance.

"*The Mother*. And these croissants and one of the personal charcuterie boards."

Surprise shone in my aunt's eyes for a brief moment before a knowing smirk tilted up one corner of her mouth. "Perfect. I'll ring you up over there and grab you a bag. Magpie, help out the other customers, please."

Other customers? I quirked a brow, then turned. *Oh*. Behind Taylor was a line of about twenty people, patiently waiting to get to the table. I was so wrapped up in getting him out of our booth that I hadn't even realized that people had walked up behind us. "Sorry, y'all. I'll be right with you!" I called out over the crowd, internally wincing at my lack of observational skills.

As Taylor stepped to the side, he leaned down and whispered, "I guess we'll have to see if this candle works, won't we, cher?"

We? Cher? That was the second time he'd called me the Cajun version of *sweetheart* in as many days, and for some god-forsaken reason, my brain and mouth were still a ball of tangled Christmas lights, so I couldn't correct him. When I met his gaze, his eyes reminded me of the blue tips of a flame burning and full of promise. Heat licked up my spine, and I had to promptly remind my libido that we did *not* like this man. We tolerated his presence because he was purchasing goods that we sold and that he was an asshole... even when he wasn't being one.

Mother above, this was confusing.

Somehow managing to unravel the tangled mess that was my mind around this man, I gave him a demure smile and said, "I guess you will." Then, I pulled my gaze from his and slipped past him to help the next customer in line.

+)) ● ((+

"You want to tell me what all that was about earlier?" Aunt Evie asked as we loaded the last of the totes into the back of her car.

"What what was?"

"Magpie, I know you're a natural blonde under all that dye, but you're not stupid."

"I think I'm more of a mousy brown now, actually." Slamming the trunk closed, I skirted the side of the car to the driver's side door as quickly as I could to avoid the seething gaze I was undoubtedly getting from my aunt.

"Magnolia Bellevue!" she screeched as my hand found the handle.

My head fell back with a groan as I watched the stars twinkle into existence overhead. "Just get in the car, Aunt Evie."

With a huff, she did as I asked, and I let out a heavy breath, doing the same. At this rate, this was going to be the longest thirty minute trip of my life. She didn't even wait until the key was in the ignition before she started up again.

"Magnolia, is that boy bothering you again?"

"Yes," I replied reluctantly before amending, "but not in the same way he used to."

"Please, be *more* vague," she deadpanned, her eyes boring into the side of my face as I merged onto the interstate.

"He just keeps... *popping up.* Everywhere. The shop, the store, *here.*"

"You know his daddy runs the clinic at the festival."

"Yeah, I know. But did *he* have to be there? What was he doing anyway?"

"Hmmm." Was her only response, but from the corner of my eye, I could see a smug smirk pulling at the corner of her lips.

"What?"

"Well, honey. When a boy just *happens to* be wherever you are, it usually means he likes you."

"Oh my god. What is this? Middle school?"

Aunt Evie's answering laugh was coupled with a slight shake of her head. "Mock all you want, Magpie. But I'll be here to tell you 'I told you so' when the time comes."

"Even if you are right, there is no way in hell I would ever date Taylor Hallows." A faux shiver ran through my body as I said his name, earning me another laugh from my aunt. "I mean it! He tormented me in high school; why would I give him the time of day?"

With a shrug, she said, "People change, Magpie. And from the drool on your chin when you were helping him, I'd say you'd want to give him more than the time of day."

"I was *not* drooling!"

"Keep telling yourself that, *cher*. Yeah, I heard him. But, baby girl, if you make those walls any higher, not even you are going to be able to knock them down."

5

Laissez les bons temps rouler, y'all!

Magnolia

Nothing quite beats riding in the car with your best friend, windows down, hair a tangled mess, as you both belt out song after song. And the ride to New Orleans with Jae was no different.

To say that we were excited for Halloween on Bourbon Street was an understatement. We hadn't been in years, and as she pulled into the parking lot in front of *Crescent Witchery*, both of us singing the final lines of Journey's *Don't Stop Believin'* at the top of our lungs—much to the chagrin of tourists passing by—we couldn't help but laugh.

I'd missed this. Yes, I saw her every day at work. Yes, she spent more time at Bellevue Manor than at her apartment. But trips like these, where it was just us and we got to let loose and just *be,* were fewer and farther between the older we got.

"Do you think Mama Jo remembers me?" she whispered as the bell over the door chimed.

"O'course I remember you, chile. Who could forget a soul like yours?" Mama Jo exclaimed as she parted the beads that hung across the doorway leading to the shop's back room.

Mama Jo was the kindest soul a person could meet in their lifetime and was a surrogate mom to everyone who walked into her store. Her deep brown eyes shone with years of wisdom in the craft and life itself. Her beautiful umber skin had permanent crinkles at the corners of her eyes and creases around her mouth from the radiant smile that was a constant fixture upon her lips. She was sunshine incarnate, especially today.

A bright yellow scarf that matched her dress was wrapped around her brow, keeping her gorgeous salt and pepper curls out of her face. A delicate chime accompanied every step she took as the crystals worn around her neck clanked against each other.

"Mama Jo!" I cried happily, quickly closing the distance between us and wrapping her in my arms.

"Hi, baby. How's my beautiful girl? Not getting into any trouble, are ya?"

"Not yet," Jaelyn scoffed amusedly from behind me, searching through the various crystals on display.

"Now, now. Samhain is not a night to go lookin' for trouble, ya hear?"

"Yes, Mama Jo," we responded in unison, both of us curling our lips inward to suppress a laugh.

Mama Jo narrowed her eyes at us, her lips pursing as she raised an accusatory finger in my direction. "Magpie, don't you go lookin' for things you're not prepared to *deal* with. I taught you better than that, and so did your Auntie."

I grasped her hand in mine and gave her a gentle squeeze. Though Jae was oblivious to the implications Mama Jo was throwing my way, I wasn't. "I promise we won't go looking for trouble."

She harrumphed in response, then shook her head. "Did your auntie send you with the supplies I asked for, or is this just a friendly visit?"

"Can't it be both?" I teased before turning to my friend, "Jae, can you grab the boxes of lavender from the trunk for me?" With a nod,

Jae headed for the door, and as it latched behind her, I turned back toward Jo. "I added some of my own goodies to your order, and Aunt Evie put some tea blends in there and restocked your candles, too."

Stars sparkled in her old brown eyes. "You girls are too good to me."

"We're not nearly good enough. You do so much for us, for the community, and for all of the local covens. It's the least that we can do. But if you need anything—"

"I'll let you know."

"Good."

"Now, before your friend comes back, I have something for you to keep you safe tonight."

"You didn't need to—"

"Shush, girl. The veil is thinner tonight; you need all the protection you can get. Even if it's just from nasty men."

"Mama Jo!"

"Baby, I may be old, but I'm not blind. And this is New Orleans," she said, winking as she headed behind her counter and pulled out a decent-sized box. "I have a few sage sticks to cleanse wherever you're stayin'. Can't be too careful down here, ya' know. Lots of spirits wandering about, especially tonight. Black candles, clear quartz, and black obsidian to put by the door for protection—plus two black tourmaline pendants—one for you and your friend."

With the size of the box, there was no way that was all that was in there. As I peered over the edge of the counter to look inside, my gasp was audible, and my eyes fell to a deep red candle at the bottom of the box. But as I reached for it, Mama Jo snapped the lid closed.

"What's with the red candle, Mama Jo?" I teased, knowing full well that they were for.

"Get your head out of the gutter, chile! It's for strength, courage, and action."

"And sex."

"Magnolia Bellevue!"

"Well, it is!" I laughed as her lips pursed, and she shook her head. "Come on, Mama Jo, I'm just teasing."

She'd just opened her mouth to retort—likely tear me a new one—when the bell chimed over the door, a couple holding it open as Jaelyn entered with the boxes from the car.

"You're lucky I've got customers, baby girl." Though her tone was serious, the slight tilt at the corner of her mouth said she found the conversation just as amusing as I did. "Now give me a hug, and then git. I have work to do."

Jae set the lavender on the counter as I boxed up the goodies from Mama Jo, her brows raised as she watched. "We doing a seance later or something?"

Laughing, I shook my head and rounded the counter to loop my arm with hers. "Come on, let's go have some fun."

+)⟩●⟨(+

It didn't matter how cold it got in Louisiana in October. Pack a few hundred people onto one street, decked to the nines in costumes, throw in some alcohol, and you've got all the makings of a sauna.

Music filtered out into the street from every bar. From pop and country to jazz, each of them added to the cacophony that was Bourbon Street. Sweat trickled down my back as I tightened my grip on Jaelyn's hand and wove my way through the throng of people, all while I attempted to avoid the puddles of unknown liquid on the ground. People stood on balconies, hollering down at passersby to show *something* to get beads that most of the hosts of those suites supplied. Was it Mardi Gras? No, not even close. But did that stop people from yelling, "Throw me something, mister", while raising their shirts in public? Also, no.

Welcome to Bourbon Street.

It's amazing how my brain blocked out *this particular* part of this holiday adventure. All I ever reminisced on was the fun time we had—the music, the dancing. But the heat from bodies pressed together and the sticky feeling of one too many drinks being sloshed onto my person as we made our way through *anywhere* somehow vanished from memory when the opportunity to repeat it appeared.

"Where are we going?!" Jae hollered above the chaos.

"*Oz!*" I yelled over my shoulder. "Just gotta find the yellow brick road."

Even though her laughter disappeared into the sounds around us, her head was thrown back, her hand flying to her stomach as her eyes crinkled at the edges.

When we finally made it past the sea of bodies and spotted our destination, my heart sank. The line to get in wrapped down the street. I figured that it would be busy since they did drag shows on Saturdays, and it was Halloween... but this was insane.

"I *really* don't want to wait in that line," Jaelyn whined next to me, her excitement dimming as we watched the line move a fraction of an inch.

"Purple Drank?" I asked, my brows winging up as I tilted my head toward the bar down the road.

"Oh, you want to get *that* kind of drunk tonight."

"We didn't stop at any bar on the way here. Not even one of the however-many-there-are *Tropical Isles*. Come on, one or two won't hurt."

Lie. That was a bold-faced lie, and we both knew it. The "Purple Drank" from *Lafitte*'s knocked everyone on their ass. It tasted like a damn grape Sno-ball, and you couldn't taste the copious amounts of liquor in it either. But it was frozen, and I was hot, so it sounded like a solid plan to me.

With a shrug, Jae extended her arm out toward the bar and quirked a brow as she said, "Go big or go home, I guess."

Taylor

When Addy told me she needed me to take her to New Orleans for her dress fitting, I hadn't expected to be roped into staying for the night so that she could go to Bourbon Street and indulge in the drunken festivities. She'd even packed costumes, for god's sake, and her fiancé, Colin, just *happened* to be in the hotel suite when we walked in.

"Come on, Tay, it will be fun! Loosen up!" she'd yelled when my deadpan expression hadn't changed since we walked into the bar.

The lights were blinding, the music blaring, and I was pretty sure there were too many people in there to be under fire code.

"Come on, man. Hang up the stethoscope for a night and have *fun*," Colin said as he pushed some kind of shot into one hand and a weirdly colored concoction into the other. "Bottoms up!"

I eyed the shot for a second, then sniffed; my stomach clenched on instinct as the smell of cinnamon liquor burned my nose. Grimacing, I met the blue-green eyes of my sister, who smirked and held up her own tiny glass in salute. "When in Rome, I guess."

Addy's whoop of excitement was barely audible over the crowd and music. We clinked our plastic glasses together, tapped them on the high-top table we'd miraculously found empty, and raised them to our lips. The cinnamon whiskey burned on the way down, but whatever was in the cup Colin had given me cut the taste and replaced it with something sickly sweet.

"What the fuck is this?" I yelled, my nose scrunching as I ran my tongue along the roof of my mouth in an attempt to dispel the taste.

"Not sure," he shrugged, his eyes glassy as he sipped from his own cup, "It's some special for Halloween. Just keep drinking; it gets better."

Yeah right. Shaking my head, I took a large swig from the cup, grimacing as I turned my eyes toward the dance floor where Addy and Colin had disappeared into the crowd.

Bodies moved in all directions, some in time with the music, others... not so much. With a sigh, I found a blank spot on the wall and leaned against it, regret settling in my stomach as something wet and sticky seeped through the fabric of my shirt. *Gross.*

As the night wore on, we hopped from bar to bar, Addy and Colin taking full advantage of the specials at each one while I nursed the drinks they pushed into my hands. By the time midnight rolled around, I was over it. I was hot. Sweaty. And Addy kept insisting I keep the mask on my face because "It would ruin the costume" if I took it off, regardless of the fact that it was annoying and itched. I'm pretty sure everyone thought I was Zorro, but she assured me that I was Westley from *The Princess Bride* and the right girl would get it. I had no clue how she thought I would find *the right girl* in the middle of a sea of drunken bodies, but she sure was adamant about it.

The *right* girl, the only one who infiltrated my mind at all hours, was probably back in Bellevue doing god knows what with lord knows who.

"Can you get me another drink?" Addy shouted as her body moved to the music, her arms swaying above her head.

"How about some water?"

"Tay Tay," she whined, her bottom lip poking out at me in the most pathetic attempt at a pout she could muster.

"Water first. *Then* I will get you another drink. Deal?"

With a huff, she nodded her head and headed back out onto the dance floor, where Colin threw an imaginary fishing line to reel her in. My body shuddered at the cringe move. I was happy for my sister, truly, I was. But they could be downright nauseating—cute, but nauseating.

Pushing my way through the throng of people, I finally made it to the bar at the back of the house. The bartenders had smiles on their faces, their painted-on makeup still perfectly in place, despite the sweltering heat inside, as they chatted with each of their patrons.

As I leaned against the bar top and waited for them to come down to my end, a familiar voice cut through the noise and pulled my attention.

"Dude, I said no. Back off."

My eyes locked onto pink and blue tresses piled into a messy bun above iridescent fairy wings. How I'd missed her in the crowd, I had no idea. Maybe it was because most everyone was in wigs, or perhaps it was because I never expected to find her on Bourbon Street. But out of all the bars in Louisiana, somehow, Magnolia Bellevue was standing a few people away.

Her irritation was palpable as she shoved the man away when he reached for her.

"Come on, princess. Dance with me. I know you want to," the swarmy guy crooned, his hands reaching for her waist once more.

Pushing away from my spot, I closed the distance and stepped between them. "I believe the lady said no."

"Who the fuck are you?" drunk guy slurred, puffing his chest out in an attempt to look intimidating.

My eyes met Magnolia's, her crystalline blues shining brightly beneath darkened lashes as she stared up at me. God, she was breathtaking. Gauzy white fabric draped down her arms and wrapped around her torso before fanning out at her hips into a delicate skirt that barely covered the tattoos on her thigh. Iridescent glitter covered every inch of her exposed skin, from her cheeks to her chest and everywhere in between.

She looked like she'd just stepped out of a fairytale.

"Hey, I asked you a question, asshole!" the guy spat as he shoved my shoulder.

Peeling my gaze from Magnolia's, I glared back at him. "It shouldn't matter who I am. The lady said no. And last time I checked, *no* was a complete sentence."

"Fuck this shit." Throwing back the rest of his drink, the man slammed his cup down onto the bar and stumbled away.

When I was sure he wouldn't come back, only then did I turn my gaze back to the ethereal woman next to me. "Sorry about that. I was down at the other end of the bar and heard you tell him no, and—"

"You wanna dance?" she asked, abruptly cutting off my rambling. Her eyes sparkled as they searched my face, a small smile tugging on the corners of her lips as her hand met my chest.

"As you wish," I replied, leaning into the insufferable costume that I was wearing.

Her smile broadened, fingers twining with mine as she began to pull me onto the dance floor. "Okay, Westley. Let's see what you've got."

I was lost. Lost in the music. Lost in the feel of her hips beneath my hands as she swayed with and against me. With the way her hands played with the hair at the nape of my neck just below the tie of my mask. The way the lights reflected off the glitter coating her body as she threw her head back in unabashed bliss.

One song shifted to another and then another, each one bringing our bodies closer together. I couldn't believe she was dancing with me. Of all the guys in this bar, she'd chosen *me*. The guy she continuously tried to light on fire with her eyes anytime she saw me.

"Air!" The huskiness in her tone pulled me from my thoughts, her eyes glowing as they met mine.

I nodded, but when I let her go, she wrapped her hand around mine, a sly smirk on her lips as she tilted her head toward the back patio and began to pull me with her.

As we turned down the hall, the crisp outside air kissed my cheeks and chilled the sweat on my skin. Good lord, I hadn't realized just how hot I was until I'd finally started to cool off. We were just about to the door that led outside when someone yelled, "Out of the way," as they came barreling down the hall with a tub full of glasses.

Yanking Magnolia to the side, I pressed her body against the wall with my own, my hands braced on either side of her head.

"Well, hi there," she breathed, her chest heaving against my own as her eyes met mine.

"Hi, yourself." Her perfume penetrated my senses this close and without a bunch of gyrating bodies around us. She smelled like sex and sin and every man's dream. Spicy with the faintest hint of floral and something sweet.

Neither of us moved away, her hands slowly sliding up my chest as her eyes flicked over my face before landing back on mine.

"So, what now?" she asked breathlessly.

"What do you want to happen?" I pressed my hips into hers, relishing in the slightest hitch in her breath.

Her fingers wrapped around the edges of the opening in my shirt, slowly pulling my face closer to hers as she arched her hips into mine. With a slight shrug, she said, "I guess we could start here."

Within the next instant, her lips were on mine. Soft and pliant with an edge of need as they moved against my own.

I had a feeling I was toast the moment I walked back into her life. But now? With her melting beneath me, her kiss growing more demanding as each second ticked by, I knew without a doubt in my mind that I was, indeed, completely and utterly screwed.

A groan slipped up my throat the moment her tongue slid across the seam of my lips, begging for entrance. I opened for her, my tongue sliding against hers in a battle of wills as her hold on me tightened. Pressing my hips back into hers, I pinned her to the wall and slid my hands down until I could untangle hers from my shirt. Pushing them above her head, I held them there as I trailed languid kisses down her neck. Fuck, she even tasted good.

"You taste like cotton candy," I said against her skin, the irony of that statement not lost on me as I kissed my way across her collarbone.

"It's the body glitter. Less talky. I need more," she mewled, her hips grinding against my thigh.

I was the furthest thing from an exhibitionist, but the needy tone in her voice lit my blood on fire. Moving my other hand from her waist, I hiked her leg over my hip and slipped it beneath the hem of her skirt. "What do you need?" I asked as my hand skimmed further up her thigh.

"Oh my god," she panted, her head falling back against the wall.

"God's not here right now, sweetheart. Just us sinners." My lips found hers once more as my fingers coasted over her center. Fuck, she was already drenched, and the feeling of it had my cock throbbing behind my zipper.

Her kiss turned demanding, her hips rocking against my fingers. As soon as I released my hold on her wrists, her hands flew to my head. Fingers twisting into the only hair she could find as I lifted her behind her knees. Her moans vibrated against my lips, but just as I was about to push aside her panties, someone yelled down the hall.

"Hey, Mag—oh, okay. Whenever you're done, girlie pop."

Magnolia's head fell back as a laugh tumbled from her throat, and she gently tapped my shoulder. As I set her back on her feet, lust-filled eyes met mine. "See you later, Westley."

Westley? Oh, fuck this costume.

Patting my chest as she passed, I gripped her wrist before she could get too far. "You're *leaving*?"

With a shrug and a wink, she pulled her hand from my grasp and fluttered down the hall like the fairy she was dressed as. By the time I got my head out of my ass and followed, she was gone.

Ripping the insufferable mask from my head, I wove through the throng of people that crowded the bar, searching for Addy and Colin. When I finally found them, my sister's eyes were as wide as a saucer as they raked across my face, an amused smile gracing her lips as she asked, "Why are you covered in glitter? Did you have an unfortunate encounter with a Cullen?"

6
Monday can kick rocks
Magnolia

THE KNOCK ON THE door made it feel like my heart was beating inside my skull, and I pinched my eyes closed as I pulled a pillow over my head to try to block out the infernal sound.

"Make it stop," Jaelyn whined next to me, the blanket shifting as she pulled it over her face.

"You make it stop," I grumbled as another round of knocks echoed through my head like a gong.

Groaning, Jae sat up and pulled the pillow from my face. "You look like you got hit by a Mack truck."

"A glowing endorsement, thank you. But an accurate one if I look anywhere close to how I feel." Everything hurt. My head, my feet, and everything in between. Last night had been a glaring reminder that I was no longer in my twenties and thirty-year-old me was not equipped to be out dancing and drinking the night away. Flopping unceremoniously onto my back, I pressed my fingers into my temples and swore that I would never *ever* drink that much again.

As the knocking continued, I rolled from the bed with a groan and shuffled toward the door, cursing the person on the other side with never having a cool side of the pillow and overcooked crawfish as each pound of their fist made my eyeballs pulse.

"I'm coming," I yelled, immediately regretting the volume of my own voice.

Keeping the chain latched, I pulled the door open. "What do you want—Mama Jo? What are you doing here?"

With a flick of her fingers, the chain fell to the side, and she pushed her way inside. "Move, chile. Your auntie called me and said you needed me, and by the state of you, I should have been here sooner."

Glancing down at my—nearly dead—watch, I scowled at the time. "It's not even eight, Mama Jo. I need to sleep."

"Hush, you. Where's the kitchen?"

Gesturing in the direction of the kitchenette in our suite, I trodded back toward the room and shook Jae. "Wake up, Mama Jo is here."

"*Whyyyy?*" she whined, burying her face into her pillow.

"I don't know, but—" the sound of a blender cut through my words and pierced my brain.

"What the hell is she doing?"

"Makin' you something to knock that drunken fog from your brains. Now, get up," Mama Jo scolded as she walked into the room and ripped the sheet from Jae.

Balling the fabric up in her hands, she left us gawking after her.

"Did she just?" Jae asked, her eyes wide as she stared out the door.

"Yep. Come on."

Putrid. That's the only word that filled my hungover brain as I stepped into the kitchenette. The whir of the blender sounded more like grinding screws and bolts than combining whatever ingredients Mama Jo kept adding to the concoction, and the sickly state of green, as it swirled around and around, made my stomach churn.

"What, in the name of all things holy, is *that*?" Jae asked, her nose wrinkling as she recoiled slightly.

"Sit your butts down and hush. This is my bonafide hangover cure. Tastes better than it smells and does the trick every time." Mama Jo poured the green gloop into two glasses and placed them on the table in front of us. Hands on her hips, she surveyed us as we eyed the cups of goo.

"I am *not* drinking that," Jae said as she covered her mouth and nose with her hand.

"Suit yourself. But you've got a long trek back home, and it ain't gonna be any fun hungover like you are."

Groaning like a petulant toddler, I picked up the glass and took a hesitant sip. It was thicker than a smoothie and slightly grainy, but it actually wasn't *that* bad. Jaelyn eyed me curiously as I took another sip and then set my glass back on the table.

"Well?" she asked, her brows scrunched together.

With a noncommittal shrug, I said, "It's honestly not that bad. A little... *weird*. But not bad."

Mama Jo watched as Jaelyn took a small sip, her lips pulling into a satisfied smirk when surprise colored my friend's face. "You're welcome. Now, drink up. When your stomachs are up for it, there are beignets on the counter for y'all." She directed her attention to me and asked, "Walk an old lady to the door?"

After another sip of her—probably magical—cure, I pushed up from my chair and escorted Mama Jo to the door. "Is everything alright?" I asked as soon as Jae was out of earshot.

"Yeah, baby. I just wanted to make sure that *you* were alright. Your aura is... *different*... today." Her eyes narrowed a fraction as she assessed me—for what, I'm not sure. But then her lips thinned into a closed-lip smile, and she bobbed her head like she had found whatever she was looking for. "Have a safe trip home, baby. And come back to see me, alright?"

With a tight hug and a peck on my cheek, Mama Jo slipped through the door with a finger-wave as she pulled it closed behind her.

Grabbing the beignets from the counter, I settled back in at the table and finished my... smoothie? Drinkable sludge? Whatever it was, I was grateful for it as the ache in my head subsided, and the sight of food didn't send me running for the bathroom. When we finished our breakfast, I grabbed my phone from its charger—thank you, drunk me, for remembering to plug it in—and shot a text off to my aunt.

MAGNOLIA

> Thanks for the house call.

AUNT EVIE

> A little kitty told me you might be feeling a little rough today.

MAGNOLIA

> I'll give them extra snuggles when I get home. Thanks again *heart emoji*

Monday could kick rocks.

After the drive home Sunday, I spent the rest of the afternoon in the kitchen with Aunt Evie and my sister. We hung various flowers and herbs to dry and planned out meals for the week. I checked and double-checked the week's orders for *CharCutie* and figured out what specials I wanted to offer. All while Maddie furiously typed away on her laptop in the breakfast nook, nibbling on whatever food I put in her radius.

It had been calm and peaceful, but that all changed the moment I walked into the kitchen Monday morning. Aunt Evie was leaning against the counter, coffee cup clasped between white-knuckled hands as she watched the news scroll across the screen.

"What's going on?" I asked as I poured my own mug. All I got was a head nod toward the TV as she took a sip from her cup and turned up the volume.

"Tropical Storm Melissa looks to be heading our way. Her current speed is fifty-three miles per hour as she slowly makes her way across the Gulf of Mexico, which means there's a good chance that Tropical Storm Melissa will become Hurricane—"

The mute icon popped up in the top right-hand corner of the screen, promptly cutting off the broadcast as Aunt Evie let out a heavy sigh. "I was hoping we'd squeak by this year without a storm."

"We still could. It could fizzle out before it ever hits the coast."

Shaking her head, my aunt pointed toward the table in the nook. "Not according to the cards."

Spread out across our breakfast table was the most extensive Tarot reading I'd seen my aunt do in a long time. Ten cards lay face up in a Celtic Cross, the answer to whatever question she'd asked glaring up from their faces.

Skirting around me to sit back at the table, Aunt Evie steepled her fingers in front of her lips, her eyes raking over the cards as if she looked hard enough, they would give her another answer. Though I wasn't as fluent in reading them as my aunt, there were two that stood out among the rest; my eyes were drawn to the ominous imagery of Death and the flames erupting from the Tower.

"I've done this reading three times now, and it's the same each time. Death, destruction, and rebuilding."

As I ran my eyes across the cards again, they snagged on the Lovers. Quirking a brow, I picked it up and twisted it between my fingers. "What's this got to do with the storm?"

"Nothing. Don't worry about it." Aunt Evie hurriedly said, snatching it out of my hand and placing it back in the spread.

"Oookay. Well, we've dealt with storms our whole lives. So, we do what we always do. Double-check our enchantments over the property, make sure there's gas in the generators, and go to the store before all hell breaks loose and all the bread and beer are gone."

"Magnolia," she breathed, her head shaking from side to side as she rested her brow in her palms.

"Okay, fine. Margarita supplies, no beer." When she didn't lift her head, I slid into the booth next to her and leaned my head on her shoulder. "It will be fine, Aunt Evie. It always is."

It had to be. There was no way we'd survived Katrina and Ida only for some bitch named Melissa to wipe us out.

We had been sitting in silence for a while, both studying the cards as we nursed our mugs of coffee when Maddie walked into the kitchen.

"What's... going on?" she asked, her brows raised skeptically as her eyes flicked between us and the table.

"Storm's coming," I supplied as I watched Aunt Evie run her hands along the card faces.

Head bobbing in understanding, Maddie poured herself a cup of coffee and came to join us at the table. "Do you need help with the enchantments on the shop, Mags?"

"Maybe? I'll check them when I go in today."

Maddie joined us at the table, and I let my mind wander as I stared out the stained-glass windows that framed the far wall, the sun's rays painting the kitchen in a kaleidoscope of colors as it shone through the panes. *The calm before the storm* wasn't just a saying down here; it was a reality. The sun was always brighter, the wind mellower. Even the sunsets were more vivid, like whatever benevolent being upstairs was determined to give false hope to those who didn't know better. But we did.

Downing the last sip of my coffee, I pressed a kiss to my aunt's cheek and went to get ready to take on the day.

·)❯●❮(·

My head fell back as I rounded the corner that led to *CharCutie*. Instead of the nearly empty street I was accustomed to, I was met with a tall, lean, frustratingly gorgeous new fixture next to my door. I swear the Mother was laughing at me. Because that's what this had to be, right? A cosmic joke?

Expelling a heavy breath, I kept my eyes straight ahead as I marched toward my shop.

"Good morning, Magnolia," Taylor said a little too cheerily for a Monday morning.

"*Taylor*. To what do I owe this displeasure?"

"Ouch. I'm wounded."

Tilting my sunglasses down to peer over the frames, I let my eyes run down his body before coming to settle back on his face. "I think you're fine." A sly smile pulled at his lips, and I rolled my eyes in response as I pushed the frames up onto my head. "You know what I mean."

When I finally got the door unlocked, he skirted around my back and pushed it open. "After you."

My foot paused over the threshold, and I cut him a glance. "We're not open yet, Taylor."

"I know," he said, palming the back of his neck as a faint flush colored his cheeks, and he met my gaze. "But I wanted to talk to you about something, if that's alright?"

With a resigned sigh, I pressed against the door to hold it open and gestured for him to enter. Flicking on the lights, I leaned against the frame and watched as he slowly looked around my little shop. He'd been there before, but it was like he was taking it in with fresh eyes. And when his gaze landed back on me, my breath hitched. Why? Who fucking knows... ok, I might have known. The man was gorgeous... *frustratingly annoying,* like a weed you can't get rid of in your garden... but gorgeous, nonetheless. His deep teal Henley hugged every curve of muscle in his arms and was pushed up to his elbows, his jeans tight in all the right places, and those infernal glasses were perched on his nose. He looked like Clark Kent without the stupid bang swirl.

Pull it together, Mags.

Mentally shaking myself for letting my mind wander, I pushed away from the door and started my opening duties. I was earlier than expected, and Jae wouldn't be in for another hour or so, but I liked it that way. It was quiet and gave me time to think. But with Taylor hovering, I wasn't going to be able to check my enchantments like I'd planned to.

"How was your Halloween?" he asked as he leaned against the counter, his sapphire eyes boring into mine.

Quirking a brow at his odd question, I turned my attention to my kiosk screen and booted up our POS system. "It was fine."

In all honesty, it had been more than fine. Despite the massive hangover that ensued, Jaelyn and I had a blast. I'd had just about enough of being around drunken idiots when a man dressed as Westley from *The Princess Bride*—arguably one of the best movies of all time—swooped in to rescue me from one. And when he'd kissed me? *Swoon*. Technically, I kissed him first, but he definitely kissed me back, and it felt like I'd melted into the wall. Maybe it was the mask or the hero act, I don't know. I didn't care then, and sure as hell didn't now. We didn't exchange names, and though it seemed like a good idea at the time, sober me was currently kicking inebriated me in the stomach over it. No one—and I mean *no one*—had ever kissed me until my knees turned to Jell-O.

"Just fine?" he hedged, a sly smirk tugging on his lips.

I could feel the blood pooling in my cheeks and pulled my lips inward as I turned away from his intense gaze. "Yes... fine. Is that what you wanted to talk to me about?"

"No, I wanted to ask a favor, actually."

"A... favor? From me? The person who is known for not caring for your presence?"

"Yep. The one and the same."

"Alright, Hallows." After loading the specials into the system, I propped my elbows on the counter across from him and rested my chin on my laced fingers. "You've intrigued me."

"I need help finding a place."

If I'd had a drink in my mouth, it would have sprayed all over his face like in a cartoon. "I'm sorry... *what*?"

"I'd like you to help me find a place, preferably a house. I just need to get out of my parents' house."

"I'm so confused right now," I mumbled, pushing away from the counter and heading into the kitchen. "Why *me*? Why not your sister or your mom?" I asked over my shoulder as I pulled the order forms from their slots.

"They're busy with Addy's wedding and engagement party. Plus, you have good taste." When I cut him a glance, he simply shrugged and gestured to the main area of my shop. "Look what you did with this place."

"Sooo, you want a pink and teal, retro diner-style house?"

"Well, *no*."

"Taylor," I huffed out his name in a breath, entirely at a loss for words.

"Mags," he said my name like a prayer, sending goosebumps down my arms. "Please?"

Please? Sweet baby cheeses. His eyes were pleading, and he looked like a wounded animal. If there was one thing I couldn't say no to, it was a poor, helpless animal.

"You do know there's a hurricane coming, right?" I asked, raising a skeptical brow as his lips began to pull upward.

"It's just a tropical storm."

"*Right now.*"

"I'm sure it will be fine. So, is that a yes?"

I couldn't help the laugh that began to build in my chest as I watched him go from pitiful puppy to giddy. With an amused scoff, I nodded as I tongued a canine. "A house? What about an apartment? You're a single guy; an apartment would work, right?"

"Yeah, I am, but hopefully not forever." He chuckled to himself and shook his head slightly. "I've done the whole apartment thing, and it's just not for me. Ideally, I'd love to have a big yard, and since I can afford it, then why not go for it?"

"In this economy? Must be nice," I mumbled below my breath, but evidently, it had been loud enough for him to hear because his brows winged upward. "Fine, I will help you look for a *house*."

Taylor's smile made me pinch my lips together to prevent myself from returning the gesture. It was so bright and infectious, radiating all the way into the deep blue swirls of his eyes, making something warm fill my belly.

"*But!*" I held up a finger, dropping my smile just a smidge and holding his gaze, "That's all this is. House hunting."

With a slight incline of his head and a knowing smile, he pushed away from the stainless-steel table in my kitchen and began backing toward the door. "As you wish."

My stomach dropped, and my eyes widened as I watched him slowly walk away, his gaze holding mine until he reached the door.

As... you... wish.

Son of a bitch.

Like wiping condensation from a window, memories from Saturday night came back to me with glaring clarity. The man from the bar had been dressed from head to toe in black with a mask covering the top half of his face and head, just like Westley, but with those eyes. *Taylor's* eyes. Deep, rich blues boring into mine. Strong hands gripping my waist. Hips pressing me into a wall while lips trailed over my skin.

Oh, fuck me.

Taylor Hallows had been two seconds from... well, from doing *exactly* that against a Bourbon Street bar wall. Which, in hindsight, was unsanitary and sober me retched at the thought. It had been Taylor-mother-forking Hallows that had made my knees turn to Jell-O. Who'd had his hand up against my... fucking hell. This, indeed, was the Monday-est Monday ever.

And I'd just agreed to go house shopping with him.

Mother, save me.

Taylor

Watching the realization that I was the one who had her pinned against an—albeit gross and sticky—bar wall two nights prior would be ingrained into my mind for the rest of my life. And the flush that crept from her cheeks and down her neck was just the icing on the cake.

It had taken every ounce of energy I'd had to dodge Addy's questions that night. Drunk or not, she had laser focus when she wanted information on something or someone.

Why are you covered in glitter? Where did it come from? Who is she? Did you get her name? On and on, she peppered me with questions, all while Colin attempted to distract her with anything he thought would work. News flash, it didn't. Nothing ever did when she set her mind to something. It wasn't until we poured her into bed, and she fell asleep that I got a reprieve. Too bad it didn't last.

Walking toward the small grocery store in town, my steps halted as my sister stepped out from around a corner. She had a knowing smile on her lips, and her blue-green eyes burned into mine.

"Whatcha doin', Tay Tay?" she asked, crossing her arms over her chest as she popped a hip out.

Damn it.

"Going to grab some stuff from the store, I hear there's a storm coming. Need anything?" I asked, looping my arm around her shoulders as I stepped past her.

She staggered, but once she found her footing, she glared up at me as we walked. "Uh-huh. And where were you *coming from*, dear brother of mine?"

"That way."

"Taylor."

"*Adelaide.*"

"Don't government-name me."

"Then stop asking me stupid questions."

"I *will* once you tell me who the girl is."

My head dropped backward as I sighed. Relentless. My sister was absolutely relentless. "I'll tell you when and *if* there is something to tell, alright?"

Her squeal pierced my eardrum, and I contemplated calling one of my audiology buddies for a consult to determine whether she'd caused irreparable damage.

"*I knew it!*" she squealed again, amplifying the annoying ringing in my ears.

"Would you stop that?"

"Sorry, I'm just excited! You've been alone for so long; I'm just happy that someone caught your eye."

Jesus, that was a low blow. Yes, it had been a while, but I wasn't a complete hermit. Years of medical school and residency weren't really conducive to relationships, and I wasn't a fan of dating in the workplace.

"Well, whoever she is, I'm sure she's great, and you'll have no trouble getting her to go out with you." Addy leaned into me as she wrapped her arm around my waist. If only she knew how wrong she was.

When we got to the store, Addy gave me a hug and backed away. "I'm going to head back home. Mom has a list of caterers for me to go through for the party. Do you work tonight?"

"Yeah, I have a shift at seven. I'll see you before I head out."

After a nod and a quick wave, I watched her walk away and pulled my phone from my pocket. I had *planned* on getting Magnolia's number today so that we could set up a time to go house hunting, but unfortunately for me, my plan hadn't gone the way I had intended it to. Did I *need* her help to find a house? No, not really. But I would use any excuse I could come up with to spend time with her, and I was still surprised she said yes. I just hoped that 'yes' still stuck after I jumped the gun and let it slip that it was me Saturday night.

Annoyed and internally kicking myself, I pulled up Facebook and searched for *CharCutie*. Sending a whisper of thanks to whatever benevolent being was watching over me, I hit the button that sent a message to the page and crossed my fingers that I hadn't just royally fucked up every plan I had.

TAYLOR HALLOWS:

> Hey, Mags. You free this Wednesday to go look at houses?

My heart leapt into my throat when a response popped up, and immediately sank when it was the auto-reply for their page explaining their hours and the specials for the day. As upsetting as it was to not have an actual reply, I was half tempted to turn around to grab their specials for the day—pumpkin tarts and cinnamon rolls? Yes, please.

Just as I was about to pocket my phone, three little dots popped up and disappeared a handful of times before her response finally filled the screen.

CharCutie:

7
Buck up, Buttercup
Magnolia

"I can't believe you're actually doing this," Jae laughed from the office doorway as I tossed my hair into a bun, took it down, and tried again. "You're even primping! Damn, girl. You are *so* screwed."

"I am not!" I shot her a glare through the mirror while wrestling my hair into something remotely presentable. Of course, today was the day my strands decided to rebel. No amount of hair ties or bobby pins could tame the mane that seemed determined to look like I'd stuck my finger in an outlet. Okay, maybe I was primping a little, but that didn't mean I had to admit it.

"You are. It's okay; he's cute," she shrugged.

"He's an ass." *Sometimes.*

"He does have a nice ass."

"Jae!" I admonished playfully. She wasn't *wrong*, though, and I couldn't fault her for stating the obvious.

"Have you touched it yet?"

"Jaelyn Marie!"

"Ooooo, full name. I'm in trouble now." She raised her hands in mock surrender, her lips pursed as she bobbed her head from side to side.

"You're ridiculous." I couldn't suppress the laugh that escaped me as I watched her make faces in the mirror, imitating my struggle to fix my hair.

"And you're in denial."

"I'm just trying not to look like a trash panda who has been in the kitchen and people-ing all day."

"You're the cutest trash panda I ever did see," she replied in the thickest Southern accent she could muster before rolling her eyes. "Here, let me." Striding up behind me, she gently pushed me into my office chair and began twisting my hair into something that resembled an actual style. "There, all better," she said, satisfaction lighting up her face.

"You're a lifesaver. Thank you."

"One more thing: *that's* not what you're wearing, right?"

I glanced down at myself, noting the flour and icing that had splattered across my jeans and caked parts of my shirt. Did I own countless aprons? Yes, yes, I did. I had an entire rack of them in the kitchen, both branded and nonsensical. But by the time I remembered to put one on, it was always too late, and I ended up wearing the ingredients instead. No one ever accused me of being a *neat* chef.

"Yes?" I said hesitantly, scrunching my nose as her eyes widened.

"Oh, hell no."

"It's not a date, Jae."

"Date or not, you're not going out in public like *that*."

Quirking a brow, I replied, "I do *literally* every day."

"No, you go *home* like that every day. Not out and about town."

I sagged into the chair, resting my head against the back support. I should *not* be this stressed over a non-date. After all, I was just helping him look at houses so he could move out of his parents' place. It wasn't a big deal. It wasn't a date. Sure, he flirted with me whenever he was around and had asked me out *once*. And yes, I'd danced with him at *The Firefly*. But this surely wasn't a date… was it? The memory of him pressing me against a wall, his hands digging into my hips, and the desire swirling in his eyes as his fingers coasted along my… *oh fuck, this might be a date*. A weird date, but it could still be construed as one, and I looked like I'd run headfirst into a cake. Groaning, I ran my hands down my face.

"Did you bring anything to change into? Do you have clothes stashed here?"

"Oh, yeah. Let me just whip out my walk-in closet that I have stashed at the back of the freezer," I grumbled into my palms.

"Trash panda? More like a *pissy* panda if you ask me."

When I parted my fingers, Jae was giving me a sardonic stare, hands on her hips.

"Sorry," I mumbled, my face morphing into something resembling that weird little emoji with the toothy grin.

"Uh-huh. When's tall, dark, and persistent getting here?"

Just then, the bell over the door chimed as if on cue, and I groaned into my palms again. "I can't do this. *Why* did I agree to this?"

"I'd say it was because he had his hand on your kitty meow-meow, and you wanted to take him for a test drive—"

"Mother, save me," I grumbled.

"*But*," she continued, ignoring my pleading stare, "you didn't find that out until *after* you'd agreed, so I've got nothing. Sorry, babe."

"Hello?" Taylor's smooth timbre filtered through the shop and into the office, making my eyes grow comically wide.

"What do I do?" I whispered, jumping out of the chair as my lungs forgot how to function. Why in the hell had I agreed to this? Why did I *confirm* the plans after finding out it was him in that dark hallway?

A sharp slap on my ass jolted me from my panic spiral, and I squeaked in response.

"Girl, get your shit together. Tell him you need to change first, and then y'all can get started. And for the love of all things holy, *breathe.* He's just a guy, and you're a badass bitch who don't need no man."

"Mags?" Taylor called out, his voice growing closer.

"We're in here," Jae yelled over her shoulder before focusing back on me. "Buck up, buttercup, and remember: no glove, no love."

"Sweet baby cheeses," I breathed, pinching the bridge of my nose.

Not a moment too soon, Taylor poked his head into my office, his megawatt smile cranked up to ten. "Hey. You ready?"

"I—uh."

"She needs to head home to change first; work was a little nuts this morning. You mind?" Jae asked on my behalf when my tongue apparently decided to glue itself to the roof of my mouth.

When Taylor stepped fully into the doorway, my mouth felt like a desert. My heart lodged itself somewhere between my stomach and my throat, just not where it belonged. Dark navy slacks hugged his legs in tailored perfection, and his button-down shirt was whiter than my namesake. Crisp, clean, and entirely put together—unlike the bridge troll standing across from him, gawking like an idiot.

"Not at all," he replied with a slight shrug. "I'll be out front whenever you're ready."

"Thank you!" Jae hollered as he turned back down the hall, and my cotton-dry mouth felt heavy.

"Ouch!" I hissed when she slapped my shoulder. "What the hell was that for?"

"Have you lost your damn mind? Or just the ability to speak?"

"Ya' know, it's quite possible that it's both."

"Jesus, Mary, and Joseph. Magnolia Lynn, if you do not get your sexy ass out there, I'm going to kick it."

"Why are you pushing this so hard?"

With a heavy sigh, Jae grabbed my shoulders. "Because despite what you keep insisting, I know you, and you seem interested. Intrigued, at the very least, and I think you should take a chance. Take him for a spin. Try on the shoes. *YOLO.* You know, all that cliché crap."

"Jae." My exasperation came out more like a groan than a word, and she narrowed her eyes at me.

"High school was a long time ago, Mags. You're both adults now. *You've* changed. Why's it so hard for you to believe he might have? But so help me, if he pulls some bullshit, I've watched enough crime TV to know how to hide a body."

"You're crazy, but I love you," I said with a laugh, pulling her into a tight embrace before grabbing my purse from the hook by the door.

Big girl panties on, I took a deep breath and headed out into the shop to meet Taylor.

"All set?" he asked when I came into view.

"Yeah. I'm parked out back, though, so I'll just meet you at the manor, okay?"

"Sure thing," he said with a smile.

Turning, I hurried through the kitchen and out the back door, my heart racing as I mentally cataloged everything in my closet.

What the hell does someone wear on a date-not-date?!

As soon as I closed my door, I fired off a text to Maddie.

MAGNOLIA

Are you home?

MADISON

Aren't I always? *crying face emoji* What's up?

MAGNOLIA

Code red: I have a thing and need an outfit stat.

MADISON

A thing?

MAGNOLIA

Yes, a thing. I'll explain when I get home, but please help me find something to wear!

MADISON

saluting emoji

"You're doing *what*?" Maddie practically screeched, disbelief radiating from every pore as I explained where I was going and with whom.

"Yep," I replied, popping the *p* with more force than was probably necessary.

"I—I don't even know where to begin with that one, Mags. *Taylor Hallows?* Really?"

"Yeah... do you remember what I told you happened on Halloween?"

"Uh-huh," she said, narrowing her eyes skeptically at me before rifling through my closet.

"Well... uh... I found out who it was."

"You gonna tell me, or are you gonna drag this out?"

"It was Taylor."

"Shut the front door!"

"Ya' know, I think this is one time 'shut the fuck up' would trump that statement, sis."

Yanking something from a hanger, Maddie chucked it at my face, a saccharine smile pulling across her lips. "Wear this. Oh, and, sis? You are *so* screwed."

"Why does everyone keep saying that?!"

"Awe, Mags. My sweet, sweet sister." Maddie perched beside me on my bed, a smile on her face and 'you're an idiot' in her eyes. "Because you like him."

"I do not," I scoffed, examining the sweater in my hands far more closely than was necessary. Yes, Taylor Hallows was good-looking. *Yes*, he'd kissed me until my bones turned to liquid. But he was still one of the reasons I wouldn't relive high school for all the money in the world. Sure, he seemed to have changed—I certainly had—but was that enough?

"Mags, honey. I don't know if this is a date or not, but promise me you'll put your best foot forward? Try not to judge him too harshly for something that happened over ten years ago. At least give him a chance to show you he's changed."

I didn't understand why everyone was pushing this. First, Aunt Evie insisted he liked me after the festival, and now both my best friend and sister seemed determined to convince me to push one of the worst years of my life aside. Some part of me wanted to. Wanted to see if there was indeed more than history had established, but there would always be that girl in the back of my mind reminding me of everything he hadn't done.

"Would you if it were Adam?" I regretted the words as soon as they left my mouth, the hurt on my sister's face striking like a knife to the heart. "Maddie, I—"

"It's fine." She cleared her throat, wiped her hands on her joggers, and stood, heading for the door. Pausing at the threshold, her sigh was audible even from across the room. "Two things, Mags," she said, looking back at me. "One: our scenarios are completely different, and you know that. Two," a small smile graced her lips but didn't reach her eyes, "let your heart lead for once, okay?"

"Okay. But Maddie?"

"Yeah?"

"I'm sorry."

Nodding sagely, she said, "Text me if you need a family emergency, okay?"

Anytime my sisters or I had a date or went out with friends and needed an excuse to leave, we'd text a random phrase to each other. Within minutes, our phones would ring, giving us an out. It never mattered what time it was, what we were doing, or if we were in a fight. We always had that—each other.

I chuckled lightly and asked, "What's the code phrase this time?"

Her brows drew together for a moment before she rolled her lips inward, mischief lighting her eyes. "Inconceivable."

"Clearly, the only logical option," I said with a laugh.

Taylor

I'd been waiting outside for approximately thirty minutes when the teal-blue door swung open, and my breath lodged itself in my throat. Mags, covered in frosting and flour, was adorable, but the woman walking down the porch steps was something else entirely. Black jeans hugged her curves and cinched her waist. Delicate lace peeked out from her off-the-shoulder dark green sweater, and her hair was twisted into a bun atop her head. Every inch of her radiated comfort and an effortless sensuality that most women worked far too hard to achieve. She was stunning, and how I'd missed that all those years ago was beyond me.

Scrambling from the front of the car to the passenger-side door, I somehow managed a simple, "Hi," as I pulled it open.

"Hi, yourself," she replied, sliding into my Bronco. Her eyes widened as she looked around, and I closed the door behind her.

Deep breaths, Taylor. It's just house shopping... with a gorgeous girl... who probably still hates your guts and is helping you out of pity.

When I slid into my seat, her eyes locked onto me. "So, what's the plan? Do you have a list of properties or open houses?"

"I, uh... just thought we'd drive around and see what we could find?"

"You're joking, right?" she deadpanned, crossing her arms over her chest.

A nervous laugh slipped from my lips as I pushed the ignition button. "My realtor should be sending me a list of properties, but it hasn't come through yet."

"Ah." She chuckled as she buckled her seatbelt. "Someone's *super* prepared." Mirth sparked in her eyes as her lips curved into a delicate smile.

Thankfully, the email from my realtor pinged on my phone just as I pulled out of her driveway and onto the main road.

"You mind checking that for me?" I asked, glancing her way before returning my focus to the road.

"You want *me* to check *your phone*?"

"Sure, why not?"

"Uh, maybe because you barely know me?"

'I know what your body feels like beneath my hands and what your lips taste like. I know the sounds you make when I kiss your neck,' was what I wanted to say, but now was not the time or place—regardless of how much I wanted to relive our Halloween encounter. Instead, I opted for something simpler... and a lot less intimate. "Magnolia, it's just an email. But feel free to snoop if that's what you want to do."

Her eyes widened, like saucers, as she hesitantly grabbed my phone from the dashboard. "You're sure about this?"

"Yes, Mags. Just click the first link so the address loads into the GPS."

Quirking a single brow, she did as I instructed, then promptly placed the phone back in its holder.

"What? No snooping?" I chuckled.

"I prefer to get to know people organically, thank you very much," she replied matter-of-factly, pulling one leg up into the seat and resting it against the door.

Silence filled the cab as Magnolia stared out the window, watching the trees roll by. Gone was the levity and joking; in its place was a heavy awkwardness that I didn't know how to dispel. The radio played faintly in the background, Jon Pardi's *Heartbreak on the Dance Floor* filling the spaces where I'd hoped conversation would thrive.

It wasn't her fault. I knew this would be awkward or weird; I just hadn't expected complete silence and didn't know where to start.

As we pulled into the first driveway, Magnolia scoffed into her palm, her lips turning inward as she dropped her hand back to her lap.

"What?" I asked, raising an eyebrow as I glanced her way.

"This is an apartment, Taylor. I thought you said no apartments?"

"It's technically a townhome."

Her deadpan expression left no room for argument, but I pushed anyway. "Would you just get out of the car?"

+)) ● ((+

The first place had been a bust right from the start because there was a yard—if you could even call it that—no bigger than a postage stamp. We didn't even make it out of the car at the second stop because it *was*, indeed, an apartment complex. By the third, I was questioning why I wanted to buy a house in the first place.

Evidently no longer trusting the listings my realtor had sent me, Magnolia pulled my phone from its holder and began scrolling through random listings to find something she deemed "appropriate."

"Oh! This one is cute!" she exclaimed, turning the screen my way.

"It looks a little small, don't you think?"

Pulling the phone away, she scrolled through the pictures. "Unless you have a wife and kids I don't know about, I think it's a good size." She shot me a sideways glance, a brow arched. "You don't, do you? Because this would be hella awkward if you did."

"No, Magnolia. I don't have some secret family stashed away in another state," I chuckled.

"Okay, good."

"Why, exactly, is that a good thing?" I asked, braking at a stop sign, a smirk tugging at my lips as hers rolled inward.

"*Because*," she drew out the word, a faint pink coloring her cheeks, "I'm no homewrecker, Taylor Hallows."

"This would have to be a date for you to be a homewrecker, Mags. *Is* this a date?" I couldn't help the smile that crept onto my lips as her mouth popped open and then promptly closed.

"So, this house has three bedrooms and two and a half baths..." I shook my head as she ignored the question and rattled off the key items on the listing. When she finally finished, her big blue eyes landed on mine. "Do you want to go see it?"

"Sure."

8

Inconceivable

Taylor

THE HOUSE IN QUESTION was surprisingly cute—a newly renovated farmhouse adorned with squared-off columns and a wrap-around porch. The yards were well maintained, and the back even boasted a new fence, making it possible for me to finally get a dog—or three—just as I had always wanted. But all the features I had been looking for in a house faded into the background the moment Magnolia and I stepped into the kitchen.

Her eyes lit up like a kid on Christmas morning; her hand flew to cover her mouth as wide blue eyes scanned the space, delicate fingers trailing along the countertops.

"Taylor," she exhaled, spinning to face me. "Do you see this kitchen?"

"Oh, I see it."

"Oh my god, if I could marry a kitchen, it would be this one," she sighed appreciatively.

"So, I take it you like it, then?" I chuckled, stuffing my hands into my pockets while I watched her flit from one side of the room to the other.

I had to hand it to her; it was a stunning kitchen. Rich cobalt blue cabinets with brushed gold accents, a white subway tile backsplash, butcher-block countertops, and a large island at the center, topped with a light gray and white marbled stone. Coordinating open shelving flanked the apron sink. The updated stainless steel appliances gleamed, and the gas stove was enormous. But what truly set the space apart were the windows spanning the back of the house, looking out over the yard and flooding the room with natural light.

"Like it?" she exclaimed. "Taylor, this kitchen is a *dream*!"

She was right; it would have been a dream. Yet all I could focus on was the light in her eyes as she pointed out every little detail—her excitement practically alive.

After inspecting every inch, she finally settled at the island. Running her hands along the marbled surface, her gaze drifted out the windows as she began to rattle off all the things she would love to create in a kitchen like this one. I could *easily* envision her here, standing with a cup of coffee in hand, something delicious baking in the oven, and a streak of flour smudged on her cheek. She just *fit*—cotton candy hair, ripped jeans, and all.

"Rolling out dough or tempering chocolate would be a breeze on this counter," she murmured, more to herself than anyone else.

I'm not sure what possessed me, but one moment I was standing by the staged dining table, and the next I was behind Magnolia, my hands braced on the counter, flanking her hips.

"You look good in this kitchen, cher," I whispered, savoring her tiny, sharp intake of breath. She had evidently been lost in her imagination more than I'd realized.

As she rotated within my arms until her backside pressed against the counter, her wide eyes met mine, and she asked in a hushed whisper, "What are you doing?"

Damn, that was a good question—one I didn't have an answer to just yet. Other than pushing my luck, I was at a loss. I had no idea how she would react, whether she had blocked out the chemistry between us after she discovered my identity last weekend. But I figured now was as good a time as any to find out.

"You never answered my question from earlier," I said, matching her tone and volume.

"What question?"

Her eyes resembled aquamarine pools with flecks of gold, flickering between mine. Stepping closer, I suppressed the cocky smile threatening to break free as her breath hitched. That tiny gasp was music to my ears as her breaths quickened.

"Is this a date, Magnolia?" I leaned down until there was barely an inch between our noses; her gaze dropped to my mouth for a fleeting moment before returning to my eyes. "Or is this just you doing me a favor?"

"Um." Her swallow was audible as she leaned back, her sweater slipping further down her shoulder and revealing more of the black lace beneath and the intricate ink that adorned her arm. "Usually there's food involved in... in a—" she cleared her throat, and I noticed her hands flexing against the edge of the counter, "date."

"Are you hungry?"

"Famished." A deep rosy hue colored her cheeks as she met my gaze, her bottom lip disappearing beneath her teeth.

I'd just pressed my hips into hers, my lips a breath away from achieving the one thing that had occupied my thoughts for the last four days when the click of heels on wood echoed into the space.

"Oh, Taylor, there you are! I'm so sorry I'm late."

Closing my eyes briefly, I expelled a disgruntled breath. When I opened them, confusion swirled in Magnolia's eyes. "We're not finished yet, cher. Not by a long shot." Straightening, I turned to smile at my realtor. "Cindy, how are you?"

"I'm fine, thanks. You didn't like any of the listings I sent you?" she asked, her brows pulling together at the center.

"They were fine, just not what I was looking for."

"Oh... okay." Her eyes grew distant for a moment, as if she couldn't fathom being wrong, before she plastered a smile back on her face. "Well, how do we feel about this place? It must have just gone on the market because it wasn't even on my radar..."

I watched as Cindy pulled up the specs for the house on her iPad, rattling them off in much the same way Magnolia had, but there was no warmth in her tone. No excitement over the newly renovated master suite that featured both a shower and a clawfoot tub, or the recently reseeded yards. It was all just bullet points meant to push a sale, and that wasn't something I was interested in hearing.

Turning back to Magnolia, I caught the hesitant smile on her lips.

"I'm going to step outside for a minute. Let you handle... this." She waved her hand in a small circle, her eyes wide as she watched Cindy prattle on about the house's history, oblivious to the interruption.

Before she could take more than a step away, I grabbed her hand and pulled her back toward me. "Don't disappear on me, cher. I meant what I said; we're not done here. Plus, I still owe you dinner."

"So it *is* a date?" she asked, her brows lifting in surprise as a playful smile tugged at the corners of her mouth.

"It can be whatever you want it to be, baby girl." I held her gaze, my thumb brushing over the pulse in her wrist. But just as she opened her mouth to respond, Cindy interrupted... *again*.

"So, what are we thinking?"

+)) ● ((+

Magnolia

We're not done here yet.

Baby girl?!

Cher.

Good lord, this man was making my head spin.

His words echoed in my mind as the crisp fall air cooled the heat in my cheeks, finally allowing me to breathe without the scent of sex on a stick filling my lungs. I was a thirty-year-old educated businesswoman. Yet when Taylor Hallows looked at me like I was the only person in the world or stepped into my space, it was like being a teenager meeting their boy band crush for the first time.

Thoughts? We evidently didn't know her. My brain cells fizzled into nothingness, leaving behind the sound of Charlie Brown's teacher—just random noises that made no sense. I didn't get it. I had never been the type of girl to swoon over a guy. I'd always been able to keep my wits about me, to form coherent sentences. But one look into those beautiful sapphire eyes, and the only thing that seemed to function with any proficiency was my libido.

Bracing my hands on the railing surrounding the porch, I took a steadying breath and pulled out my phone.

SISTA SISTA CHAT

MAGNOLIA

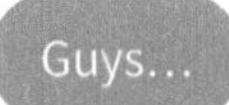

MADISON

Oh, shit. Already?

MEREDITH

Wait, what's going on? What did I miss?

MADISON

Do you ever check your phone? Mags is on a date-not-date with Taylor.

MEREDITH

I've been in class, Maddie, geez.

Taylor who?

Wait, are you talking about that sexy smart type from the mixer?

MAGNOLIA

How do you remember that?

MEREDITH

Mind like a vice. But what's happening? I'm so lost right now.

MAGNOLIA

Yes, that Taylor. Also known as Taylor Hallows.

MEREDITH

The guy who was an ass in high school? Why are you on a date-not-date or whatever with him?

MADISON

One and the same. But what's going on, Mags? Do you need an out?

MEREDITH

Wait, what's the code word? No one told me the code word!

MAGNOLIA

sighing emoji No, I don't need a rescue. I don't know what I need.

MEREDITH

SOMEONE TELL ME THE CODE WORD!

MADISON

It's "inconceivable." Happy now?

MEREDITH

brow raised emoji

MAGNOLIA

Mer, when are you coming home? I'll explain everything then.

MEREDITH

Possibly this weekend? But with the weather coming, I'm not sure. I might have to hunker down here.

MAGNOLIA

Have you checked/enhanced your enchantments on the apartment?

MEREDITH

Yeah, they're good to go.

MADISON

Can we get back on track, please? Mags, what's going on?

MAGNOLIA

He almost kissed me.

MEREDITH

WHAT?!?!?!

MADISON

WHAT?!

MAGNOLIA

Oh, shit. I think he's finishing up with the realtor.

MADISON

Magnolia Bellevue, don't you dare drop that bomb and then ghost us!

Taking a deep breath, I glanced back at the door to ensure he wasn't near and hit the little red voice record button.

MAGNOLIA

"Okay, I'm sending this in a voice message because it's faster. We were looking at a house, and I was fawning over the kitchen—as one does when house hunting. The next thing I know, he's got me caged against the counter, and his lips are a hair's breadth from mine. I don't know what to do! He said he's taking me to dinner when we finish up here. Do I go? Do I chicken out? HELP!"

MADISON

Yeaaaah, remember when I said you were screwed?

MAGNOLIA

Shut up.

MADISON

Rude.

MAGNOLIA

Not helpful.

MADISON

But I told you so.

Now go have dinner, and don't text us again unless you need an out. I expect a full recap when you get back home.

MEREDITH

Sissy, if you don't go to dinner with that fine piece of ass, I will never speak to you again.

Kidding… kind of. *winking smiley face emoji*

MAGNOLIA

Y'all are the worst.

MEREDITH

You love us.

MAGNOLIA

Always. Thanks, girlies. *heart emoji*

As soon as I slipped my phone back into my pocket, Taylor pushed the screen door open. His gaze locked onto me, shining like the tip of a flame as it raked down my body and sent a shiver down my spine.

Knock, knock. Who's there? No one. Magnolia's brain has once again left the building.

"Everything alright?" I asked, leaning against the rail in what I hoped was a nonchalant manner, convinced I couldn't trust my knees around this man—especially when he looked at me like a man starved, and I was the only thing on the menu.

"Yeah. Cindy is going to put the key back in the box and lock up." His steps were slow and methodical as he closed the space between us, but he didn't crowd me against the rail like he had in the kitchen. Instead, he held out his hand for mine. "You ready to go?"

"Mmhmm." It came out more of a squeak than anything else, but it was all I could manage at the moment. I ran my tongue across my dry lips as I slipped my hand into his, and it wasn't lost on me how he tracked the movement.

+)) ● ((+

Dinner passed in a flurry of awkward, heavy glances and little conversation. It was as if neither of us knew what to say after what had happened in the kitchen. We stopped for burgers at a place called *Somewhere*—yes, that was actually the name, which was brilliant marketing if you asked me—and I made sure to keep my mouth full the entire time we sat in that tiny diner. The food was amazing, but my stomach was rebelling against me for the speed at which I'd inhaled my dinner.

The ride back to Bellevue Manor wasn't much better.

I could feel his eyes on me every time he glanced my way, and it took everything I had to keep mine focused out the window. Tension settled in the cab like a weighted blanket as dusk filled the sky, painting it with color behind the massive oak trees. Louisiana sunsets never got old. The way mandarin and violet tones splashed the sky before stars danced in the navy backdrop was breathtaking.

"I didn't know you sang." Taylor's voice startled me out of my reverie, and I whipped my head toward him.

"I—I don't." Had I been singing? I hadn't even realized he turned on the radio, but slowly, the tail end of *Rainbow* by Kacey Musgraves filtered into my ears. If there was a song that could make me sing without knowing it, it would be that one.

"You do, and quite well, actually."

"Okay, well, I don't *typically* sing in front of people I don't know." Heat crept into my cheeks as I turned my head back toward the window.

"Why not?" His question caught my attention. It was only a few sentences, but it was becoming the longest conversation we'd had so far.

"I don't know," I shrugged, wrapping my arm around my knee propped against the door. "I guess I don't like being the center of attention? I don't like people staring at me, especially when it's something I don't think I'm very good at."

Taylor hummed in response, the corner of his mouth lifting slightly before his gaze met mine. "You've got a beautiful voice, Magnolia. Thank you for sharing that piece of yourself with me, even if it was unknowingly."

Well, slap me sideways and call me Sally. This man was full of surprises, and each one left me speechless. I honestly didn't know how to respond; "thank you" didn't seem adequate.

"You really don't know how to take a compliment, do you?" he asked with a chuckle.

"I think I'm just still trying to figure you out."

"What do you mean?"

Expelling a heavy breath, I shifted my gaze out the windshield. Did I really want to get into this right now, in the cab of his car where there was no escaping the conversation? No. Not even a tiny bit. But the furrow in his brow and the softness in his eyes as I finally met his gaze pulled the truth from my lips before I could think better of it.

"You were one of my tormentors in high school, Taylor. You, Kyle, and all your idiot friends made my life a living hell. And now? I... I just don't know what to think."

"I know."

His words were a heavy exhale, settling between us as a new kind of tension hung in the air. It lingered for the rest of the ride back to the manor, silence reigning until he put the Bronco in park.

With a murmured thanks, I gripped the handle on the door, but he caught my opposite hand, stilling my movements as his thumb brushed across my knuckles.

"I know I fucked up back in high school. I know that nothing I say or do will change the past. All I'm asking is that you give me a chance to get to know you. To show you that I'm not that person anymore."

"Why? Why are you so interested in getting to know me? I'm just—"

"You're just Magnolia Bellevue?" When I nodded, my eyes falling to my lap, he pressed his finger beneath my chin and lifted it, forcing me to meet his gaze. "You're far more than just a name. I may not know all that much, but I do know that."

"Why, though? Why me?"

"Because despite growing up in this small town, surrounded by all the Sophies and Kyles, you're still authentically *you*. It took me leaving to discover who I was outside of this place and its people, while you found yourself within it." His thumb swept across my chin, sapphire eyes flicking between mine before shifting down to my lips.

With my heart lodged firmly in my throat, I had to swallow *hard* to push it back where it needed to be before I did something stupid—like lean across the console that separated us and kiss the man who had me feeling so foolish. Mustering all the sanity I could gather, I gently pulled away from his grasp and opened my door. "Thanks for dinner."

His hand dropped between us, a melancholy smile lifting the corners of his mouth as he nodded solemnly. "Goodnight, Magnolia."

"Night."

I breathed deeply as I closed the car door and walked up the porch steps. Once safely inside, I leaned against the door and pulled out my phone.

MAGNOLIA

Don't forget to put a bid in on that house.

Peering out the window framing the front entryway, I watched as confusion creased Taylor's brow while he pulled his phone from the stand on his dash. Mine pinged in my hand, and I couldn't suppress the grin spreading across my face as I glanced down at my screen.

TAYLOR

So you did snoop. *smirking face emoji*

Adding my number to your phone and yours to mine is not snooping; it's being proactive.

Plus, I figured this would be easier than you messaging the shop when you have more house questions.

I'm going to use this for far more than house questions.

Oh?

I meant what I said, Mags. I want to get to know you.

How'd you put it earlier?

Organically?

I couldn't suppress the smile on my face no matter how hard I tried. Despite myself, I had actually enjoyed tonight. The fact that he was so determined to get to know me for me should not have been as endearing as it was, but alas, the bar for men was below the depths of hell, and that one minuscule amount of effort put him firmly above ground level.

Snickering to myself, I sent off one final text as I walked into the kitchen.

Goodnight, Magnolia.

"Spill," Maddie demanded, pulling my gaze from where it was still glued to my screen.

She and Aunt Evie stood at the kitchen island, brows raised expectantly, giddy smiles stretching across their lips.

Shit.

9
Damn cat

Magnolia

THE REST OF THE week blurred by as I prepped for upcoming catering gigs and readied the shop for the impending hurricane. Because, of course, Louisiana's coastline couldn't catch a break for even one season. I hadn't seen Taylor since he dropped me off at the manor on Wednesday night, but each morning brought a random question from him.

Today's was, "What's your favorite color?" When I responded with "*blue*," it was evidently too vague for his tastes. When I joked about giving him the exact Hex code, I could practically hear his laughter through the flood of laughing emojis he sent back. But other than a few texts exchanged, it felt as if Wednesday had never happened.

The sound of Lewis Capaldi's *Before You Go* filled my earbuds, drowning out the whir of the drill as I drove another screw into the plywood, somehow managing to hold it in place while precariously balanced on a *very* unstable plastic milk crate. Could I have asked for help? Sure. *Should* I have asked for help? Absolutely. But I was a strong, independent woman—who apparently thought she could hold a four-foot-long piece of wood, nearly wider than my arm span, while drilling it into place. So far, I was... *managing*. But I still had four more windows to go, and my muscles were already screaming at me.

When the screw was flush against the plywood, I dropped my arms, exhaling heavily as I took a moment to look around.

Everyone in town seemed to move about in a calm state of panic, finishing last-minute storm preparations. Boards covered most windows on the street, and sandbags were stacked in front of storefronts—including mine. Smaller windows were taped in an X pattern in hopes that, if they broke, shattered glass wouldn't litter the store or street. The local grocery was completely out of bread, non-perishables, and, of course, beer—because you can't survive a hurricane without the essentials. But aside from that, it was a typical Sunday afternoon; the sun still shone brightly, warming the chill that had settled in over the last few weeks.

"Need a hand?" The deep timbre of Taylor's voice pierced through the music in my ears, startling me so much that I nearly toppled off my makeshift stool. "Easy there, sunshine," he chuckled, his hand bracing my lower back to keep me steady.

"Make a damn noise, Taylor. Geezums!" My hand flew to my chest as I struggled to steady my racing heart. At that moment, I couldn't tell if my pulse was racing from the near fall or from the warmth of his palm pressed against the small of my back, his thumb rubbing in little circles along my spine.

He laughed, "I did... many times. I think I called your name at least three times before I realized you had earbuds in."

"So your solution was to sneak up on me while I'm holding a power tool?"

His head shook slightly, a teasing smile playing on his lips. "What are you going to do, Mags? Drill me to death?"

"The idea might have merit." I pulled the trigger, the drill whirring to life as I struggled to suppress a smile.

Fiery sapphire blues locked onto mine, and suddenly, the thought of *me* drilling *him* wasn't what was on my mind. That thought needed to be squashed immediately.

"So," he said, taking a step closer, hands shoved into his pockets, "do you need help?"

"Hmm?" My mind was still swirling along the gutter, eyes sweeping over the impressive expanse of his chest behind a button-down shirt that had no reason to be that fitted.

"Do you need help?" he asked, slowing his cadence as he dipped his head until his face filled my view.

"What? Oh! Help. Uh... sure? Yeah, help would be nice."

Stupid. Stupid. Stupid.

Taylor's eyes locked onto mine again as he stretched out his hand, a smile curling one side of his mouth as I placed the drill into his palm. "Mind somewhere else today, cher?"

You have no idea.

+)●((+

The storm was slated to hit on Tuesday as a CAT two hurricane, but in true hurricane fashion, Melissa stalled just beyond the coast, soaking up the warm Gulf waters like a sponge before unleashing havoc along the coastline. That prolonged time in the Gulf ramped her up to a CAT four, and she was now heading straight for Biloxi.

Which was good news for us, since it put us on the "good" side of the hurricane—as if such a thing existed—but her bands stretched clear into Alabama and Texas.

The wind outside had picked up, and the rain began to trickle down the window panes. Other than that, it was a normal Friday evening. Aunt Evie stood at the stove, her arm in constant motion to keep the roux for her gumbo from burning, filling the house with a mouthwatering aroma while the news broadcasters droned on in the background.

With a flick of her finger over her shoulder, she switched off the broadcast and turned on the kitchen speakers; *"Seven Nation Army"* by The White Stripes filled the space. With a pep in my step that the song deserved, I sidled up beside her, grabbed a cutting board, and the andouille links. Silence lingered—the only sounds coming from the music and the rhythmic chop of my knife against the board as I sliced the sausage into little rounds, ready to be browned. We bobbed our heads along to the beat as we focused on our tasks, but when *Thousand Miles* by Vanessa Carlton infiltrated the speakers, we couldn't help but belt out the lyrics.

It was hysterical, really.

Grown women singing into spoons and dancing around the kitchen while Mother Nature threatened to tear into our home. The scene grew even more comical when Maddie slid into the room on fuzzy sock-clad feet at the start of the chorus, pulling moves that Terry Crews would envy.

But as the song came to an end, thunder crashed overhead, causing the lights to flicker and the sky to darken.

"Here comes Melissa," Maddie sing-songed as we all turned our attention to the bay windows.

Lightning crackled through the sky, illuminating the gray in bright whites tinged with blue, as the rain began to pour in heavy sheets.

Aunt Evie sucked in air through her nose, closing her eyes briefly as she let it out, then turned back to the stove. Spoon moving in figure-eight motions with one hand, she clutched her crystal cage around her neck with the other. She hated hurricanes—though I wasn't sure there was a single person along the coast who *liked* them. It didn't matter how long you lived on the Gulf Coast; they never got any easier—you just got better at preparing.

Maddie padded over to the stove and silently picked up where I'd left off with the sausage, tossing the rounds into the skillet where we'd melted a pat of butter. That clap of thunder seemed to steal all the levity from the air, replacing it with anxiety over something we couldn't control.

A strangled meow pulled my focus, along with the incessant pawing at my calf. Bending down, I scooped up my ginger familiar and stroked her long coat. "What is it, Hermeownie?"

Taylor

The power lines held strong as the first bands of Hurricane Melissa dumped rain over Bellevue.

"I can't believe Michael decided to be on Team A at the hospital," my mother grumbled, more to herself than to me, as she angrily flicked between fabric swatches.

"I offered, Ma."

Blowing out a harsh breath, her hazel eyes locked onto mine. "I know, baby. Your father is just as stubborn as a mule."

Where my father and I worked, hospital staff was split into three groups for natural disasters. Team A stayed at the hospital during the storms. Team B—which I had been assigned to—came in when the all-clear was given so Team A could go home. Then there was Team C, which included all non-essential personnel like the billing office, doctors' office staff, etc.

Of the three, I preferred Team A. I was already used to working twelve-hour shifts; the only difference was that I had to sleep on a cot at the hospital when my shift ended instead of going home. I *hated* waiting out the storm at home. My mother was a frantic mess, despite having grown up in this sleepy little town we called home. And I could only play Battleship with Adelaide so many times before I wanted to flip the game and chuck it out the window.

It had only been a few hours since the first band hit, and I was already getting cabin fever.

Deciding to see if Magnolia was as stir-crazy as I was, I pulled my phone from my pocket, thankful I still miraculously had service. We hadn't talked much, which was more my fault than hers. I'd been helping my mom prepare the house for the storm on top of working the graveyard shift at the hospital, making it nearly impossible to have a normal conversation outside of sporadic texting.

TAYLOR

> Lovely weather we're having, isn't it?

I watched and waited for those three little dots to pop up, but when none appeared, I stuck my phone back in my pocket and padded into the living room. Addy was stretched out on the couch, her phone clutched in her hand as her fingers moved furiously over the screen.

"Hey!" she protested when I moved her feet out of the way and plopped down beside her.

"What are you so engrossed in right now?" I asked, draping my arm across the back of the couch. "Colin not agreeing with your entrée choices?"

"Oh, fuck off." She huffed as she readjusted on the cushions. "For your information, *sir*, Clara just told me she saw Magnolia Bellevue walking around town, screaming some gibberish."

What the hell?

"Is she sure?"

"Kind of hard to mistake her for someone else, don't you think? How many people in town have pink and blue hair?"

"There's a hurricane. There's no way she's out there in this." I scoffed, turning my gaze toward the window, away from my sister's probing stare.

"Know a lot about Magnolia, do you, brother?" I didn't need to look at her to know her perfectly manicured brows were arched in suspicion.

"What? No. I mean, I know who she *is*. We went to high school together for a year. But no one in their right mind would be out in this weather."

Right?

"Well." Addy shrugged, turning her attention back to her phone as I slipped mine back out from my pocket.

TAYLOR

Magnolia, please tell me you're not out in this mess.

When a response still hadn't come through five minutes later, I stood from the couch and made my way toward the back door as calmly as I could manage.

"Where are you going?" Addy hollered after me.

"To check the generators."

+)) ● ((+

Rain battered against my Bronco as I wove through the slowly accumulating debris along the road. I still hadn't heard from Magnolia. I even tried calling her, but it went straight to voicemail.

"Come on, Mags. Where are you?" I muttered to myself, keeping my head on a swivel, scanning for any sign of cotton-candy hair amid the dreary gray blanketing our town.

I turned down the street that housed *CharCutie* when I spotted her. She was soaked from head to toe, her hair plastered to her back and face as she hurried down the sidewalk.

Finding a place to park where I hoped it wouldn't get crushed by a tree, I jumped out and began making my way toward her.

"Magnolia!" I yelled over the howl of the wind. "Mags!"

"Meowfoy! Meowfoy! Where are you, buddy?"

Meow-what? What the hell did she just say?

"Meowfoy!"

"Magnolia!" I yelled again. This time she heard me, her head whipping in my direction, eyes wide.

"*Taylor?!* What the hell are you doing?"

"I could ask you the same thing!"

"My... my cat got out. We can't find him!" Her voice cracked, and then I realized tears were mingling with the rain on her cheeks.

"Mags, baby, we need to get inside somewhere."

"I can't! I need to find him!"

Son of a bitch.

I pushed all the air from my lungs into my cheeks and shook my head. "What's his name?"

Her lips curled inward for a moment before she scrunched her nose. "It's Meowfoy."

"Allllrighty, then. Let's go find this cat." No sooner were the words out of my mouth than the wind picked up and sent a branch crashing onto a power line, sparks flying into the air. "Fuck. Mags, come on, we need to get inside."

"No!" she protested, trying to pull her wrist from my grasp. "I can't leave him!"

"*Please*, Mags. Cats are smart. He's probably hunkered down somewhere safe, and we need to do the same." Tightening my grip on her wrist, I pulled her down the street. Branches and water were piling up in front of her shop, making that route impossible.

Panicked eyes darted around the town square, her lip trembling as she continued to search for her fuzzy friend.

Swearing to myself that I would kill this damn cat if it got *her* or *me* killed in this storm, I pulled her toward the back of her building.

"Keys, Mags. I need your keys." With shaking hands, she pulled them from her pocket and handed them over. But as soon as I opened the door, she bolted.

"Meowfoy!"

"Dammit, Mags. Get inside!" I demanded when I caught up to her.

"No!"

"So help me, woman, if you don't get inside—"

"What, Taylor? What are you going to do?"

Her outburst had me raising an eyebrow. She was cute when she was mad, and my next choice would likely only infuriate her further.

"Put me *down*!" Her screech was swallowed by the storm as I flung her over my shoulder like a sack of potatoes. Her fists slammed into my back as I walked toward the back entrance of her shop.

"Not until we're inside," I yelled loud enough for her to hear.

With a disgruntled groan, Magnolia ceased her assault on my spine when she realized it wouldn't change my mind.

Once the door was closed and locked behind us, I gently set her back on her feet. But that single action had me back at square one, as she glared up at me, looking like she could incinerate me with her eyes.

"What the fuck is your problem?!" she yelled, pushing against my chest.

"*Me?* I wasn't the one wandering around town in the middle of a *hurricane!*"

"I was looking for my cat!"

"Yeah, about that. *What* was this furry little escape artist's name?"

A flush bloomed in her cheeks, dimming the fiery hate in her eyes. "That's... that's none of your business."

"Oh, on the contrary, sunshine. I believe it's one hundred percent my business since I just drove into a hurricane to save your ass."

"Save my?" She huffed out a breath, then turned to storm further into the space. "Look here, Taylor. I didn't *need* you to 'save my ass.' I was perfectly—"

"Safe? Please tell me you were not just about to say safe."

"*Fine.* I was perfectly *fine.*"

My head fell back, and I counted the speckles on the ceiling to calm my nerves. "Mags."

"I was just trying to find my cat." Her voice cracked at the end of her sentence, and when I met her gaze, her eyes shimmered with unshed tears.

"Dammit, Mags." I closed the space between us in a few strides and pulled her into my arms. I shouldn't have felt relieved when she melted into my embrace, her face burrowing into my chest as her tears fell, but I did. God, I loved the feeling of her there. Of being the one who could bring her even a little bit of comfort. And sure, I was the only one around at the moment, but that didn't mean she had to *accept* the solace I offered.

We stayed that way until her shoulders stopped shuddering. When she pulled her face from my chest, a wary grimace spread across her lips.

"I'm sorry."

"For what, baby?" That was the second time I'd called her that. It wasn't intentional; it just slipped out. But it felt good. *Right*. And the fact that she hadn't recoiled either time made my heart beat a little faster.

"Well, I'd say for soaking your shirt with my tears, but you already look like a drowned rat," she said with a light chuckle.

"Oh, like you look like Miss America right now?" I joked back, but even soaked through her clothes, she was a vision.

"A sense of humor, I like that." Her smile was infectious, making her eyes sparkle brighter than any gem in a jeweler's case. Her hand wrapped around mine, fingers threading together as she pulled me toward the kitchen. "Come on, I've got some towels we can use to... well, mop up some of the water anyway. I don't think they'll get us *dry*."

10
Peachy keen, Jelly Bean
Magnolia

FAMILY CHAOS

MAGNOLIA

Couldn't find Meowfoy. Are we sure he's not hiding in the house somewhere?

AUNT EVIE

We've turned this place upside down.

MADISON

Even shook his favorite treats, and nothing.

AUNT EVIE

Magpie, where are you? The storm is getting worse.

MAGNOLIA

I'm at CharCutie waiting it out.

MADISON

large eyes emoji

MAGNOLIA

zipped lips emoji

MEREDITH

What's going on?

·)) ● ((·

SISTA SISTA CHAT

MADISON

Why do I feel like there's more to this story?

MAGNOLIA

Maybe because Taylor Hallows hauled me over his shoulder and brought me into my own shop?

MEREDITH

Holy Mother. *wide eyes emoji*

MAGNOLIA

And now he's looking at me with a weird look on his face.

MEREDITH

Do you have a weird look on your face?

MEREDITH

Side note: can we please get an italics function in text messaging? I want my inflections inflected!

MAGNOLIA

I'm going to go. Need to save my battery life since I don't think I have my charger here, and I don't know how long I'll be stuck.

MADISON

Yeah, okay, Mags. I'm sure it's torture being 'stuck there' with the guy you've been drooling over.

By the way, I'm using this in a book. K, thanks.

Though we couldn't see it, the sound of rain hammering against the roof and wind whipping against the building told us the storm was still having a field day with Bellevue. It had only been an hour at most, but the heavy silence settling inside my little shop was louder than the chaos outside.

We'd taken up residence on *CharCutie*'s kitchen floor, leaning against one of the stainless-steel tables as we tossed random objects into one of my mixing bowls across the room. It was the only thing I could think of to occupy ourselves, especially after Taylor peeled his rain-soaked shirt from his body—his impressive physique on full display. It wasn't like he was carved from granite, but good lord, he was fit in all the right ways. Strong arms and chest, with just a hint of cushion around the middle. The kind of body that's nice to look at but even better to curl against. After all, who likes to lay on a rock?

I, on the other hand, had sprinted out of my house in a dingy t-shirt with bleach stains and sweatpants that had seen better days. And since I had been at home, I didn't even have a bra on under my shirt. Given that I'd just endured the freezing rain, there was no way he hadn't noticed.

"Soooo," Taylor drawled as he launched a piping tip toward the bowl, the metallic clang echoing through the air as it hit the lip and ricocheted away. "Dammit."

A snicker escaped me before I could stop it as I launched my own toward the bowl, achieving the same result. "So?" I parroted back.

"Are we going to talk about it?" He threw another piping tip, a muffled '*yes*' escaping his lips when it landed inside the bowl.

"Talk about what?"

"Well, we could start with why you thought chasing your cat in a hurricane was a good idea."

"And the conversation would end there. Just like it has every other time you've tried." Pushing up from the floor, I rounded the table in search of something to keep my hands busy and to distract myself from the inquisition in his eyes.

"Magnolia."

As soon as he said my name, the lights flickered a few times before the entire space went dark. If I'd been there alone, it wouldn't have been a big deal; a little wiggle of my fingers would have illuminated the place in a magical glow. But with Taylor here, I had to fumble around the kitchen, searching for a flashlight. A curse slipped from my lips as something clattered to the floor just before a beam of light landed on me.

"You alright over there?" he asked, concern lacing his tone.

"Yeah, I'm fine. Where'd you get the flashlight?" When I turned around, I suppressed the urge to facepalm as Taylor held up his phone and shrugged.

Of course. A fucking phone.

"Mags, are you okay?"

"Oh, I'm peachy keen, jelly bean. There's only a hurricane outside, my familia—*family* cat is missing, the power is out, and I have a half-naked man standing in the kitchen of my business. Just another Friday." My words rushed out in a breathless stream, my head spinning slightly from the abrupt lack of oxygen.

"Mags, I'm sure your cat will be fine."

"You don't get it." I threw my head back, taking a deep breath as I ran my palms down my face. "Meowfoy is more than just a family cat. You... you wouldn't understand."

"You're right; I don't. We never had pets growing up. But uh, *Meowfoy*? You named your cat Meowfoy?"

"And Hermeownie."

"*Hermeownie*?"

"Don't be an ass."

After throwing his hands up in surrender, Taylor placed his phone face down on the countertop to spread the light out a little more. "Just explains why Clara told Addy you were walking around screaming gibberish, is all."

"Wait. *That's* why you were out in this mess?"

"Yeah." A hesitant smile curved his lips as he palmed the back of his neck.

"Are you out of your mind? There's a hurricane outside!"

"You have *got* to be kidding me," he deadpanned, resting his hands on the tabletop. I shouldn't have noticed how his muscles flexed as he put his weight onto his palms. I shouldn't have traced every line and divot across his arms. The tiny uptick on his lips when I finally forced my gaze to his face cemented that fact.

"Mags," he drew my name out in a husky whisper that sent a shiver down my spine.

"Uh-huh." I couldn't concentrate—not with him stalking toward me like a lion hunting a gazelle. His eyes burned as they locked onto mine, and I couldn't tell if it was the thunder outside or my own pulse roaring in my ears.

"What's going on in that head of yours, sunshine?"

"Sunshine?" I squeaked, then cleared my throat.

He hummed in response, taking calculated steps toward me. "Bright and beautiful, but will burn you alive if you get too close."

Raising my brows, I huffed out a breath. "Is that what you think of me?"

"Give me a reason that I shouldn't."

"Excuse me?"

"We've been dancing around each other for the better part of two weeks. Neither of us has taken the steps to open the conversation on whatever *this* is," he said, gesturing between us.

"Taylor, I... I don't know what you want me to say."

"I want you to tell me what's going on in that beautiful brain of yours."

I had to turn away, had to unglue my eyes from his or I was bound to burst into flames. "I, uh... I think I have some food in the walk-in that we could eat. I'm hungry; are you hungry?"

"Magnolia."

Pushing away from the counter, I attempted to skirt past him to the cooler on the other side of the kitchen, thankful that my charms had held and the refrigerators were still running despite the lack of power.

I didn't make it more than a step before his hand wrapped around my wrist, pulling me back toward him. My hands landed on his chest, his body heat searing into my palms as his heart thumped beneath at a pace as rampant as my own. Dropping his hold on my wrist in favor of my waist, he lifted my chin with the other.

"Talk to me, sunshine. Tell me I'm not alone in this. Tell me you feel what's between us as strongly as I do." His voice was barely above a whisper, his words washing over me like a summer breeze as his sapphire blues flicked from my eyes to my mouth and back again.

"Are you asking me, or telling me?" My words came out breathier than I'd intended, but it was hard to get oxygen to my brain when he was this close. Hard to do anything other than stare into his eyes as he held mine, the dim glow of the phone's light carving out every chiseled feature on his face.

"I'm *hoping* you feel the same."

"And if I don't?"

"Then I guess that's just something I'll have to live with." His eyes bore into mine as he reverently stroked his thumb across my chin. I could feel his heart rate rising, could sense the shift in his breathing as he tried to keep it slow and steady while mine turned ragged.

"We barely know each other." I don't know if I stepped back or if he moved forward, but suddenly I was back in that gorgeous kitchen in the farmhouse. Only this time, his body pressed against mine, and instead of marble, cold steel bit into my still-wet sweats.

"That's kind of the point of dating, is it not? To get to know each other?"

"But your friends—"

He leaned in further, his face a breath away from mine, cutting off all streams of consciousness. His man-candle-worthy scent penetrated my nose, causing my head to spin.

"I'm not friends with them, Magnolia. I haven't been in a long time. And if those are your only concerns, then..." A smirk tugged at the corner of his lips as his eyes flicked down to my mouth.

"Then what?" I breathed.

"Then I don't see how this could be a bad idea."

"Oh, there are many reasons this could be a bad idea." Did I mean to rise up on my toes? No, not really. But he was like a planet, pulling me toward him with gravitational force.

"Care to share them?"

"Not right now."

Taylor

When Magnolia's lips met mine, I didn't know how to react. Had I wanted her to kiss me? *Was the sky blue?* I'd thought of little else since Halloween. But it had taken me by surprise, so it took me a moment to get my bearings—which had evidently been a second too long because she began to pull away.

Not wanting—or willing—to let the moment end, I wrapped my arm around her waist and pressed her into the counter behind her. She melted against me, her arms snaking up my chest to wrap around my neck, leaving a trail of fire in their wake. Everything about her was intoxicating: the way she smelled, the way she felt beneath my hands, and the feel of her lips on mine. But when I swept my tongue across the seam of her lips and she moaned? Good lord. That one little sound vibrated against my lips and down into my groin.

Running my hands down her sides, I hooked them beneath her thighs and lifted her onto the counter surface. Her gasp was silenced by my mouth, and she widened her legs enough for me to step between them.

Kissing Magnolia Bellevue was like burning alive and breathing fresh spring air, all wrapped into one. Her touch ignited every fiber of my being, but the little sounds she made? God, the crimes I would commit to hear those over and over again.

Our kiss slowed to a languid tangle of tongues as her hands slowly slid down my frame, wrapping around my back like she was mapping every inch of my torso. Desperate to do the same, I fingered the hem of her t-shirt and pulled away enough to rest my forehead against hers.

Breath ragged and coming in low pants, she asked, "Why'd you stop?"

"Because as much as I want to touch you, I'm not going to do it without your explicit permission."

"Oh," she squeaked. "I should have done that, too." Her hands shifted against my waist, but before she could remove them, I wrapped her wrists in my own, holding them in place.

"You can touch me anywhere you want to, cher." Her breath hitched, and I couldn't help the smile that tugged at my lips. Relinquishing my hold, I moved to wrap my hand around the side of her neck. Running my thumb along her jawline, I tilted her face up until those aqua eyes locked onto mine. God, she was breathtaking. Even in the dim light, her eyes sparkled; the little flecks of gold in her irises putting all the glitter of Mardi Gras to shame. "May I?"

Pulling her bottom lip between her teeth, her eyes flicked between mine as she gave me a breathless nod.

"You sure, baby? Because I don't know if I'll be able to go back to keeping my hands to myself if you let me."

"Oh, good god, Taylor. Just fucking touch me."

I melded my mouth to hers, tightening my hold on her neck as I pulled her closer. When I broke away again, her disgruntled groan was music to my ears.

"Stop doing that," she whined, wrapping her legs around my hips, her feet digging into my ass as she attempted to pull me to her.

"You're awful bratty, you know that?"

"There's one surefire way to shut me up, you know?"

"Point taken." As I reclaimed her mouth, I slipped my hands beneath the hem of her still-damp shirt. My groan was swallowed by her lips as my hand met skin softer than velvet and smoother than silk. I wanted to take my time, to map out every inch of her, commit every freckle that dotted her cheeks to memory, and find what made her writhe or gasp.

I wanted to make her *mine*, and if the way her head dropped back as I trailed my lips across her jaw was any indication, it seemed I was well on my way.

Her hands found my biceps, her grip tightening as my hands moved north, pulling her shirt up with every inch I traversed.

"Taylor," she gasped as I sucked the sensitive skin where her neck and shoulder met.

"What do you need, sunshine? Tell me what you want."

"More. I need... I need *more*."

Rotating my hands to slide up her back, my head fell to her shoulder with a groan. "Magnolia," I growled against her skin.

"What?" she panted, panic lacing her tone.

I lifted my head to meet her gaze. "Mags, baby, you mean to tell me you haven't been wearing a bra the entire time we've been locked in here together?"

Pink flushed her cheeks. "You mean you didn't notice?"

"I do try *not* to stare at women's chests, Magnolia," I deadpanned, earning a small smile as her flush deepened.

"I was so cold you could have cut glass with my nipples."

My nostrils flared as I inhaled deeply, my cock throbbing in my pants as a very different visual came to mind: Magnolia topless, nipples hardened into peaks for an entirely different reason, her mouth parting in a little *o* as her head fell backward and she rode my—

Nope. I needed to get my thoughts back on track before they completely derailed. I was already harder than I had any right to be, and she hadn't even touched me below the waist. But it was hard not to let my mind wander when she looked at me the way she was—her breath slow and heavy, her lips swollen from mine, and a lustful haze shining in those aqua orbs.

Slowly, I slid my hands across her back until they spanned her ribcage. Keeping my eyes trained on her face, I watched for any inkling of doubt to flash in her eyes. There was none—not as my hands moved along her sides, nor when my thumbs brushed the edges of her breasts.

"Taylor, *please*," she pleaded, her grip tightening on my arms as she arched her back slightly.

"You're sure?"

"Yes, dammit." Apparently fed up with me, Magnolia sat up abruptly and wrapped her hands in my hair, pulling my mouth down to hers.

Throwing caution to the proverbial wind, I cupped her breasts, groaning when they felt like literal perfection. Soft and pliant—not too big or small, they fit perfectly in my hands.

Tweaking a nipple with one hand, I used the other to lift her shirt higher. I wanted—no, *needed*—to have them in my mouth. But just as the fabric reached her chest, the soft tinkling of a bell had Magnolia shoving me off of her and jumping down from the counter.

"Magnolia," I ground out, banding my arm around her waist to haul her back.

"Hush!" She slapped my arm a few times until I let go, straightening her shirt as she frantically looked around her kitchen. "Meowfoy? Here, boy!"

"Baby, the cat's not in—" The sound of a meow had the words dying on my tongue. Surely there was no way in hell that the cat had gotten through a *locked* door... right?

Before I could voice my opinion, a ball of wet, matted fluff wriggled out from beneath the counter where I'd just had its owner on top of.

"You have *got* to be kidding me," I muttered to myself, pinching the bridge of my nose as Magnolia's excited squeal echoed in the small space.

Scooping up the large snowball she insisted was a cat, Magnolia nuzzled the big—seriously, a cat that big belonged in a zoo or something—fuzzball. "What are you doing here? You're supposed to be home!"

The cat bumped its head against hers, its purrs loud enough that I could hear them from where I was standing a few feet away. Nodding like she'd had some kind of telepathic communication with the thing, she placed Meowfoy back on the floor and turned for the large walk-in cooler in the kitchen.

My gaze shifted from the soft sway of Magnolia's hips down to the cotton ball on the floor. Its bright blue eyes were locked on me, and I was pretty sure it was scowling. But that wasn't possible, was it? Cats couldn't scowl... could they?

When Mags returned with a small dish, the cat tilted its head, eyeing me with a knowing gaze. It felt as if he understood exactly what he'd interrupted, as if he had been biding his time for that precise moment to make his presence known.

This was the third time something—or someone—had thwarted our progress. I was slightly relieved it had happened the first time since she hadn't realized it was me, and we were both, at least, tipsy. But this was becoming absurd.

My arousal effectively diminished as the cat continued to stare me down—yes, I was certain that's exactly what he was doing. I grabbed my shirt from where I'd draped it across the counter to dry. It was still damp and cold from lying on the metal table, but what could I do?

"I don't think your cat likes me," I said, pulling the shirt over my head.

"What? No, you're fine. He's just crabby because he's wet."

"If you say so." I watched Magnolia settle on the floor by her pet, stroking her hand down his coat. I could have sworn the little bastard smirked at me before dipping his head to indulge in the food she'd placed in front of him.

I guess he took after his namesake.

Cat: one.

Taylor: still zero.

11
Man Hating Cat Club
Magnolia

HOURS HAD PASSED, AND I could hear the storm subsiding; the wind shifted from a howl to a whistle, the rain dwindling to a gentle pitter-patter on the roof. Yet, despite the calm settling in, I couldn't get closer than a foot to Taylor. Every time I tried, my furry little bodyguard would whine, stretching his long body up my side or twining in circles around my legs until I finally scooped him up.

The *one* time he ventured close enough to brush a strand of hair behind my ear, Meowfoy growled. *Growled*! I'd never heard him make that sound in my life.

When his interference escalated to the point where Taylor and I couldn't even have a conversation, I scooped him up and made my way to the vinyl booths lining the main area of my shop.

"What is your deal?" I whispered as I settled him in my lap.

His head nudged my cheek, his thoughts trickling into my mind as if they belonged there. *"I don't like him."*

"You're a cat. You don't like anyone."

"Not true. I love my witches. It's these mundane *beings that I don't like."* Disdain dripped from his words, prompting me to roll my eyes.

"Why don't you like *him*?" I kept my voice low, but I was sure I looked like a crazy cat lady scolding her fuzzy companion.

His purr resonated like a dull roar as he rubbed his head beneath my chin. *"He's a man. I don't trust him."*

I snorted softly, shaking my head slightly as I stroked his back and tail. "Meowfoy, you don't even know him."

"I know enough. I remember the tears from all those years ago. I remember his name. I know what he did to you."

Mother, help me. It felt like the thoughts still tickling the back of my mind funneled into his, and were parroted back with startling clarity. I tried to use the same logic thrown at me. "We were children. I've grown. I've changed. He seems to have, too."

Meowfoy huffed through his nose, those icy blue eyes landing on my face, filled with skepticism. I knew cats could be judgmental, but geez.

"Just give him a chance. And if he hurts me, I give you permission to shit on his pillow."

His eyes narrowed slightly before shifting over my shoulder, likely to where Taylor was watching us. *Yep, don't mind me—just a crazy cat lady.*

Groaning internally, I pressed my brow against Meowfoy's head as his words came out as a low growl. *"Fine."*

"Thank you," I whispered, kissing his furry little head before setting him down on the bench. He turned in a circle twice before finally sinking down onto the vinyl, his front paws curling under him until he resembled a loaf of unbaked bread dough.

When I returned to the kitchen, I let out a heavy breath. "Sorry about that."

Taylor raised an eyebrow, his gaze flicking to the blob of fur across the room before quickly redirecting back to mine. "Everything alright over there?"

"Yeah," I said with a nervous chuckle. "He's just a little... *protective*."

With a slight nod, Taylor hesitantly wrapped his hand around mine, pausing as his eyes darted back toward the bench before gently pulling me closer.

"As much as I would love to pick up where we left off—"

"It'd be a bit awkward with my cat glaring at you?" I finished for him, a wry smile lifting my lips.

"Yeah, something like that," he chuckled in response.

Silence settled between us, but my heart thundered in my ears as Taylor's thumb traced circles around the pulse point in my wrist. I opened my mouth to say something—*anything*—to break the tension taut between us, like a rope in a tug-of-war, when his phone beeped from the counter behind him.

"Shit." He grabbed his device, flipping it screen up to reveal a red, blinking battery symbol.

"Oh, crap. I'm sorry. I think I have a flashlight somewhere in the kitchen or the office. Why don't you look around out here while I check in there?" Hesitancy flickered in his eyes for the briefest moment, as though he feared I would vanish if he let me go. Tightening my grip on his hand, I offered him a small smile. "I'll be right back."

Pulling my phone from my pocket, I switched on the flashlight and headed toward my office, exhaling a heavy sigh as I slipped through the door. There had to be a flashlight *somewhere*. But after drawer after drawer yielded nothing, I sank into my chair with a groan.

"Find one?" Taylor called from down the hall.

"No. You?"

"No. It looks like there are emergency lights, but they should've turned on when the power went out."

Fucking hell. I'd completely forgotten about those stupid things. I hadn't needed them in the past, having magic on my side, but hindsight was twenty-twenty, I guess.

Taking a deep breath, I muttered an illumination incantation, releasing a tendril of magic to kick-start the emergency lights—crossing my fingers that it worked since I'd never bothered to see if they even functioned. A faint glow filtered down the hall and into my office, followed by a yelp and a crash that had me leaping from my chair.

"Taylor? What happened—" I slapped a hand over my mouth, *desperately* trying to stifle the laughter bubbling in my throat.

Taylor—who was now sitting on the floor surrounded by bowls and cake tins—pointed an accusatory finger at me, his brows knitted together as a smile threatened to break free. "Don't. You. Dare."

The tiniest chuckle escaped my lips, and his eyes widened.

"*Magnolia,*" he growled, attempting to push himself up from the floor. But every move he made sent metal clattering against metal, creating a symphony of *clangs* that filled the space.

I tried, I really did, but I couldn't hold back any longer. My laughter erupted from my chest, intensifying when he nearly slipped on a bowl behind him.

My stomach cramped, my cheeks ached, and tears threatened to spill from my eyes as I leaned against the counter for support.

When he finally found his footing, his eyes locked onto mine, retribution gleaming in their sapphire depths as a cocky smirk played at the corner of his lips. "You're going to pay for that."

"What?" I gasped through my hysteria.

Carefully navigating the scattered baking supplies, Taylor began to stalk toward me. My laughter faded as I swallowed hard, my heart pounding as his eyes burned into mine. I felt like a deer caught in headlights, rooted to the spot by the flames in his gaze.

"Taylor," I breathed, finally finding my voice and willing my feet to move.

"You want to laugh, sunshine? I'll give you something to laugh about."

"Taylor... what... what are you doing?" I asked as he slowly advanced.

"Are you ticklish, Magnolia?" he asked, tilting his head slightly as that smirk deepened.

"What? No." My eyes widened like a full moon on a clear night. When my brain finally caught up, my feet finally started moving. "Nononononono. *Taylor*," I admonished, holding my hands out as if warding off a wild animal.

"*Magnolia*," he said my name in a tone heavy with the promise of torture.

No one in their right mind liked to be tickled, but the butterflies in my stomach hadn't received the memo because they were currently taking flight, performing acrobatics.

With each step I took back, Taylor advanced. I hadn't realized we'd rounded the entire island until my heel struck a bowl, the sound ringing through the quiet and pulling my focus for the briefest moment.

But that second was all he needed, and he pounced.

Strong and determined, yet still gentle, his fingers danced along my sides, sending me into a fit of giggles. When a snort—unbidden and without my permission—escaped, I clamped my hands over my mouth and shut my eyes tight.

Taylor's hands stilled on my waist, and I felt him lean closer, his breath warm against my ear as he whispered, "Did you just *snort*, sunshine?"

Oh, ruler of the underworld. Open your depths and swallow me whole, because there is no way in hell I can face him after that absurd sound came from my face holes.

Taylor

Magnolia's face could make a red rose envious, and it was the cutest thing I'd ever seen. Her hands shifted from covering her mouth to completely shielding her face as she thudded her head against my chest.

"Mags, baby. Look at me," I said with a soft chuckle. When she simply shook her head, I gently grabbed her wrists and nudged her head away from my chest. "Why are you hiding?"

"Because that was embarrassing," she groaned into her palms. Slowly, her hands fell from her face, revealing piercing aqua orbs that locked onto mine. "You could've been a gentleman and ignored it, but *nooo*."

A snort of my own escaped at her dramatics, and her bright eyes narrowed. "Why would I ignore something I find endearing?"

"*Endearing?*"

"Yes, Mags. Endearing. In the span of, what, five minutes? I've learned two new things about you." Her brow quirked, and she looked at me like I'd lost my mind. Who knows, maybe I had. But I also wasn't wrong. "I now know you're ticklish, and when your laughter really gets going, you make the cutest little snorting sound this side of the Mississippi."

She turned her lips inward, trying and failing to suppress her smile as she rolled her eyes in response.

"You keep blushing like that, and I'm going to want to see how far down it goes."

Her bottom lip disappeared between her teeth, her eyes locking onto mine as flames danced in their depths. Then she pinched them closed and groaned out my name—not in the good way, either. "What is it?"

"We—" she rested her palms on my chest, her fingers rubbing along the fabric of my t-shirt. "We should probably slow down."

"Slow down…" I repeated, running my hands up her arms and down her sides to her waist, relishing in the way goosebumps followed my touch. Her lips curled inward as she finally raised her eyes to meet mine.

"Yes," she breathed, her hands curling into fists around the fabric.

"Mags, baby. Your lips are saying one thing, but your body is saying something else entirely. Help me out here."

"We have… There is…" Blowing out a sharp breath, Magnolia pressed her hands against my pecs and gave me a gentle shove. "There. Maybe now my brain can form words."

"Come again?" I asked, chuckling.

"You're basically a… a… walking sex stick, and you smell like a man-candle. It makes my brain go all liquidy, and I can't do the *words* into sentence *putting*."

My mouth opened and closed, brows knitting together as I struggled to wrap my brain around the words that just came out of her mouth. I wasn't sure how, and I was pretty sure that Ms. Bourgeois—my old high school English teacher—would have had a stroke hearing that sentence, but somehow it made sense.

I took a few steps back until I collided with the counter that filled the center of the kitchen. "Better?"

"Yes, thank you." She exhaled all the air from her lungs as she propped herself up on the countertop, leaning back on her hands. "So."

"So."

"Slower."

"As you said. Care to elaborate on that, sunshine?"

"There's obviously something..." She gestured between us, and I watched her throat bob as she swallowed, her eyes locked onto mine. "*Between us.*"

"Uh-huh."

"But I'm not really into the whole..." Her gaze traveled down my body, her breathing slightly labored as her lip disappeared between her teeth, and a flush blossomed on her cheeks.

"The whole *what*, Magnolia?" It took every ounce of self-control I had to remain on my side of the kitchen. There was no denying the attraction between us, especially when the hunger in her eyes matched the fire raging inside me.

"Friends with benefits," she squeaked out, her cheeks deepening in color.

"It's a good thing that's not what I want then, isn't it?"

"You don't?"

Expelling a heavy sigh, I shook my head and brought my gaze back to hers. "Permission to approach?"

"What is this, a courtroom?" she asked, a flicker of that fire I was used to igniting in her tone, melting away the meekness from moments before.

"No, but you asked for space so your brain could do the 'words into sentence putting,' so I wanted to make sure it was alright first." When she nodded slightly, I slowly closed the distance between us. Her legs parted, giving me room to step between them, and I rested my hands just above her knees. "I told you, Mags. I want to get to *know* you. I know we started off kind of strong, but if you want to slow it down, then that's what we'll do. We just need to set some ground rules."

"Ground rules," she echoed, nodding. "Like what?"

"Texting?"

"Obviously."

"Phone calls?"

"That's a given."

"Telling people?"

"Telling *who*? And what?" she asked, a quirked brow lifting.

"Family and friends, and that we're seeing each other."

Her nose scrunched, head tilting to the side. "Not yet?"

"Okay, but may I ask why?"

"I don't want everyone staring at me any more than they already do. You're still the town golden boy, even after all those years away. And I'm still... well, *me.*"

I didn't agree, but I understood her perspective. She'd spent her life enduring sneers from townsfolk because someone started a rumor years ago that she and her family were witches. It was part of why Kyle had tormented her in school, still finding twisted joy in it. Ridiculous, but it was Magnolia's reality. If it were up to me, I'd shout it from the rooftops. I wanted to walk around town with her on my arm, do mundane things like grocery shopping, cook her dinner, or share a bucket of popcorn at the movies. But she had her limits, and I didn't want to push those boundaries—not yet, anyway. She wanted to go slow, so just call me a tortoise—at least he won in the end.

I nodded sagely and released a steady breath. "Fair enough. But that brings me to my next question. How are we going to go on dates if you don't want the town knowing about us?"

"Convenient run-ins?" she suggested, grimacing.

"Mags."

"I don't know, Taylor. I don't know how to do *this*."

"Date?"

"No, I know how to do *that*. It's been a while, but I'm pretty sure the premise hasn't changed. Can't we just, I don't know, figure it out as we go?"

A stone sank in my stomach as I nodded, and silence settled between us. But then her hands found my hips, gently pulling me closer as she stared up at me.

"Kissing?" she asked hesitantly, her eyes flicking back and forth between mine.

"Do you want me to kiss you?" I brought one hand to her waist, the other cupping her cheek as I held her gaze—and my breath—because if she said no, I was pretty sure I would shrivel up and die on the spot.

"Definitely."

"Just not in front of anyone." Her chin dropped, her eyes falling to my chest before I coaxed her gaze back up to mine. "I'm not big on PDA, anyway."

And then I kissed her.

It started off soft and slow, but when a contented little moan vibrated against my lips, fire surged through my veins. Slipping my hand around to the back of her head, I tangled my fingers in her hair, tilting her head back to devour her.

Her hands fisted into my shirt, pulling me closer as she wrapped her legs around my hips. Banding an arm around her back, I slid her to the edge of the counter until her center pressed against me. She gasped against my lips, then slowly began to rock her hips along the hardened ridge of my cock, and I nearly came from just that.

With a disgruntled groan, I released her hair, grabbed her hips to still her movements, and rested my forehead against hers. "Mags, baby, are you *trying* to kill me?"

Our labored breathing mingled in the space between us for a moment before she gently separated us. "No. Sorry. I told you... liquid brain."

"The feeling is mutual. Trust me."

Her gaze raked down my body to the tent pitched in my joggers. "I can see that."

"Magnolia," I ground out, "if you keep looking at me like that, this whole 'taking it slow' thing is going to be a lot harder than it should be."

"Pun intended?" she asked, a devilish smirk curling her lips.

"I think you lied. I think you *are* trying to kill me."

"I'm sorry," she said with a light chuckle, then cleared her throat and fixed me with a determined gaze. "Let's start over."

When I quirked a brow, she made a shooing motion with her hand until I backed up enough for her to hop off the counter.

"Magnolia Bellevue." She held out her hand, a sweet smile stretching across her face as her eyes met mine.

Chuckling, I shook my head as I took her hand. "Taylor Hallows."

"Charmed." She gave our hands a gentle shake, her smile widening as she inclined her head slightly.

The scoff that escaped me was involuntary, but the smile that followed was entirely for the woman in front of me. Eyes locked onto her aqua and gold irises, I ran my thumb across her knuckles and gently pulled her toward me. Wrapping my opposite arm around her waist, I watched her eyes widen as I tilted her back. "I'm sure."

And then I kissed her to the sound of the wind whipping against the building, rain hammering on the roof, and the soft jingle of her damn cat's bell as he sauntered across the shop.

12

Save a horse

Taylor

"Whatcha got for me, Chels?" I asked, sinking into a chair in the corner of the nurses' station.

"We've got a back pain in bed two, a snake bite in trauma one, and a puncture wound in bed four."

"Do we know what kind of snake it was?"

"Not sure. EMS just got them settled in the room. Britt is taking the report, and Dr. East is in there now, so I think you're off the hook on that one."

Swiveling my chair toward the computer, I pulled up the triage notes for the other two patients I needed to see and let out a heavy breath. I was exhausted.

It was midnight by the time the storm passed through our sleepy little town, only the outer bands sweeping across the parish with light wind and rain. By then, Mags and I were both worn out and ended up dozing on the vinyl benches of her shop. Well, "sleeping" might be a stretch. Even propped against the wall, my feet dangled off the edge. It didn't help that Meowfoy's bright blue eyes seared into mine all night, as if he were just waiting for me to drift off.

A cat. I was a grown-ass man, and I was scared of a damn *cat* that looked like a giant cotton ball with feet.

By the following morning, the coast was clear to leave our little bubble, but I hadn't seen or heard from Magnolia since watching her walk up her front porch steps. By the time I made it back to my parents' house, my dad had called my mom on the landline and asked her to inform me that Team B would be implemented as soon as the roads cleared. That brought us to today—two days since the storm started, one since I saw Magnolia, and I was already itching to be in her orbit again.

But as storm cleanup continued outside the hospital doors, patients flooded through them, and it was my job to ensure they could return to their lives as quickly—and safely—as possible.

Rolling my neck, I slid back my chair and stood. "Bed four first?"

After a quick nod from Chelsea, I motioned for her to lead the way to the patient's room while I repeated their information in my mind. Bedside manner was crucial in the medical field, and I took pride in it. I wanted my patients to feel safe and comfortable talking to me, especially after going through something traumatic.

Clyde Jarvis, 45 years old.

Male.

Pronouns: he/him.

Reason for visit: puncture wound to the right hand from handling a fallen fence board while cleaning up his yard.

With a steadying breath, I plastered on as non-exhausted a smile as I could muster and stepped into the room. "Hey, Mr. Jarvis. I hear you've got a nasty puncture on your palm. Let's get you fixed up so you can get out of here. How'd y'all fare during the storm?"

·))●((·

By the time seven a.m. rolled around, I was nearly dead on my feet. One shift down, two more to go before I got a day off. Not that it would be much of a day off since I needed to help my parents pick up the yard. That was where I was heading now, even though everything in me wanted to drive down that gravel drive leading to a bright teal door.

As I put my Bronco in park, I leaned my head against the headrest and closed my eyes for a brief moment, willing the exhaustion to disappear as I prepared for the inevitable onslaught of questions that would undoubtedly be hurled my way as soon as I stepped foot inside.

I'd managed to evade my mom's prodding the morning after the storm, claiming I needed to sleep so I would be "bright-eyed and bushy-tailed" for work. But Addy was a different story altogether. She was relentless in her inquiries, and there was no way I was escaping her scrutiny two days in a row.

Blowing out a breath, I left my car and headed around back to check on the generators. The house was dark since the power was still out, but it was blissfully cool thanks to the Big Ass Fan we had set up in the French doors off the breakfast nook.

I sighed in relief when I stepped inside and didn't encounter the ever-present scent of coffee. No coffee meant no Addy... at least not yet.

Grabbing one of the lanterns we kept by the door, I turned it on to the lowest setting and crept through the house like a teenager sneaking back in after curfew. I decided to shower after my sister vacated the premises later that day. I closed my door with a soft click and sagged against it.

"You ready to talk to me now?"

Adelaide's voice shattered the silence, my heart rate skyrocketing as I swung wide eyes toward her. She lounged across my bed with her arms crossed over her chest.

"Jesus, Addy! Are you trying to give me a heart attack?" I demanded in a hushed tone.

"No, but it would serve you right for running out into a hurricane and avoiding me afterward."

Her eyes narrowed as I held her gaze. I couldn't tell her where I went without mentioning Magnolia. And if I told her about Magnolia, my mom would find out, and then the whole town would know because my mother couldn't keep a secret to save her life.

Shaking my head, I pushed off the door and crossed the room to my closet. Avoidance. I could manage that as long as I didn't look too closely at my sister.

"*Taylor Michael Hallows,*" she screeched, her hands flying to cover her eyes as I pulled my shirt over my head.

"Adelaide Jane Hallows," I mocked, wadding up my shirt and tossing it into the hamper. "You're the one in *my* room, baby sister." Running a hand through my hair, I huffed out an exhausted breath and turned toward her. "Look, Addy. I've been at work for the last twelve hours. I smell like a hospital, and I'm tired. Can we pick this up another day? Another year? A century?"

"You promised you'd tell me what was going on—"

"*When* there was something to tell. And right now, there isn't. So just let it *go*. Please, for my sanity."

Her eyes narrowed to slits as she slipped from my bed and pointed an accusatory finger at me. "I'm watching you, Hallows."

"Ooo, so *scary*," I teased, grabbing her finger and pulling her into a hug. I hated keeping secrets from my sister. She was one of the best people I knew and one of my best friends. But this wasn't just my secret to share. I could handle her prodding, could deal with the murmurs around town—at least I thought I could. But Magnolia had been subject to their scrutiny her whole life, and I didn't want to be the one who added to it. Not again.

Addy sighed against my chest, her arms tightening for a brief moment before she pulled away with a wrinkled nose. "You stink."

"No shit, Sherlock." Grabbing her shoulders, I spun her toward the door and ushered her out. "Now, out. Shoo. Be gone."

With the door closed and locked behind her, my brow hit the wood with a soft thud as I heaved out a sigh. Keeping this secret wasn't going to be easy.

Magnolia

Cleaning up after a hurricane was never a fun task. It was always hot, humid, and inevitably, the power wouldn't be back on for a few days. Hurricane Melissa turned out to be no different. The house was sweltering, sweat dripping down my spine in little beads, and it was only nine in the morning.

Trudging into the kitchen after a restless night of zero sleep, I groggily mumbled a good morning to my aunt and sister, who sat holding cold glasses of sweet tea to their faces and necks. But as I poured myself into a stool at the island, I couldn't miss the sly grin on Aunt Evie's face.

"What?" I asked, bringing the cold pitcher to my forehead and sighing as the cool drops of condensation slid down my nose and cheeks.

"Oh, nothing. *Beautiful* day today, isn't it?" The waggle of her brows shot mine into my hairline, my eyes following hers as they drifted toward the bank of windows framing the breakfast nook.

Lungs robbed of air and mind spinning like a top, I nearly dropped the pitcher onto the counter as I watched Taylor swing an ax down onto a large branch that had fallen in the side yard.

Dark wash jeans hugged his legs, covered in wood chips and dirt. His shirt clung to him as if he'd been in a wet t-shirt contest, and those strong forearms glistened in the early morning light. And he was wearing a goddamn baseball cap.

Time seemed to move in slow motion as I watched him bring the ax down on the branch. My eyes zeroed in on the way his gloved hands wrapped around the wood handle, and memories of how those hands felt sliding along my sides, cupping my head, tangling with my hair flooded back—

My core clenched, and I shook myself to cut off that train of thought.

"What's he doing?" I asked, swinging my head back around toward my snickering family members.

"Looks like he's chopping up that branch," Aunt Evie joked, her brows wagging as she took a sip from her glass.

"Quite well, if you ask me," Maddie added, her head tilting slightly as she kept her gaze trained out the windows. When she turned back toward me, her eyes narrowed as she pointed at my mouth. "You've got a little *drool*, just… there." Her finger poked my bottom lip, and I recoiled with a scoff.

"Stop that!" I hissed, smacking Maddie on the shoulder and placing the pitcher back on the countertop. I hadn't seen Taylor in four days. Hadn't heard from him either, since cell service was still spotty around town. And there was no way in hell I was going to let our first encounter after everything that happened at *CharCutie* be with me dressed in a ratty tank top and shorts that barely covered half my ass.

Slipping off the stool, I took another glance toward the windows and hurried out of the kitchen, my escape trailed by Aunt Evie's laughter as she yelled, "Have fun!"

+·))●((·+

I was pretty sure that the column I was leaning against was the only thing keeping me on my feet at this point.

After I'd changed into leggings and a tank-top sports bra, I threw my hair into a ponytail and pulled it through the back of my favorite hat before heading outside to help Taylor clean up *my* yard. A satisfied smile spread across his lips when I confessed to telling my sisters about him being at *CharCutie* with me during the storm. His brows rose in disbelief when I swore up, down, left, and right that I hadn't told them anything else.

I hadn't... not really. But Maddie could read it on my face as easily as revisiting her favorite novel.

We worked in relative silence for most of the morning, but when my muscles started screaming at me from overuse, I slipped inside to grab us some sweet tea. That led me here—leaning against the column at the top of my porch steps, glass of tea pressed against my neck as water dripped down between my breasts, my eyes glued to the man loading wood into a wheelbarrow. He'd stripped off his shirt hours ago, and I watched each muscle flex beneath his golden skin as he worked. I swear it was the heat that made me want to lick the sweat off his pecs.

When his eyes met mine across the yard, I stood a little straighter, trying to pass off my blatant ogling as casual. But the smirk on his lips told me I had failed. *Miserably.*

I couldn't even keep myself from muttering *"sweet baby cheeses"* when his eyes locked onto mine as he twisted his hat backward and started crossing the yard toward me. Don't ask me why that's sexy. I have no clue. But it is. Always has been, always would be.

My eyes roamed over his frame of their own accord. My teeth bit my bottom lip without my permission, and my thighs clenched together when his gaze honed in on the movement.

Slow. We're supposed to be taking this slow, I reminded myself as he drew closer.

"See something you like, sunshine?" he asked, propping his foot on the bottom step as he tugged off his gloves and pulled the rag I'd given him earlier from his back pocket, swiping it across his brow.

A shudder ran through me as I descended the steps on uncharacteristically wobbly legs, holding out his glass for him to take; nearly dropping the damn thing when his fingers brushed mine.

I'd just opened my mouth when Aunt Evie poked her head out the front window and yelled, "Hey, y'all! Yard's looking great, but come on in and grab some lunch. I made cold-cut sandwiches."

Before either of us could reply, she slipped back inside, and I was left with a grinning, half-naked Taylor staring at me expectantly.

"Meeting your family already? Gee, Mags, I don't know. We're supposed to be taking this slow."

My mouth dropped open in an astonished gasp as I slapped his shoulder. "Shut up. You hungry or not?"

"Starving."

Suddenly, I wasn't so sure we were talking about Aunt Evie's cold-cut sandwiches. His eyes perused my frame languidly before landing back on my face. His hand wrapped around my waist, the rough calluses on his palm rasping against the thin strip of skin that poked out between my top and leggings as he pulled me down one more step and into his body.

"What are you doing?" I asked breathlessly as my hands came to rest on his chest.

"Kissing my girl." He ran his nose up mine, our breaths mingling between us.

My girl. With just those two words and his mahogany and vanilla scent mixing with the sweat on his skin, I was a puddle of goo. It shouldn't have been as intoxicating as it was, but once again, this man rendered me stupid.

"Someone might see." I knew it was a stupid excuse. No one but us was outside, and I really didn't care if my aunt or sister saw us kissing.

His chuckle vibrated in my chest as he banded his arm around my lower back. "It's been four days, Mags, and I'm dying over here. And I know you are too. Don't think I missed the way you've been eye-fucking me all day. No one will see us, plus it was a ground rule we agreed to, remember?"

Fucking ground rules. That had simultaneously been the best and worst idea I'd ever had.

"Where'd you go, baby?"

"What?" I asked, watching as his eyes flicked between my own.

"You retreated somewhere inside yourself. I don't know where you went, but if this is too much..."

When his grip loosened on my waist, I slid my hands up his chest and wrapped them around his neck. "It's not too much." Then I pressed my lips to his, his arm tightening around me, pulling me flush against him as his fingers dug into my side in the most delicious way. I could feel him hardening in his jeans, and try as I might, I couldn't keep my moan to myself.

Taylor's hand slipped down my body, gliding over my ass until he could palm one side, giving it a hard squeeze as he pressed his hips into mine.

Giggles from inside the house filtered into the lusty haze clouding my brain, and I pulled back with a groan, resting my brow on his.

A disbelieving chuckle rumbled out as he palmed both sides of my ass, grumbling, "One of these days, I'm going to get you alone, and there won't be another living soul around to get in my way."

"We'll see about that," I chuckled, spinning his hat back around as I pulled out of his hold. If the way he'd palmed it said anything, it was that he would probably be staring at my ass as I walked away. So I made sure to put a little swing in my stride as I sauntered up the steps, laughing when I threw a glance over my shoulder and caught him red-handed. "Come on, cowboy. Let's get some lunch."

"*Cowboy*?" he barked, eyes wide as he took the steps two at a time to catch up to me. His hands gripped my hips as he hauled me back against him, his breath hot on my ear as he whispered, "Save a horse, baby."

Sweet baby cheeses.

13

Alligator or chicken?

Magnolia

I COULDN'T CONCENTRATE IF my life depended on it. Today marked my first day back at *CharCutie* since the storm, and every—*every*—inch of the space reminded me of being there with Taylor.

The shop had fared well, thanks to the protective charms and enchantments, but after being closed for a week, I was woefully behind. I still needed to prepare for two catering gigs booked during the last Meat-Cute—one of which was only three days away. Jaelyn and I had decided to push this month's event back a week, but I still had to plan the menu, update my table rental order, and, of course, go shopping for the whole thing. On top of everything else, I also had to finalize the menu for my storefront. But everywhere I looked, I saw Taylor.

Rolling out and laminating dough for croissants? My mind took that moment to remind me of when he'd been in my bubble, his rough palms sliding up my sides as he kissed me senseless in that exact spot.

Pulling out bowls? I was bombarded with flashes of him chasing after me after I laughed at him while he sat among a pile of those infernal things.

I could see him lounging on the benches in the main area, leaning against the counters with that megawatt smile. I felt him like a phantom's kiss along every inch of my body that his hands or lips had traversed.

"Earth to Magnolia," Jaelyn chimed, waving her hand in front of my face, a sly smirk settling on her lips.

Startled back into reality, my rolling pin slipped from my grasp and clattered against the stainless counter. A curse tumbled from my lips as I scrambled to catch it before it rolled onto the floor. "Damn it, Jae. Don't sneak up on me."

"Sneak up on you? Girl, I don't know where you are, but it sure as hell isn't here," she said with an amused chuckle, her coils bouncing around her face as she shook her head. "I've been talking to you for the past..." She checked the nonexistent watch on her wrist, her gold bangles jingling as she turned her hand. "Five minutes? Well, I guess I was more or less talking *at you* since I didn't realize your brain had left the conversation."

"Sorry, Jae," I replied with a grimace. My mind was there in that kitchen—it just happened to be focused on a past-tense version of it.

Giving myself a mental shake, I began rolling out the dough until it was a quarter of an inch thick, then folded it over itself twice before starting again. "What were we talking about?"

"*I* was discussing the menu for the party on Friday. Did you still want to do sauce-piquante? If so, are we doing chicken or alligator? Or did you want to switch to passed hors d'oeuvres?"

After repeating the process twice more, I wrapped cling wrap around the dough with a groan and walked it to the cooler. The trick to achieving perfectly layered and flaky croissants was ensuring the butter stayed cold. It took time to complete all the lamination, but it was always worth it.

When I returned to the counter, I grabbed a wet rag and began cleaning up my workspace. "I should probably call them and see what they want to do. I didn't even think of that when I called to confirm they still needed catering."

Though most of my catering jobs revolved around charcuterie boards and pastries, someone occasionally requested an actual meal, and this just so happened to be one of those cases. I both loved and loathed it. I enjoyed dusting off culinary skills that I didn't get to use often, but the prep for actual meals, along with everything else, was a lot more work than I had time for at the moment.

With the counter sufficiently clean, I tossed the rag in the sink and walked over to where Jae leaned over the island, scribbling on a notepad while scouring the forms spread across the surface.

"Okay, so *if* they want to do a full meal, maybe we can simplify it?" she asked, one dark brow rising as her caramel eyes met mine.

"Sauce-piquante isn't hard to make; it's just time-consuming. As long as the number of guests doesn't increase, it shouldn't be a big deal. But we do need to find out if they want alligator or chicken so that I'm not running around last minute. It's going to be hard enough to find everything I need as it is."

Jaelyn nodded as she swept the forms into a neat pile. "I'll give them a call and finish up the list so we can grab everything later. *You* need to pop some Excedrin and chug some caffeine."

"Get out of my head," I teased, bumping my hip against hers. We'd been friends long enough that she could see my migraines coming from a mile away. It was the little things—a pinch in my brow, the squinting to block out some light, or because my vision would start to blur. She was always there with a snack, water, caffeine, and some kind of pill that she knew I wouldn't take unless she watched me like a clucking mother hen.

"I think *you* need to get out of your own head." Before I could respond, my phone pinged in my pocket. Pulling it out, I glanced down at the screen before quickly tucking it back into the back pocket of my jeans. Apparently, I wasn't fast enough, as Jaelyn's eyes widened, her lips pursing as she ran her tongue along her teeth and chuckled to herself. "Tell Taylor I said 'hey.' I'll go take care of this; you lock up the front and see what Mr. *'As you wish'* wants."

"You're never going to let him live that down, are you?"

"Not a chance." She waved over her shoulder as she made her way toward the office.

Slipping my phone back out of my pocket, I swiped the screen and opened my messages.

Taylor

> Hey, sunshine. You busy on Friday?

Magnolia

> Hey, cowboy. Unfortunately for you, I am.

As I waited for his response, I placed my phone on the front counter and began going through my closing duties: blinds dropped and closed, front door sign flipped, display case lights off. I had just finished pulling the last tray of leftover pastries from the front case when my phone dinged. Sliding the tray into a slot on my rack, I dusted off my hands and picked up my device.

Taylor

> Oh?

Magnolia

Yeah, I've got a gig.

Taylor

I didn't know you were in a band! That's so cool; maybe I'll come check you out *winking emoji*

Magnolia

A catering gig, asshole. *side-eye emoji* You know I don't sing in front of people.

Taylor

I consider myself special, then.

Magnolia

raised eyebrow emoji

Taylor

I got my own personal concert on our first date. Now we just need our schedules to line up so we can have another one.

And no, Magnolia. Cleaning up your yard while you stared at my ass was not a date.

MAGNOLIA

Hey! I helped!

And last time I checked, I caught you staring at MY ass, Mr. Hallows.

TAYLOR

Can you blame me?

A laugh bubbled up, and I rolled my eyes at my screen as I typed out my response.

MAGNOLIA

I can, but I won't.

I watched as three little dots popped up then disappeared twice before his response finally came through.

TAYLOR

> So when are you going to let me take you
> out?

My thumbs paused over the screen as my endless to-do list scrolled through my brain. I wanted to go out with him; I really did. But our timing was always off. I still didn't know what he did, and I kind of liked it that way. It kept some of the mystery that this town—where everyone was in everyone *else's* business—severely lacked. Whatever it was he did, our schedules rarely aligned, and with the holidays approaching, finding time to do anything outside of work would be next to impossible.

Make time, the little voice in the back of my head chided.

I tilted my head to the side, narrowing my eyes on the screen when a thought popped into my head just as Jaelyn poked her head around the corner.

"Hey, I just talked to Mrs. Thibodeaux. They want to keep the dinner and asked for alligator if you can find it, but chicken is fine if not. She also said you're welcome to use her kitchen so you don't have to cook it here and then transport it all the way to Baton Rouge."

My shoulders sagged with relief at Jae's words. "Thank God for that. Is the rest of the shopping list finished? And can you give Gary a call to see if he can help us out?"

"Yes and yes. You want it?"

"Yeah. I'll finish up front, and then head out."

"Do you want me to come with?" she asked, curiosity swirling in her eyes.

"Nah, I just kind of want to disassociate while I shop. Plus, I have a new audiobook I can listen to." *One truth, one lie.*

"Uh-huh." Her eyes narrowed as she asked, "What book?"

Scrunching my brow, I replied, "Uh, I don't remember the name, but it's some small-town, age-gap, grumpy-sunshine, something or another that Maddie suggested."

"Mmhmm," she hummed in response, her lips pursing in a way that said she knew I was full of shit. "Whatever you say, Mags. I'll leave the list on the desk. Call me if you need anything or want *company*, okay?"

"Yep." I popped the *p* with a little more force than necessary, and Jae shook her head as she turned back toward the office. "Love you!" I hollered at her back.

"Uh-huh. Love you too, liar."

Did I hate lying to my best friend? Absolutely. But I couldn't break my own ground rule, could I? Plus, I was about ninety-nine percent sure she knew and was just waiting for me to blurt it out. After all, she was one of the people who pushed me toward him, so it's not like it would come as much of a shock if I *did* tell her.

One step. I made it one step toward the office, determined to spill the beans about me and Taylor—because there was no way I could keep this from her for long—when another text came through on my phone.

TAYLOR

Mags?

And that's what we call the universe intervening. Blowing out a raspberry, I looked up toward the ceiling and then typed out a response.

MAGNOLIA

Can you meet me at my house in twenty?

Sure.

You gonna tell me what you have in mind, or are we flying by the seat of our pants?

How do you feel about grocery shopping?

·))●((·

Taylor

Grocery shopping? I've been on a few unconventional dates in my time, but going to the grocery store is certainly a new one. A smile pulled at the corner of my lips as I parked my Bronco in Magnolia's driveway nineteen minutes later. I hadn't even unbuckled my seatbelt before she came bounding down the front steps and stole the breath from my lungs. She looked like the girl next door—if the girl next door had pink and blue hair, tattoos, and the attitude of a mountain lion. The emerald green dress she wore flowed down to her shins, and the cream sweater had slipped off her shoulder. It felt like time moved in slow motion as I watched her jog toward the car, and I still hadn't unglued myself from my seat by the time she threw open the passenger door.

"Hey," she said in a breathless exhale as she pulled the door closed, her cheeks slightly flushed as she briefly met my gaze before digging through her purse.

"Hey, yourself." It came out smoother than I felt, and as I took a deep breath to calm the nerves that sprang to life anytime she was near me, her spicy floral scent filled my lungs, and all I wanted to do was breathe her in.

Angling my body toward hers, I silently watched and waited for her to finish whatever she was doing. My God, she was beautiful. The golden-hour sun shone through the windows, highlighting all the little hairs that had slipped from her braids and framed her face. It caught on the ends of her long lashes, traced the delicate contour of her nose, and accentuated the fullness of her lips.

With a quick puff of air, she blew the strands out of her face and brought her gaze to mine. "Sorry, I thought I left my list at the shop, but I found it," she said, holding out a sheet of blue paper with a triumphant grin. Tilting her head, she quirked a brow. "What? Do I have something on my face? In my teeth?"

"What? No—"

Hastily flipping down the visor, she continued. "Sorry, I was trying to eat before you got here so I wouldn't go to the store starving—"

"Mags—" I tried to cut her off, but there was no slipping between the words tumbling from her lips at sixty miles per hour.

"And I didn't have time to check the mirror before I ran out the door—"

"Mags!" I chuckled, reaching across the console to grab her hand as she frantically searched her face for an imperfection that wasn't there. When her gaze finally landed on mine, I said, "You're perfect. I was just admiring the view."

Faint pink colored her cheeks, and she pursed her lips to hide her smile. "Smooth, cowboy. Real smooth."

"I speak only the truth, cher," I replied, releasing her hand as I pushed the ignition button. Even though I wasn't looking directly at her, I didn't miss the sarcastic side-eye or the mouthed "*oh, okay*" as she rolled her eyes and pulled her seatbelt across her chest. That just wouldn't do. Unlatching my seatbelt, I turned her way, wrapped my hand around the back of her neck, and pulled her toward me.

Shock widened her eyes as my nose brushed against hers, and I felt her swallow hard. But in less than a fraction of a second, heat filled her gaze as it traveled down to my lips and back. Sliding my hand around to grip her chin, I held her still as I whispered, "Hi."

"Hi," she replied in the same tone.

"I'm going to kiss you now, okay?"

Her breath caught in her throat as she pulled her bottom lip between her teeth and nodded against my hand. "Yeah, okay. Sounds good."

My lips brushed against hers, and I felt her melt in my hold. I intended for it to be a quick, simple dusting of lips, but as her sweet little hum vibrated from her mouth and into mine, I pressed harder. My hand rotated from her chin to around her nape, tugging her across the console as her hand gripped the front of my shirt for balance. But before it could go too far, I pulled away, resting my brow on hers, our ragged breaths mingling as the air in the cab grew heavy with tension.

"That was one hell of a hello, cowboy," she whispered, a smile evident in her tone.

Chuckling, I pressed my lips against her forehead and tucked a stray hair behind her ear. "You sure you want to go grocery shopping?" I asked when I finally settled back into my seat. "I can think of a few alternatives, one of which includes a lot more of that hello."

"As promising as that sounds, I *need* to go to the store. Are *you* sure you want to come with me?" she questioned, a singular brow rising as she readjusted her seatbelt.

"Sunshine, if the store is where you need to be, then the store is where we'll go. *But* I do have an idea."

"Oh yeah?" she asked saucily, her brows inching toward her hairline as she tried to mask the smile on her lips.

"Yeah, baby. When it comes to you, I've got *loads* of 'em." I winked, then threw the car in reverse.

+)❭●❬(+

"Good Lord, woman. Are you buying the whole damn store?" I jested as we turned down another aisle. The contents of Magnolia's cart ranged from fresh produce to liquor to toothpaste, and a little bit of everything in between.

"Shush you. I have to shop for this Friday, restock things for the shop, and pick up some stuff I need at home too."

Shaking my head, I looked down at the list she'd handed me when we walked in and called off the next item. "The next line says alligator/chicken? What's that for?"

"I'm making some variation of sauce piquante for a dinner party on Friday, just not sure which one yet. Hence the slash." She placed a large bag of powdered sugar and a bottle of vanilla the size of my face into the buggy, then turned toward the butcher counter at the back of the store.

"Ooowee, lookin' good, cher!" the plump man behind the counter hollered as we approached.

"Hey there, handsome. Did Jae call you?"

"Yeah, hang tight, and I'll go grab it for ya from da back."

As the butcher walked through the stainless door behind him, I leaned on the cart and raised my brows. "Who's that?"

"Gary," she stated matter-of-factly.

"And who might Gary be?"

"Jealous?" she asked with a cheeky grin.

"Just need to know if I need to step up my game, sunshine." I winked as Gary emerged, carrying a foam cooler.

"Here ya go, cher. T'ree pounds of fresh gator. You lucky I still had me some in my icebox from 'da end of 'da season."

"Ugh, Gary, you handsome, handsome man. You're a lifesaver. Seriously, you just rescued my dinner."

"Shoo, cher. You can't be talkin' to me like dat with your beau standing right there, yeah." Gary gestured toward me, and I took the cooler from his hands and slid it onto the rack beneath the buggy.

"Yeah, well, when he starts bringing me fresh alligator to save my dinners, then I'll call him handsome too." Magnolia's head fell back as she laughed, her eyes locking onto mine as a smile tugged at her lips. She seemed so free away from town, unbothered by people staring or making comments behind her back. The fact that she chose to share that part of herself with me warmed my chest. I liked every version of her I'd glimpsed already, but this one—the one not many got to witness—was slowly becoming my favorite.

The sun had set by the time we loaded everything into the trunk and headed back toward Magnolia's house.

"You hungry?" I asked casually when her driveway came into view.

"Yeah, but I can just grab something from the fridge when you drop me off."

I hummed in response, but when I took a left instead of the right that led back to her house, her head whipped my way.

"Uh, Taylor? My house is that-a-way." She hiked her thumb over her shoulder, her brows drawn together.

"I'm aware. But I need to go *this-a-way* for my idea."

"Your idea?"

"Yeah, baby. My idea."

14
Freaking man-candle
Magnolia

Settling back into my seat, I narrowed my eyes at Taylor and leaned forward to turn up the volume on the stereo. When *Make Me Wanna Die* by The Pretty Reckless filled the cab, a smirk pulled up one corner of his lips as I whipped my head his way. Outside of Jae and occasionally Maddie, I hadn't really met many people who listened to the same hodgepodge of music that I did.

"You listen to The Pretty Reckless?" I asked incredulously.

"Among others, but yes. Why?"

"No reason, just... not many people around here even know who Taylor Momsen is outside of her playing Jenny Humphrey in *Gossip Girl*. That's all."

"I forgot she was in that." When I opened my mouth to retort, he shot me what I assumed was meant to be a withering stare and continued. "Addy watched it religiously when we were growing up, so I caught a few episodes."

"Addy watched it, huh?" I chuckled. He rolled his eyes, but a smile tugged at his lips.

Minutes ticked by in silence, and with each passing moment, my anxiety mounted. No amount of curious glances or pleading made him budge on telling me where we were going, and I hated it. I despised surprises. I preferred plans—needed to know who, what, when, and where. Though I hadn't explicitly *told* him that, I was pretty sure he was picking up on it and enjoying my squirming.

I fidgeted in my seat, fiddled with the ends of my braids, scrolled through my phone, and sent a text to my sisters, saying I was pretty sure I was being kidnapped. Their response? A flurry of crying-laughing emojis. I tried anything to keep myself occupied and distract from the countless crime shows and podcasts that swirled in my mind.

But when he turned down an unlit road, I sat up straighter, my head on a constant swivel as I tried to make out any distinguishing landmarks—just trees, lots and lots of trees.

"You're a serial killer, aren't you?" I asked, one eye narrowed and arms crossed as I turned toward him.

A laugh tumbled out, full and loud, before he croaked out, "*What?*"

"It's dark, we're driving down an unlit road leading to God only knows where, and you've been awfully silent on the drive. Highly suspect, Mr. Hallows."

"Jesus, Mags," he said with a laugh, shaking his head as he pulled into a makeshift parking spot.

"Just so you know, I won't go easily. I'll fight you tooth and nail. Literally."

"It's a *picnic*, sunshine. I brought you out here for a picnic. Or did you not notice the stuff I added to the cart at the store?"

My mouth dropped open in a little *o* before I promptly closed it and rolled my lips inward. Had I noticed him adding things to the cart? Nope. I was too busy worrying about my own list and running through recipes in my head to make sure I hadn't forgotten anything. It hadn't even crossed my mind as odd when he insisted on putting the items on the conveyor belt at the checkout.

"God, you are something else, you know that?" he joked, his shoulders shaking with laughter as he unbuckled his seatbelt.

"Sorry," I squeaked, a laugh of my own building as I watched him dissolve into more laughter.

"Come on, let's eat." I watched as Taylor climbed out of his seat, walked around to the back of the car, and began pulling out bags—plural. How had I missed that?

"You comin'?" he asked when I hadn't budged.

"You want me to get *out*?" Disbelief filled my voice. There was no way in hell I was getting out of this car. It was pitch black outside, and even though the car was still running with the headlights on, there was no way I'd be able to see more than my hand in front of my face.

Laughing. He was laughing at me *again* as he closed the hatch and walked to my side of the car. I watched through the tinted glass as he set the bags on the ground and looked up to the sky, his shoulders dropping in what seemed like a heavy sigh before he opened my door.

Every cell in my body seemed to come alive as he reached across me and clicked the latch on my seatbelt. Butterflies awoke in my stomach, fluttering delicately as if just emerging from their cocoons, as he gently turned me in my seat until I faced him. Those same butterflies took flight as he pressed his way between my knees, his broad palms running up the outside of my thighs until he reached my hips and tugged me toward him.

My hands flew to his chest as my butt met the edge of the seat. His nose was only a hair's breadth from mine. Add that to the flames in his eyes that made getting burned seem like a good idea, and the way he huskily whispered, "Yeah, sunshine. I want you to get out of the car," and he had all the makings of Magnolia soup.

"Okay." I breathed, my fingers curling into the charcoal Henley he wore. "But what about my groceries?" The words came out in a breathy exhale, my mind lost in the depths of his gaze.

"Your groceries are all in cooler bags, remember? They'll be fine for a picnic."

Neither of us moved, and I was pretty sure I stopped breathing altogether. At least until he scooped me into his arms and slowly slid me down his body until my feet found the ground, filling my nose with the warm scent of sandalwood and vanilla. *Freaking man-candle.*

All I could do was stare. Well, stare and breathe in his heady scent that made me want to force my aunt to create a candle that smelled just like him. I don't know how long we stood there in silence. It could have been a decade for all I knew, with how my brain turned to goo whenever he was around.

"You alright?" he asked when I still hadn't acknowledged his statement about my groceries being safe.

Alright? I wasn't even sure I understood what that meant at that moment. His hands were warm on my waist, his hold firm, and I just wanted to melt into it. Talking became increasingly complicated the longer he held my gaze, and all I could manage was a high-pitched, "Mm-hmm."

A small smile tugged at his lips before he pressed a gentle kiss to my brow and bent to pick up the bags with one hand while the other wrapped around mine.

+))●((+

Either he'd somehow planned ahead, or he had picnics often because he seemed to have thought of everything.

Giant blanket to sit on? Check.

Plastic cups and silverware? Yep, he had those too.

A food spread fit to feed twenty? I had no idea how I missed him adding all of that to the buggy.

After setting everything up, he rolled down the windows of his Bronco and turned the stereo up so that the music filtered out into the quiet as we sat in the glow of the headlights, the sound of crickets adding to the melodies. We'd just finished off the croissant sandwiches he'd bought the fixings for when the first few notes of one of my favorite songs—*Neon Baby* by Annie Bosko—came through the speakers. Dusting off my hands on the skirt of my dress, I got to my feet and held my hand out toward a very confused-looking Taylor.

"Dance with me?" I asked, wiggling my fingers.

A contented smile stretched across his lips as he stood and placed his hand in mine, pulling me close. As we began to sway to the music, his arm slipped beneath my sweater and around my waist, his thumb brushing lightly against the skin above the top edge of my dress.

Every stroke of his thumb set my blood on fire. Every step that somehow brought me closer, even though we were already flush against each other, made my heart race. There was something magical about being in the middle of nowhere, dancing in the grass beneath the stars with headlights as our spotlight.

Taylor made it feel magical.

It was more than the undeniable chemistry between us—and believe me, I *tried* to deny it. It was more than how a simple touch or look made my heart skip or my breath catch. It was this man who cleaned up my yard without asking, who agreed to an asinine "date" at a grocery store just because our schedules never aligned and he wanted to see me. It was the man who snuck date-night items into my cart to turn a mundane trip into something more. That was the man worming his way into my heart, gently soothing the hurt girl that lived in the back of my mind and kept reminding me this was a bad idea.

And it was that man I pushed up onto my toes to kiss as the song came to an end.

Taylor

A bomb could have gone off at that moment, and I wouldn't have noticed—not as every cell in my body sparked to life like I'd stuck my finger in a socket. Magnolia's lips were soft and hesitant against mine, her spicy floral scent wrapping around me like a blanket I never wanted to take off. When she tried to pull away, my arm tightened around her waist, my other hand slipping from hers to cradle the side of her neck, holding her close.

A contented sigh vibrated in her throat as her hands wound their way around my neck and her fingers tangled in my hair. God, every slide of her skin on mine, every movement of her lips, was like setting fire to gasoline. She could burn me alive, and I'd thank her for it.

Warm skin met my palm as I slid my hand up her back, my fingers tangling in the delicate ties crisscrossing her spine. All it would take was one little tug, and it took everything I had not to act on that thought. I wanted to take my time—wanted her writhing beneath my hand and tongue before giving in to our basest needs. But as her fingers pulled at the hair at the base of my neck, I needed her like I needed air in my lungs. I needed to taste her like my very life depended on it.

Grabbing the back of her thighs, I lifted her into my arms, and her legs wrapped around my waist, heels digging into my ass as I made my way toward my car.

"What are you doing?" she squeaked, giggles escaping her lips before they moved across my jaw. When she reached my ear, she nipped the tender flesh, and I dug my fingers into the pliant muscle of her ass. I'd never been an 'ass man,' but as my hands tightened around her, all I could picture was her bent in front of me, my handprint red and angry against her skin as she moaned my name.

Something like a growl rumbled in my throat when she sucked my earlobe into her mouth, and I hastened my steps. Throwing open the back passenger door, I sat her on the bench seat and claimed her mouth with mine. Time ceased to exist. The music faded into nothing as every synapse and thought focused solely on Magnolia. On the sounds she made as I sucked the skin where her shoulder met her neck or dipped my tongue into the hollow at her clavicle. Every nerve lit up like fireworks when her hands delved beneath my shirt, my muscles jumping as she tenderly ran her hands along my back. I wanted to explore her in the same way, but I *needed* her consent. I needed to know she wanted this as badly as I did.

"Magnolia," I breathed, resting my brow on hers as her hands continued to push my shirt upward. "Mags, baby, I need to know—*ow*, fuck!" I slapped the side of my neck, pulling my palm away to reveal a little splat of black and red.

A motherfucking *mosquito*.

"Taylor?" she asked hesitantly, her brows pinched together as she nervously brushed her skirt back down from where it had gathered at the tops of her thighs. Beautiful, sun-kissed thighs I'd barely gotten to explore; one of which was decorated with a portrait of... was that Audrey Hepburn?

Groaning, I leaned forward until our noses brushed. "Mosquitos."

"Pardon?"

"There are mosquitos, sunshine."

"They might as well be the state bird. There are *always* mosquitos, cowboy."

"*That mouth*," I ground out before pressing my lips to hers, relishing the way she melted into the kiss before I broke it off. "I am aware, Magnolia." I slowly trailed my lips along her jaw, sealing each statement with a kiss. "But the first time we do *this...*" kiss. "The first time I get to feel you..." *kiss*. "Get to taste you?" *kiss*. "It's not going to be with tiny vampires flying around." Dragging my lips to her ear, I whispered, "If anything is going to be biting you, it's going to be me."

A shiver ran through her body, and I pressed a chaste kiss to her cheek as I pulled back. Her eyes were wide, her lips parted as her chest rose and fell with labored breaths. "Any questions?"

Seeming to give herself a mental shake, she leaned back on her hands, tilting her head to the side, a smile that could bewitch a soul painting her full, thoroughly kissed lips. "Just one." When I raised a brow, she asked, "You got that house yet?"

My nostrils flared as I stepped back into her space and pulled her behind the knees until her ass was nearly hanging off the seat, forcing her to wrap her legs around me to keep from falling. "Baby, if I had a house, we'd be there already."

"Pity," she whispered as wide baby blues locked onto mine and she pulled her bottom lip between her teeth.

Fucking hell.

+·))●((·+

The car ride back to Magnolia's house was uncomfortable, to say the least. My dick was painfully hard behind the zipper of my jeans, and it seemed Mags was just as tortured as I was. Every few minutes, she'd squirm in her seat, readjust her dress, or mess with her seatbelt. I couldn't miss how she clenched her thighs together anytime our eyes met or the hungry way she looked at me when she thought I was paying attention to the road and not her. News flash: I was always paying attention.

By the time we reached her house, a gentle breeze could have snapped the tension between us. But there was nowhere for us to go to work it out. She lived with her aunt and sister. I lived with my goddamn parents and occasionally my sister. Screw our schedules being unconducive to a relationship; everything about our situation was fucked. We were in our thirties and dating like teenagers.

As I cut the engine, Magnolia blew out a heavy breath through pursed lips and turned my way. "Can you help me with the bags?"

I held her gaze for a moment before nodding. "Yeah, baby. Hang tight, and I'll grab your door."

"You don't—" I was already out the door and on my way to hers before she could finish. When I pulled it open, she rolled her eyes but gave me a demure smile. "You don't have to do that."

"A, I'm pretty sure my mother would smack me upside my head if I didn't. But aside from that, and more importantly, B, I *want* to."

Something like shock flashed in her eyes before she quickly masked the emotion. It made me wonder how many douchebags she'd been with who didn't treat her like the goddess she was. Then a pang of guilt slammed into my chest at the realization *I* had been one of them. It didn't matter that it had happened what seemed like lifetimes ago. I had contributed to the look in her eyes—the one that said she didn't think she was worthy of having her door opened for her, and God only knows what else.

We worked in silence, each of us taking trips back and forth to the car until all the bags were lined up on the porch by the door. "You sure you don't want help carrying them in?" I asked as she turned her key in the lock.

"I'm sure. It's not that many, and I don't want to risk waking Aunt Evie or Maddie up. It's fine, really. I've got it."

Not that many? I was pretty sure there were at least thirty bags surrounding our feet, but I didn't want to overstep her boundaries. So instead of arguing, I stepped into her space and cupped her cheek in my palm. "I know you *can* do it, sunshine. But that doesn't mean you always *have to.*"

"Thank you," she whispered, her eyes darting between mine as the tension between us tugged tighter.

"For what?" My face moved toward hers on its own accord, inching ever closer like magnets drawn together.

"Tonight. The store, the picnic. Everything."

"You don't have to thank me, Magnolia."

"I know, but I *want* to," she echoed back my words, and I couldn't help but smile.

"Goodnight, sunshine." I pressed my lips to her brow, letting them linger for a few seconds as her hands gripped my shirt at my waist.

When I pulled away, she whispered, "Goodnight, cowboy," and let me go.

I watched her watch me leave through the rearview mirror until she was nothing more than a blip, then focused on getting home. I had work the following night, which meant I usually slept most of the day, but I needed to make sure I called Cindy first thing in the morning. My bid on the house had been accepted, and we were in the waiting game of inspections and escrow and everything else that came with closing on a house. Six weeks. That's how long Cindy said it would take for everything to line up and go through. I knew I needed to be patient and that the wait would be worth it in the long run. But I wanted to move in—not just because I was ready to have my own space and roots, but because, in my *professional* opinion, there was no way in hell I would survive another cockblock. Between Halloween, the freaking cat, and those pesky mosquitos, my balls were no longer blue; they were purple.

I needed a cold shower... probably two.

15

Turtle Mochasippi with the works

Taylor

I SAT IN MY car in the hospital parking lot, taking a moment to breathe and gather my thoughts. *Exhausted* didn't even begin to describe how tired I felt, and it wasn't because of work. I was accustomed to long hours, and I was only on day two of my stretch of three-twelves, so my schedule wasn't crazy this week. Yet my mind refused to shut off when I finally had the chance to slow down for the day, spinning stories about how differently Wednesday night could have unfolded under different circumstances.

God, images of Magnolia smiling up at me while we danced played like a movie behind my eyelids. The sweet sounds she made when I kissed her echoed in my memory, the soundtrack to every quiet moment. Blowing out a resigned sigh, I hooked my badge on my scrub pocket and grabbed my phone. Magnolia was in Baton Rouge for the night for her catering gig, and I knew I probably wouldn't see her until Sunday—at the earliest. But I missed her, so I pulled up our thread and sent her a quick text before heading inside.

MAGNOLIA

I groaned at my screen as her text came through. Did I appreciate that she wanted me to have a nice night at work? Hell yes. Did she know I was a doctor and that the "q" word was forbidden in the medical field? Nope. It didn't matter that it was just a text or that she had no clue; the word had been invoked, and now I was probably in for one hell of a night.

Friday nights in the emergency room usually went one of two ways: either it was busier than a beehive, or it was more dead than a corpse six feet under. Unfortunately, tonight turned out to be the former. When I walked in for my seven o'clock shift, chaos reigned. Code blues blared left and right; ambulance gurneys lined the walls in front of the nurses' station, their patients waiting for rooms to open up; doctors and nurses ran back and forth. I overheard our charge nurse saying that the waiting room had a wait time of over four hours.

I released all the air from my lungs as I dropped my belongings in the corner that would become my home for the next twelve hours, settling in for what was undoubtedly going to be a long night. And boy, was I right.

By the time I finally sat down to catch my breath, it was nearing ten o'clock, and I was starving. I would have given anything for some of whatever Magnolia was cooking tonight. With that thought in mind, I slipped behind the nurses' station to the break room to grab my Dr. Pepper from the fridge, inhale a protein bar, and check my phone. My eyes widened when I saw the little green bubble by my messages indicating ten unread messages, and a red bubble over the phone icon with a two. *What in the hell?* No one ever texted me while I was at work, let alone called unless it was an emergency. I clicked on the messages first and breathed a sigh of relief at the couple from my mom and Addy, but it was the six next to Magnolia's name that drew my attention.

Magnolia

I got a flat. *face palm emoji*

There's a wreck on I-10, and now I'm going to be late.

I swear, if the trip here is any indication of how this night is going to go, I'm screwed.

I know you're working, but just to keep you updated on the fuckery happening tonight: I burnt my roux. ME! I burnt the roux.

> If you're still following along, that home-
> made ice cream I made? Yeah, it's frozen
> solid because I forgot to put the sugar in it.
> *crying emoji*

> Fuck, Taylor, I'm sorry. Here I am blowing
> up your phone, and you're working. I don't
> know why I'm doing this. I just... I'm sorry.

I didn't respond. Instead, I clicked on her picture at the top and called her as I walked down the hall, the din of the emergency room fading into the background. When she didn't answer, I hung up and tried again... and again. When she finally picked up on the third ring, I didn't even get a "*hi*" out before her tear-laced words came through the speaker.

"Taylor? Oh my god, I'm so sorry. I—I know you're working, I shouldn't have called you—"

"Mags, baby, what's wrong?"

"Everything that could go wrong has. I've never had so many dishes fail in one go, and I just—I don't know what got into me. I just needed to hear your voice. I'm sorry."

I had to admit, hearing her say she needed me made me preen a little. This woman who seemed so self-assured, who always wanted to do things on her own, wanted to hear *my* voice when she was in distress. "Baby, don't ever apologize for calling or texting me, especially if you're upset. I'm sorry I wasn't available when you needed me. Are you okay?"

She sniffed a few times before answering with an unconvincing, "Yes."

"Oh, then those are happy tears coming through the line?" I jested, hoping a small joke would bring some light back to her otherwise dark night.

"Mmhmm," she hummed, followed by a quick sniff.

"*Magnolia.*"

"I'm okay, Taylor." She took a ragged breath and blew out a raspberry before continuing, "Jae pulled me up by my bootstraps, and we figured everything out. I redid my roux, and it was perfect. Then she ran to the store to grab a gallon of Blue Bell while I threw together the bananas foster bread pudding. We just finished cleaning up."

"You sure you're alright?"

"Yeah, I'm sure." She paused for a second, then said so softly that I almost missed it, "At least I am now."

"Oh?" I couldn't keep the smile from my face if I tried. "Why might that be, sunshine?"

"Oh, shush you."

"I think I'm growing on you, Bellevue."

"Yeah, yeah. Don't let it go to your head, Hallows." The levity returned to her tone, and I couldn't help but wonder if she wore the same smile I had on my face.

"*Dr. Hallows, you're needed in trauma three. Dr. Hallows to trauma three.*"

"Shit." The PA system cut off, and I glanced down the hall to where my nurse, Sam, was waiting with wide eyes that clearly asked, *what the hell are you doing? Let's go!*

"Taylor? Is everything okay? What was that?"

"Hey, baby, I'm so sorry, but I've got to go. Are you sure you're okay?"

"Yeah, I'm fine. I've got to head back in anyway to help Jae haul stuff to the car."

"Okay. Be careful driving back tonight, and let me know when you're home safe."

"Oh, um, we're going to stay at Mer's apartment tonight, actually. After the night we had, neither of us wants to drive the two hours back, and it'd be nice to see my sister."

"Oh, okay. Let me know when you make it there?"

"Checking up on me, cowboy?"

"Just making sure you don't get kidnapped by someone other than me, sunshine. I'll talk to you soon." I started heading back down the hall at a slow jog when Sam threw her hands up in the air, mouthing "*sorry*" as she rolled her eyes and headed toward the trauma bay.

"I'll let you know when I'm safely behind Mer's door with a daiquiri in my hand. Have a good night."

"You too." I disconnected the call and tucked my phone into my scrub pants pocket as I followed in Sam's wake.

"I hope you enjoyed that call, Dr. Hallows, because I don't think you'll be getting another chance tonight," Sam chided as I stopped at the sink to wash up before grabbing my gloves.

"Worth it," I said with a smile as Sam shook her head and took her place next to the gurney. Scrubbed and dried, I grabbed gloves from the rack on the wall and braced myself for the incoming trauma. *Here we go.*

+)⟩●⟨(+

The sky was awash in pinks and oranges, and there was a bite to the air when I finally stepped out of the emergency room the next morning. I was bone tired, but throughout the rest of my shift, the only thing on my mind when I wasn't with a patient was Magnolia. When we got off the phone the night before, she seemed to be in better spirits than when I'd first spoken to her. But I still wanted to make things better, wanted to see the smile on her face and be the one to put it there.

Leaning against the seat while my car heated, I pulled up my messages again. She'd texted me when she got to her sister's apartment, then sent a picture of herself, Jaelyn, and Meredith—who I realized was the same woman at the door during the Meat-Cute. But it was the text from said sister that caught my interest.

MEREDITH BELLEVUE

> Hey, I stole your number from Mags' phone when she passed out.

Was that odd? Just a tad, and I had been too busy to respond when I'd received the text. But as I stared at that message, an idea popped into my head.

TAYLOR

> Well, this is my lucky day because I need to ask you something.

MEREDITH BELLEVUE

> It's fucking 7 am, and you're texting me why?

> Fuck me, this is what I get for not putting my phone on Do Not Disturb.

> What do you want, Hallows?

TAYLOR

> Good morning to you, too. I just got off work, so sorry for waking you up. But if you give me your address, I'll bring you coffee.

The gray bubble indicating someone was typing popped up and disappeared a handful of times before the response came through.

MEREDITH BELLEVUE

> Shouldn't you be bringing Mags coffee?

TAYLOR

> That's the plan, little Bellevue.

MEREDITH BELLEVUE

> Ew, don't call me that.

> 515 Azalea Park Drive Apt 206.

> And if you go to CC's, I want a GIANT Turtle Mochasippi. Mags will want one too.

> Actually, make that three giant Turtle Mochasippis, with the works and an extra shot since you woke me up at the ass crack of dawn.

I chuckled to myself as her texts rolled in, then put the address into my GPS. It would take a little over two hours to get there, and I still needed to head home first to shower and change clothes.

I tried to give myself a pep talk as I backed out of my parking spot, but that had never been my strong suit, especially when logic was applied.

"Exhaustion is just a state of mind." *No, it's not; your body needs rest to recharge. Exhaustion is your body's way of saying you need to slow down.*

"Two hours isn't that long of a drive." *True, but it's a hell of a lot longer after a cluster-fuck of a twelve-hour shift when you haven't really slept in three days.*

"I just need to drink some coffee. Maybe grab an energy drink when I hit the gas station." *Yeah, because that's a super healthy alternative to actually sleeping.*

As I came to a stop sign, I tilted my head back against the headrest and heaved a sigh as the last piece of my pep talk sank into place, which was the only thing that logical me could agree with.

"Seeing Magnolia will make it all worth it." *Yeah, it will.*

It was just about a quarter after eight by the time I got back in the car, so I sent a text to Meredith to let her know I was on my way and what time I should arrive. When her text response popped up on my navigation screen, I clicked it and let the system read it to me in its femininely robotic voice.

"Meredith Bellevue says: 'thumbs up emoji, bring coffee or else.' Would you like to respond?"

"No," I answered with a chuckle. I might not know much about Magnolia's sisters, but it seemed they were three peas in a pod from the limited interactions I'd had with them.

"Okay," the navigation chimed, then faded out so the stereo could play; *Hey Ho* by the Lumineers filled the cab as I hopped onto the highway.

Magnolia

I'd never been an early riser or a morning person, and today was no different. After the clusterfuck that was my first full catering job in months and after falling asleep on Meredith's uncomfortable couch, I was sore. I was crabby. And I was in desperate need of a large cup of coffee.

Sunlight streamed through the windows in Meredith's living room, but it was the clanging echoing from the kitchen that pierced through my slumber—if you could even call it that.

"What the fuck is going on?" I groaned as I sat up, brushing my messy hair out of my face so whoever was in the kitchen could fully appreciate my annoyance.

"Shut *up*," Jae moaned from her spot on the floor opposite the coffee table.

"Both of you shut up. Bunch of whiny babies," Mer said as she began moving around the kitchen, mumbling to herself.

"What the fuck are you on about?" I asked as I stood and stretched, my bladder waking with the movement and sending me scurrying to the bathroom.

"None of your fucking business!" Mer hollered as I pulled the door closed.

Okay, so *none* of us were morning people.

With a roll of my eyes, I did my business and then decided to shower while I was in there. The hot water washed over me, gently pulling the last threads of sleep and exhaustion from my bones, soothing muscles that ached from the lumps in the cushions. I let myself soak in the streams of hell's finest water for a few minutes, then bathed and grabbed a towel from the hook next to the shower.

I dried quickly, wrapping the fluffy purple towel around me. But as I scrunched the water out of my hair with another towel, I heard the faint sound of a knock on the door.

"Hey, who was that?" I asked as I exited the bathroom, steam billowing out behind me as I walked toward the living room.

"Uh, Mags?" Jae questioned, her brows shooting into her hairline over wide eyes.

"What?" I quirked my own brows as I turned toward the door. There stood Taylor Hallows, holding a cup holder with three huge coffees, all topped with fluffy whipped cream and drizzled in chocolate and caramel.

His wide eyes raked down my frame, a faint pink coloring his cheeks while his throat bobbed as he swallowed. "Hey, sunshine. I thought... uh... I'd bring you some coffee."

I had to hand it to him—he had a lot more willpower than I did. I don't think I could have averted my eyes from a towel-clad Taylor as quickly as he pulled his gaze from me. And if it hadn't been for the way the pink in his cheeks deepened, and the way he cautiously handed the tray of coffees to Meredith as he turned his back to me, I probably would have been hurt.

What the fuck!? I mouthed. My eyes must have been as wide as saucers when they met the gazes of my friend and sister, both trying desperately not to laugh. They both mouthed *"sorry"* with a shrug, then Meredith flicked her head back toward her room.

Right.

Clothes.

Clothes would be good.

"Uh, thanks. I, um… I'll be right back." I had never run so fast in my life. Hand gripping the top of my towel, I sprinted toward the other side of the apartment. Throwing Meredith's door closed behind me, I sagged against the white wood and expelled a ragged breath.

Why was he here? *How* did he know where *I* was? I mean, obviously, I knew I had *told* him I was at Meredith's apartment, but how did he know where *that* was?

Panicked, I scrounged through Meredith's closet, searching for anything that would work for an outfit. We were the same size—though I had her on height—but we were *not* the same person. I tended to gravitate toward jewel tones and dark shades. Granted, there were days I could go for bright colors, but those were few and far between. I liked jeans and comfortable tees, flowy skirts and dresses that toed the line between cottagecore and flirty grunge. *Was that a thing? Surely that was a thing, right?*

Meredith, on the other hand, was a college student. One who opted for tiny shorts and oversized shirts that covered said shorts, making it look like she wasn't wearing any.

And that was all I was finding at the moment.

I'd just sagged down the wall when my wonderful sister, with her limited wardrobe, came in with a mischievous grin on her face. But one look at me in a heap on the floor turned that grin into a grimace.

"Shit, Mags. I'm sorry. I didn't think he'd show up when you were half-naked," she said with a laugh, her eyes scanning the small panicked mess I had made. "Not finding what you're looking for?"

"All of your shorts are teeny-tiny, and your shirts are made for giants."

"I'm sorry. *You* try sitting through two-hour lectures and see if you want to spend it in uncomfortable clothes," she deadpanned, her hip cocking to the side as she crossed her arms.

She had a point. Burying my face in my hands, I screamed silently, muffling the sound.

"Feel better?"

"No," I huffed into my hands before pulling them away.

"Breathe, sis. I have some bootcut jeans hanging in the back of the closet that should fit you, and you can borrow one of my purple off-the-shoulder sweaters. I've got some cute game day earrings you can loop through your tunnels."

"Game day?"

"Yeaaah, you know, where guys in tight pants run around and catch a ball? And where us normal people drink and eat all day?"

"*Please* tell me he's not planning on taking us tailgating."

Meredith scoffed, then headed into her closet, presumably to pull out the clothes she mentioned, but her voice filtered out. "*Us*? Nah, sis. *You*. And I don't know what he's planning, Mags. But you can't walk around campus on game day without the right colors on. Learned that the hard way. Here," she said when she emerged, her arm outstretched to help me to my feet while the other held two hangers draped over her shoulder.

Meredith stayed and chatted while I got dressed, then helped me put my still-damp hair into twin fishtail-French braids. But as I placed my hand on the doorknob, I paused and glanced down at my feet. "Uh, Mer?"

"What *now*? You look fabulous, if I do say so myself. I haven't even worn those jeans yet because I need to get them hemmed, and I don't think they'll fit me quite as well as they fit you. Now I'm jealous."

"You're delusional, but thank you," I replied with a chuckle. "But I need shoes. I wore my nonslip Danskos to the gig last night, and I don't want to ruin your masterpiece."

Meredith threw her head back with a groan, then rolled off her bed and stomped back into her closet. "You owe me!" she hollered from the depths of her walk-in.

When she emerged, the gasp I gusped was completely involuntary. "No. Mer, I can't."

"You can, and you will. But if you mess them up, you owe me *two* pairs."

She skipped across her room with a sassy smile on her face and thrust the boots into my hands—her *favorite* boots. Gorgeous warm brown leather with an eagle overlay and wingtips on the toes. She'd saved for weeks to afford these Corral boots, and I'd only seen her wear them a handful of times since she got them.

"You're sure?"

"Definitely. Now come on. Chop chop. The man drove two hours to see you *and* brought you coffee. If you don't jump him, I might." She threw a wink over her shoulder as she pulled the door open and headed into the living room.

Taking a deep breath for what seemed like the thousandth time that morning, I grabbed some socks from her dresser, plopped down on the edge of her bed, and pulled on the boots. Guess it was time to see if they were made for walking.

16
Geaux Time
Taylor

"OH. MY. *LANTA*," JAELYN exclaimed, taking another hefty sip from her frozen coffee, her eyes rolling back in her head as she let out an appreciative hum.

"I'm glad you're enjoying it," I replied with a chuckle. Footsteps echoed against the hardwood in the hall, and I jolted upright from where I had been leaning against the small island, my head snapping in that direction.

"It's just me," Meredith trilled, her arms raised in mock surrender, a teasing smile tugging at her lips. "Mags will be out in a sec. Now, where—" she drew out the last word, glancing around the small kitchen. "Ah! There it is!" Swiping her coffee from beside the sink, she took a deep sip and hummed in the same way Jaelyn had.

"Is it really *that* good?" I asked skeptically.

"It's coffee, chocolate, dairy, and caramel. It's basically all the food groups." A slurping sound punctuated her statement as Meredith's eyes bore into mine, holding a challenge akin to her sister's.

I had just opened my mouth when I heard the soft click of boot heels. I still hadn't closed it by the time Magnolia stepped into view, rendering me speechless. Her jeans hugged her curves before gently flaring around her feet, and the purple sweater somehow made her eyes shine even brighter. Those incandescent blues seared into mine, a faint pink coloring her cheeks as a teasing smile lifted her lips.

"You're gonna let a fly in, cowboy."

I snapped my mouth shut, and when I smiled back at her, the pink in her cheeks deepened.

Jaelyn's laughter was barely muffled as she buried her face in her arm on the countertop. From my periphery, I could see Meredith cover her mouth with a hand before composing herself.

"So, wait." Jae's head popped up, her eyes wide before narrowing on me and flicking to her friend. "Are y'all… *dating*?" she demanded incredulously.

"I guess the coffee kicked in," Meredith whispered to no one in particular.

My eyes widened as the color in Magnolia's cheeks deepened. Had she not even told her best friend? The look on her friend's face suggested she hadn't. When neither of us answered, Jaelyn spun the stool she was perched on, fixing her friend with a look that could only be described as "*What the fuck*?"

"Magnolia Lynn Bellevue! I can't believe you didn't tell me!" Jaelyn screeched.

"Oh, come on, Jae." Magnolia crossed her arms and met her friend's gaze head-on. "You *knew*."

"*No*, I suspected. But *you* never *told* me. I'm disappointed. Hurt. My flabber is gasted."

"Jae, cut the crap. You knew. I knew. We *all* knew. How the town gossips haven't picked up on it yet is beyond me." Meredith waved a dismissive hand at Jaelyn's gaping stare before continuing, "Either way, they aren't as good at keeping it a secret as they think they are. She—" she pointed an accusatory finger at her sister, "just hasn't grown the balls to say it out loud yet."

"Hey!" Mags yelled, hurt edging her voice as her brows scrunched together, glaring at her sister.

"Well? Am I wrong?"

Magnolia's gaze flicked to mine, and I held it. I watched her take a deep breath, a sheepish smile tugging at her lips as she said, "No, you're not wrong. Not entirely, anyway. I just wanted to stay in our bubble a little while longer."

Her eyes never strayed from mine, and though her words were directed at her sister and friend, they felt like they were meant for me. She knew I wanted to tell people. Knew I wanted to take her out where anyone could see, to properly introduce her to my family instead of them just knowing her name because she lived in town. But I understood that she needed time before opening herself up to any potential criticism she suspected would come her way, so I followed her lead and would continue to do so.

"Bubble, shmubble. You tell your best friend who you're banging," Jaelyn huffed, taking another long pull from her straw.

Jesus Christ. This was definitely not a conversation I needed to be—or *wanted* to be—a part of, and by that point, I was pretty sure my face was the color of a freshly boiled crawfish. Thankfully, no one was paying me any mind.

"Jaelyn Marie!" Magnolia and Meredith screeched in unison.

"What?!"

"Sweet baby cheeses." Magnolia pinched the bridge of her nose and huffed out a sigh. "One, I'm not *'banging'* Taylor." Her eyes cut to mine, and a crimson flush crept across her cheeks again. "Two... I don't even remember what two was, because what the *fuck*, Jae?!"

All three women began talking over each other, their voices growing louder as their hand motions became more animated. The conversation was hard to follow, and after about a minute, I stopped trying to. Instead, I opted to de-escalate... or try to, anyway.

"Uh, Mags?" Eyes full of fire met mine, and it wasn't the kind I wanted directed at me. Palming the back of my neck, I asked, "You wanna get out of here?"

"Good god, yes." Snatching her purse from the counter, she shot her friend a withering stare that would have had me shaking in my boots if it had been directed my way, then stormed past me and through the door, her coffee completely forgotten on the countertop.

I caught the edge before it slammed, then turned back to the other two women, who seemed to be having some kind of wordless conversation. When they finally looked my way, I said, "Thanks for the assistance this morning, Meredith. Jaelyn—"

"You comin', cowboy?" Magnolia called from the hall.

"You better go. She's all riled up," Jae said with a sobering chuckle, shooting Meredith a look I didn't quite understand.

"Right. See y'all around."

"Good luck!" they hollered in unison as the door clicked closed behind me.

By the time I made it out into the parking lot, Magnolia was already halfway to my car, her fists bunched at her sides, boots clicking purposefully against the concrete. When she reached my Bronco, she yanked on the handle of the passenger side door, and I couldn't help but chuckle when she threw her head back and groaned because it was locked.

"In a hurry, sunshine?" I asked as I approached.

She whipped around to face me, lips pursed as she folded her arms across her chest. "Unlock it, please." It wasn't a question; it was a statement that dripped with her frustration from the conversation that had just transpired. I guessed Jaelyn wasn't kidding when she said she was 'riled up.'

I shook my head as I closed the remaining distance between us, relishing the way her eyes widened and her lips parted slightly. Her head tilted back as I stepped into her space, forcing her back against the car door. "It's been quite a morning, cher." She scoffed and rolled her eyes, but it was the unintentional tells from her body that I honed in on. It was the tiny, sharp intake of breath when I gripped her waist, the way her pupils dilated incrementally, and the beautiful pink hue coloring her face that set off the freckles dusting across her cheekbones and nose. "That wasn't *exactly* how I planned this morning to go."

"Oh?" she whispered, her throat working around a swallow as her eyes flicked between mine.

I let my eyes roam down her frame and slid one hand up her side until I could wrap it around the side of her neck. "No, sunshine. But seeing you flushed and in a towel was certainly a highlight."

Before she could reply, I pressed my lips to hers. She went stock-still for a microsecond before her hands fisted into my shirt, tugging me closer. Kissing Magnolia was as easy and natural as breathing, and the way she always melted into me felt like nirvana for a mere mortal like myself.

Pulling away, I swept my thumb across her bottom lip as a contented smile lifted the corners of her mouth. "That's more like it."

"I'll say."

I pressed a kiss to her brow, then stepped out of her space. "You really didn't tell Jaelyn?"

Her entire body sagged with the sigh she expelled. "I wanted to. Almost did the day we went shopping."

"So why didn't you?" I asked as I pulled her away from the car and opened the door for her.

"Honestly, I don't know. I tell her everything, and she actually *pushed* me to give you a chance. I guess I liked it just being us. I liked our bubble."

Mags slid into her seat, and I closed the door, pausing the conversation until I slipped into my own. "But your sisters knew. Your aunt, too."

"Kind of hard to keep it a secret when you're showing up at our house to clean the yard, cowboy," she said sardonically.

"True," I replied with a chuckle. "Sorry about that."

Silence filled the cab for a moment as I backed out of my space and headed out of the lot.

"Don't be. Honestly, it was like a weight lifted. It was nice not having to hide you from my family. I should have told Jae; she's just as much my sister as Maddie and Mer."

A heaviness settled across her features, and I reached across the console to entwine our hands. When Magnolia turned toward me, her smile didn't quite reach her eyes, so I tightened my hold, warmth filling my chest when she returned the squeeze.

It was time to turn this day around.

"What do you want to do today?" I asked as I wove my way through the game day traffic.

"You mean you didn't have everything planned down to the minute? Speaking of, how in the hell did you know where Meredith's apartment was?"

"Are you hungry?"

"Taylor."

"Your sister stole my number from your phone and texted me last night. Still don't know why, but I'm not complaining. Now, are you *hungry*?"

Her eyes pinched closed as she muttered, "I'm going to kill her," before blowing out a breath and answering my question. "I'm always hungry."

"Great, we have a reservation at *The Windchime* in twenty minutes."

⁌⁌⁌●❨❨⁋

"Holy shit, this is so good. Do you want a bite?" Magnolia asked, cutting off another piece of her omelet.

I'd been to *The Windchime* for brunch before, but I'd always opted for the Eggs Benedict. Magnolia, on the other hand, had gone for the Boudin Omelet—something I had never even considered.

"No, I'm alright."

"Oh, come on, cowboy. Live a little." Magnolia stabbed the bite she'd just cut with her fork and held it out to me. Her eyes sparkled with mischief, the fork swaying slightly as her hand moved closer to my side of the table.

Challenge accepted, sunshine.

Shock widened her eyes as I wrapped my hand around hers and guided the fork to my lips. Her mouth popped open in a surprised little *o* as I held her gaze and took the bite. Flavor exploded on my tongue—creamy cheese, spicy sausage and rice, peppers, and seasoning, the pillowy texture of the eggs. Who would have thought eggs, boudin, and pepper jack cheese would work so well together?

Magnolia and the chef apparently, but who's keeping track?

A knowing smile spread across her lips as she watched me chew, her brows rising as she asked, "It's good, right?" Swallowing, I reached for her plate, but she swatted my hand away. "Dream on, cowboy. This is *mine.*"

"Oh, come on!"

"Nope. Sorry, big boy. Maybe next time you'll listen to the person with *superior* culinary knowledge." She gave me a saucy smile as her fork slipped between her lips, doing a little happy wiggle in her chair.

The rest of our meal passed with laughter and easy conversation. The more time I spent with her away from Bellevue, the more her walls came down, and the smiles she gave me came easier.

"Can I ask you a question?" I asked, snatching the bill from the tabletop and cutting her a disapproving glance when her hand hovered above it.

She narrowed her eyes at me, but there was an upward tilt to her lips as she said, "Didn't you just?"

"Hardy, har, har."

I watched as she dabbed her mouth with her napkin and placed it on the table, folding her hands beneath her chin as she looked at me expectantly.

"What's the connection between your family and the town?"

Her lips turned inward as she adjusted in her seat. "What do you mean?"

"Well, your last name is Bellevue—"

"It is."

"And we *live* in Bellevue—"

"Thank you, Captain Obvious," she sniped, her gaze shifting out the window as her arms crossed defensively on the table.

Closing the bill fold, I set it on the edge of the table for our waitress to grab, then reached across to take her hand. "Hey." When her eyes cut to me, they were wary. Something about this subject made her uncomfortable. "We don't have to talk about it, Mags. I was just curious."

She watched as I rubbed my thumb across the back of her wrist, blowing out a breath through her nose. Her eyes closed briefly before finding mine again. "It's not that. It's just—" Her gaze shifted back down to where my hand wrapped around her wrist. "It's the reason everyone in town calls us witches."

I sat in silence, letting her work through whatever was running through her mind, but I couldn't deny the anxiety curdling in my stomach as the seconds ticked by.

"My family came here from England a long, long, *long* time ago and settled around Salem. Generations came and went as the colonies grew around them. Throughout those years, they were known for their use of herbs and natural remedies. But when people began accusing women of being witches for doing precisely that, they fled to the South and settled here. The town of Bellevue was already established, and my however-many-great grandmother married into the founding family. Since then, we've just kept the name—regardless of marriage."

Her gaze grew distant as she spoke, as if she were reliving a history drilled into her brain her whole life, and for all I knew, it might have been.

"My family never stopped doing what they did best, but as the accusations of witches traveled further South, the name was once again assigned to the women in my family. Only down here, they were revered for their abilities... until they weren't."

She paused when the waitress came by the table to grab the bill, then began again once she walked away.

"To this day, it doesn't matter what my aunt, my sisters, or I do. That brand has been attached to our family name. It's one of the reasons my mom moved out of Bellevue as soon as she could and just... never came back."

Even though she wasn't looking at me, I didn't miss the tears she blinked away as she cleared her throat and continued.

"Anyway, depending on who you ask, it's either a miracle or a curse. Unfortunately for me, 'curse' seems to be the favored term."

"Mags, I'm so—"

"Please don't. I don't want your pity. I just want you to understand why I'm so hesitant about *this*. That town will never accept me or my family as we are. All they see is what they want to see, and screw the people affected by it." There was a silver sheen to her eyes as they met mine, and it gutted me.

When the waitress returned with my card, I signed the receipt and stood, extending my hand. Mags gave me a hesitant smile as she slipped her hand into mine, and I pulled her to her feet and into my embrace. I didn't care that we were in the middle of a restaurant, didn't care that countless eyes turned our way.

Lifting her face to mine, I gently swiped my thumb along her cheekbone. "I see you, Magnolia Bellevue. I see your kind and fierce heart. I see your stubborn determination and the love you hold for those around you. You're so much more than those town clowns give you credit for."

Before she had a chance to argue, I pressed my lips lightly against hers. When I pulled away, her eyes were softer than I'd ever seen them, and it made my heart skip. "Come on, let's walk around a bit before we have to head back home."

+)) ● ((+

A sea of purple and gold flowed around us, the warring music from tailgates blaring around campus as we walked through the throngs of people. None of that mattered, though, not when Magnolia clung to my arm, one hand wrapped in mine as the other gripped my bicep.

We meandered in and out of shops, stopped to grab tea from a food truck, and soaked in the electric atmosphere around us. I hadn't been home during football season in years, let alone on campus during a home game, and just being around all the hype sent adrenaline coursing through my veins.

A slight tug on my arm had me following Magnolia into a store called *Geaux Time*, my eyes drifting appreciatively down her frame before snapping back up.

"Hey, y'all. Welcome in. Let me know if I can help with anything," the sales clerk hollered.

"Thanks," Mags replied cheerily as she dragged me across the small store.

I followed like a lost puppy as she wove her way through the racks until a small squeal erupted, and she released my hand. Picking up a baseball cap from a table, she placed it on her head and turned back toward me. "What do you think?"

She struck a pose, her head turning from side to side to give me the full effect, and all I could do was smile. She looked downright edible. How something as simple as a baseball cap could flip a switch and send blood rushing south, I had no idea, but it did, and I sure as hell wasn't complaining.

Okay, I was complaining a little because, once again, there was nowhere to make good on the promises we'd been dancing around whenever we were together.

Something in my expression must have shifted because she straightened and sauntered the few feet between us, running her hands up my chest. "Like it?"

"You have no idea, sunshine." My voice came out gravelly even to my own ears.

She pushed up onto her toes and whispered, "How's house hunting going?"

Fuck me sideways. My eyes rolled back, and I had to suppress a groan as she nipped lightly at my ear, then sank back to her heels.

"I'm going to get it." She tapped me twice on my pec, then walked toward the checkout.

Escrow was going to be the death of me... or my balls. Probably both. Dragging in a ragged breath, I thought of things that could quell the swelling in my pants.

Colonoscopies.

Severed fingers.

Mom.

It helped—until it didn't. When I turned around, Magnolia was leaning on the counter, her pert ass sticking out and just begging to be slapped. She was chatting animatedly with the sales clerk as the woman scanned the tag and then cut it off. But before Magnolia could pull her wallet from her bag, I slapped my card down on the counter and leaned down until my lips were next to her ear. "Don't argue, cher. Let me buy the damn hat." When she opened her mouth to protest, I whispered so low that only she could hear, "It's more for me than it is for you anyway."

My lips brushed against her cheek as I pressed my hips into hers, and her sharp inhale was music to my ears. But apparently, two could play that game because I had to suppress a groan when she pushed her hips back.

The sales clerk—Alyssa, if her tag was correct—didn't seem to notice the rise in tension. She swiped my card, handed it back to me, then handed Magnolia her hat with a cheerful smile and a chirpy, "Y'all come back and see us."

Wrapping my arm around Magnolia's waist, I slipped my hand into her back pocket as we walked toward the door. Once we were outside, I pulled us out of the flow of foot traffic and pried the hat from her grasp.

"Hey!" she protested, reaching out to steal it back.

I placed the cap on her head, then tugged her toward me, my arms encircling her waist, hands slipping back into her pockets as her arms wrapped around my neck. "Ya know, I'm starting to understand the hat appeal."

She giggled and pushed up on her toes to press her lips against mine. It was short and sweet, but her whole demeanor shifted when we pulled apart. All the lightness that had surrounded her died away like someone snuffing out a candle. Her eyes grew wide, and she jolted out of my grip, pulling the cap further down on her brow.

What the fuck?

"Mags?"

I watched the color drain from her face as her eyes locked onto something across the street. With one word, one *name*, every wall I'd torn down was built back up.

"Sophie."

17

Swords, and lightsabers, or whatever

Magnolia

Sophie-mother-fucking Larson.

All I wanted was one Mother-damned day where everything went my way. But no, the universe evidently took some perverse pleasure in popping my proverbial bubble. Say *that* three times fast.

I'd felt eyes on me the moment my lips touched Taylor's. That sixth sense, the one no one could quite pinpoint—the one that flashed a giant red sign in your mind screaming *WARNING*—blared to life as I pushed up on my toes to kiss the man I was falling for. I should have listened. I *always* listened to that intuition. So, of course, the one day I didn't was when it bit me in the ass.

Sophie's eyes locked onto mine, her lips pursing as she slowly dragged her gaze down my frame before flicking it toward Taylor. The only saving grace at that moment was that all she could see was his back... at least until he turned around. It felt like a scene from a movie, where the hero and the villain stand across a battlefield, and everything else blurs around them—just without swords, or lightsabers, or whatever.

Taylor stiffened as Sophie's gaze returned to me. Her lips curved into a menacing smile as she pulled her phone from her purse. *Shit.*

"We need to leave." I meant for my voice to come out stronger than a mutter, but dread settled in my stomach, making my throat feel swollen. If there were a yearly trophy for the biggest gossip in Bellevue, Sophie would need an entire room to display her collection. If she knew, it wouldn't be long before everyone in town did, and that made my brunch threaten to make an unwanted reappearance. We were well and truly *fucked*.

When Taylor still hadn't averted his gaze from across the street, I wrapped my hand around his wrist as he shifted in that direction. "Taylor, please. Let's just go."

His muscles relaxed slightly when I threaded my fingers with his, but when his eyes met mine, there was a fire in them that screamed ret-ribution—though for what, I wasn't entirely sure. Yes, I'd just spilled the cliff notes version of my family's history, and he had firsthand knowledge of how I was treated in high school. Yes, I'd dealt with this my entire life, and this was his first time facing that vicious glare beneath the perfect Southern Belle facade. But now was not the time to go all *'Hulk smash'* on Sophie.

I held his gaze, my hand tightening around his as I began to step away from where we'd frozen on the sidewalk. He followed for a mo-ment before his strides became purposeful, overtaking me and pulling me behind him through the crowd until we turned a corner.

I followed blindly, weaving through throngs of fans while avoiding bumping into those carrying drinks, all the while keeping my eyes locked on his back. His shoulders were taut, his back rigid, and his grip on my hand unwavering as we made our way around campus. When the crowd finally thinned, he turned down a quiet street and released my hand before running both through his hair.

"Taylor?" I hedged, slowly approaching where he perched on some steps, his head bowed into his palms, elbows resting on his knees.

When a moment passed and he still hadn't answered, I knelt in front of him and pulled his hands away. "Talk to me, cowboy."

Blowing out a breath, Taylor wrapped his hands around mine. "I'm sorry, Mags. I... I never thought we'd run into someone from town here. And the way she looked at you? Fuck—" His gaze fell to where our fingers intertwined, his thumb running soothing circles around my knuckles.

"Hey," I cooed, lifting his gaze back to mine. "First and foremost, you are not responsible for knowing where everyone in town is at all times. Secondly, don't let little Miss Priss get to you. I've been on the receiving end of those cold, calculating eyes more times than I can count, and I always come out unscathed."

At least I do now, anyway.

There was a time when Sophie's glares and menacing smiles would send me cowering, or running with my tail between my legs. But that time had long since passed, and I wasn't about to revert now.

Taylor's sapphire blues searched mine, sadness and guilt swirling in their depths. "I don't know how you do it, Magnolia. I truly don't. The moment I saw the way she was looking at you, I just—" Something akin to a growl emanated from his throat, and that sound, coupled with the protective edge in his voice, ignited a fire in my veins. I'd never had a man want to go to bat for me, and seeing someone as kind and sweet as Taylor channeling his inner macho man over someone as insignificant as Sophie lit me up like fireworks.

I could feel the warmth flooding my cheeks, and the intensity of his gaze fanned that flame. Seconds, minutes—I don't know—passed before I could form words again, and when they finally came, they escaped as a breathy whisper. "Welcome to this side of the fence, cowboy. And as for how I 'do it'? I have to. I don't really have a choice. I ran after high school—"

"But you came back."

"I did," I said, nodding solemnly. "I came back because despite everything that town has put me and my family through, I love it there. That town is as much my home as anyone else's, and I'll be damned if I let them take it away from me."

Taylor slid his hand to the back of my neck, pulling me toward him, his brow resting against mine. Sandalwood and vanilla filled my nose and saturated my senses. "I am in awe of you, Magnolia Bellevue."

I chuckled and shook my head against his. "Hold on to that thought, because life's about to get really real around here."

⊹))●((⊹

The weeks leading up to Thanksgiving blurred by. I had two more catering gigs that, thankfully, went off without a hitch. The Meat-Cute was just as successful as before, and the shop over-flowed with orders for seasonal treats. It was wonderful—*amazing*, even—but I couldn't focus on the success when every time I stepped outside my door, it felt like every pair of eyes in town was drilling holes into my back.

There hadn't been any more whispers than usual, no harsher glares than I was accustomed to. But there was a distinct shift in the air, making me look over my shoulder, just waiting for the proverbial shoe to drop. That shoe felt more like the anvil from the old Wile E. Coyote cartoons, and I was nowhere near as fast as the Road Runner.

"How's the chopping coming?" Aunt Evie asked from across the kitchen island, measuring out ingredients.

"What? Oh, it's fine. The onions and bell peppers are finished and split into bowls for each recipe."

"Good. Good. So what's next?" Her eyes flicked to my cutting board... my *empty* cutting board.

"Shit. I'm sorry, Aunt Evie. I don't know where my head is at."

Tonight was Thanksgiving Eve, which meant all hands on deck in the kitchen to prep for tomorrow's meal. I loved cooking for the holidays. The house always smelled warm and savory around Thanksgiving, and sweet and downright *divine* during Christmas. But no matter the holiday, we always premixed and prebaked most dishes, so all we had to do was heat them while the turkey fried. Yes, we fried turkey for both major end-of-the-year holidays.

My aunt hummed in response, her eyes rolling back in her head before returning to meet my gaze. "Your head is across town where Mr. Hallows is."

She was right—and wrong—all at once, but I kept that to myself.

"Is he gracing us with his presence tomorrow?" Maddie asked from her spot at the stove, sautéing corn, peppers, and garlic.

Mother above, that smells good.

"No, I don't think so. His sister and her fiancée are coming down." *I think.* I hadn't heard from Taylor much since the incident. Well, I hadn't reached out to him much. It wasn't intentional at first, but the more anxious I became, the more I tended to pull away, and I didn't want him caught in the crosshairs of whatever was inevitably coming my way. Because it would come. It always did.

"Well, that's too bad. I even got a sixteen-pound turkey this year," Aunt Evie said with a sigh.

Despite our history, both my aunt and my sisters had warmed to Taylor, which brought a smile to my lips.

As if speaking his name had summoned him, my phone began vibrating on the counter a moment before the chorus from Big and

Rich's *Save a Horse (Ride a Cowboy)* filled the sudden silence in the kitchen.

"He has his own *ringtone*?!" Meredith screeched from the breakfast nook, surrounded by a mountain of potatoes she was putting off peeling. "Oh my lanta, the 'cowboy' comment makes so much more sense now."

I glared at my sister while hastily wiping my hands on a towel, snatching my phone from the counter, and heading out the door, laughter trailing from the kitchen in my wake.

Once outside, I inhaled deeply and slid the green circle to answer the call. "Were your ears burning?" I asked, then pinched the bridge of my nose at the sheer stupidity of that greeting.

"You talking about me, sunshine?"

"Wouldn't you like to know?" I retorted with a light laugh.

Silence filled the line as I walked to the porch swing overlooking the front yard. Fireflies danced in the sage green moss hanging from the oak branches. A crisp wind wove through my hair, bringing with it the earthy scent of fall. It was peaceful—something I hadn't felt in recent weeks. Something I hadn't realized I desperately needed.

"How are you?" I asked when the quiet lingered.

"I'm alright. Tired, but fine. You?"

I hummed in response, my head bobbing on its own before I said, "The same, really. Work has been crazy lately. I sold out just about every day this week, which is amazing. But if I see one more pumpkin pie, I might vomit."

His laugh was warm through the speaker, washing over me like that first breath of fresh, balmy air in spring—the kind that carried the scent of honeysuckles and azaleas. I closed my eyes and just existed for a moment, letting go of everything that had plagued my mind since we left Baton Rouge. I let my worries over what would come from Sophie seeing us together vanish. Just for a minute, I allowed myself to *be*.

Taylor and I talked for a while, about nothing and everything simultaneously. It was easy—effortless—and just what I needed.

When an hour had passed, the front door creaked open, and Maddie poked her head out. "Hey, we need you in here. Mer is planning a coup."

"I'll be right there. And tell her to keep away from my recipes," I said with a chuckle. When the door clicked closed behind her, I returned my attention to my phone. "Hey, I've got to go. Mer is threatening to dismantle my dinner for tomorrow, and I'd rather not have to resort to takeout."

I could hear his stifled laugh, and if I closed my eyes, I could picture it. I could see his megawatt smile and the little creases forming by his eyes, the way he would shake his head before it fell forward, his shoulders moving with amusement. I could see it all, and I missed it. I missed *him*.

A burning sensation filled my nose, and I tilted my head back to stare at the porch ceiling, trying to quell the tears threatening to spill over.

Maybe I wasn't as silent as I thought, or maybe he just inherently knew, but whatever it was, Taylor's voice softened as he asked, "Mags, baby, what is it?"

"Nothing," I squeaked, sniffing back emotions that wouldn't surrender to my control. It had to be hormones. My period was coming or something because I did *not* cry at the drop of a hat.

"Mags."

"I just... ugh. I miss you, okay? Happy now?" I swiped a hand beneath my eyes as traitorous tears began to fall.

"Ecstatic." I could hear the smile in his voice, and I pinched my eyes closed, waiting—and hoping—for him to continue. When he did, my heart leapt into my throat. "I miss you too, baby."

Taylor

The sound of Magnolia saying she missed me echoed in my brain long after the line had disconnected, a smile etched on my face as I stared down at my screen. The last few weeks had been rough. Our lives felt more out of line than ever. She was busy at work—more than usual with the upcoming holidays and all the extra catering gigs. My job was always busy, so that wasn't anything new. But she'd been steadily pulling away since the incident in Baton Rouge, and though I understood to an extent, it still hurt.

From where I stood, nothing around town seemed different. Then again, as she so pointedly pointed out, I'd never been on her side of things when it came to the people here. Since we'd barely had a moment to talk, I had no clue what was going on on her end.

Blowing out a heavy breath, I stood from the wicker loveseat my mom had set up on the back deck.

"Soooo, who's the girl?" Addy drawled, her sudden presence nearly making me jump out of my skin.

"Jesus f-ing Christ, Adelaide!" My hand flew to my chest, my heart hammering against my ribcage. "Why do you insist on sneaking up on me?"

I whipped my head in her direction just in time to see her give a nonchalant shrug and slide a spoon from between her lips. "Why do you make it so easy to startle you?"

"Do you *need* something, oh loving baby sister of mine?"

She padded over to where I stood, plopped onto the cushion I'd just vacated, and held out a second spoon. "I *was* going to see if you wanted to share this ice cream with me—"

"That's *my* ice cream, Addy."

"It's in the main freezer, TayTay, therefore it's now communal ice cream," she said with another shrug. "*Anyway*, I will still share, but now it comes with a price."

"You're *blackmailing* me over my own ice cream?"

"I am." She nodded decisively. "Now, who's the girl? And don't even try to deny it. *I heard you, Taylor.*"

The fact that my sister was asking me *who* I was talking to made my heart feel a little lighter.

"I told you I would tell you when there was something to tell." A small smile tugged at my lips as I sank down next to my sister and snatched the proffered spoon. Perhaps Sophie hadn't told every Tom, Dick, and Harry about seeing us. Maybe, just *maybe*, she'd changed her ways like I had.

That misguided thought died with the next words out of my sister's mouth.

"Fine. But you wanna tell me why Claire is saying you were in Baton Rouge with Magnolia Bellevue, of all people?"

Shit.

Shitshitshitshit.

"What?" I countered, trying to sound calm as I dug the spoon into the silky, frozen cream.

Every second felt like an eternity as Addy took another bite of Rocky Road and adjusted her position. My nerves prickled as I waited, my breath catching in my lungs, my mind spinning on how to direct this conversation.

After what seemed like a lifetime, Addy said, "Claire texted me a bit ago and said that Sophie wouldn't shut up about how she had '*the gossip of the century,*' or some bullshit like that." When I just stared at her, she rolled her eyes and continued. "Evidently, she *swears* she saw you and Magnolia in Baton Rouge a few Saturdays ago."

"Addy, you know better than to believe anything that Sophie Larson says," I said with a slight scoff, trying to mask the rising panic in my chest.

"True, but then Claire sent me this." Her phone screen illuminated her face before she turned it toward me.

That fucking bitch. Everyone knew that Sophie was a blabbermouth, and most people brushed aside whatever she had to say. But this time, she'd apparently taken it upon herself to acquire *proof.* I'd seen her pull out her phone, but I never suspected she'd stoop that low. Thankfully, the picture glaring at me from my sister's screen was blurry at best. My face was obscured by pixels, and Magnolia's was blocked by the bill of her hat. But there was no mistaking the hair peeking beneath the edge of the cap.

I could feel Addy's eyes drilling into my face as mine stayed glued to her screen. It was as if she were testing me, trying to see which path I would take when the facts were staring me in the face. I could either tell her everything and hope that Magnolia would understand, or I could continue to feign ignorance.

I knew which way I *wanted* to go, but it wasn't just me in this scenario, and the words tasted like acid as they fell from my lips.

"Why on Earth would I be hanging out with Magnolia Bellevue?"

Shock widened Adelaide's eyes, her mouth gaping slightly before she tongued a canine, bobbed her head in disbelief, and let out a mocking scoff. Disapproval flashed in her eyes, her lips turning down at the corners as she patted me on the shoulder before unfolding herself from the cushion. "I'm going to bed."

"What about my ice cream?" I called after her as she rounded the edge of the loveseat.

"You don't deserve ice cream," she shouted over her shoulder. "Oh, and Taylor?" When she reached the French doors, she turned halfway, narrowing her eyes at me in the best impersonation of our mother I'd ever seen. "I may not have all the details, but you and I both know you're lying. So do us both a favor and just stop, mmkay?"

I'd love to, sis. Trust me.

With a heavy sigh, I nodded. "Goodnight, Addy."

"Night-night," she sing-songed, throwing a finger wave over her shoulder as she walked back into the house.

With Addy gone, I was once again left with my thoughts—only this time, worry edged every single one. Gossip would eventually trickle out and die. But what do they say about a picture? That it's worth a thousand words? I had a feeling that pixelated image of Mags and me would be worth a lot more than that in this podunk town we called home.

Life's about to get real, indeed.

18
Holiday hangovers

Holiday hangovers were a thing, right? They had to be. Because there was no other reason for the fatigue dragging me down, making me want to crawl under my desk at *CharCutie* and take a nap. Groaning, I let my head fall onto my folded arms and blew out a heavy breath.

"What are you doing?" Jaelyn's familiar voice drifted in, laced with a sigh. I didn't even have to look up to know she was standing in the doorway.

"Solving world hunger, obviously," I muttered, my voice muffled by my arms.

Silence. The kind that carried an exasperated glare you could feel.

"Wallowing, Jae," I clarified, lifting my head just enough to meet her unimpressed gaze. "I'm wallowing."

"Why?" she asked, drawing the word out as her boots clicked against the tile. She crossed the small office and dropped into the chair across from me.

Pushing back into a sitting position, I shrugged. "Not really sure, honestly. Woke up in a messy-depressy mood. Plus, the shop is basically dead today."

Not to mention the fact I hadn't heard from Taylor since the night before Thanksgiving—five days ago. It was official: I was a lovesick puppy pining over a stupid boy. Or maybe just a "like-sick" puppy, because I wasn't going there.

"Uh-huh. Get up." Jae stood abruptly, motioning for me to do the same.

"Why?" I hedged, raising a confused brow as she stared me down.

"Because you've been wallowing for days, your hair's a mess, and we've got menus to plan and shopping to do for that party next week." When I didn't budge, she huffed, rolled her eyes, and rounded the desk to tug me out of my chair. "I made you an appointment at *Belle Amour* with Greyson to fix..." She waved vaguely at my head, her lips pulling into a disapproving scowl. "That."

"What? What's wrong with my hair?"

"Mags, sweetheart, I say this with all the love in my heart." Her hands landed on my shoulders, caramel eyes soft but edged with a tough-love gleam. "Your roots are almost two inches long, you're leaning more toward muddy water than vibrant cotton candy swirls, and your ends are so split I could see them from across the room."

"Ouch, Jae. Tell me how you really feel, why don't you?"

Her brow quirked, and I quickly amended, "On second thought, maybe don't."

"Your appointment's in forty-five minutes. Throw on some mascara, swipe on a little gloss—something to make you look less like you rolled out of bed at one o'clock on a Monday afternoon—grab a coffee from *The Magic Bean*, and get your ass over to Greyson's."

"Jae, I don't have time to—"

"You're going, Magnolia Lynn." Her tone brooked no argument. "You haven't made time for yourself in far too long, and if I have to walk you there myself and wait outside the door, I will."

She wasn't bluffing, and we both knew it. But it also meant closing the shop early—not that it mattered. Business had been oddly slow today. Our usual Monday rush had turned into a trickle, which was concerning. I had a sinking feeling Sophie had something to do with it.

With a heavy sigh, I looked to the ceiling and groaned, "Fine."

"Atta girl." Jae patted my shoulder and pulled me into a quick hug before exiting the office.

I stood there for a moment, the silence deafening when there were usually voices filling my little shop. Blowing out an aggrieved breath, I made my way toward the mirror on the wall and winced. Jaelyn hadn't been wrong. Actually, she'd been *nice* about it. I looked like a Mother damned bridge troll—a trash panda. Even Mother Gothel at the end of *Tangled* had me beat.

Spindly strands of hair stuck out like hay from my bun, there were dark circles under my eyes that I was pretty sure concealer would laugh at, and—great—a zit the size of Mount Vesuvius had taken up residence on my chin. Groaning again, I pulled the elastic free, letting a tangled mess of faded, orange-tinged pink and Old Gregg blue tumble over my shoulders. I couldn't believe I'd forgotten to renew the enchantments on my hair. Every four weeks, like clockwork, I respelled it to refresh the color, seal the ends, and bring back its bounce and wave that I could only achieve with magic—hot tools were *not* my friend. Now it was just... sad.

Jae was right. I needed to make time for myself again.

With a nod of determination, I bundled my hair back into a bun, swiped on some concealer and mascara, glamored the zit out of sight, and headed for the door.

+))●((+

The last time I'd set foot in a salon was years ago, back when I lived in Baton Rouge, and the memory still haunted me. That so-called "salon"—if you could even call it that—was a disaster of chipped paint and broken appliances, reeking of overly perfumed shampoo, hair dye, and enough hairspray to choke a horse. The woman working on me had stunk of cigarettes and seemed to be taking all of her frustrations out on my poor scalp. After that ordeal, I'd sworn off salons, opting for home trims and magical enchantments instead. But Jae had booked this appointment for me, so I yanked on my big-girl panties and braced myself for disappointment. If you set your expectations low enough, they can only go up. Right?

Clutching a giant peppermint mocha for courage, I pulled open the glass-and-gold door to *Belle Amour*, and—holy shit. My jaw dropped as I stepped into the most adorable space I'd ever seen. Plush blush couches framed a cream-and-pink rug in the lobby, a whimsical chandelier of twigs and flowers glowing softly above. Floating shelves made of raw-edge cypress lined one wall, neatly stocked with endless rows of beauty products. White sheers framed the windows, letting in natural light that bathed the space in a warm, welcoming glow.

I silently vowed to buy Jaelyn *something* for insisting I come here. Maybe a new purse. Or shoes. Or—

"May I help you?" A cheerful voice pulled me from my thoughts. The receptionist stood behind a stunning cypress desk with a raw, wavy edge. A pink neon sign reading *Belle Amour* glowed across its base.

"Oh, hi!" I moved away from the door, offering a sheepish smile. "I have an appointment with Greyson. I think I'm a little early."

"No problem!" She smiled warmly, her fingers flying over the keyboard. "What's your name?"

"Magnolia."

"Got it! You're all checked in. Have a seat wherever you like, and Grey will be with you shortly. Would you like anything to drink? Water? Tea? Wine?"

Wine? While getting my hair done? What alternate universe had I stumbled into? I raised my coffee with a polite smile. "I'm all set, thanks."

"Alright! If you change your mind, just holler. I'm Liv."

"Thanks." I turned toward the couches, expecting to settle in for a wait. But before I could even sit down, someone called my name.

"Magnolia?"

Startled, I spun around, sloshing coffee onto my hand. "Shit—sorry! Yes, that's me."

The man approaching me laughed, shaking his head. He gestured silently toward Liv, who handed him a cloth for my mess. "No biggie. Jae warned me you might be a bit of a mess, but don't you worry, honey—I'll get you right as rain and ready to take on the world in no time."

Flustered, I cleaned up my spill and followed him to his station. Greyson was, hands down, the prettiest man I'd ever seen.

The back of the salon was just as charming as the front. Cream walls and polished concrete floors created a clean, cohesive look. Blush chairs sat at every station in front of gold-framed mirrors with uplifting sayings across the tops—Greyson's said 'do it for yourself, no one else'. There were twinkle lights intertwined with floral branches draped across the ceiling, giving the space an ethereal, fairy-like quality. I already loved it here.

"So, what are we doing today?" Greyson asked, freeing my hair from its elastic. His smile faltered slightly as he assessed the chaos that was my hair.

"Color and a trim, I guess." I chuckled nervously. "I'm usually better about upkeep, but life's been a little... hectic."

He nodded, grabbing a brush to gently work through the tangles. "What's your usual routine? Your hair history—or *hair-story*, if you will."

Panic fluttered in my chest. How was I supposed to answer *that*? It's not like I could say, '*Oh, ya know. Same as anyone else, really. Magical enchantments.*'

"Oh, um, the usual," I hedged. "I shampoo twice, condition from the mids to the ends, and do a mask once or twice a month."

"Good, good. And the color? How do you maintain it? Do you use heat tools?"

I laughed outright, shaking my head. "Greyson, I know my hair color would say otherwise, but I'm pretty low-maintenance. I rarely use hot tools, and I usually handle color touch-ups in my kitchen sink."

He grinned, shaking his head in mock disbelief. "Well, prepare for the most high-maintenance day of your life, my darlin'. That bossy friend of yours left strict instructions to pamper you, and pamper you I shall. You ready?"

I swallowed thickly, nodding as our eyes met in the mirror. His face lit up with excitement, his full lips curling into a smile that showcased perfect, pearly teeth. "Let's do this."

+)) ● ((+

"Girl, if you don't close your eyes, it's creepy," Greyson admonished, massaging shampoo into my scalp.

"What? Oh!" I snapped my eyes shut, and he chuckled. "Sorry."

"It's okay. It just looks weird from this angle, and you're supposed to be relaxing. So keep those peepers closed and just breathe."

Taking a deep breath, I focused on the sensation of his strong fingers kneading my scalp and the back of my neck. The warm water cascaded down, washing away the stress that had been building. It felt amazing. I was half tempted to come here once a week just so Greyson could wash my hair.

But just as I was reaching a state of zen, sharp, needling voices pierced the air and shattered my peace.

"You can't believe everything that Sophie girl says," voice number one snapped. "I know, Geraldine, but she had a picture this time," voice number two responded.

Well, at least I knew who one of them was now. I groaned internally. So much for a peaceful day at the salon.

And it had been going so well.

"Oh, snap," Grey whispered, excitement lacing his tone. "One of the best perks of this job is the old biddy gossip. I wonder who they're talking about."

"I'm sure it's no one special." I took another deep breath, trying to find my zen again—but it was nowhere to be found.

"I just don't see what that sweet boy sees in her. It's Magnolia Bellevue, for goodness' sake. And that hair!"

"Oh, I know! And they say that whole family of hers are witches. Witches, Dorothy! He could do so much better."

My eyes flew open at my name, and I was met with Greyson's wide hazel gaze.

"It's fine, Grey. I'm used to it," I whispered, trying to muster a convincing smile.

The truth was, I was used to it—used to people talking about me behind my back, judging me for my looks or how I lived my life. But hearing that people in town didn't think I was good enough for Taylor stung more than it should.

Greyson's lips pressed into a thin line, fire flickering in those golden-green irises. "I'm going to say something."

"No," I whisper-shouted, reigning in the anxiety churning in my gut. "Please don't. I'll handle it. I always have."

I forced another smile to my face—though I was sure it looked as deflated as I felt. Thankfully, Greyson just huffed out a breath and went back to rinsing the conditioner from my hair.

When he finished, he wrapped a towel around my head, and we returned to his station—my appearance shocking the hell out of Geraldine and Dorothy. Their cheeks flushed crimson, and their eyes bugged out as they sat under the dryers clutching their gossip rags. Figures.

"Ladies," Grey said curtly, shooting them a scathing look that had me biting my lips to suppress a laugh.

The rest of my appointment was depressingly awkward. The playful banter between Greyson and me was gone, replaced by pitying glances in my direction and disdainful glares in the mirror aimed at the two women behind him. At least my hair looked incredible. Greyson had worked his magic, and I was sorely tempted to nix the enchantments altogether just so he could do my hair more often.

"What do you think?" he asked, his hazel eyes glowing as he fluffed the big, bouncy curls cascading over my shoulder.

"You are a miracle worker, Grey. Thank you." My sinuses burned as I met his gaze in the mirror. "For everything."

"You are a queen, Magnolia Bellevue. Don't let anyone make you think otherwise."

"Do it for yourself..."

"And no one else," he finished, wrapping his arms around my shoulders and pressing his cheek to mine.

He'd just removed the cape from my shoulders when *Tennessee Whiskey* by Chris Stapleton drifted out of my purse.

"Thanks again, Grey," I said, scrambling out of the chair to grab my phone. Aunt Evie's photo lit up the screen.

Sliding the green dot to the right, I pressed the phone to my ear. "Hey, Aunt Evie."

"Hey, Magpie." Exhaustion thickened her voice as she blew out a heavy breath. "You gonna be home soon?"

"Yeah, I just finished up at the salon. I need to run by the shop—"

"I already called the shop. Jae's going to close up for you." Another sigh crackled across the line, and the hair on the back of my neck stood on end.

"What's going on?"

"Some hooligans egged the house."

19

I could do it in heels

Taylor

My muscles screamed in protest as I shoved the barbell back onto the rack, exhaling a shaky breath. Even with lighter weights in all my circuits, I felt like I might keel over and die—and I still had cardio to tackle. Convinced I couldn't move even if I tried, I stayed sprawled on the bench, sweat trickling down my temples and soaking through my shirt. Skipping the gym for weeks hadn't been in the plan when I moved back to Bellevue, but between work and trying to see Magnolia, my fitness routine had taken a backseat. Now, I was paying for it.

Magnolia.

Her name invaded my thoughts at every moment of the day, no matter what I was doing. Yet, I hadn't reached out to her in days. She'd sent me a few texts—one with a dancing turkey gif wishing me a Happy Thanksgiving and a couple of "just checking in" messages—but I hadn't replied. Not once. It wasn't that I didn't want to; I just didn't know what to say after Addy had confronted me. I was tired of lying to the people I cared about, but I also couldn't shake the fear that I was wrecking the best thing in my life.

Sitting up with a wince, I swung my legs over the bench and leaned forward, elbows on my knees. *Paralyzer* by Finger Eleven blasted through my earbuds as I dragged myself toward the treadmills. Did I want to run two miles today? No. Not even a little. Cardio was the bane of my existence, but I'd earned the ice cream and beer I'd planned for afterward. Life was about balance, even if mine was a disaster.

Half a mile into my run, my earbuds betrayed me, dying right at the guitar solo of *Back in Black*. Groaning, I decided to push through to at least a mile. But no way in hell was I slogging through the rest of it without music to drown out the pounding of my feet and the treadmill's whirring.

I tried to focus on my breathing and the steady thrum of my pulse, but not even noise-canceling earbuds could have silenced what I heard next: her name, falling from someone else's lips.

I glanced at the domed ceiling mirror and spotted Kyle and Spencer by the weight racks behind me. Their stupid grins instantly brought back memories from high school—the same smirks they wore when they tormented anyone they deemed beneath them, especially Magnolia. My stomach twisted.

Fuck.

Screw finishing my run. If they were talking about Magnolia, they had my undivided attention. Slowing the treadmill to a walk, I yanked out an earbud, angling to hear them better. They either didn't notice me or didn't care because their conversation continued like they were the only ones in the gym. Every word stoked my fury.

"Man, it was just like old times," Spencer bragged, laughing. "And the look on her aunt's face when it hit the wall right next to her head? Classic."

Kyle high-fived him. "Serves them right. They don't belong here. High time we drove them out of town."

"Bellevue witches? More like Bellevue bitches," Spencer sneered. "That Magnolia chick is the worst of 'em."

"She's got Hallows brainwashed or something. Sure, she's hot as hell now, but no piece of ass is worth losing your friends over—not with her brand of crazy."

Red. A fiery blaze of rage. My finger slammed the treadmill's emergency stop button, and I ripped out the other earbud. *Do no harm,* the angel on my shoulder reminded me as I stomped over to the two idiots. I'd always taken that oath seriously, but I'd also never wanted to deck someone as much as I did right then. If ruining my career weren't a possibility, Kyle and Spencer would have thirty-pound weights embedded in their faces by now.

I marched toward them, fists clenched. My reflection loomed over them in the mirror, but they didn't flinch. Kyle's gaze caught mine, his slimy grin widening.

"Well, well. Finally come to your senses, Hallows?" he drawled, setting his weights down.

"What the fuck did you two idiots do now?" My voice was low, seething.

"Calm your tits, Taylor. It was just a harmless prank," Kyle said, shrugging as Spencer snickered.

Do no harm was becoming harder to stick to by the second.

"What the fuck did you do?" I demanded again, stepping closer.

Spencer grinned. "You think they like their eggs sunny side up or scrambled, Ky?"

Laughter erupted between them.

I snapped. One second, I was standing there, and the next, my hands were fisted in Kyle's shirt, his wide-eyed panic fueling my fury as he barked, "The fuck are you doing, Hallows?"

"If you hurt them..." My voice was a growl.

Kyle squirmed as Spencer grabbed my bicep in a weak attempt to intimidate me. When I didn't let go, his gaze darted nervously around the gym.

Finally, I shoved him back and jabbed a finger into Kyle's chest. "Stay the fuck away from Magnolia and her family, asshole. I won't warn you again."

Kyle's eyes flared with anger, but I didn't stick around to see what he'd do. Grabbing my bag, I stormed out of the gym.

It only took about fifteen minutes to get to Bellevue Manor, and though I hadn't known exactly what to expect, what greeted me was far worse than I'd imagined. Bright yellow yolk dripped down the white siding, pooling on the porch below, where scattered eggshells littered the wooden planks. Evie and Maddie were scrubbing the railing, but it was Magnolia who instantly grabbed my attention. She always did—especially when she stood at the top of the steps, hands on her hips, a rag clenched in her fist, and a scowl darkening her beautiful face.

I hadn't even stepped out of the car before she shouted, "Go home, Taylor."

Not exactly the welcome I'd hoped for, though I couldn't blame her. Slamming my car door harder than necessary, I ignored her outburst and crossed the yard toward her aunt. "Can I help?"

"No!" Magnolia snapped, folding her arms across her chest. The move might have been meant to intimidate, but all it did was draw my gaze to where her breasts pushed higher. When my eyes flicked back to hers, fire blazed in her aqua blues, and a pretty crimson flush spread across her cheeks.

Evie turned to me with an exaggerated eye roll. "Ignore her. You'd think after a day at the salon, she'd be a little more mellow—"

"I was mellow," Magnolia huffed, throwing her arms out to gesture at the mess on the house. "Until you called me about this shit."

"Anyway," Evie cut her off with a pointed glare before turning back to me. "We'd love some help, Taylor. Thank you."

"We don't need his help—"

"Cheese and crackers, Mags. *Shut. Up.*" Maddie abandoned her spot at the railing, stalking over to me. "Here, you can take over for me. I need a break." She shoved a sponge into my hand, wiped hers on the towel tucked into her back pocket, and headed for the stairs.

Their aunt came to stand beside me as I watched the women bicker. She whispered, "Come on, honey. I'll show you what we're working with."

"Is she alright?" I asked, nodding toward Magnolia.

Evie barked a laugh and clapped my shoulder. "Is anyone ever really alright?" When I shot her a questioning look, she shook her head with a chuckle. "She'll get over it. Now, come on."

A few minutes later, Magnolia joined us. She didn't acknowledge me, just dunked her rag into the soapy water and got back to work. For fifteen minutes, she scrubbed and ignored me, her silence gnawing at my patience. I couldn't take it anymore. I didn't want to go back to square one. I didn't want her gaze filled with disdain. I wanted the fire—the longing I'd grown used to over the past few weeks.

"Mags—"

"Oh, so you do remember how to speak."

"Magnolia—"

"Your fingers don't seem to be broken, either."

"Magnolia, stop."

"Stop what?" Her tone was nonchalant, but her knuckles turned white as she scrubbed at the siding with unnecessary force. Her movements stilled when I wrapped my hand around hers. Her eyes snapped to mine, her lips pressed into a tight line as she gritted out, "Let go."

"Talk to me, and I will."

"Excuse me?" she scoffed.

"You heard me."

"Why should I? You've been ignoring me for five days. What's a few more minutes?"

"Sunshine—"

"Don't 'sunshine' me, Taylor Hallows." Her voice sharpened, growing louder with every word as she yanked out of my hold. "You've been ignoring me for days, and then suddenly, when your stupid-ass friends decide to egg my house, here you are. Riding in on your white horse, in shining armor, coming to my rescue. Well, guess what? I don't need you or your stupid horse. I can save myself—and I could do it in heels."

Behind her, I caught her aunt's wide-eyed expression as she retreated into the house. She must've thought we needed privacy to hash this out. But the whole damn town could've been there, and I wouldn't have cared. Magnolia was going to listen to me, whether she wanted to or not.

Blowing out a frustrated breath, I grabbed her wrist and pulled her down the steps, around the side of the house.

"What the hell do you think you're—" Her tirade ended in a squeak as I pinned her against the siding, caging her between my arms. Her pupils dilated, her breathing quickened, and hell, having this conversation was the last thing I wanted to do right now.

I leaned closer, taking in her spicy floral scent. I was close enough that I could count her freckles and make out every shade of blue and gold that colored her irises. Every defiant spark in her eyes had me wishing we were somewhere far more private.

"Listen up, sunshine," I whispered. "I've said it once, but I'll say it a thousand times if that's what it takes to get through to you." My hips pressed against hers, and her breath hitched. "I am not friends with those idiots. I nearly beat them with a fucking weight when I found out what they did."

Her mouth opened—probably to argue—but I covered it with my hand. "It's my turn to talk, cher." Her glare turned icy, but I didn't waver. "I'm sorry I didn't call or text. After we talked, Addy confronted me about being with you in Baton Rouge, and I panicked. It was a dick move, and I shouldn't have done it. But I did, and here we are."

Something wet and warm hit my palm, and I yanked it back. "Did you just *lick* me?"

"Serves you right," she snapped.

"Goddamn it, woman." Wiping my hand on my joggers, I cupped the back of her neck, bringing my face inches from hers. "Baby, you think glaring at me and biting my head off is going to scare me off. It won't. It just turns me on."

I felt her throat work as she swallowed. Her ragged breath coasted across my lips, words spilling out in a heated whisper that seared my skin. "You... you can't just come over here and... crowd me against a wall and expect me to forgive you."

"I don't," I whispered back, my thumb brushing over her plump bottom lip.

She shifted her face away from my hold, locking her gaze with mine. "Then what do you want?"

What I wanted was to kiss her until we forgot our names. Until neither of us could tell where one ended and the other began. I half-expected her to laugh in my face when I said as much, but instead, her eyes widened, and her lip disappeared between her teeth.

"I'm still mad at you," she breathed as I inched closer to her mouth.

"I know."

"You can't just ghost me and expect everything to be fine."

Her protests were growing weaker, breathier, as her head tilted instinctively to the side, our lips drawing closer. I smiled and repeated softly, "I know."

"I... I'm still mad at you," she murmured, her resolve cracking.

"So you've said." When she started to pull away, I tightened my hold just enough to keep her close. "Baby, you can be mad at me all you want. It just means I get to make it up to you." Her breath hitched as I ran my nose along hers. "Now, if you're done arguing, I'd like to start making amends."

Her mouth parted, likely with another flimsy excuse, but I didn't give her the chance to voice it. My lips claimed hers, and she melted into me. Her hands slid up my chest, fingers tangling in my shirt as she pulled me closer.

Letting go of her neck, I gripped her hips and lifted her against the wall. She wrapped her legs around me, her hands threading into my hair as I trailed my lips down her neck, pushing aside the collar of her shirt to nip at the sensitive skin where it met her shoulder.

"Taylor," she mewled, her hips rocking against mine.

God, that felt good. Too damn good.

Dropping my head into the crook of her neck, I gripped her hips tighter, stilling her movement as a groan tore from my throat. "Sunshine, you're going to make me lose it if you keep that up."

"I need... fuck, Taylor, I need you. Please."

"I know, cher." Sliding one hand around to cup her ass, the other drifted closer to her center. Her black leggings hid nothing—I could feel her heat, her wetness, through the thin fabric. "Jesus, Mags," I groaned, running my fingers along the seam of her pants. She shuddered, her fingers tightening in my hair as her legs locked around my hips.

I adjusted my touch, reading every cue her body gave me. I varied the pressure, traded long swipes for slow, deliberate circles that narrowed into faster, smaller ones. My lips grazed her neck, my teeth teasing the tender skin, while my free hand explored her curves. When I found the rhythm that had her back arching and her head falling against the wall, a deep male pride swelled in my chest.

Her body quivered and tightened as she shattered, her cry of release vibrating against my lips as I kissed her through it. She melted into my arms, boneless and trembling.

We stayed like that, our heavy breaths mingling, my forehead resting against hers. When she squirmed in my hold, I gently lowered her to her feet, though I couldn't step back. I didn't want to. Seeing her unravel like that was intoxicating. And I knew it was only a glimpse. I needed to see her laid out beneath me, my name falling from her lips as I pushed her to ecstasy again and again.

"Sweet baby cheeses, cowboy. That's... that's never happened before," she murmured on a breathy exhale, her hand sliding down my chest.

"Really?" I asked, just as breathless.

She nodded. When her fingers reached my waistband, I caught her wrist gently, halting her descent. Confusion flickered in her eyes as they met mine.

Cupping her cheek, I brushed my thumb across her soft skin and smiled. "I'm fine, cher."

She raised a brow, amused. "The tent in your pants would beg to differ, cowboy."

Didn't I fucking know it. "I'll be fine, Mags. That was about you, not me. I'll have my turn. And when that time comes…" I pressed my hips against hers, earning a soft gasp. "I'm going to take my time. This won't be a quick romp in the sheets."

"Setting some high expectations there, big guy."

Tilting her face up, I grinned. "Guess you'll have to see for yourself." I stole a quick kiss before lacing my fingers with hers. "Now, come on."

She groaned, dragging her feet as I led her back toward the front of the house.

"You expect me to clean up eggs after *that*?"

"We could always go inside and finish what we started." Her face paled as I veered toward the front steps.

"Nonono."

"Didn't think so."

Come here often?

Magnolia

Good morning, beautiful.

Oh, so you do still have my number.

I see you're still upset with me.

One orgasm does not equal forgiveness, cowboy.

What about multiple?

MAGNOLIA

Side eye emoji

TAYLOR

It's okay, sunshine. I'm a patient man.

I wore you down once, I can do it again *winking emoji*

·)）●（（·

"Delivery!" Jaelyn sing-songed sardonically over the chime of the door. "*Again.*"

I looked up to see a massive bouquet of flowers obscuring her face. "Another one?"

Between the arrangements Taylor had sent to *CharCutie* and my house, I looked like I was running a florist shop. It had been cute and sweet the first couple of times. Now? Ridiculous.

"That boy is working overtime for your forgiveness," Jae quipped, setting the vase on the kitchen counter. "What is this? Number five?"

"Seven, actually."

"You're joking."

"Nope." I popped the *p* with enough force to make it echo. "He's been sending them to my house, too."

"Geezums, Mags. What did he do that he thinks requires drowning you in flowers?"

I walked around the counter and buried my face in the petals. Roses the color of a sunset, deep-pink daisies, crimson chrysanthemums, and a few blooms I recognized but could never remember the name of, brushed against my cheeks. The floral scent was heady, intoxicating. Of all the bouquets so far, this one was my favorite.

"He ignored me for days," I muttered, pulling the card from the center.

A reluctant smile tugged at my lips as my eyes skimmed the messy scrawl: *I could totally go for some you right now.*

Persistent didn't begin to cover it.

"So, what? You're ignoring him back?" Jae's caramel eyes sparkled with mischief as she waggled her brows.

"Not exactly. But a little groveling never hurt anyone."

"God, I love when you're in your villain era." She laughed.

Sliding the card back into its holder, I carried the flowers to the office. Just as I returned to the kitchen, my phone vibrated, Taylor's ringtone spilling through the air.

"Do you own a monopoly on flowers or something?" I asked instead of greeting him.

"Hello to you, too."

"Taylor, you need to stop. This is too much," I chided lightly.

"Have you forgiven me yet?"

Had I?

I flopped into my chair, swiveling back and forth as I propped my elbow on the armrest. It had been a week since the incident—and the orgasm. I could understand freaking out over Addy confronting him. I might have done the same. But shutting me out afterward? That still stung. And no amount of flowers could fix it.

"I'll take your silence as a no," Taylor surmised. There was a lightness to his tone, though, one that told me he wasn't giving up anytime soon. Against my better judgment, a small smile crept onto my lips.

"You can't buy forgiveness, cowboy. And as pretty as the flowers are, they're not really... *me*."

"What do you need me to do, Mags?"

I exhaled heavily. "I need communication, and ours is absolute crap. If this is—if *we're*—going to work, we have to talk."

"So, there's still a chance?" he asked animatedly.

I groaned, and the line went silent for a beat, then two, before he spoke again. "Sorry. I know you're right. But it's something we'll have to work on—*both* of us."

"I know," I admitted softly. I wasn't blameless. I had my walls—thick, reinforced ones, built from a childhood full of letdowns. My sisters always said I was like a grimy window: people had to scrub away the dirt to find the clear glass beneath.

Maybe they weren't wrong.

"Are you busy this weekend?" Taylor asked hesitantly.

"I have a catering job on Saturday," I said, grateful for the work. Business at the shop had slowed to a crawl, and every little bit helped.

"What about Friday?"

"Prepping all day. Sunday?"

"That should work. Brunch?"

"Mags, do you want me to lock up so we can go to the store?" Jae hollered from somewhere in the shop.

"Yeah, that's fine!" I called back. Returning to the phone, I added, "It's a date."

"Great. I'll text you the details."

"Bye, cowboy."

"See you soon, sunshine."

+)) ● ((+

"Can you fix the tablecloths on the banquet table and adjust the centerpieces on the high tops, please?" I asked one of the waitstaff as they passed.

They nodded briskly, and I thanked them profusely before heading back to the kitchen.

I was a nervous wreck.

This was the biggest party I'd ever catered, and the sheer number of moving parts had me two seconds away from hyperventilating into a paper bag.

"Ms. Bellevue?" A smooth, lilting voice interrupted my spiral.

"Oh, Mrs. Stephens! Hi, hello. How are you today?" My nerves seeped into every syllable, and I internally groaned. I was supposed to be a professional, and I was quite certain I looked like a floundering idiot.

"I'm well, dear. Thank you."

Mary Stephens looked like the archetype of an uptight principal, with her slicked-back bun, pressed slacks, and small, rimmed glasses perched on her upturned nose. But she was one of the sweetest people I'd ever had the pleasure of working with.

"Everything looks gorgeous out front, and the food smells divine. You're going to make my clients very happy, of that I'm sure."

"I can't wait to meet them," I replied with a nervous smile.

I still had no idea who this party was for, and that was seriously unnerving. Mary had been the middleman for every step of the process, from the tasting menu to the final selections. All I knew was that the clients were a young engaged couple hosting an intimate gathering.

A delighted squeal from the backyard drew our attention. Mary turned back to me with a grin. "Guess now's as good a time as any to introduce you."

Taylor

My mother was going to kill me.

I should have been here over an hour ago. She'd been blowing up my phone, alternating between angry texts and increasingly impatient voicemails.

But I'd finally gotten the keys to the little house Magnolia and I had looked at over a month ago. The entire day had been spent hauling boxes, unpacking, and making lists of all the things I still needed to buy to fill that very empty house. Sure, I had some stuff in storage, but it was all broke med-student and barely-ever-at-home residency furniture that was practically falling apart when I picked it up off of one of those buy, sell, trade pages on the internet.

So yeah, I was late.

"Fuck me," I muttered, pulling into my parents' driveway. Cars lined up and down the drive, and halfway down the street. I hit the call button on my steering wheel. "Call Dad."

"You better be lost or dying, son," he answered with a chuckle.

"I'm here. Where am I supposed to park? Did Mom and Addy invite the whole damn parish?"

"Feels like it. She blocked off parking near the shed. I'd hurry, though. She's about to send out a search party."

"Yeah, yeah. I'll be in in a minute." Hanging up, I navigated toward the family parking area—complete with a sign, because of course, there was.

Christmas music assaulted my ears as I stepped out of the car, and I groaned. For weeks, my mom and sister had tortured me with their carefully curated playlist.

I wasn't a Scrooge. I liked Christmas. But my mom was basically Mrs. Claus with a southern accent as soon as Thanksgiving dinner ended, and Addy was her protégé. So naturally, her engagement party was Christmas-themed.

At least it was December and not in the middle of the summer.

Bing Crosby's *White Christmas* filled the air as I rounded the house. Strings of white lights crisscrossed the backyard, framing a makeshift dance floor. The oaks at the yard's edge shimmered under their own strands, and a giant fake tree stood in the living room. They'd really gone all out, not that I was surprised in the slightest.

My dad spotted me first. He gave a quick head shake toward the bar before I could greet him.

I barely turned when my mom's voice cut through the crowd. "Taylor Michael Hallows, you're late."

Sighing, I spun on my heel and met the harsh, disapproving gaze of my mother. "Hi, Ma. You look lovely tonight."

"And you're late," she repeated, her tone still sharp.

Crossing the distance, I kissed her cheek and felt some of the tension ease from her shoulders. "Sorry, I got buried in boxes and lost track of... time."

I trailed off as a familiar flash of pink and blue caught my eye. My breath hitched.

What she doing here?

"Taylor, are you even listening to me?" my mom demanded and I pulled my attention from where I could have sworn Magnolia was chatting with one of my cousins.

"Sorry, Ma. What were you saying?"

She groaned, threw her hands up, muttering something about no one ever listening to her, as she stalked off.

By the time I looked back, the flash of color was gone. Maybe my mind was playing tricks on me.

Convinced it was my imagination playing tricks on me, I headed toward the bar. If I was going to have to hug and make small talk with a bunch of extended family that I only saw for major life events, I was going to need a drink... or three.

"What'll you have?" the woman behind the bar asked as I approached. She looked twelve, and I had to bite my tongue to keep from asking her if she was old enough to even be near alcohol.

"Whiskey neat."

"Can I get a glass of cab, please?"

My head snapped toward the voice. Aqua-blue eyes locked with mine, a sheepish smile tugging at her lips as she held my gaze.

She was stunning.

Her high ponytail fell over her shoulder, the black bow tied at the top making her look effortlessly playful. But her eyes—god, her eyes—had always been my undoing.

"Come here often?" she teased, one brow arching as the bartender handed her the wine.

Before I could answer, Addy's voice rang out. "Tay Tay!"

Magnolia bit her lip, no doubt hiding a smirk as Addy threw herself into my arms.

"You made it!" Addy beamed before gesturing toward Mags. "And I see you've met my fabulous caterer."

Magnolia's lips twitched. "Tay Tay?"

"Watch it, *Magpie*," I warned. "Only Addy gets to call me that."

Magnolia's eyes narrowed slightly, but the ire they'd held the last time I saw her was missing. The lights from the tree danced in their aquamarine depths, and I had the overwhelming urge to kiss her. Right there. In front of everyone I knew.

Instead, I gave her a wink and shifted my attention back to my sister, nearly missing the faint blush that colored her cheeks as I turned. "You look beautiful tonight, sis. You and Mom certainly outdid yourselves."

"Oh, please. I tried to scale it back, but you know Mama."

That I did. Our mother couldn't do anything less than two-hundred percent, and her only daughter's engagement party—and subsequent wedding—was no exception.

Addy, oblivious as ever, continued gushing about Magnolia's food. When she called it "orgasmic," Mags sputtered, nearly choking on her wine. The ensuing blush on her cheeks nearly undid me.

"I—I'll just go check on the kitchen," she stammered before hurrying off.

I watched her weave through the throng of people, then once she turned in the direction of the kitchen, I snapped my gaze back to my sister. "You really couldn't come up with a better adjective?"

Addy shrugged. "I'm going to go hunt down my future hubby. Make sure he's not cornered somewhere by nosey aunties." Then with a wink and a jerk of her head toward the kitchen, she disappeared into the crowd.

Fucking sisters, man.

After dodging relatives for close to an hour, I slipped into the kitchen.

The noise hit me first—a chorus of "Yes, Chef" echoed as Magnolia directed her team. She moved effortlessly, checking sauces, tasting dishes, and adjusting plating with the precision of an artist.

I leaned against the wall, captivated.

This was her element, and aside from seeing her put together charcuterie boards at the one Meat-Cute I'd been to, I'd never seen her like this. She was flawless as she flitted back and forth from the stove, stirring and tasting before moving back to her cutting board on the island. I'd seen my mom cook when I was growing up, hell, even I knew my way around a kitchen, but watching Magnolia was like watching a dance—fluid, graceful, and every step done with a purpose.

When the staff cleared out, I broke the silence. "Come here often?"

Magnolia jumped, dropping her knife. "*Shitfuckgoddamnit*," she groaned, clutching her hand to her chest. Her eyes were pinched closed as she bounced from foot to foot.

"Mags?" I closed the distance in seconds. "You okay?"

"No, I'm not okay! Don't you know better than to sneak up on someone with a knife!?"

"You cut yourself?"

Magnolia's eyes flew open, her gaze crashing into me with fury blazing in their depths. "No, asshole, I just felt like doing a little jig in the middle of the kitchen while spewing expletives."

"At least your vocabulary's intact."

"Bite me."

"Love to, cher. But first, let me see your hand."

"Why?"

"Because I want to finish chopping off your finger, obviously. Now, *let me see it.*"

She finally unfurled her fingers. Blood coated her palm.

"Run it under cold water. I'll be right back."

"Where are you—wait. Don't get your dad. I'll die of embarrassment."

I smirked. "Why would I get my dad?"

"For stitches?"

Shaking my head, I turned to retrieve my medical bag as confusion twisted her features. "Keep your hand under the water, I'll be right back."

When I returned, she was hunched over the sink.

"Alright, that's probably good," I said, resting my hand on the small of her back.

Magnolia groaned and stood upright, wincing as she examined her fingers. When I placed my bag on the counter, her brows quirked and she asked, "What's that?"

"It's a medical bag."

"Just because your dad is a doctor doesn't mean you are, cowboy."

"You're right," I said with a chuckle. "But my doctorate in emergency medicine and job at West Baptist does."

"Wait... *what*?"

I opened the bag and started pulling things out. "Okay, lemme see."

"Woah, hold up. You're a *doctor*?!"

"Mags, baby, you can ask me all the questions you want to *while* I look at your hand. Now, let me see it."

Magnolia hesitantly placed her hand in mine, and I cautiously dabbed away the water and blood as it began pooling again. "It doesn't look too bad," I explained as I gently rotated her knuckles in the light. "Good news is that you don't need stitches."

"Is there bad news?" she asked.

"I'll have to wrap it."

She groaned, her head falling back in exasperation. "But I need my hand."

"I know, I'm sorry. You'll still be able to bend them, but the more you do, the more the cuts will reopen."

"Great," she groaned. "Anything else?"

"The antiseptic burns like a bitch."

21
Alas, there's no knob
Magnolia

"Fucking hell!" I spat through clenched teeth as Taylor poured what felt like molten lava over my knuckles.

"I'm sorry, baby. Almost done."

"Mother above, that *hurts*."

I bounced on my toes, exhaling a shaky breath when he finally stopped and dabbed at my hand with a blue towel he'd pulled from his bag.

"You doing alright, sunshine?" he asked, his tone laced with amusement.

"You're enjoying this, aren't you?"

"Maybe a little."

"You're the reason I'm injured, and you're laughing at me?"

"Whoa, now. *You* were holding the knife, Mags, not me."

"You *startled* me!"

I couldn't believe what I was hearing. My irritation flared, and I fought the urge to slap him—or at least aim for his shins.

"I know. I'm sorry," he said, a note of sincerity softening his voice. Then his lips twitched at the corners, betraying his amusement.

"I can't believe you're enjoying my pain," I huffed.

"No, baby." His hands were gentle as he smoothed ointment over my knuckles and wrapped them in what looked like a fancy Band-Aid.

"What I'm enjoying is taking care of you. And maybe"—his voice dipped, sending a shiver through me—"the fact that I get to touch you while my family and their friends are just on the other side of that door."

His words hit me square in the chest, igniting a flurry of butterflies. His eyes held mine with a tenderness that made my breath hitch. As he brushed a stray strand of hair from my face and cupped my cheek, goosebumps erupted along my skin.

"Are you okay?" he murmured, his voice impossibly soft.

"I think I'll live," I whispered. Had he moved closer? His lips hovered a hair's breadth from mine, his gaze flicking down to my lips and back up, over and over.

"I'd really like to kiss you right now," he said, his breath warming my skin, "but I don't want to overstep—or mess up your lipstick."

"It's a stain," I replied, my voice barely audible. *It's a stain?* What the hell was wrong with me? I was supposed to be mad at him. But one superhero moment, a few sweet words, and I was a puddle of goo. Being around Taylor Hallows was like riding a rollercoaster: thrilling, unpredictable, and downright dizzying.

"Is that permission?" he asked with a low chuckle, tugging me closer.

I opened my mouth to answer—yes, no? Honestly, I wasn't sure what I was about to say—when the kitchen door swung open. We leapt apart like shrapnel.

Jae stood in the doorway, hands on her hips, her wide eyes dancing with mischief. "I was going to ask if you needed a sock on the door, but alas, no knob."

"I cut myself. Taylor was just helping me bandage it," I said in a rush, my cheeks flaming. Jae's raised brows said it all. She wasn't buying any of it. I knew it. She knew it. Hell, the crickets outside probably knew it, too.

"Uh-huh. And did you also require mouth-to-mouth? Because it sure looked like his lips were on yours when I walked in."

"Jae!" I chided, but she just grinned.

"Fine, fine. I'll be over here if you need me for more 'medical emergencies.'"

Before I could respond, Mary Stephens entered, glowing with happiness. "Magnolia! Everyone *loved* the food. The bride is over the moon!"

Hearing praise for my creations never got old; my heart flipped at the compliment. "I'm so glad to hear it. Is there anything else the couple needs?"

Mary shook her head. "No, they're winding down out there. The bride sent me to insist you take a break and enjoy the rest of the party."

"Oh, I can't—"

"The bride insists," Mary interrupted, her tone firm. "And what the bride wants—"

"The bride gets," Taylor finished with a smirk.

Mary beamed at me. "Thank you, Magnolia. You were a dream to work with."

"So were you, Mrs. Stephens."

"Please call me Mary. Mrs. Stephens is my mother-in-law, and plus, I have a feeling we'll be seeing a lot more of each other in the future." Her gaze flicked knowingly between Taylor and me before she left.

"Well, you heard her." Jae clapped her hands together. "Go enjoy the party."

"But the kitchen—"

"Will be fine," she cut in. "The waitstaff and I have it covered. Now, go."

Taylor packed up his supplies, his hand warm on the small of my back as he guided me toward the door. "Shall we?"

"But the kitchen—"

"Will be fine without you," Taylor said, his tone leaving no room for argument. "Bride's orders, remember?"

I hesitated, glancing around the room. The kitchen was my sanctuary, my refuge in the chaos. Sure, it wasn't a complete disaster—I cleaned as I worked—but there was still plenty left to do.

Jae seemed to sense my reluctance. "I have your list, Mags. I know what needs to be done and where everything goes. I've got this. Go have some fun."

With a resigned groan, I let Taylor steer me out of the kitchen and into what remained of the party.

Most of the guests had already gone, but laughter still spilled from the living room, where a few stragglers mingled. Taylor's hand stayed firmly on my lower back, grounding me as he led me past the noise and out into the crisp night air.

The backyard looked like something out of a holiday movie. Twinkling Christmas lights draped across the trees, casting a soft glow over the empty dance floor set up in the middle of the expansive yard.

"Do you think anyone even used the dance floor?" I asked, leaning against the deck railing.

Taylor stepped behind me, his warmth seeping into my back as he wrapped his arms around my waist. I felt his shrug more than I saw it.

"Someone's about to."

"What?" I turned, only to find him holding out his hand, an invitation in his eyes.

"Dance with me, cher."

"But your family—"

"Is either preoccupied or drunk off their asses." His voice was low, his expression soft. "It's just you and me out here. Dance with me. Please?"

"But there's no music," I protested weakly, grasping for an excuse.

Taylor quirked a brow, pulling his phone from his pocket. Moments later, Norah Jones' *Come Away With Me* flowed into the stillness.

"Have you run out of excuses yet?" he asked, his lips curving into a teasing smile.

"I'm sure I could come up with a few more," I mused, sliding my hand into his.

"But?"

"But I don't want to."

His grin widened, and my knees nearly gave out. This—these small, unspoken gestures—was what I needed. Not grand declarations or sweeping gestures, but the little things. The slow dances, the stolen moments, the quiet intimacy of just being.

As Taylor pulled me into his arms and swayed to the music, careful of my bandaged hand, a feeling I hadn't allowed myself to embrace in a long time unfurled in my chest. His touch was steady, his presence grounding, and the world melted away as the song wrapped around us.

"What are you thinking about?" he asked when the track shifted into another melody.

I hadn't been thinking much, to be honest—just losing myself in the feeling of being held by him. But his question brought the outside world rushing back in.

"Were you going to invite me to be your date tonight?"

"What?"

"For this. The engagement party."

His sheepish expression told me everything I needed to know before he spoke.

"Taylor..."

He blew out a heavy breath. "No. I thought it might be too soon to meet my family when we haven't even been on a public date yet."

"So why did you ask me out tonight?" I demanded, my voice rising.

Taylor grimaced. "I thought... I don't know. I just wanted to spend time with you. Alone."

"Taylor Hallows, tell me you were not planning to ditch your sister's engagement party."

"Okay, I won't tell you," he muttered.

"Taylor!" I tried to pull away, but he tightened his hold on me, and—sweet baby cheeses—either he'd stashed a salami in his pocket, or...

His smug grin confirmed my suspicions, and I groaned.

"I asked you out tonight because I wanted to show you something," he said, his voice dropping an octave.

Is it the sausage in your pants? My mind veered straight into the gutter, but I managed to bite back the words.

"What do you want to show me?"

Instead of answering, he twined his fingers with mine and started leading me toward the side of the house.

"Wait, where are we going?"

Taylor glanced over his shoulder, his smile sly. "You'll see."

I pulled my hand free and stepped back. "Not until you tell me."

With a low growl, he closed the gap between us in two strides, wrapping me in his arms. His lips descended on mine, and I melted like butter on a hot skillet. Kissing Taylor was intoxicating—my mind hazy, my body light, every nerve alive with sensation.

When he finally pulled back, his breath warm against my cheek, I could barely string two words together.

"Are you going to tell me now?" I managed, my voice embarrassingly breathless.

He shook his head, grinning as he laced his fingers through mine again. "Trust me."

"Can I at least grab my purse?" I asked, still trying to regain control of the situation—or at least my heart rate.

"It's already in your car," Jae called from the doorway.

"Jesus, do you have a GPS tracker on her or something?" Taylor yelled back, exasperation tinging his voice.

"No, but maybe I should, considering how often you try to whisk her away," Jae shot back, her grin audible in her words.

I stifled a laugh as Taylor pinched the bridge of his nose in frustration.

"Would you be nice?" I whispered, nudging him with my elbow.

"Baby, we've been interrupted more times than I care to count. *Three* of those times were by *her*," he muttered, nodding toward Jae.

"I thought you weren't counting," I teased, earning a playful glare.

He stepped closer, his hand brushing a strand of hair behind my ear. The intimate gesture sent a shiver down my spine. "I just want you to myself for once. Is that such a bad thing?"

"No, it's not," I admitted, my voice softer than I intended. Rising onto my toes, I pressed a quick kiss to his lips, savoring the way his arms instinctively tightened around me.

"If y'all are quite finished," Jae interrupted, her tone dripping with mock impatience. "Mags, would you kindly grab your purse so I can go home?"

"Go," Taylor murmured, tugging me toward the car.

•)❯●❰(•

Taylor

"Taylor," Magnolia drew out my name, her voice tinged with suspicion as I turned onto the winding driveway of my new house. She leaned forward in her seat, squinting into the darkness as if it might reveal my intentions.

I hummed in response, unwilling to trust my mouth—or my brain—to form coherent words.

Nerves prickled along my spine as the gravel crunched beneath the tires. The feeling caught me off guard. I'd been so sure about this step, about planting roots and starting a life of my own. But as I stole a glance at Magnolia, her face a mixture of curiosity and unease, one thought consumed me: *I hope she likes it.*

The headlights illuminated the front of the house, and Magnolia gasped.

"What are we doing here?" she demanded, sitting bolt upright. "Taylor, we can't be here!"

"Why not?" I asked, fighting back a grin as I put the car in park.

"Because it's *someone's house*! You can't just show up at someone's house uninvited!" She was whisper-yelling, as if the homeowners might overhear.

"It *is* someone's house, sunshine." I pulled the keys from the console, dangling them in front of her. "It's mine."

Her eyes went wide. "You...you bought the house?"

"I did."

"But why?"

Instead of answering, I stepped out of the car and rounded to her side, opening her door. Magnolia stayed rooted in her seat, staring at me as if I'd just told her I was the heir to a secret kingdom.

"Taylor, what are you doing?" she asked, her voice tinged with disbelief.

Sliding my hands up her thighs, I let my thumbs brush the hem of her dress. Her breath hitched, and I leaned closer, steeling myself for what I was about to say.

"I bought this house—*this* house—because you fell in love with it," I said, my voice low and steady. "Because I couldn't picture anyone else in that kitchen. I couldn't imagine anyone else swinging on that porch swing, watching the sunset with me. I want you here, Magnolia. I want *us* here. I'm all in."

The words hung between us, heavy with meaning. My heart pounded as I waited for her response.

Magnolia launched herself at me, her arms wrapping around my neck as her lips found mine. The force of her kiss knocked me back a step, but I recovered quickly, my hands locking around her waist to hold her close.

Her kiss was everything—fierce, desperate, and all-consuming. Weeks of pent-up tension ignited between us, burning away every doubt, every hesitation.

When I finally pulled back, it was only because I needed to hear her say it. Needed to know where she stood when it came to *us*.

"Everything okay?" she asked, her voice breathless, her hands resting over my thundering heart.

"Mags, what are we?" The words came out rougher than I intended, but I didn't care. I needed to know. "Are we just...seeing what happens? Are you my girlfriend? Are we—"

"Do you *want* me to be your girlfriend?" she interrupted, her voice barely above a whisper.

"Do you want to be?" I countered, my heart hammering in my chest.

Her cheeks flushed, and she dropped her gaze, but I wasn't letting her hide. Tilting her chin up, I held her gaze.

"I want you to be my *everything,* Magnolia," I said firmly. "I told you—I'm in this. Both feet, firmly planted, with you."

"You really bought this house because I loved it?"

"I did."

Her lips curved into a slow, radiant smile. Then, like a magnet, she leaned into me, her hands fisting in my shirt.

"Well, *boyfriend,*" she murmured, her voice teasing but her eyes shining, "I guess you'd better show me inside."

Fucking hell.

Release the kraken

Magnolia

WE'D BARELY MADE IT through the front door before I was trying to climb Taylor like a goddamn tree.

The front door of the house he bought because I loved it.

If I wasn't already falling for the man, I sure as hell would be now.

My arms wrapped around his neck as he kicked the door closed with a resounding *boom*. His hand fisted in my ponytail, a gentle burn of pain where the strands tugged against my scalp. The other was splayed across my lower back, anchoring me to him in the most delicious way. With one swift movement, he backed me against the wall with enough force that I gasped against his lips, his hips pressing into mine as he slid his hand down my side to hike my leg over his hip. A groan rumbled against my mouth as his fingers glided from the silk of my tights to the bare skin just above them.

I whined when he pulled his lips from mine, heat pooling low in my belly as his gaze roamed over my body. It felt like his eyes were touching me, caressing every inch of skin until they settled on where his fingers gripped my thigh.

"Fucking hell, sunshine," he ground out, his hold tightening. His thumb brushed just beneath the band of my stockings, and even with his head tilted down, the smirk curling his lips was unmistakable. "You are a walking temptation, Magnolia Bellevue."

The intensity in his eyes when he looked back up made my knees weak. If he didn't have me pressed against the wall, I'd be a puddle on the floor.

"One I fully intend to indulge in."

Mother, Maiden, and Crone, give me strength.

This wasn't how I thought my night would go, but Blessed Mother, I was grateful I'd picked this outfit. It wasn't anything special—a maroon corduroy dress layered over an ivory turtleneck—but I'd paired it with black thigh-high stockings instead of tights. I hated the way full stockings sagged by the end of the night, but apparently, my fashion annoyance was a blessing in disguise. The heat in his eyes could have melted the iceberg that sank the Titanic.

If this were a movie, there'd be some sultry song playing in the background, like *Play With Fire* or *You Put a Spell on Me*. But this wasn't a movie. This was real, and my brain was still catching up to the fact that I'd gone from loathing this man to craving him pressed between my thighs.

The only thing grounding me was the solid weight of Taylor's body against mine.

"Bed," I panted as his lips blazed a path from my mouth to my jaw. I'd let him take me against the Mother-damned wall—maybe one day he would—but right now, I needed to feel his weight on top of me, his skin against mine.

Taylor's eyes locked with mine, and he slowly lowered my leg to the floor before sliding his hand back to my waist. The glow from the porch lights streaming through the windows illuminated his face, catching the sapphire blue of his eyes like moonlight on the ocean.

I may have been a witch, but the way he was looking at me made me feel like I was the one under a spell.

Suddenly, the inches between us were unbearable.

On second thought, the wall was fine.

I cupped his cheeks and pulled him back down to me. Our lips collided, fierce and desperate, tongues tangling in a battle for dominance. Clothes were tugged and discarded as Taylor backed us out of the foyer. We paused only long enough for me to pull his sweater over his head and toss it aside.

Our movements were hasty and clumsy. My fingers fumbled with the buttons of his shirt as he worked to undo my dress. It slid from my shoulders, catching on my boots and nearly tripping me.

This was an accident waiting to happen.

The thought had barely crossed my mind when Taylor stumbled, pulling me down with him. I yelped as we tumbled to the floor, landing in a tangle of limbs.

A loud crash followed, and our eyes snapped to a pile of toppled boxes beside us. Silence stretched for a beat before laughter spilled out of both of us.

"When I imagined you on top of me, cher, this wasn't what I had in mind," he teased, grinning up at me.

"Taylor!" I swatted his chest.

When I tried to climb off, his arms tightened around my waist, his smile turning wicked. "I'm not complaining, sunshine."

"I am. Your house is a hazard, Hallows."

I shifted in his hold, and he loosened his grip just enough for me to sit up. That turned out to be a mistake, as it left me acutely aware of every inch of him pressed against me.

It also gave him a very clear view of the most intimate parts of me.

Heat flushed my cheeks as his gaze drifted to the thin strip of cotton between my legs. A thrill raced down my spine as his hands skimmed down to bare skin before squeezing. The heat that had dimmed moments ago reignited into a roaring flame.

Was I nervous? Hell, yes. It had been embarrassingly long since I'd been with anyone other than my handy-dandy vibrator, Vib-ritzio. Yes, I named it. Don't judge me. Not to mention, most of my partners hadn't exactly prioritized my pleasure. There had been a handful of moments where I'd reached the finish line, but those were the exception, not the rule.

But the way Taylor was looking at me? I had a distinct feeling that wouldn't be the case this time. Those nervous little caterpillars in my stomach transformed into fluttering, anticipatory butterflies.

Taylor's grip tightened as I shifted over him. Feeling emboldened, I rocked forward slightly, a delicious zing sparking through me at the friction against my clit.

"Magnolia."

The way he ground out my name had my heart pounding. His gaze flicked between my face and the place where our bodies pressed together, raw and hungry. It was intoxicating—empowering—and I wanted to see how far he'd let me push him, how long it would take for his restraint to snap.

Lifting his chin with my finger, I held his gaze as I worked my hips in slow, deliberate circles. The fabric of my panties dragged against me with every roll, sending shivers of pleasure through my body. I could feel him twitch against me, and the sensation only stoked the fire.

A muscle in his jaw jumped, his breaths coming in heavy exhales like it took every ounce of control he had not to take me right there. His fingers flexed against my thighs before sliding around to my behind to guide my movements.

"Are you trying to kill me?" he asked, voice strained.

"No," I replied, feigning innocence. "Just seeing what it takes to unravel you."

I sounded far more confident than I felt, but his villainous, panty-melting smirk made my boldness falter. My whole body thrummed with heat. If he so much as breathed on me, I might combust.

Without warning, he sat up, pulling me flush against him. One strong hand slid around the back of my neck, his whispered words tickling my ear.

"Two can play at that game, cher. And I'm very competitive."

Oh, shit.

Taylor pulled me into a kiss that could only be described as punishing—one that promised my lips would be red and swollen by morning. His arms slid beneath my thighs, lifting me effortlessly as he stood. Mother above, that was an amazing feeling.

A moan escaped as his grip tightened on my ass, my legs locking instinctively around his waist. His lips never left mine as he carried me through the house, weaving between the maze of boxes.

When we reached the master bedroom, he set me gently on the bed. The kiss broke only long enough for him to strip my shirt over my head. I tugged at the last buttons of his dress shirt as he shucked it off, and for a moment, I just stared.

Sweet baby cheeses. I'd almost forgotten what shirtless Taylor looked like.

His chest was all sharp lines and lean muscle, with just enough softness to make snuggling feel like heaven instead of curling against a brick wall. The urge to run my tongue down the groove between his pecs was almost overwhelming.

Clad in only a matching black bra and panties—yay for wearing coordinating underwear for once—my thigh-high stockings, and boots, I watched as he took a step back. His gaze raked over me like a man starved, his fingers working his belt free from the loops with deliberate slowness.

My breath came in shallow pants, my body trembling with anticipation as I waited for him to release the kraken. I was soaked, my panties clinging to me uncomfortably. Watching him saunter forward, all swagger and intent, made heat rise from my cheeks down to my chest.

"You know," I squeaked, swallowing thickly, "I could help with that."

"Oh, I know you can," he replied, his voice a low rumble. "And you will. But as I said, two can play this game. And, baby, it's my turn."

Holy forking shirt balls, Batman. I was sweating.

Figuratively, of course. Women don't sweat—we glisten. And I was glistening like a damn Washington vampire in the sunshine.

Taylor didn't just walk to me. He prowled. Each step was purposeful, like a predator cornering its prey. I couldn't help the shiver that ran down my spine.

His hands moved to my boots, slipping them off with ease. He trailed his fingers up my calves, his touch featherlight, until one hand hooked behind my knee. He hitched it over his hip as he knelt on the bed, his other hand cupping my cheek with a gentleness that contradicted the intensity in his eyes.

His lips brushed against mine, soft and unhurried, parting them just enough to allow his tongue to slide in and coax mine into a dance. Every move was delicate, deliberate, and maddeningly restrained.

It was driving me insane.

"Taylor," I whimpered, arching beneath him as he moved his lips along my jaw.

"What do you need, Magnolia?"

The gravel in his voice sent shivers cascading down my spine, pooling heat low in my belly.

"I need you to touch me. Fuck me. Something. I'm dying here," I groaned, raking my nails down the muscles of his back.

The bastard smirked—actually *smirked*—against my neck before pulling away and piercing me with his Southern sky blues. "Tell me exactly what you want, cher."

He was asking me...what I wanted...? *The fuck?*

I blinked, thrown. No man had ever asked me that before.

Not knowing how to respond, I defaulted to my usual defense: sarcasm. "What, no quips about being a doctor who can teach me things about my body that even I don't know?"

That cocky smirk broadened and the heat in his eyes could've scorched the earth.

"I could say that," he murmured, his hand ghosting down my body, "and I'd probably be right."

His fingers skimmed the valley between my breasts, grazing just enough to make my nipples pebble beneath the lace of my bra. They trailed lower, so achingly slow that I thought I'd crawl out of my skin.

"But even with every anatomy book, lecture, and residency, the only person who can tell me how to make you come, how to make you scream my name until your lungs give out, sweet Magnolia,"—his hand flattened against my stomach and slid to my hip, grinding me against his thigh—"is you."

Holy Mother of fucks. I was so beyond screwed.

"You know your body better than anyone... for now, anyway."

Yep. Totally screwed.

His fingers teased the edge of my panties, his pinky dipping just beneath the elastic. My breath hitched, every nerve ending sparking to life. Every word I knew seemed to evaporate.

"Talk to me, sunshine."

"Lower," I managed to whisper, barely audible.

He started to pull back instead, a devilish grin tugging at his lips. Instinctively, I grabbed his wrist.

"Be more specific, Magnolia," he murmured, brushing his nose against mine. His lips were so close, his voice so deep and intimate, I shivered. "Or I'll do it my way."

The worst part? That didn't sound like a threat—it sounded like a promise. And part of me wanted to let him. To let him decide, to give him full control and see what he'd do.

But I knew what he was asking for. He wanted me to take ownership of my own pleasure.

Of course, my brain had turned into goo and could barely form words, much less a coherent response. The first thing it managed to come up with slipped out before my filter caught it.

"I'm not very good at following directions."

Smooth, Mags. Real smooth.

Taylor's grin softened into something warm and unbearably tender. He freed his wrist from my hold and cupped my cheek, his thumb brushing lightly along my skin. "Lucky for you, I am."

He pressed a soft kiss to my lips, then whispered, "Think of it like a recipe."

"A recipe?" I squeaked, tilting my head back as his mouth moved to my neck.

"Mmm." His lips grazed the sensitive spot where my shoulder met my neck, and I swore my brain short-circuited. "One for your pleasure."

Sweet baby cheeses.

"I need to know the ingredients, and only you can give them to me."

His hand slid down my body again, inching closer to where I wanted him most. My breath hitched, every thought scattering.

"I need your words, Magnolia."

Words. Right. What were those again?

"I, uh. I need you to touch me," I stammered, feeling heat bloom in my cheeks.

"I am touching you, sunshine. Be more specific."

When my brain still refused to cooperate, he pulled back just enough to look at me, one brow quirking in challenge.

"Don't tell me the firecracker who could set me ablaze with a glare is shy in the bedroom."

I scoffed. "No!" Though it didn't even sound convincing to me.

"I'll tell you what," he began, the glint in his eye making my heart stutter. "If I'm doing something you don't like, tell me to stop. Otherwise, I'll do what I think you need. Deal?"

I swallowed hard, nodding. "I can do that."

His smile turned wicked, sending a thrill straight through me. "Good girl."

23
That... what... no.
Magnolia

Any response I had died on a gasp as Taylor dropped his head, his mouth capturing my nipple through the thin lace of my bra. His fingers slipped beneath the cotton of my panties, finding my soaked center. A shiver raced down my spine as he circled my clit and then dipped lower. The tip of his finger teased inside, and my breath caught, my heart pounding like a drum in my ears. Stars danced behind my closed eyelids, each sensation more electrifying than the last.

"So fucking wet for me already." His husky whisper was velvet and whiskey, steeped in desire that sent a flush racing across my skin. "Eyes on me, baby. I want to see you when you come on my hand."

"That—that's not going to happen," I panted, reluctantly forcing my eyes open.

"Our track record would beg to differ."

"Beginner's luck," I said through a gasp as he slid a finger inside.

Taylor raised a brow, his fingers slowing. "Is that a challenge, cher?"

"N-no. Just a f-fact." Though even I knew that fact was crumbling under his touch.

"It won't be for long."

"Wha—" My words choked off as two fingers slid inside me, curling to press against a spot that made my back arch.

Heat licked up my spine as his thumb resumed its delicious circles on my clit. My gasp turned into a moan when he tugged my bra cup down and drew my nipple into his mouth. The mounting ecstasy built with each stroke of his fingers, but when his thumb pressed a fraction too hard, I flinched, retreating from the edge of release.

"What is it?" Taylor's voice was gentle, his brow furrowing.

"I—uh..."

"Words, cher. You promised me your words."

Blowing out a nervous raspberry, I muttered, "It's not a button, cowboy." His eyes widened in surprise, and I bit back a laugh. "I just mean, you don't have to press so hard. Firm, but gentle."

He nodded, his expression thoughtful. Slowly, he adjusted his movements, the new rhythm nearly perfect. The shift must have shown on my face, because he narrowed his eyes at me.

"Words," I reminded myself, feeling a blush creep up my cheeks. "A little harder."

He obeyed without hesitation, his touch becoming exactly what I needed. I sank into the sensations, more confident now in voicing my desires. Taylor followed every whispered direction with precision, his focus unwavering as he laved my breasts and adjusted his rhythm to match my needs.

My breath turned ragged, tension coiling in my core as his fingers worked magic inside me. My limbs grew heavy, tingling warmth spreading from my toes to my fingertips.

"Taylor, I... I'm—"

"I know, cher. Tell me what you need."

"More. You. I—"

His lips silenced me, swallowing my moan as he slipped another finger inside and quickened his pace. Three fingers stretched me, filling me so completely I could hardly think.

"Be a good girl and come for me, Magnolia."

The sound of his voice—dark and velvety as he said my name—pushed me over the edge. My climax hit like a wave, my body clenching around him as he wrung every drop from me like it was his damn job. His tongue tangled with mine, his touch unrelenting until my muscles gave out and I melted into the bed.

Taylor withdrew his fingers, and I watched, wide-eyed, as he slipped them into his mouth, groaning at the taste. "Fuck, you taste good. But as much as I want to fuck you with my tongue, I need to be inside you."

Say less, sir.

I reached for the button on his slacks, but he caught my wrist, pinning it above my head. His lips brushed mine briefly before he pulled back.

"Baby, if you touch me right now, I'm going to blow," he said with a soft laugh, kissing me again.

When Taylor pulled away, he climbed off the bed, taking me with him until we were both standing at its edge. His heated gaze swept over my body, making me feel deliciously exposed. Backing up a step, he gave me a playful smirk.

"Take it off, cher. Let me see you."

"I'll show you mine if you show me yours," I countered, lifting my chin.

His brow quirked as he moved to unbutton his slacks, his movements slow and deliberate. When he pushed them down, my jaw nearly hit the floor. His cock was fully hard, standing at attention like it was pointing straight at me—a goddamn homing beacon.

"Your turn, sunshine."

I froze. It wasn't absurdly big like the exaggerated heroes in Maddie's romance novels, but it was enough to make my pulse quicken.

"Mags," Taylor said, taking a step closer.

"That... what... *no*." My words tumbled out in incoherent fragments, and I forced myself to meet his gaze. "Where the hell have you been hiding *that*?"

Good lord, would my filter ever work around this man?

His low chuckle sent heat straight to my core. "See something you like, cher?" He brushed a loose strand of hair from my face, tucking it behind my ear with a gentleness that belied the hunger in his eyes.

"Like? Yeah. Slightly intimidated by the anaconda you've been hiding in your pants? Also, yeah."

"That mouth." He shook his head with a grin before capturing my lips in a searing kiss.

Deft fingers unclasped my bra, and it joined the growing pile of clothes on the floor. My hands skimmed over his chest and shoulders, wrapping around his neck as he lifted me with ease. This time, instead of gently laying me on the bed, he tossed me onto it. A startled squeak escaped me before he grabbed my ankle, dragging me closer until I was at the edge.

With a deliberate slowness, he hooked his thumbs into the waistband of my panties and slid them down my legs, leaving me in nothing but thigh-high stockings.

"Fucking hell, Mags. You're sexy as sin."

"I don't think sin is supposed to be sexy," I teased, my voice breathy.

His hands traced up my thighs, leaving a trail of fire in their wake. "Do you have a favorite position, cher?"

Who does what now?

The question threw me off balance, heat rushing to my cheeks. My gaze darted to his hand as he gripped his cock, stroking himself with lazy confidence.

"Magnolia," he drew out my name, his voice a sinful caress. Crawling over me, he kissed a line down my collarbone, slipping his fingers back into my center. Every nerve in my body lit up at his touch. "I know you have one. I can see it written all over your beautiful face."

My breath hitched, and I forced myself to answer. "It's called the flatiron."

When I peeked up at him, his wide eyes made me backpedal. "But I'm not picky! Anything is fine—"

His mouth covered mine, cutting off my rambling. After thoroughly silencing me with his lips, he pulled back and flipped me onto my stomach.

Oh. *Oh.*

Fucking hell, he actually knew what that was?

His warm hands caressed the curve of my ass. The anticipation built like a storm as I heard the unmistakable sound of a condom packet tearing. Excitement and nerves tangled in my belly when I felt the head of his cock nudge against my slick center.

"Fuck," he groaned as he pushed inside, inch by inch, filling me to the brim.

My body stretched around him, the ache sweet and satisfying. When he was fully seated, his weight settled over me like a comforting blanket, and I moaned, "As amazing as this feels, I need you to move, cowboy."

"I know, sunshine." His voice was tight with restraint. "But give me a second."

I wiggled my hips, testing his control, and his grip tightened immediately. The sound of his palm meeting my ass echoed in the room, followed by the sting that sent a jolt of pleasure straight to my core.

"Well, well, well," he murmured, his hand kneading the sting away. "Do you like being spanked, cher?"

"Y-yes." The word tumbled out unbidden, and I pressed my hips back toward him, inviting more.

Taylor chuckled darkly, driving into me with a force that made my breath hitch. "Good to know."

Taylor's pace turned punishing, his thrusts precise as they hit that perfect spot inside me over and over. My grip on the sheets tightened, knuckles whitening as I braced myself against the headboard. Every motion sent a jolt of pleasure through me, and it wasn't long before the familiar pressure began building low in my belly.

"Yes, yes, yes," I moaned, my voice breaking as the tension coiled tighter.

But just as I teetered on the edge, Taylor pulled out, and I whined in frustration, shooting him a glare over my shoulder.

"Easy, sunshine," he said with a smirk, his hands gripping my hips to flip me onto my side. Lifting my leg, he draped it over his shoulder, the new position bending me in ways I didn't think possible.

"Hey—*oh*," I gasped as he slid back inside, the angle hitting even deeper than before.

"You okay?" His ocean-blue eyes searched mine, softening slightly even as his movements remained firm.

"Yeah, just don't stop."

"Wasn't planning on it, cher."

Taylor leaned down, bending me further as he captured my lips in a bruising kiss. His hips rocked into me with unrelenting rhythm, the friction against my clit pushing me closer to the edge. Warmth flooded my body as his hands roamed over my curves, caressing, kneading, claiming.

Every nerve ending was alight, and my head tilted back, breaking the kiss as a ragged moan escaped. My fingers tangled in his hair, pulling him closer, needing more of him.

Wherever his hands were, his mouth followed. There wasn't a doubt in my mind that concealer would become my best friend over the next few days with the way he was sucking at my skin.

I needed to feel every inch of him. Needed to be consumed by him.

Pressure built low in my belly as I neared the release I so desperately craved, and I whined as Taylor pulled away from my lips and sat up straight. His eyes burned into mine, desire flaming in those ocean blues as he pressed his hand flat against my abdomen and swirled his thumb on my clit. I gasped at the sensation, my back bowing as pleasure swept through me.

"I'm so close," I mewled, my eyes sliding closed as it all became too much.

"Eyes on me, baby. I want to see you when you come on my cock for the first time." My eyes flew open, latching onto his. "That's it. Fuck, you're so beautiful."

"Taylor," I breathed, barely able to form words as the pressure built to an unbearable height.

"I've got you, baby," he whispered. The circles he drew were firm but teasing, coaxing me higher with every pass. "Come on, Magnolia. Give it to me. I want to feel you fall apart."

My body obeyed before my mind could catch up. The orgasm tore through me like a lightning strike, stealing my breath and blurring my vision. My walls clenched around him, drawing a deep groan from his lips as he continued to drive into me, prolonging the ecstasy until I was trembling.

"Fuck," he growled, his thrusts becoming erratic. With a final deep stroke, he buried himself inside me, his release triggering another wave of pleasure that rippled through my oversensitized body.

When he collapsed beside me, his chest heaving, I felt the echo of his heartbeat against my skin. I'd never been so sated in my life. Never had my needs met in such an expert manner and I knew that any man who tried to come after Taylor would pale in comparison.

But I didn't want any other man.

I wanted Taylor.

I wanted him between my thighs six ways from Sunday, and all the pleasure that promised. But more than that, I wanted all the things he'd promised while we stood in his driveway. The front porch swinging and singing in the kitchen. But there was always that little voice in the back of my mind that liked to rear her ugly head at the most inconvenient times.

He doesn't know the real *you.*

Only this time, she was right. He didn't. He didn't know the rumors surrounding my family were real, and telling him terrified me.

"Mags?" Taylor's voice pulled me from my thoughts, and I turned my head to meet his gaze. "Where'd you go, sunshine?" he asked as he pressed a kiss to my shoulder.

"Sorry, I just got lost in my head for a minute."

"Everything okay?"

Concern filled his eyes, and I rolled onto my side to cup his cheek. "Everything is perfect."

Pressing my lips to his stoked a fire in my belly, desire sparking and spreading as our kiss deepened, growing more demanding with each passing second.

The voice in the back of my head could shut the hell up. I wasn't about to let her ruin this—wasn't about to let her snuff out the joy of being wrapped in his arms. Taylor finding out I was a witch? That was a problem for future Magnolia.

Swinging my leg over his waist, I straddled his hips and rocked against him. I was so lost in my thoughts that I hadn't even noticed when he'd gotten up to remove the condom. The silky feel of him beneath me nearly made me fall apart.

"Again? Already?" he asked with a low chuckle, his hands framing my hips and guiding me along his length.

"I'm ready if you are."

His laugh was warm, rich, and it made my heart feel like it might burst right out of my chest.

"Baby, when it comes to you, I'm always ready."

Taylor's hand slid up to cradle my neck, pulling me down to meet his lips. He kissed me until every thought, every worry, evaporated, leaving nothing but him.

24

Shit, the cinnamon rolls!

Taylor

I hated mornings. Probably more than most people. But I despised them even more when I woke up panicking on my day off, my brain conveniently forgetting that detail. Not that I could blame it—working every weekend for the past month and a half would do that.

Groaning, I tossed my phone back onto the makeshift night-stand—a random box that still needed to be unpacked—and flopped onto the bed, crossing my fingers that my frantic movements hadn't woken Magnolia.

Last night had exceeded every expectation I'd dared to hope for, surpassing the dreams that had sustained me these past few months. It had taken her a bit to open up about what she needed, but once she had, watching her repeatedly unravel beneath my hands was a memory I'd carry for the rest of my life.

Smiling, I rolled to my side and reached for her. My fingers, expecting soft, warm skin, brushed cool emptiness instead.

Sitting up, I grabbed my glasses from the box beside the bed and looked around. Her side of the bed was untouched—the covers pulled back neatly, the pillows propped against the headboard. The bathroom was dark and empty, and the bedroom door was closed. If it weren't for her clothes still scattered across the floor, I might have thought she'd slipped out without saying goodbye. Which raised an interesting question—was she walking around the house naked?

Dragging myself out of bed, I pulled on sweatpants and headed for the door. The sweet scent of cinnamon and freshly brewed coffee hit me as soon as I opened it. I let out an appreciative sigh. I could get used to this—waking up to coffee and baked goods.

The smell lured me through the house. Sunlight poured into the living room, bathing the space in buttery light and highlighting the sea of packed boxes. I hesitated, half a step toward the nearest box, the urge to organize tugging at me.

Then music drifted from the kitchen, along with Magnolia's soft singing, cutting through the stillness.

Taking a deep, steadying breath, I approached the kitchen and leaned casually—at least, I hoped it looked casual—against the doorway. Not that it mattered. Her back was to me.

Magnolia was a vision—and a tease—as she danced around in my button-up from last night. The sleeves were rolled to her elbows, the hem brushing her thighs. Her hair was piled haphazardly on her head, swaying slightly as she sang along to *Love Drunk*. When she lifted her arms and swayed them above her head in time with the music, I lost any hope of keeping my cool.

The hem of my shirt inched higher, teasing me with a glimpse of skin just below her ass, and it took every ounce of self-control to stay put.

I stood there, watching, as an absurd sense of pride swelled in my chest. She moved around the kitchen like it was hers, not mine. My cheeks ached from smiling, but I couldn't help it. She had me utterly captivated.

I was just about to make my presence known when she flicked her hand toward the sink. My words caught in my throat as water gushed from the faucet, and soap spilled into the basin. Then, with another wave of her hand, steam rose from a mug as a spoon inside it began to stir itself.

What the actual fuck?

Blinking, I rubbed my eyes, sure I was hallucinating from exhaustion. But then, with yet another flourish of her fingers, the music skipped to a new song mid-chorus.

My pulse thundered in my ears as my thoughts—slow as dial-up internet—latched onto one, unavoidable conclusion. Those rumors weren't just rumors. Magnolia really was a witch.

How many times had she used magic around me without my noticing? Was she a good witch? Were bad witches even a thing? How many witches lived in town? Was it hereditary?

A thousand thoughts spiraled through my mind, but there was one that played on repeat.

"She's really a witch."

Shit. Did I just say that out loud?

Magnolia spun around, her wide eyes locking onto mine as her hands flew to her mouth. Everything stopped—the water, the spoon, even the air in the room.

"Taylor, I... I can explain," she stammered. Tears welled in her eyes, and even from across the room, I could see her chest rising and falling in unsteady breaths. She looked *terrified.*

"Mags—" I started, stepping toward her.

"I'm so sorry," she blurted, backing away. "I never wanted you to find out like this."

When she hit the island behind her, I quickened my steps.

"Taylor, I'm so sorry. I—"

"Shhh. Mags, baby, it's okay."

Her tears spilled over as she crumbled. Wrapping my arms around her, I pulled her close. Relief washed over me when she didn't pull away.

Sure, it was shocking to learn witches weren't just a fairytale. And yeah, dating one was... different. But she was still Magnolia.

My Magnolia.

The biggest highlight was that she wasn't green like that one from the play my mom and sister loved so much.

Or was that just the *Wizard of Oz*?

Damn it, focus, Taylor.

Holding her tightly, I stroked soothing lines down her back until her breathing steadied. Then, lifting her by the waist, I set her gently on the counter and tilted her face up to mine, swiping away her tears with my thumb.

"Magnolia," I murmured, "I need you to hear me. Are you a witch?"

She hesitated, then nodded.

"Cool. I don't care."

Her teary eyes widened in shock.

"I mean, I care a little that you didn't tell me," I admitted, pressing my forehead to hers. "But I understand why you didn't."

"Taylor—"

"Nope. You're listening right now."

Her lips snapped shut, and I suppressed a laugh.

"Mags, I told you I wanted to know everything about you. That includes this. You're awe-inspiring, beautiful, brilliant, and one hell of a baker. None of that changes just because I know you've got a little magic."

"It's more than a little," she whispered, a small smile tugging at her lips.

"Oh, good. We've moved on to humble bragging. That's a positive sign."

Magnolia let out a small chuckle, wiping her cheeks. "Just setting expectations, cowboy. But seriously, if you don't want to—"

"Mags, don't even think about finishing that sentence."

"I'm being serious. Being with me before you knew was going to be hard enough, but now that you know what I am—what my aunt and sisters are—it adds another level of difficulty."

Placing my hands on the counter beside her thighs, I leaned in until our noses nearly touched. "Sunshine, what I said last night hasn't changed. I'm in this. For all the ups, downs, and mystical." I punctuated the word with a dramatic wiggle of my fingers, earning a smile that hit me square in the chest. "Should I prove it to you?"

She raised a skeptical brow as I took a half-step back, sliding my hands down her thighs to her knees.

"Taylor, what are you doing?"

"Proving it." With a gentle tug, I brought her to the edge of the counter and nudged her legs apart. A flash of pink lace caught my attention, and my pulse quickened. "Where did those come from?" I asked, running my thumb over the delicate fabric in slow, teasing circles.

Her voice hitched as she replied, "My purse. I... ran out to the car and grabbed it this morning."

I stilled, my thumb pressed against her. "You keep panties in your purse?"

Her sharp, blue eyes met mine. "You never know when you'll need fresh undies, Dr. Hallows."

"That mouth is going to get you in trouble, cher." Resuming the gentle strokes she loved, I reveled in the soft moan that escaped her lips.

"Maybe I like trouble."

"I know you do."

Without waiting for a response, I dropped to my knees and ran my tongue over the lace, savoring the taste of her even through the thin fabric. Her sharp intake of breath spurred me on as I slid her panties aside and pressed a finger into her slick heat.

Her head fell back, and she groaned my name.

I paused, glancing up at her flushed face. "You wouldn't happen to have more stashed in your purse, would you?"

"What? No, why?" she panted, her eyes hazy with need.

"Pity." Hooking my finger into the lace, I grinned.

"Taylor," she warned, her eyes narrowing. "Don't you dare."

"They have to come off, cher."

"Then take them off!"

I was rendered stupid as I watched her pull my button-up higher on her body. I'd seen her completely bare before me not even twelve hours ago, and somehow, seeing her skin kissed by the late morning glow was so much better. It wrapped around her in a halo of golden light, accentuating every line and curve of her body that she exposed. The sharp dip of her waist. The flare of her hips. The delicate line of her nose, and the full fan of her lashes when she turned her head just so...

"Are you going to help me?" she asked as she wriggled on the counter, trying to shimmy her panties off without getting down.

"I don't know, cher. I'm kind of enjoying the view." I waggled my brows, and she cocked hers in response Smirking, I replaced her hands on the waistband. "Lean back and lift your hips for me."

She did as I asked, and I slipped the garment down her legs, stuffing it into my pocket with a satisfied grin.

"I'm going to need those back," she said, cocking an eyebrow.

"Maybe." I shrugged, spreading her legs wider and settling between them. "But until then"—I patted my pocket—"these are mine."

Whatever retort she'd planned evaporated into a gasp as my mouth found her again, my tongue working in tandem with my fingers. Her thighs quivered around me, and her sweet cries filled the kitchen as I brought her closer to the edge.

Sliding one hand under her shirt, I cupped her breast, rolling her nipple between my fingers. Her breathing turned shallow, her body trembling. She was a sight to behold, her body glistening beneath the recessed lighting and the golden rays of sunshine through the windows.

"Taylor—" she panted as my cock throbbed in my pants. "I'm going to... I'm gonna—" The sound of the oven timer blared through the kitchen, jarring us both. "Shit! The cinnamon rolls!" Magnolia exclaimed, wriggling in my hold.

"Don't you fucking dare, sunshine," I growled, my grip shifting down to her hips, anchoring her in place.

"But they'll burn."

"So don't let them." Doubling my efforts, I added a third finger and sucked hard on her clit.

Magnolia whined, nervous eyes flicking from me to the oven across the kitchen where the buzzer was still sounding. "Son of a bitch."

With a frantic wave of her hand, the timer ceased, and the oven door dropped open with a clang.

"We good?" I asked before dragging my tongue lazily up her center, smirking as she pinched her eyes closed and whimpered.

"Those better not burn, cowboy. No amount of—*motherfucking-dammit.*" With one swirl of my tongue against her clit and a curl of my fingers inside her, her tirade over the baked goods fell away, and we were back to where we'd been before the interruption.

If I were someone who believed in the universe having some divine plan, I'd think it didn't like the idea of us being together with as many times as we'd been interrupted. But I wasn't, and the universe could, disrespectfully, fuck itself. There wasn't a chance in hell that I was letting her go now that I'd had a taste.

She moaned my name, her muscles clenching around my fingers as her release tore through her.

When her body stilled and her breathing evened, I pressed a final kiss to her inner thigh and stood, sliding my arms around her to hold her close.

"I don't think even your cinnamon rolls can top that breakfast," I teased, laughter bubbling up as her wide-eyed, incredulous expression morphed into a playful glare.

"Oh, you—" With a flick of her hand, she swiped a dollop of frosting from the counter and smeared it on my nose, giggling when I sputtered in mock outrage.

"Where did that come from?" I demanded, trying not to smile as she slipped the offending finger into her mouth.

"*Magic,*" she said with a shrug, then licked the tip of my nose.

"Why you little..." Hoping there was still some icing on my nose, I sandwiched her head between my hands and ran my nose along her cheek. My chest warmed with the sound of her unabashed laugher and squeals of joy as she wiggled in my grasp trying to escape.

"Taylor, stop!" she said between giggles. "I need to get the cinnamon rolls!"

Reluctantly, I let her go, watching as she hopped off the counter and hurried to the oven. The golden rays of sunlight streaming through the windows wrapped around her, highlighting every curve and line of her body. She was mesmerizing.

Substantial breakfast first, she'd said.

But the way her sea glass eyes sparkled with promise made one thing clear—breakfast wasn't the only thing on the menu today.

25

Not like a ritual sacrifice, or anything.

Taylor

"How long have you known you're a witch?" I asked, popping the final bite of my third—don't judge, they're that good—cinnamon roll into my mouth.

Magnolia shrugged, taking a long sip from her coffee. "Since I moved here. So, eight? My mom hadn't said anything before that—not that I can remember, anyway. But Aunt Evie spilled the beans as soon as she brought us to Bellevue Manor." Her gaze dropped as she spoke, but a soft smile tugged at her lips, the memory clearly bringing her joy. Turning to the window, coffee cup cradled in her palms, she added, "I felt it, ya know?"

"Felt what?"

"The magic." Her voice was soft, wistful. "As soon as I stepped foot in that house, it was like the warmest hug you could imagine—wrapping around me, like it was welcoming me home. Like I was meant to be there. It's just too bad the rest of this godforsaken town doesn't see it that way."

Her eyes dropped to her mug as she set it down on the floor where we'd been sitting. Plates, napkins, and coffee cups littered the space around us as we leaned against the cabinets. I really needed to go furniture shopping.

Wiping my hand on a paper towel, I grabbed her wrist and tugged her toward me until she settled across my lap. Gently, I tucked a loose strand of hair behind her ear and turned her face to mine.

"You are meant to be here, Magnolia Bellevue. And if the people in this town haven't figured that out yet, that's on them. No more hiding, sunshine. Especially not from me."

"It's not that simple, Taylor." Her voice was firm but tinged with sadness. "I can't just go around town throwing spells this way and that. All that would do is start a witch hunt. People already treat me like a pariah; I'd rather not give them an actual reason."

"Okay, fair. And also totally unfair. But can you promise not to hide from *me* anymore?"

A tiny furrow formed between her brows as her eyes searched mine. After a deep inhale, she nodded. "I can promise to try. This is new for me, too, cowboy. Not even Jaelyn knows."

"Really?" I couldn't hide the shock in my voice. When she shook her head, I pressed, "But she's your best friend, right?"

Magnolia nodded, sadness flickering in her gaze as she looked down at her fidgeting hands. "She is. But even the best of friends can start a witch hunt. It's why my mom stopped practicing—at least, that's what Aunt Evie told me."

I must have looked confused because she sighed and shifted until she was straddling my legs.

"According to my aunt, Mom had a friend—Susan... Suzanne? Something like that—who was her best friend through high school, college, even nursing school. They were as tight as two people could be."

"Two peas in a pod," I offered.

"Exactly. Anyway, one day, Mom found a spell in the grimoire…" She paused, catching my raised brow, then rolled her eyes. "A grimoire is like a family spellbook. Or a witch's cookbook, I guess. It's full of spells, incantations, rituals, stuff like that."

"How big is this book?"

"Big. But that's not the point. Focus, cowboy."

"Right. Sorry. So your mom and… what's-her-face?"

She huffed out a chuckle but continued. "Mom found a spell that lasted twelve hours and would reveal a person's innermost thoughts and feelings about a posed question or action."

"Sounds simple enough."

Magnolia scrunched her nose, a clear sign she was bracing for my reaction. "It is… but it requires a drop of their blood. Just a drop, it's not like a ritual sacrifice or anything, just a simple prick of the finger—nothing dramatic."

"Baby, calm down," I said with a chuckle, cutting off her nervous rambling. "What happened next?"

"Well, Mom cast the spell and told her she was a witch. She even did a few minor tricks to sell it. And Mom got the answer she needed. Susan—or Suzanne, whatever—freaked out, and Mom had to give her a sleep tonic to get through the next twelve hours."

"What happens when the time runs out?"

"They forget. It's like it never happened."

I let that sink in for a moment—possibly too long, judging by Magnolia's concerned expression—then finally responded with a contemplative, "Hmm."

"'Hmm'? That's your response? 'Hmm'?"

"It makes sense, honestly. It's a good way to test the waters without risking everything."

"Who *are* you?" she asked with a disbelieving laugh.

Wrapping my arms around her waist, I pulled her closer. I loved how perfectly she fit against me, like two puzzle pieces coming together. "Taylor Hallows. Nice to meet you."

"Fuck off," she said, laughing as she playfully pushed at my chest.

"How about I fuck you instead?" The words barely left my lips before Magnolia's mouth was on mine, her hands tangling in my hair as she ground against me.

"Is that a yes?" I asked when we came up for air.

"Absolutely."

᛭))●((᛭

"Where do you want these?" Magnolia asked, rummaging through yet another box. "Looks like a bunch of medical textbooks. Don't you have to return those?"

"Only if you don't buy them outright," I replied, pulling random odds and ends from my own box. I really should've Marie Kondo'd this stuff before packing.

"Okay, Mr. Fancy Pants. But where do you want them?"

When I looked up, Magnolia was standing across the living room by the built-in bookcase, a hefty medical textbook in each hand. I had no other explanation for why all the blood in my body suddenly traveled south except for the fact that it was her—standing there in the t-shirt and sweatpants I'd, begrudgingly, loaned her. But hot damn, if seeing her in my clothes wasn't one of the biggest turn-ons there was.

"Earth to Taylor," Magnolia sing-songed, waving one of the books before letting out a grunt and pulling it to her chest. "Fuck, these are heavy."

"That they are." Palming the back of my neck, I scanned the room, trying to figure out where to put them, and came up blank. Did I mention I really needed to go furniture shopping? With a sigh, I said, "I guess just stack them on the shelves for now. I'm planning on setting up an office-slash-guest room eventually, but those shelves will do for now."

Magnolia muttered something like "okie doke" before returning to the task at hand.

We worked in relative silence for a while, but when I opened the next box and found my Bluetooth speaker, I let out a whoop of excitement.

"Did you find gold?" she asked with a laugh, peeking out from behind a blanket she was folding.

"No, but I found this." I held it up as she dropped the blanket, her lips pulling into a smile. "Want some music?" "Always."

Thanking whatever benevolent being presided over electronic devices and their battery life, I turned the speaker on and pulled my phone from my pocket.

"Any preference?"

She hummed, then said, "Maybe nineties or early two-thousands?"

"Seriously?" I deadpanned.

"As a heart attack, Doctor Hallows."

"Hardy har har," I retorted as she laughed, shaking my head while connecting my phone to the speaker. Typing "early 2000s" into Spotify, I scrolled until I found something tolerable. I settled on *Fireflies* by Owl City and hit play. Magnolia's face lit up, and she started singing along, her hips swaying as she unpacked another box.

Okay, maybe the playlist wasn't so bad if that was the reaction I got from my girl.

My phone hadn't been back in my pocket for more than thirty seconds when it pinged repeatedly with text notifications. Sighing, I perched on the windowsill and opened the thread from Addy. There was a collage of pictures from the night before: shots of her and Colin, a quick selfie of the two of us where she beamed while I looked like I wanted to be anywhere else, and a few more with me in the background looking sullen—complete with laughing emojis in the captions.

I'd just finished scrolling through the last one when another text popped up.

ADDY

> Mary sent this to me. It's cute! But you've got a lot of explaining to do, big bro. *smirking emoji*

Before I could even process what she was talking about, another image loaded. It rendered me speechless. Though the resolution was still decent, the picture had clearly been taken from inside the house and zoomed in so far that the Christmas lights strung above the dance floor had starburst streaks. And right below those twinkling bulbs were me and Magnolia, standing impossibly close, our faces lit with moony smiles as we gazed at each other.

"Goddammit," I muttered, pinching the bridge of my nose beneath my glasses.

Was I pissed that our privacy had been invaded—again? Yeah. But I couldn't help the smile tugging at my lips as I stared at the photo. Magnolia looked incandescent under the glow of the lights, her smile radiant as she looked up at me. We just fit.

"Everything alright over there, cowboy?"

+)〕●〔(+

Magnolia

Taylor's mouth was taut as he stared down at his phone, his hand absently rubbing his jaw.

"Taylor?" I hedged, stepping closer to him.

"What? Oh, yeah. Everything's fine. Just..." He trailed off, squeezing his eyes shut as he pulled off his glasses and pinched the bridge of his nose. "Here."

He extended his phone to me, and I took it, glancing at the screen. Two emotions hit me in rapid succession.

One: Awwe, look how cute we look. This would make a great wallpaper.

Two: What the actual fuck? Who? What? How?

"Uh, Taylor. How did you get this picture?"

He let out a heavy sigh, dragging his palms down his face before slipping his glasses back on. "Addy sent it. She said the wedding planner passed it to her."

That tracked, especially given the look Mary had shot me as she left the kitchen earlier.

I set his phone on the nearest box and stepped between his knees, framing his face in my hands as he'd done to me so many times. His eyes avoided mine, so I pulled out the big guns. "Babe."

Deep sapphire blues locked onto mine instantly. I felt his smile against my palms before I saw it.

"What did you just say?" he asked, his voice soft with disbelief.

"You heard me."

"I don't think I did."

"Taylor."

"No, that wasn't it."

I tried—and failed—to look disapproving. Even with narrowed eyes, I couldn't mask the smile tugging at my lips. "I called you babe. Don't make a big deal out of it."

"Oh, but it is a big deal." Taylor's arms slid around my waist, pulling me closer until my knees bumped the windowsill.

"Either way, I'm not mad about the picture," I said.

"You're not?" He sounded genuinely surprised.

"No, I'm not. A little annoyed that our private moment wasn't so private, but it is what it is. I just hope Addy didn't send it to everyone and their mom."

"She wouldn't," he assured me. "She is, however, giving me shit for not telling her about you. But that's my problem."

"Then there's nothing to be mad at. Actually, can you send it to me?"

Taylor's eyes lit up with joy, and the sight was more heartwarming than I could have anticipated. "I don't know why you look so surprised that I want a copy," I teased.

"Not surprised, cher. Just happy."

In one swift movement, Taylor stood, lifting me with him. My laugh dissolved into a gasp as his lips met mine, and I wrapped my arms around his neck.

When he started walking, I squealed and wiggled in his arms. "Taylor! You need to unpack!"

"True. But that's not what I want to do right now." To punctuate his point, he tossed me over his shoulder like a sack of potatoes and smacked my ass.

"Taylor!"

"Ahh, memories."

"What?!" I squeaked, propping myself up on his back to glare at him.

"The last time I had you like this, you were screaming like a town crazy person in the middle of a hurricane looking for your cat. I can't believe you don't remember."

Oh, I remembered. I remembered appreciating his ass before remembering I was mad at him. I remembered hating how attractive he was when I was supposed to despise him.

And yet, here we were. Somehow, in the short time we'd been reacquainted, my tune had changed.

Taylor was kind. He was generous.

And he was mine.

Mine? What kind of fantasy novel bullshit was that thought?

"Trust me, I remember," I said. "Kind of hard to forget you falling off my counter and into my baking supplies."

Taylor froze in the doorway to the hall, and I couldn't help but laugh—until he slowly slid me down his body, my feet finding the floor.

"You're going to pay for that, cher."

"Taylor..."

He stepped back, dropping his hands. The look on his face was menacing in the best, most delicious way. He looked like he wanted to devour me, and the heat pooling in my belly told me I wouldn't stop him.

"You've got a two-second head start, sunshine. Don't waste it. Because when I catch you..." His slow, predatory smile was all the incentive I needed to bolt down the hall and straight into his bedroom.

Sure, it was a little on the nose. But the sooner he caught me, the sooner I got to have him.

26

Truth hurts, witchling.

Magnolia

THE LATE AFTERNOON SUN painted the Spanish moss draping from the old oak trees in a warm, peachy glow as Taylor drove me back to Bellevue Manor. I stared out the window, unable to suppress the smile on my lips even if I tried. All things considered, the day had been blissfully perfect. Yes, I had inadvertently given him a glimpse into a world he didn't know actually existed, but he had taken it in stride—a lot better than I had expected, if I was being honest. It was, for lack of a better word, magical—more than I could have ever hoped for. Now, I just had to hope Aunt Evie and my sisters understood.

My smile faltered for only a second, but it was long enough for Taylor to notice. He always noticed.

His hand tightened around mine where they were interlaced over the center console, then he brought my knuckles to his lips, drawing my attention to him.

"Penny for your thoughts?" he asked, his eyes flicking to mine before returning to the road ahead.

"Hmm? Oh, it's nothing, really."

"Cher, I thought we agreed you wouldn't hide from me anymore."

Blowing out a raspberry, I met his gaze as he rolled to a stop at the lone traffic light in town. "I have to tell my aunt and sisters, and if I'm being one-hundred percent transparent, I'm scared shitless. I have no idea how they're going to react." The words tumbled out at the speed of a freight train. I sucked in a ragged breath and blew it back out.

"You don't think they'll be happy for us?" he asked tentatively, worry lacing his voice.

Oh, sweet baby cheeses, this beautiful, beautiful man. "Honey, I'm never going to hear the end of it when I tell them we're officially dating."

"Honey?"

"No? You don't like it?"

"Sunshine, you could call me Mary Poppins and I'd come running, as long as you call me yours."

"Did you leave any cheese for the rest of us after that line?" I teased with a chuckle.

Taylor's eyes narrowed, his expression turning mock-serious, which only made my chuckle spiral into full-blown laughter. He was adorable when he pretended to be mad.

By the time we made it to my driveway, I had managed to calm myself, but as soon as he made that turn, my anxiety shifted from nervous flutters into a full-blown, Mother-damned T-Rex rampaging in my stomach. My lungs ached with every breath, sharp pain ripping through my sternum as my heart pounded like a drum in my chest.

"Mags, baby, what's wrong?" There was no panic in his voice, but his wide eyes told another story as they frantically searched my face. I hadn't even realized we'd parked until he cursed under his breath, jumped out, and threw open my door in seconds. Ripping off my seatbelt, Taylor turned me in my seat and pulled me into his arms. "Magnolia, I need you to breathe for me, okay? Just focus on my voice and try to match my breathing."

"I—I can't," I managed between the needling breaths I was able to take.

"Baby, you're talking, which means you're breathing. That's good. Just close your eyes and focus for me, okay? In..." He inhaled deeply, pressing a steadying hand down my spine to straighten my back as I mirrored him. "Out."

I felt his exhale brush the top of my head, and with every rise and fall of his chest, my own breathing began to even out, my thundering heart slowing to a more bearable pace.

"Good. Keep going," he whispered, his hand tracing soothing lines up and down my back.

When I was calm enough for him to let go, Taylor pulled back and tilted my face toward his. I hadn't realized I was crying until his thumb swept across my cheeks, whisking away the tears.

Fucking panic attacks.

I hadn't had one in about a year, but when I did, they hit with the force of a meteor crashing to Earth. If I had to have one, though, at least I was in the presence of a hot doctor. Silver linings, I guess.

"Are you alright?" he asked, his beautiful blue eyes flicking between mine now that my breathing had steadied.

"Oh, you know, just wanted to show you another facet of my amazingness." I tried for lighthearted, but it came out more self-deprecating, and I winced when he let out a heavy sigh.

"Don't do that. Panic attacks are no joke. I'm just glad I was here to help you regulate. Was it because you're scared to tell them about us?"

"God, no!" I framed his face in my hands. "Taylor, no. I'm not scared to tell them about us. I'm scared to tell them that you *know*. No one knows. We've never told anyone... well, other than others in the coven, obviously."

Shit. I should not have said that.

Taylor's eyes flared with interest, and I could almost see the questions forming in his mind. But something on my face must have said *now is not the time*, because he blinked them away and returned to the matter at hand.

"Do you have to tell them? Right now, I mean?"

"They have a right to know." Even if the thought made me want to vomit, they deserved honesty. I had screwed up, and it was time to face the music.

"Well, lucky for you, it doesn't look like anyone is home at the moment. So you'll have at least a little time to run through all the doomsday scenarios you're thinking of right now."

"Wha—*I am not.*"

He didn't need to say a thing—his face did it for him. Lips tugged down at the corners, brows arched, head tilted slightly. Every inch of him screamed *I don't believe you for a second.*

It was infuriating. And endearing. But mostly annoying. How dare he call my bluff? It didn't matter that he was right—I should be allowed to live in my delusional la-la land for as long as I wanted.

With a roll of his eyes and a shake of his head, Taylor scooped me into his arms and set me on the ground in front of him. "Come on, cher. You've got a battle plan to make, and I have a sister to appease before she does something stupid like tell my mother."

"Sounds like we both have battle plans to make."

Taylor linked his fingers with mine and held my gaze as he brought my knuckles to his lips again. In that moment, I finally understood all those swoon-worthy historical romance scenes, as butterflies erupted in my stomach and heat rushed to my cheeks.

"I'll never get tired of that," he murmured, dropping our joined hands between us.

"Of what?" I asked, cheeks burning under the intensity of his stare.

"The way your body reacts to the simplest touch." He waggled his brows, and I was certain I now resembled a red Christmas ornament.

With a playful smack to his shoulder, I said, "Come on, cowboy. Battles to plan, victories to procure."

"Yes, ma'am." He punctuated his words with a mock salute, and we both laughed as he followed me toward the door.

·))●((·

In the hour since Taylor dropped me off, I'd panic-cleaned nearly all of the downstairs, and I had to admit—Bellevue Manor had never looked so good. The floors gleamed under the pendant lights, sconces, and chandeliers, the dust bunnies having met their untimely ends. I'd loaded and run the dishwasher, tackled two loads of laundry, and scraped all the cat hair off the stair runner. Now, my arm was killing me.

Could I have done this with a little sprinkle of magic? Sure. But I always felt more accomplished when I did it with my own two hands. Besides, no amount of magic could quell the anxiety still churning in my stomach.

Plopping down on one of the barstools at the island, I paused my audiobook, pulled off my headphones, and chugged the last of my water. I needed to get a grip before my aunt and sister got back. Letting my head fall onto my crossed arms, I took deep, steadying breaths. Surely it wouldn't be that bad... right?

A soft bell jingle pulled me upright as Hermeownie trotted into the kitchen, letting out a trill of greeting before stretching up on her hind legs, her paws resting against my thighs. The moment we touched, her thoughts brushed into my mind.

"Up, please."

"Yes, ma'am," I said with a laugh, scooping her into my lap.

She circled twice before collapsing into a warm puddle of orange and white fur, her purrs vibrating against me. *"Evie and Maddie just turned down the drive. Are you ready?"*

"Ready?" I echoed, but Hermeownie only stared, her strong Maine Coon features on full display. "Am I that obvious?"

"You've been anxious since you stepped through the door. And you never clean like that unless you think you're going to get into trouble for something."

"Ouch!"

"Truth hurts, witchling. But I will stay with you if you'd like."

"I think I would, actually. Thanks."

Hermeownie gave a satisfied nod, then closed her eyes, settling in for the conversation I really didn't want to have. I hadn't even figured out how to start it before the front door swung open.

"Hiya, Magpie! I didn't know you'd be home." Aunt Evie's smile felt like a sledgehammer to my heart.

This was going to suck.

"Did you clean?" Maddie's voice pitched up an octave as she scanned the pristine room in disbelief.

"Magnolia, what's—"

"Taylor knows I'm a witch."

"Well, that was one way to do it, I guess," Hermeownie's sardonic tone wrapped around my mind.

"Shush," I admonished in a whisper to the orange fluff ball teetering on the edge of getting dumped off my lap. She only purred in response, smug.

"Excuse me?!" Aunt Evie's sharp voice yanked my attention back to where she and Maddie stood frozen in the doorway, grocery bags looped over their forearms, fingers going red from the weight.

"I, uh... Taylor caught me using magic at his house this morning."

"Mother, Maiden, and Crone." The words rushed out as Aunt Evie stalked toward the counter, dropping her bags. Maddie, meanwhile, had gone stark white, her feet seemingly rooted to the floor.

"Mads? You okay?" I asked hesitantly. My middle sister was usually the calm one, but when someone pushed the right button at the wrong time, she went off like a firecracker. And I had the distinctly unfortunate feeling I'd just jammed my finger into that button.

"Am I—You did *not* just ask me that asinine question." Jarred from her stupor, she stormed across the kitchen and dropped her bags with a thud.

"Careful! One of those might have the eggs in it, Madison!" Evie snapped. Then, with a deep breath, she fixed her gaze on me. "Explain."

It only took a few minutes to run through the events of the morning, but it felt like the longest minutes of my life. Aunt Evie's face shifted from irritation to something resembling understanding—though I wouldn't go so far as to say she completely got it. Maddie, on the other hand, was unimpressed, her brows knitting together in a way that looked permanent by the time I finished.

"Are you certain he won't say anything?" my aunt asked.

"Of course he's going to say something! He's Taylor Hallows!" Maddie screeched.

"Hey!" I shot back.

"What? He tormented you in high school, didn't he? Why wouldn't he go blabbing this all over town?"

"Hold up—weren't you one of the ones who *pushed* me to go out with him? Said we were adults now, and if I'd changed, why couldn't he?"

"Oh, don't you put this on me. You—"

"Ladies!" A tickle of magic brushed my skin as I tried to interject, but no sound came out. Maddie suffered the same fate, her mouth opening and closing like a fish as she clutched her throat and glared at Aunt Evie. "Blessed Mother, I haven't had to do that in ages," our aunt muttered. "Now, that's quite enough. If you two can behave, I'll return your ability to speak."

Maddie met my glare with one of her own, but we both nodded. Within seconds, Aunt Evie's magic fluttered over my skin again, and I let out an exasperated huff.

"Magnolia, obviously this isn't ideal," she said, rubbing her temples. "But if you believe he'll keep our secret, then I see no reason to intervene. Should that change, however..." She trailed off, unspoken words hanging heavy in the air.

If Taylor spilled our secret, we'd have to take retroactive action with a memory spell. None of us liked doing them—unpredictable things, memory spells. Either they erased exactly what they were meant to, or they took more than intended.

Magic was finicky on its own. Add a mundane, and the results were even less certain.

"I can't believe you're letting this stand," Maddie muttered, arms crossed, eyes downcast.

I understood her frustration. Truly, I did. She'd been in an on-again, off-again relationship with someone who'd meant the world to her. And the last time they'd broken up, it was because he thought she was keeping something from him. And she had been—just not what he'd assumed. So hearing that I'd spilled the family secret to someone I barely knew and was basically getting a pat on the wrist for it? Yeah, that probably stung.

"Maddie—"

"Magnolia, just stop." With a sigh, she pushed away from the counter and turned for the door. "Let me know when dinner's ready."

And with that, she was gone.

Aunt Evie's raspberry and the rustle of grocery bags redirected my attention. "Help me with these, would you?"

"Uh... sure." Hermeownie let out a squeaky meow as I deposited her on another stool and stood, rounding the island to begin pulling items from the bags.

Silence reigned as we sorted the groceries into their places. When the last bag was shoved under the sink with the rest, Aunt Evie braced herself against the counter and blew out a breath.

"Magpie, I trust your judgment. But are you sure you can trust him with this?"

That question had rolled around and around in my brain all day, and every time, I landed on the same answer. "I am."

With another heavy sigh, she nodded. "Well, then I hope you're right. Now, let's get to work on dinner, shall we? Fried chicken and biscuits sound good?"

"Sounds perfect."

"Good. And then we'll call your *other* sister."

Greeeat.

27
Touché, Dr. Hallows. Touché.
Taylor

"WHAT ABOUT THIS ONE?" Magnolia asked, plopping down on what had to be one of the most uncomfortable-looking couches I'd ever seen. She stretched her arms over the backrest, a barely concealed smirk playing on her lips.

We both knew there wasn't a chance in hell that monstrosity was coming anywhere near my house, but I sank—and I do mean *sank*, because the cushion practically swallowed me whole—down next to her anyway. "Could work. Just needs a little—"

"More stuffing? New fabric? To be burned in a bonfire and never thought of again?"

I gasped in feigned outrage, hand flying to my chest as I met her aqua gaze. "How very *dare* you. This is a masterpiece."

"A masterpiece for a dumpster fire," she shot back with a laugh.

"Hey, you picked it, and I'm a sucker for anything related to you. So, *obviously*, this is the winner."

"I know you're joking. But just for clarity's sake, if this couch goes home with you, I won't."

The mischief in her eyes told a different story, so I leaned in, close enough that my nose brushed her ear. "Yes, you would. And you'd love every single second of me sinking you into these cushions."

A shiver ran down her spine as she turned to meet my gaze, but the quirk of her lips had my smirk faltering. "I think the couch beat you to it, cowboy."

A laugh exploded from my chest, Magnolia joining in as we both slipped deeper into the cavernous trap somehow marketed as a couch.

"How we doin' over here, folks?" A bubbly redheaded sales clerk appeared, her grin far too wide to be endearing.

"We're fine, thanks. Just looking," I said, stifling a laugh as Magnolia wiggled against the deep-seated cushions, her escape attempts failing spectacularly.

"Well, if y'all need anything, my name's Katie, and I'll be around."

"Thanks, Katie," Magnolia grunted, still flailing in the couch's grasp.

"Hang on, sunshine," I chuckled as Katie walked away.

"She could've at least offered to drag us out of this devil's nightmare," she grumbled, blowing a stray strand of hair from her face.

Scooting to the edge, I pushed to standing and held my hands out. "Upsy daisy, sunshine."

"You're so weird." Laughter laced her voice as she grasped my hands and let me tug her to her feet.

"Perhaps," I said matter-of-factly, pulling her into my arms and pressing a quick kiss to her lips. "But then again, so are you."

"Touché, Dr. Hallows. Touché." Wrapping her arms around my waist, she kissed me briefly before turning to scan the rest of the showroom. "Want to look at the sectionals?"

Words died on my lips as I took her in. She looked everywhere but at me, oblivious to the way my heart tried to claw its way out of my chest every time she touched me. I wasn't sure when this feeling would stop—if it ever would. I didn't think I'd ever tire of her presence, of wanting her in my grasp, even if it was just basking in her gaze from across a crowded room. She'd become a source of light in my life, her smile brightening my days, her wit and sarcasm keeping me perpetually on my toes. And like a kick to the gut, that elusive four-letter word I'd been fighting back with a goddamn two-by-four came skipping to the forefront of my mind.

"Taylor?"

My name on her lips pulled me from my thoughts. All I could do was smile. She was simply breathtaking—clusters of freckles dusted across her cheeks and nose like tiny constellations, full lips tinted the barest hint of pink from the lip balm she'd applied before we walked in. Effortlessly beautiful. And I was the lucky bastard who got to call her mine.

"If you stare any harder, cowboy, you're going to bore holes into my face."

"Sorry, sunshine." I pressed a kiss to her brow. "Can't help it."

Despite the snarky roll of her eyes, a flush colored her cheeks. "Come on, Casanova. Let's find you some furniture."

We meandered through the store for the better part of an hour, testing every couch that seemed even *remotely* reasonable. Magnolia, ever the planner, had brought a measuring tape despite the clearly labeled dimensions—not that I pointed it out. I loved watching her determination to make my house a home, transforming it from just a space with four walls and a roof into something lived in, something ours. Little did she know, I would have been happy with just a mattress on the floor and candlelight, as long as she was the one I shared it with.

When we'd—or rather, *I'd,* since she insisted the final decision was mine—finally settled on everything, Magnolia practically skipped toward Katie with the list of item numbers. I may be a doctor, but even I was grateful for payment plans as we walked back to my car, my wallet significantly lighter. I was now the proud owner of a sectional with way too many pillows, a dining table and chairs, a rug I didn't actually hate, a coffee table, an accent chair—whatever the hell that meant—and some actual bedside tables to replace the boxes I'd been using. There was still more I needed, but at least the main areas of the house were covered.

"So, what's next?" I asked as we settled in the car, flipping Magnolia's seat warmer on since Louisiana had apparently decided to take December seriously this year.

"How do you feel about Christmas decorations?"

I quirked a brow at the giddy smile spreading across her face. "They're fine, I guess?"

"*Fine?* You *guess*?! Taylor, whatever-your-middle-name-is, Hallows—"

"Michael."

"What?"

"My middle name is Michael, sunshine."

"Ah, thank you. Taylor *Michael* Hallows!" She clapped her hands together. "Christmas is the best holiday. The lights, the sparkle, the *whimsy*!" Each word became more wistful as she listed reasons to love it.

But I only needed one.

And that reason was sitting beside me, waving her hands around in excitement.

"Okay, okay, you've convinced me." I grabbed her hands, pressing a kiss to her knuckles simply because I could—and because it made her cheeks turn a delicious shade of pink. "We can decorate the house."

The house.

Not *my* house.

Because the more time I spent with her—the more I didn't want to ever let her go. And the more those four walls became just as much hers as they were mine.

Magnolia

The smell of freshly baked cookies wafted through the whole of *CharCutie*, their sweet scent seeping into every nook and cranny—and, judging by the way people paused outside the windows, likely drifting into the street as well.

I loved Christmastime—the food, the festivals, the lights—but this time of year was always carried a bittersweet edge. The pain of losing my parents all those years ago still lingered day to day, but as the anniversary of their deaths loomed closer, it flared into an agonizing ache. Christmas had been my mom's favorite holiday, and she always went out of her way to make it special. She let Maddie and me help her bake cookies—planting the seed of my love for all things baking—while singing carols and dancing around the kitchen with my dad. *White Christmas* played on the TV as we decorated the tree, and we spent hours driving through neighborhoods, admiring the light displays.

After we went to live with my aunt twenty-two years ago, she made sure to keep those traditions alive. She just added the Winter Solstice celebration to the mix when we'd learned about our heritage.

We still decorated a tree, hung mistletoe, baked gingerbread, exchanged gifts, and otherwise made merry like everyone else. But we also honored something deeper. There were rituals and dancing to ground ourselves in nature's rhythm, a way to wait for the darkest days to end and the light to return. It was invigorating. Healing. And this year, I needed it more than ever.

Still, we strung icicle lights—Mom's favorite—along the porch and watched every cheesy Christmas movie we could find, even though they were all the same story with different actors. *White Christmas* still played as we hung ornaments on the tree, each of us taking on a character's role and reciting their lines—I was always Betty. And I still sang every holiday song at the top of my lungs like the merriest, most off-key caroler in the history of Bellevue. Or, at the very least, hummed along—which was what I was doing as I plopped another ball of dough onto the cookie sheet.

It would have been easy to let my grief overwhelm me, to let it drag me into the winter darkness. But it took effort to embrace the joy of the season, and that was what my mom would have wanted. So I did my damndest to try.

Dusting my hands off on my apron, I covered the final tray of prepared cookie dough in cling wrap and slid it onto the rack bound for the cooler. By the time I finished cleaning, the last batch of cookies was ready. And so was I.

Tonight was the town's Winter Festival, and I was beyond nervous. I went every year, but somehow, I'd let Taylor talk me into going *with* him. Which meant walking through town, hand in hand, in front of *everyone*. This wasn't a soft launch of our relationship—it was a headfirst leap off a cliff. A giant, blinking neon sign that screamed *Look at me! I'm with Taylor Hallows!* It took everything I had not to melt into a puddle of panic.

With a deep breath, I shook out my hands and tried to expel all the anxiety that was determined to take root. Then I hung my apron back on its hook, packed the warm cookies into a box, and headed toward the office to grab my purse and keys.

With the festival happening, all the shops in town were closing early—including mine. And since it was only two in the afternoon, I still had plenty of time to help Aunt Evie and my sisters decorate the tree before Taylor came to pick me up.

Taking a quick glance back out the front windows to make sure there wasn't anyone standing around outside, I sent a wave of magic through *CharCutie*, closing the main area for the night. As the overhead lights and display cases dimmed, the warm white Christmas strands I'd draped across the windows and the flocked tree—complete with bakery-style ornaments and pink crystal garland—beside the door lit the space in a warm, happy glow.

Purse, keys, and cookies in hand, I stepped out the back door—only to halt when it hit something with a dull *thud*.

I peeked around the edge and found a long, rectangular crimson box resting on the stoop, tied with a white ribbon. A smile tugged at my lips as I let out a soft laugh, already pulling my phone from my pocket.

MAGNOLIA

I snapped a picture, sent the text, and tucked my phone away before bending to pick up the box. Something faintly rancid filled my nose as I made my way toward my car. I glanced around, searching for the source, but decided it had to be the dumpsters. It sure as hell wasn't the cookies I was carrying.

After jostling all of my belongings, I slid into my car, tossed my purse onto the passenger seat and gingerly placed the cookies beside it. The moment the engine purred to life, I cranked up the heat and connected my phone, and let my holiday station play.

Settling in, I lifted the lid of the mystery box—

And gagged.

The rancid stench from outside thickened, mingling with something that smelled like dirt.

Every warning bell in my soul blared. My fingers stilled, the lid hovering millimeters from its base.

I *should* close it and toss it in the nearest dumpster. Walk away. Forget I ever saw it.

But some stubborn, reckless part of me *had* to know. Had to *see* with my own eyes what I somehow *knew* I would find in that box.

Swallowing hard, I took a fortifying breath and lifted the lid the rest of the way.

Nestled inside, on a bed of black silk, lay a dozen long-stemmed, wilted roses. Their petals were coated in dirt and something else—something that made my stomach churn. Tiny movements caught my eye. *Something was crawling in the soil.*

A strangled noise scraped up my throat. I threw my door open and flung the offending *gift* to the ground as I dry heaved.

Sweat dampened my brow as I braced myself against the car, breath coming in ragged pants. *Who the hell would do something like that?*

Anger surged, hot and blinding. My jaw ached from clenching my teeth, from swallowing back the tears that were fighting to get free.

With a growl, I reached down to grab the lid from where it had landed in the footwell. I was about to chuck it out the door with the rest of that *disgusting* gift—

Then I saw it.

A slip of paper, tucked beneath the ribbon.

You should throw it away.

But I didn't.

Jaw tight, I yanked out the note and tossed the lid onto the pavement. Someone else could deal with that mess. I *wasn't* touching it again.

Shutting my eyes, I took a deep breath and unfolded the paper.

Bonfire Night is coming.

And last time I checked, witches make great kindling.

My breath caught in my throat. My stomach twisted, nausea rising again.

Bonfire Night was supposed to be *innocent*. A Southern tradition, where fires lined the Mississippi to light Papa Noël's way. And with one hastily scrawled message, someone had stolen that innocence.

We hadn't even made our relationship public and it was already starting.

A disbelieving laugh bubbled up my throat, a lone tear streaking down my cheek.

Then my car speakers chimed with Taylor's reply.

TAYLOR

> Wasn't me, sunshine. But if I've got competition, let me know. *winking emoji*

> Can't wait to see you tonight.

28
Southern winter wonderland

Taylor

Growing up in Bellevue, I'd never been one to get excited about the Winter Festival. The glittering lights suspended from poles, zigzagging across the square before coalescing at the gazebo in the center, never filled me with the joy they seemed to bring others. I didn't understand the need for sparkling snowflakes, garland draped with baubles, or the craving for the copious amount of sweets that lined the streets, their scents wafting from the tents and thickening the air.

It never made any sense to me. Didn't strike me as a necessary experience to be had every. Single. Year.

Until I saw the joy this time of year brought Magnolia.

I'd never forget her excited skips through the rows of Douglas firs as she scoped out each one in search of what she deemed perfection. Or the way her eyes would flutter closed as she broke off a few needles and inhaled their piney scent. How the Christmas lights she'd convinced me to hang sparkled in her aqua-blue eyes as we swung on my porch, or the sound of her laughter as she twirled to ridiculous Christmas songs while we hung ornaments on my tree.

She'd shown me what Christmas meant to her. And, in turn, the joy she bared for the holiday had begun to seep into my Scrooge-like heart.

At least, it had—until today.

If someone asked me to make a list of words to describe Magnolia Bellevue, *quiet* wouldn't even be in the top fifty. And yet, that's exactly what she'd been since I picked her up from the manor.

Quiet.

Not the comfortable kind, like when we sat on my porch, wrapped in an easy silence, or when we drove home from an errand. No, this was the other kind. The kind that made your head spin with all the terrible things that could be spiraling in your partner's brain—but you're too chicken shit to ask what's wrong because if nothing *is* wrong, then you've just created a problem by assuming one existed in the first place.

And I hated it.

The ride to the festival had been eerily silent, which I might've attributed to her being tired from work—except I knew better. It was the way her gaze stayed trained out the window, how she leaned as far away from me as possible, that had my mind spinning through an obnoxious amount of—likely irrational—scenarios.

Every answer was minimal. One or two simple words. A hum to signal she'd heard me. There may have been a smile stretched across her crimson-painted lips, but it was forced and subdued, never quite reaching her eyes. And those sparkling winter blues I loved so much? Dim.

Not even the sight of the town decked to the nines in a Southern winter wonderland seemed to lift her spirit. She just looked on with indifference, a gray cloud hovering over her head as we made our way toward the vendor stalls.

When I helped her out of the car, I'd tried to take her hand—she shoved hers into her coat pockets so fast I barely saw the movement. When I wrapped an arm around her shoulders, she stiffened before sidestepping around a puddle and away from me.

I had no idea why she was so tense, but I was bound and determined to coax her shoulders away from her ears and bring some ease back into her uncharacteristically rigid frame.

The smell of spiced cider filled my nose, and I nearly groaned, my mouth watering at the scent. Resting my hand on the small of her back, I didn't miss the way her muscles tightened, her eyes pinching shut for the briefest second before she relaxed—just barely—into my touch. Ignoring the pang of hurt in my chest, I plastered on a smile and asked, "Would you like some?"

"Hm? Oh, uh, sure. Sounds good."

She met my smile with a hesitant one of her own before her eyes flicked around the booths. I wasn't sure what—or who—she was looking for, but whatever she saw had her stepping away from my touch, curling in on herself.

"You okay, sunshine?" I asked as we stepped forward in line.

"What?" It came out in a nervous breath, her eyes roving cautiously over our surroundings before settling back on me. Whatever she saw there made her gaze soften, and she pulled her hand from her pocket to grab mine.

"Sorry, I'm just a little—"

"Distracted?" I questioned, raising a brow.

"Yeah," she answered sheepishly.

"Baby, what's going on? You've been in your head since I picked you up," I asked in a hushed whisper, tightening my hold on her hand. Now that I had her in my grasp, the last thing I wanted to do was let her go.

Unfortunately for me, she didn't seem to share that sentiment.

"It's just been a long day." We took another step forward, and she sucked in a sharp breath as she glanced over my shoulder. "I, uh... I need to use the restroom."

I quirked a brow at the rapid—and random—shift in conversation before scanning the area for signs pointing to the porta-potties. But before I could point her in any direction, she patted my chest.

"I'm just going to run down to the shop for a minute. Meet me there?"

CharCutie was a good block and a half away, and while I didn't think anything would happen, it was dark. And bad shit still happened in small towns.

"I can walk with you."

"It's not that far. I'll be alright."

Before I could respond, she pushed up onto her toes, pressed a kiss to my cheek, and was off.

⊹)) ● ((⊹

I'd been standing outside *CharCutie* for what felt like hours—but had realistically only been about ten minutes—when the front door finally swung open.

Only, instead of the cotton-candy ball of sunshine I'd been hoping for, I was met with a sober-faced Jaelyn, her caramel eyes boring into me with a mix of irate anger and sympathy.

It was confusing, to say the least.

"Hey, Jae. How's it going?"

Her brows shot up, and she just stared at me for a moment. "How's it...? Seriously, Hallows?"

"You know something."

"And obviously, you don't." She blew out a breath, muttering, "Fuck my life," before scrubbing her hands down her face.

"Jaelyn, if there's something I should know—"

"Slow your roll, Westley." She exhaled sharply. "Look, I don't want to be the one to tell you, but it doesn't seem like ya girl is going to. So, here's the facts."

Rage wasn't an accurate word for the emotion coursing through my veins as Jaelyn relayed the information Magnolia hadn't seemed inclined to share with me. My eyes widened with each revelation, jaw tightening until my teeth ached.

When she finished, only one word, one burning question, spilled from my lips in a growl.

"Who?"

Jaelyn's eyes softened, her head shaking slowly. "She didn't know. But you need to pull it together, Taylor. There's a reason she didn't tell you. And it probably has something to do with the look on your face right now."

"The look on my face?" I ground out, forcing my fingers to loosen around Magnolia's cup of cider.

"Yeah. You know, the one that screams 'I will seek retribution for the wrongdoings against my woman.'" When I quirked a brow, she smirked. "Don't get me wrong, we all love a cinnamon roll turned villain, but I don't know that morally gray is your color."

"What?" I barked.

"Pick up a book other than a medical textbook, Dr. Hallows. Your world will be a lot more colorful."

With a pat on my shoulder, Jaelyn skipped away, leaving me staring after her—more confused than when this night started.

Dead roses.

Ominous notes.

Morally gray?

I didn't know why Magnolia hadn't told me about the flowers. Didn't know why I hadn't pressed her. But at least now, part of the puzzle was solved.

And it was about damn time this town got the memo.

Magnolia Bellevue was mine.

And I was hers.

Whether they liked it or not.

Magnolia

The cider Taylor had gotten me had long since chilled, abandoned in my grip as my stomach twisted itself into knots so tight I was scared anything I tried to consume would come right back up.

After hiding in my office at *CharCutie* for the better part of fifteen minutes, spilling my guts to Jaelyn about what had happened, I'd finally emerged—only to find Taylor leaning against a lamppost. A smile was on his face, but there was something else in his eyes. A simmering ember of anger.

At what, I wasn't sure.

But if I had to guess, I'd say it was directed at me.

Not that I could blame him—I was terrible company tonight.

We walked around for about an hour, but the longer we stayed, the more overstimulated I became. My back ached from how tightly I'd been wound since I left work. The music blaring from the loudspeakers sounded like rusted gears grinding in my ears, and it took everything I had not to slap my hands over them to block out the noise.

Every brush of an arm against mine as we wove through the crowd made me want to crawl out of my skin. Even when Taylor—poor, sweet, wonderful Taylor—tried to gently guide me with a comforting hand on the small of my back, every muscle in my body locked up, bracing for something.

And he felt it. I could see it written all over his face, even when he tried to hide it behind a smile. A smile that never reached his eyes. A muscle in his jaw jumped with the effort.

I felt awful. This wasn't how tonight was supposed to go. Even as anxious as I'd been, I never wanted it to turn out like this. But no matter how hard I tried, I couldn't shake the feeling of being watched.

Couldn't ignore how the crowd split whenever we passed, giving us a wide berth.

And I sure as hell couldn't stop noticing the eyes that watched our every move.

Blessed Mother, there were *so many eyes*.

Glares and sneers trailed us as we walked. Whispered words—much too loud to be inconspicuous—swirled around me, growing into a deafening roar that drowned out everything else. The laughter of happy couples and children. The music. All of it, gone.

What is he doing with her?

She's not good enough for him.

She's got him under some kind of spell.

I'd heard it all before. I would hear it for as long as we were together. Hell, even if we weren't. It was always the same story, no matter who was on my arm.

But it still stung.

It didn't matter what I did or how nice I was to the crotchety people in this town—I was, and always would be, *less than*. Never good enough. Always too much for their delicate sensibilities.

"Dance with me, sunshine."

Taylor's deep timbre cut through the whirlwind in my head, slicing through the storm like a blade of sunlight piercing the clouds. His sapphire eyes held me captive as he extended his hand.

I hadn't even realized we'd made it back to the gazebo—the *center* of the entire festival. A giant spotlight, shining right on us, ensuring that everyone could see.

I shrank under the weight of it, curling into the nobody this town was so determined to make me.

Trying desperately to keep the rising panic out of my voice, I whispered, "Everyone is staring, Taylor. I... I don't think this is a good idea. Maybe we should just leave."

He didn't look away. Didn't check to see if I was right.

He just held my gaze.

And in those eyes—steady and warm, filled with unwavering adoration—I felt my chest tighten.

"Let them."

Linking our hands together, Taylor pulled me in, his voice clearer than crystal as he said, "Even if they are, all I see is you, Magnolia. All I ever see is you."

Cupid takes aim... fires...

"Taylor, I—"

"Please, sunshine." His hand came up, fingers warm as they cradled my cheek, his thumb sweeping soft, soothing lines along my cheekbone. He leaned in, voice dropping to a whisper meant only for me.

"I don't care if they're watching. They can look all they want, because it's about damn time they learned—I don't care what they think. I don't care what they want. What *I* want is to dance with the woman of my dreams. To hold her in my arms while I tell her that I am falling head over feet in love with her."

Straight through the heart. Hook, line, and sinker, folks.

Before I could even begin to form the words his confession deserved, his lips were on mine—soft and slow, like we had all the time in the world.

And in that moment, we did.

Because the world, the festival, the people—it all fell away as he pulled back, guiding us toward the open lawn beside the gazebo.

All I saw was him.

His eyes, glowing beneath the warmth of the Christmas lights strung for the festival.

His smile, bright enough to make even the Grinch love Christmas.

An instrumental version of *Christmas Time Is Here* played over the loudspeakers as I followed him into the grass.

But the only thing looping through my mind was the sound of his voice—telling me he was falling in love with me.

29
Love Shack
Magnolia

Everything around me blurred, except for the sapphire blues searing into my own. Clothes fluttered to the ground like feathers. Hands moved languidly along skin, tracing curves and muscles, while lips parted and teeth nipped.

Pillowy softness met my back, a sharp contrast to the fiery line of kisses trailing down my sternum, broad palms sliding along my sides before cupping my breasts. My fingers wove their way through chestnut locks, silky strands slipping between them as I arched beneath his touch.

My back bowed as he filled me, his name falling from my lips like a plea or a prayer as he rocked into me with agonizing slowness. His hands never stilled, his mouth a constant murmur of sweet words that washed over me like sun-soaked ocean waves.

"More, Taylor, please. I need more," I begged, sweat-slicked skin sliding against his as his lips traversed my neck and shoulder.

Sitting up, Taylor pulled me into his lap, guiding me until I was straddling him, his cock nudging insistently at my center. Bliss like I'd never known radiated through every cell in my body as I sank down onto him, taking him fully.

We moved together like a call and answer, giving and taking all we wanted, all we needed. Pleasure built, coiling tight and fierce inside me, the crescendo rising with each thrust. Grunts and moans, whispered affirmations and praise filled the room, a symphony of need that made my soul sing. I was teetering right on the edge, right at the precipice of something divine.

All it would take was one... more...

Beep.

Beep.

Beep.

Beep.

Something between a groan and a whine escaped as I rolled over, slapping my hand around blindly until I found my phone on the nightstand. Yanking it under the covers, I silenced the infernal thing and shoved it under my pillow.

Of all the times for my alarm to go off, it had to be while I was reliving the amazing night I'd had with Taylor?

Mother above, the universe had jokes.

After the shitshow that was most of the Winter Festival, he'd flipped the night on its head with one simple sentence that still had my head reeling hours later.

Of all the people on this Mother-damned planet, he'd picked me.

Was *choosing* me.

He was falling in love... with me.

Warmth washed through me as his confession echoed in my mind, the way his eyes had locked onto mine, pleading with me to hear him.

And I had.

I'd heard him. Felt him, from top to toe, and cemented his words in my heart until all the sneers around us floated away like dust in the wind.

Cracking my eyes open just a smidge, I peeked out from under the covers. Late morning light filtered through Taylor's bedroom curtains, illuminating the space and highlighting one glaring fact—he wasn't here.

Breathing deeply, I rolled toward his side of the bed—*which, I guessed*, technically *was the whole bed, but that was neither here nor there*. My chest warmed as my gaze landed on something lying across his pillow.

A small bundle of mistletoe, tied with a red ribbon and a tiny gold bell, perched atop a folded piece of paper.

For a moment, unease slithered through me. After the last unsuspecting note I'd received, I had to take a deep breath and remind myself—I knew, for a fact, this one was from Taylor.

And that someone wasn't trying to scare me off... *again*.

At least, not at this very second anyway.

Sitting up, I wrapped the sheets around myself and picked up the berries and note, the bell's delicate chime ringing through the quiet room as I flipped the paper open.

You looked so peaceful, I couldn't bear to wake you.

Coffee is set to brew and should be finished by the time you wake up.

There are also pastries on the counter, though they're not as good as yours.

I work until 7 p.m. tonight, but I'll text or call you when I can.

Oh, and hold onto that mistletoe. I have plans for it later.

Toe-curling thoughts raced through my mind at his final words. Visions of one—or both—of us holding that bunch of berries over intimate places, teasing and tasting until we were a tangled mess of limbs, had me desperate to go back to sleep and let my subconscious work its magic.

But my stomach growled, and the scent of freshly brewed coffee called my name like a siren's song.

Begrudgingly, I rolled out of bed.

After throwing on a pair of Taylor's sweats—because why not?—I grabbed my phone and made my way toward the kitchen.

With liquid nirvana procured, I padded to the breakfast nook. A plastic clamshell of raspberry danishes sat on the table, and a—

Wait.

Was that a *key*?

It was.

A mother-forking *house key*.

Beneath it sat another folded piece of paper, but I couldn't seem to make my hands, arms, lungs, or brain work as that little silver piece of metal glinted up at me from the tabletop.

A house key.

Were we even there yet?

Apparently, he thought so.

But staring at the physical representation of where he saw us, suddenly, I wasn't so sure.

Hands trembling, I nudged the key aside like it was radioactive and picked up the note.

Don't freak out.

Who am I kidding, you're probably spiraling right now, aren't you?

"Just a tad," I mumbled, willing my hands to quit shaking as I kept reading.

Take a deep breath, sunshine. This doesn't have to be some big proclamation... though it seems pretty tame compared to what I said last night.

"Psh, speak for yourself, sir."

Great. Now I was having a full-blown conversation with a piece of paper.

It's just a key, Magnolia. It's not going to bite you or harm you in any way.

But if you're staying at the house, you need a way to lock up if and when you leave and I'm not there.

See? Practical.

He had a point.

And it was hard not to notice that he hadn't called it his house. Now that I thought about it, he never did. It was always *the* house. Something about that realization settled my anxiety just a fraction.

If you're not ready to keep it, I completely understand. But I'd like for you to.

Either way, this goes at your pace, baby.

So, take a deep breath, drink your coffee, eat some pastries, and just… think about it, okay?

By the time the breath I'd taken left my lungs, my phone chimed.

TAYLOR

> You're spiraling, aren't you?

Blessed Mother. Did he have a sensor on this thing? I flipped the paper back and forth, scanning for an electronic bug like something out of a *James Bond* movie.

Was I being overdramatic? Maybe. But I couldn't help it.

MAGNOLIA

> Did you add cameras to the house without telling me?

TAYLOR

crying laughing emoji No, but I'm assuming that I did, in fact, time that correctly.

MAGNOLIA

A key, Taylor? Really?

TAYLOR

Stop overthinking it, sunshine.

MAGNOLIA

Do you really think we're there?

TAYLOR

I do. But, baby, I will meet you wherever you're at.

I reread his words until they blurred.

Was I there?

I wasn't sure.

But as my gaze dropped to the key, I couldn't deny the warmth swelling in my chest. Maybe I wasn't all the way there—but he'd met me step for step in every way.

So maybe... just this once... I could meet *him*.

I picked up the key, letting it dangle from my index finger, and finally noticed the keyring attached. Large and shaped like an old motel tag, its teal enamel coating shimmered in the morning light. One side read Est. 2025, but when I flipped it over, I let out a breathy laugh. *Love Shack* stood out in metallic gold letters against the teal.

MAGNOLIA

Love Shack?

TAYLOR

Hey! You picked it up, that's progress!

MAGNOLIA

How do you know I hadn't picked it up before now? Hmmmmm?

TAYLOR

Because that would have been the first thing you sent me, sunshine.

MAGNOLIA

Shouldn't you be, I don't know, saving lives or something?

TAYLOR

Probably.

MAGNOLIA

Worst. Doctor. Ever.

TAYLOR

I really should go, though. Text you later?

MAGNOLIA

You better.

TAYLOR

Have you stopped spiraling?

MAGNOLIA

Maybe…

Are you sure this thing works?

TAYLOR

> Guess you'll have to use it and find out.
> *winking kiss emoji*

> See you later, sunshine.

Chuckling to myself, I sat down at the table, popped open the clamshell, and inhaled the buttery, sweet scent of raspberry jam. Maybe I was just really hungry, but the moan that rumbled up my throat at the first bite was damn near pornographic. They might not have been as good as mine, but I'd be damned if a free pastry didn't taste just as sweet.

I'd just popped the last bite of my third one into my mouth when my phone vibrated against the table, followed by the unmistakable chorus of *Ms. Jackson*. I let it play for a beat before swiping to answer.

"Hey, Jae. What's up?"

"Uh, hey, Mags." Her voice was uneven. "I, uh. I don't know how to tell you this, but you need to get down to *CharCutie*."

+)) ● ((+

Red and blue lights strobed through the front of *CharCutie*, casting flickering shadows against the shattered shards of glass littering the black-and-white tile and spilling onto the sidewalk outside. Tiny fragments, like crushed diamonds, reflected in the fluorescent lights and early evening sun, crunching beneath my heel as I stepped forward.

All that time. All that hard work and love I'd poured into this place—fractured and broken, much like the decimated front windows.

I hadn't even planned on coming in today. Jaelyn was scheduled to open around lunch. But when she arrived, this was what she'd found.

Bricks through my motherfucking windows.

Not just one or two—*all four* of the massive panes, along with the front door.

I'd been in disbelief since her frantic phone call, refusing to believe that even in a town that hated me so much, someone would stoop this low simply because of who I was dating.

But I'd been wrong.

Oh, so very wrong.

I stood in the middle of my shop, my entire body numb as the police car lights painted streaks of blue and red across the back wall and display cases. I'd been here for hours—answering questions, filling out paperwork, watching my dream shatter at my feet. I still needed to call my insurance company, but I was exhausted. Physically. Mentally.

My throat tightened as I took in the damage, so lost in my grief that I barely registered the crunch of another set of footsteps before a throat cleared behind me.

"Can you think of anything else I need to put in the report, Magnolia?" Sheriff Jackson asked, his deep amber eyes full of concern.

He looked so much like Jaelyn when he wore that expression, and I was beyond grateful to my best friend for calling in her dad instead of dialing the sheriff's office.

"I—I don't think so, Mr. Bill. Thank you, though."

"Alrighty. Well, in that case, we're all done here. But if you think of anything else..."

"I'll be sure to give you a call. Thanks again."

Bill Jackson nodded, then pulled me into a brief embrace before handing me his card. "You call this number, alright? It's my direct line."

"I will."

"Alright."

With one last nod, he turned and left, leaving me alone in the wreckage of my dream.

And now that I was alone, the numbness dissolved, giving way to blistering rage.

I was *done*.

Done with this town.

Done trying to be the bigger person.

It wasn't getting me anywhere, so why the hell should I keep appeasing these pearl-clutching, Bible-toting masses?

I needed to go home. Needed to *do* something.

As if reading my mind, Sheriff Jackson called my name from his squad car. When I turned, he asked, "You need a ride home?"

+)❍●((+

The second the Sheriff's car disappeared down my driveway, I bolted into the kitchen, flinging magic left and right, yanking herbs and ingredients from their resting places in the cabinets.

I had no idea what I actually needed—so I called for *everything*.

"Ostende te. Veni ad me," I demanded, clearing space on the island.

A warmth washed over me as the family grimoire shot from the shelf, floating to rest in the open space before me. Its cover flew open, pages flipping of their own accord before settling on the index of incantations.

My magic churned in my veins, feeding the fire in my belly as I ran a finger down the list.

But there was nothing.

I needed something *more*.

I wanted to—no, *needed* to punish this godforsaken town for all the shit it had put me and my family through.

"Maledictio," I growled, teeth clenched, watching as the pages fluttered toward the back of the book.

Nothing. Just a blank, time-stained page staring back at me.

"Fuck!" I slammed my hands onto the counter so hard my wrists ached. My eyes squeezed shut as frustration clawed at my ribs. But when I opened them again, an icy chill ran down my spine.

Words had begun to appear.

Cautela, maga.

Tenebrae ultra imminet.

Maledictiones omitti non possunt.

Latin. Of course, it was fucking Latin.

Taking a slow, measured breath, I forced myself to focus, calling on the long-buried lessons Aunt Evie had drilled into my head since childhood.

"*Caution, witch. Darkness looms beyond. Curses cannot be undone*? No shit!".

Ignoring the blatant warning, I tried to flip the page—but it wouldn't budge.

"Help me!" I screamed, trying to force the paper to move. Then one final line appeared at the bottom of the page.

Solus sanguis ligabit.

Only blood will bind.

The words burned into my vision. I read them once. Then again.

Frustrated beyond reason, I grabbed a knife. I'd no sooner pricked my finger, a whirlwind of magic whipped through the room.

"Magnolia Bellevue!"

Aunt Evie's sharp voice sliced through the air just as the grimoire *vanished*—summoned to her hands as she and Maddie stood across the kitchen, their eyes wide in horror.

"What in the name of the Triple Goddess were you thinking?" she hissed. "We do *not* do dark magic."

"We don't do *anything*!" I screamed back. My heart was hammering in my chest as I fisted my hands in my hair and tugged, looking for something—anything—to ground me.

"Magpie—"

"No. Absolutely not." My voice was calm—too calm. Like the air before a storm. "You don't get to stand there and coddle me like I'm still the little girl who came into this house twenty-two years ago. For years we have sat around and done *nothing*. Years of being sneered at and ridiculed. Of being the fucking town pariahs. And I ignored it like you taught me, held my head high and let it roll off of me like water. But enough is enough."

Maddie's face paled. "Mags, come on—"

"No." My tone was steel, cold and sharp as I met their gazes. "I'm *done*. Done with the jabs. Done with the dead flowers. Done with bricks through my fucking windows. And if you won't help me, then—"

"Mags!"

Taylor's voice thundered through the house, and every pair of eyes snapped to the closed pocket doors.

"Mags!"

I locked eyes with my sister, seething. "How fucking *dare* you. This doesn't concern him!"

"You're about to curse half the damn town, and you don't think that *concerns him*?" she fired back, and my eyes widened slightly.

Maddie *rarely* cursed, opting for phrases like 'fudge' and 'cheese and crackers'. So when an expletive did fly from her lips, you knew she was *pissed*.

Well, baby sister, so am I.

The doors slammed open.

Taylor stood in the doorway, red-faced and wide-eyed.

"Tell me I didn't just hear what I think I just heard."

Taylor

"I can't believe you called him!" Magnolia yelled, raking her hands angrily through her hair as she locked eyes with her sister.

"I didn't! I texted Meredith—"

"She has his number! What the fuck did you think she was going to do?!"

"How was I supposed to know that?" Maddie shot back, voice rising to match her sister's.

"Maybe if you would fucking talk to me, you would!"

My eyes volleyed back and forth between the two sisters. It was like watching an angry tennis match—or two lionesses circling each other—and I had no idea what I was supposed to be doing. Clearly, Magnolia didn't want me here, but after seeing the numerous texts and missed calls from her sister, and getting the full rundown of what had happened, she was just going to have to get over it.

I was here—scrubs and all—and she was going to talk through this with me.

"Magnolia?"

For the first time since I'd stepped foot in that house, her eyes flicked to mine—just for a second—before shifting to her aunt, who clutched some old, fat book against her chest like a shield.

"We're not finished here," Magnolia damn near hissed.

"Yes, Magnolia. We are." Her aunt's voice was calm, but firm. "And if I have to bind the grimoire from your magic until you calm down, I will. I don't want to, but I will."

With a frustrated groan, Magnolia stormed toward us. Her family stepped aside, but she breezed past me like I wasn't even there.

"Go after her," Madison ground out, jerking her head toward where Magnolia had stomped off.

Turning on my heel, I followed, calling her name as she slammed the screen door behind her.

"Mags, talk to me," I said gently, stepping out onto the porch. There was a bite to the air, and as much as I wanted to wrap my arms around her, I knew better than to push.

"Taylor, stop. You shouldn't even be here—this doesn't concern you." Her tone was icier than a snowball, and though the last thing I wanted was to fight right now, it seemed she was itchin' for one.

"Doesn't concern me? You just said you wanted to curse the whole goddamn town."

"No, Maddie said that." She spun on her heel, fixing me with a hard glare.

"Was she wrong?"

Her nostrils flared, but she didn't deny it.

"Fuck, Magnolia. What has gotten into you?"

"Gotten into me?!" She threw up her hands. "They threw bricks through my windows, Taylor! Sent me dead flowers with Mother only knows what crawling around in the dirt. Egged my house. Do I need to go on? What would you have me do?!"

"I don't know! But sure as shit not that."

I ran my hands through my hair, inhaling deeply in an attempt to quell my rising anger. I wasn't mad at her—I was mad *for* her. And yelling wouldn't get us anywhere. So, with a calmer tone, I asked,

"Why didn't you have spells or something on the windows? You know, to keep something like that from happening?"

Fire blazed in her eyes, and her mouth popped open in shock. "Why didn't I? Gee, I don't know, Taylor. Maybe because having unbreakable windows when a brick is thrown at them isn't the best idea for a suspected town witch."

She fell silent after that, breathing heavily through her nose as she held my gaze. And when I didn't respond—because what the hell could I say to that?—she turned, walking toward the railing.

I gave her a few moments, letting the tension settle so neither of us said something we'd regret. But the silence was unbearable.

"I'm sorry," I finally said. "I... I shouldn't have said that. Shouldn't have questioned you or how you use your magic."

Her head bobbed slightly, but she didn't say anything.

"Mags, baby, please talk to me."

"I can't do this," she whispered into the night, her gaze never straying from the yard.

"Can't do what, baby?" I asked, cautiously closing the distance until I could lean on the railing beside her.

Tears tracked down her cheeks, and the sight gutted me. I hadn't even realized she was crying. When I reached for her, she jerked away, squeezing her eyes shut.

"Please don't. I can't—" She took a shuddering breath. "I can't do this right now."

The tremble in her voice. The tears on her face. The way she wouldn't look at me or let me touch her...

My stomach bottomed out.

It wasn't a this she couldn't do—it was us.

And though I knew that deep in my bones, some masochistic part of me needed her to say it. I needed to hear the words.

"What can't you do, Magnolia?"

Glassy eyes met mine, her bottom lip quivering. "You already know what I'm going to say, Taylor."

"Then say it." There was more bite to my tone than I intended, but I couldn't help it. Fissures formed in my heart, spreading wide and deep, and it fucking hurt.

"Us."

It came out as more of a croak than a word, like it hurt her just as much to say it as it did for me to hear it. And that was something—I guessed. It meant she still cared, still wanted this. She just didn't believe she could have it.

But when I opened my mouth to say as much, she shook her head and wrapped her arms around herself like a shield.

"Don't you get it? They want me away from you. I'm not good enough for the town's golden boy, and I can't do this anymore. I'm just. So. *Tired.*"

"Please, Magnolia, don't do this."

"Taylor, I don't want to, but I can't do this right now. I need time. Space to figure out what's best for both of us."

"You mean what's best for you."

She flinched like I'd struck her, and I immediately regretted my words. Taking a breath, I cupped her cheek in my hand, my voice softer now.

"The town has already decided what they think is best for us. Don't give them that power. Please, sunshine, don't do this to us."

"I don't want to," she whispered again, leaning into my touch the barest amount. "But I need the dust to settle. They've targeted me, my home, and now my business. All because I fell for a guy out of my league."

"One: I'm not out of your league—if anything, you're out of mine. And two: I'll give you what you're asking for. But, baby?" I waited until she met my eyes. "This? Us? It isn't over. So take the time you need, but know that I'll be right here waiting for you."

Not willing to give her the chance to argue, I pressed a kiss to her brow and turned away, heading down the porch steps.

Walking away—when all I wanted was to be her safe harbor in the storm—was one of the hardest things I'd ever done. But I did it.

For her.

For us.

Because I meant every word.

I was in this.

And if her admitting that she'd fallen for me told me anything, it was that she was, too.

She just needed time to realize it for herself.

30

Sucks to suck, bro

Taylor

MY CHRISTMAS-TIME TO-DO LIST generally consisted of the following: work, eat way too much, and avoid malls and any other shopping centers—except the grocery store—from Thanksgiving until the new year. Those items were still very high on my list, but over the last month, one more task had been added: finding Magnolia the perfect gift.

I'd planned to do what any sane person would do around the holidays—shop online. Unfortunately for me, my dear, sweet sister Adelaide didn't agree with that plan. She'd waxed poetic about how *Magnolia deserved better than online shopping* and *you can't get a feel for the gift through a computer screen*, insisting on dragging me out to New Orleans with her to shop.

She wasn't entirely wrong. Magnolia *did* deserve better than that, and I'd even been mildly excited to brave the crowds for her. But after what happened a week ago, I just didn't have the mental capacity to deal with the Christmas hellscape that was shopping in person. I hadn't told Addy why I no longer wanted to go, but no matter the excuse I threw out, her response always landed somewhere along the lines of *sucks to suck, bro.*

So, I went.

And as expected, I was hating every single second of it.

So far on this little adventure, I'd been run into by at least ten people with no spatial awareness—none of whom had so much as muttered an *excuse me* or *sorry*. My heels had been clipped by overstimulated moms desperately trying to wrangle kids and push strollers, mumbling apologies as they went. I'd also been cussed out by a man who'd come *this close* to backing his car into mine. But that's what I got for shopping five days before Christmas, I supposed.

It was fine. Completely and totally fine.

Woosah, and all that.

Who was I kidding? We'd only been here an hour, and I was already ready to go.

"This way, TayTay," Addy sing-songed, looping her arm through mine, the fluffy ball on the end of her sequined Santa hat bouncing with every step.

"Must you call me that in public?" I groaned.

"Must you be so grumpy?" She furrowed her brows, jabbing me in the ribs when I scowled down at her. "What's got your knickers in a twist? Trouble in paradise?"

"Something like that," I muttered, shoving my free hand into my jacket pocket.

"Seriously?" she squeaked. "I was joking, but shit, Tay. What happened?"

"Magnolia pressed pause."

"What? Why? Huh? I don't get it. I thought things were going well with y'all."

"They were."

"Then what happened?"

I exhaled a heavy breath, shaking my head as I gestured for her to lead the way—right into... *oh, for fuck's sake.*

"I am *not* going into *Victoria's Secret* with my baby sister. Hell to the fuck no, Adelaide. I really don't want to pour acid into my eyes or get a lobotomy."

"Quit being a ninny and come on. I just want jammies and workout clothes."

I quirked a brow. "Since when did you start working out?"

"I don't. They're comfy." She shrugged. "Now come on, and keep talking."

I spilled my guts as Addy rifled through an astronomical amount of clothing, watching as she went from nodding in understanding to her cheeks flaming pink with rage.

"What the actual *fuck* is wrong with people in that town? Does she have any idea who's been doing it?"

Shoving my hands into my pockets, I shook my head. "Not that I know of."

"And you haven't heard from her at all over the last few days?"

Another shake of my head.

"Have you reached out?"

"She asked for space. It's killing me, but I'm trying to do what she asked."

Addy paused her rummaging and met my gaze, her eyes soft, tinged with the kind of sadness that made me want to sprint away from this conversation. She'd always been able to read me, to see through any mask I put on, and this was no different.

Rounding the table, she wrapped her arms around my waist and squeezed. "You're a good man, Taylor Hallows. She knows that. She'll come around."

"I hope you're right." I returned her embrace, exhaling a heavy breath. "I really hope you're right."

By the time Addy finished her shopping—my arms full of *her* bags, and none of my own—we were heading back toward the car.

"I'm starving," she groaned dramatically once she was settled in the passenger seat.

"We were just by a food court, Adelaide," I deadpanned.

"Yeah, I know. But I still need to go to *Mignon Faget* to grab something for Mom, so I figured we could grab lunch over that way."

"What am I, your chauffeur?"

"*No?*" My eyes narrowed at her innocent tone, her lips twitching as she fought a smile. "Okay, I hadn't *intended* for you to be my chauffeur, but it's not my fault you didn't find anything at the mall. *Maybe* you'll have better luck there?"

With a roll of my eyes and a groan, I pulled up the address for the jewelry store and grumbled, "Doubtful."

+)) ● ((+

An hour and a half later, we were back in the car, and I didn't particularly care for the cocky smirk my sister was giving me as she shook *my* tiny bag from the jewelry store in my face.

"I *told* you," she sing-songed.

"Hush."

I hadn't expected to find anything for Magnolia at a jewelry store—it was always so cookie-cutter and commercial, and my girl was neither of those things. But *Mignon Faget* was different. Their pieces were crafted for locals, for people who loved Louisiana. A little chunky, a little funky, but artfully made. Unique. Just like Magnolia.

Hell, the *whole store* screamed Magnolia, and it had been a struggle to settle on just one piece. But when I saw their Sol collection, I was sold.

It wasn't anything extravagant—just an open, sterling half-sun pendant with a black opal and mystic topaz charm hanging in the center. I didn't know much about gemstones, but I *did* know they mattered to Magnolia. So, I did the only thing I could think of—asked the internet.

Did you know black opal was supposed to protect against negative energy?

Yeah, me either.

And after all the *negative shit* that had been happening lately, I figured it couldn't hurt.

"You're just mad that I was right," Addy chided playfully as she buckled her seatbelt.

"No, I'm annoyed that you're rubbing it in."

I couldn't help but laugh when she stuck her tongue out at me.

"Thank you, Addy. Really." My fingers tightened around the bag. "I just hope Magnolia gives me the chance to actually *give* it to her."

Addy was silent as I backed out of the parking spot, merging into the thick holiday traffic of New Orleans.

"She will," she said, her voice laced with a confidence I didn't feel.

But the smile she gave me sparked the tiniest flame of hope in my chest.

Things would be okay.

They *had* to be.

I wasn't giving the universe—or any higher being—the option otherwise.

⁺))●((⁺

"Ten hours down, two to go," I mumbled as I sank into my chair at the nurses' station.

"You got any fun plans for the holidays?" Chelsea asked, tapping away at a patient's chart.

"Not really. Just looking forward to a few days off. You?"

"Yeah, heading to my parents' house for Christmas Eve, then just doing the family thing with the kids on Christmas Day. You're not doing anything with that new girlfriend of yours? Magnolia, right?"

I pressed the heels of my palms into my eyes and groaned. This was exactly why I didn't bring up my personal life at work—people in the medical field were nosey. All it took was one person overhearing a conversation, and it spread through the department like wildfire.

Taking a deep breath, I said, "No, we don't have any plans."

Chelsea quirked a brow.

"It's complicated."

"Well, uncomplicate it, doc."

She said it so bluntly that my head snapped in her direction, eyes wide enough to pop out of their sockets. "I didn't complicate it."

Chelsea huffed, unconvinced, and turned back to her computer, her nails tapping away at the keyboard.

"Chels—" Before I could get her name out, Dr. Fredmont pulled out the chair between us and swiveled toward me.

"Hey, Taylor, can you take bed four for me?"

"Maybe. What is it?"

"It's one of the MVA patients that came in on the ambulances. They're stable, but I've got my hands full with the other one right now." The latter part of her statement was dripping with annoyance—which meant that whoever that patient was, they were being a pain in the ass.

"You sure you don't want to give me the problem child?" I asked with a chuckle.

"Nah, I can handle him. He's not nearly as scary as he thinks he is."

"Alright. Yeah, I've got a bit before I have to round again, so I can pop in for you."

"You're the best. I owe you one."

"Don't hurt 'em, Meg," I called as she spun around and stood.

"*Never*. But I think he might need a catheter," she said with a wink before striding out of the nurses' station.

I chuckled as I swiveled back toward the computer and logged into the system. "Hey, Chels, can you give me the rundown on the ambulance notes for bed four while this thing loads?"

"Yeah, give me a sec."

The spinning wheel of death continued to circle as Chelsea tapped away, and by the time she had the patient information pulled up, my screen still hadn't loaded.

"Okay, let's see here. Two-car MVA... Looks like Fredmont's problem patient t-boned the patient in bed four—ouch. Uhh, front and side airbags deployed, unresponsive at the scene, superficial facial laceration—"

Her words fell on deaf ears.

My screen had finally loaded, and the second I saw the last name of my new patient, I was out of my chair, rounding the nurses' station before I even had time to think. My heart pounded so loudly in my ears that I barely registered Chelsea calling my name. It wasn't until I saw her pacing the hallway that my steps slowed.

"Magnolia?"

She turned at the sound of her name, just briefly, but long enough for me to see the flush in her cheeks, the smears of black running in rivulets from her eyes as she whispered into her phone.

As if her brain took an extra second to register that it was me who had called her name, her head whipped back toward me, eyes wide, mouth agape. "I'll, uh... I need to call you back, Jae."

Her gaze flicked over my face as she took a hesitant step forward, tucking her phone into her pocket. "Taylor, what... what are you doing here?"

I pointed to the hospital name and logo on my coat. "I, uh... I work here."

It was a statement, but good God, it sounded like a question.

Recognition flashed in her eyes, and she nodded. "Right. Sorry."

It had been over a week since I'd seen her—since we'd said anything to each other—and this being the reason she was finally back in my orbit was killing me. In that moment, I wasn't Dr. Hallows. I was just Taylor, and all I wanted was to pull her into my arms and tell her that everything was going to be okay.

"Magnolia—" I stopped when her eyes snapped to mine, a fresh well of tears lining her lashes. "Shit, baby, come here."

I barely took two steps before she launched herself into my arms, burying her face against my chest, her body shaking as her tears soaked into my scrub top.

This wasn't the reunion I wanted.

But fuck if it didn't feel like I could finally breathe again.

"I was so worried that it was you in that bed," I murmured against her hair. "Fuck, I was so scared."

Her arms tightened around my waist, and I ran a hand up and down her spine, some of the tension I'd been holding onto finally ebbing away now that I knew she was in one piece.

"I'm alright. It's Aunt Evie," she choked out, her words muffled against my chest.

"Dr. Hallows?" Chelsea's voice was soft, her eyes flicking between me and the back of Magnolia's head.

I swallowed hard. "Go on in, Chels. I'll be there in a minute. But after, I need to let Fredmont know I can't take this patient."

Magnolia jerked out of my hold, her eyes frantically scanning my face. "What do you mean you can't take this patient? Why? What's going—"

"Shh. Mags, baby, breathe." I pulled her back toward me, nodding at Chelsea, who slipped inside the patient's room with a wary look over her shoulder. Once the door clicked shut, I turned my full attention to Magnolia.

"I can't treat your aunt because it's a conflict of interest."

"What conflict of interest?" she demanded, panic rising in her voice.

"*You*, Magnolia. You're my conflict of interest. Evie deserves the best care she can get, and I can't give that to her because I'll be too worried about *you*."

"Oh."

"Yeah. *Oh*."

I pulled her into my arms again, resting my chin on top of her head, relishing the steadying cadence of her breathing against my chest.

"Why don't you go grab a coffee while I check on Evie, okay? I'll update you when you get back."

She nodded against my chest, and I pressed a kiss to the top of her head before letting her go, watching as she took slow, defeated steps down the hallway before disappearing toward the lobby.

With a steadying breath, I turned and headed for her aunt's room, bracing myself for what I was about to see.

"How we doing in here?" I asked as I stepped through the door, keeping the question general in case Evie was awake. She wasn't.

"Vitals are good, but she's been in and out of consciousness. Probably got a gnarly concussion."

I nodded, rounding the bed as I pulled my stethoscope from my coat pocket. After rousing her just enough to get consent for an examination, I checked her over, grimacing every time I inadvertently caused her pain. I never wanted to hurt a patient. But when it was someone you knew—someone you *cared* about—it made it that much worse.

One of the many reasons medical professionals weren't supposed to treat people they had personal ties to.

By the time Magnolia returned, I'd ordered something to manage Evie's pain, Chelsea had drawn blood for the lab, and we had her scheduled for a CT scan and x-rays. The concussion was obvious—we just needed to determine how severe. I also suspected she'd at least fractured her left arm, but imaging would confirm. Unfortunately, radiology was backed up. It was going to be a while before they could get her in.

Magnolia took in the information in stride, nodding as each fact was laid at her feet. But she looked exhausted. Sitting in the chair outside her aunt's room, her head rested against the wall, eyes drooping, her entire body folding in on itself.

Squatting next to her, I brushed a strand of hair from her cheek and whispered, "Why don't you head home? She's staying overnight—you might as well go get some rest."

"I... I can't." Her voice was so quiet I almost missed it. "I don't want to be alone. Not after everything that's happened."

"Where's Maddie?"

She sighed, heavy and worn. "I called her, but she's out of town at some book thing. She can't get a flight back until tomorrow."

"Meredith?"

A slow shake of her head. "Still taking finals. I didn't want to distract her."

"Come home with me." The words left my mouth before I had the chance to think them through, but I didn't regret them.

Her eyes snapped to mine, wide and piercing, and I swallowed before clearing my throat.

"I get off in"—I checked my watch—"about an hour. Come home with me, baby. Let me take care of you."

She hesitated. "I don't want to intrude, Taylor."

"It's not intruding if you have a key, sunshine. Besides that, I want you there."

"You're sure?"

"Never been more sure in my life."

+)>●((+

"Goddammit," Megan seethed as she stepped back into the nurses' station, radiating pure annoyance.

"What's up, doc?" I asked, trying to lighten the mood.

The rest of the shift had flown by in a blur, and I was ten minutes away from getting out of here with my girl. Yeah, the circumstances weren't ideal, but I'd take what I could get.

"That little"—she paused, scanning the floor to make sure no patients were within earshot, then dropped her voice to a whisper—"shit in bed two just left AMA."

I grimaced. A patient leaving against medical advice always meant more paperwork—paperwork they were supposed to sign before walking out. But I guessed her patient didn't feel like sticking around.

"Shit. I'm sorry. Need help with anything?"

"Yeah, can you mark him AMA in the system and print the forms for me? I'd ask Rhonda, but she's already up to her elbows in triage, and I really need to pee."

I made a face. "I really didn't need to know that."

"Buck up, Dr. Hallows. And thank you!" she called as she darted toward the staff bathroom.

My laugh died the second I pulled up Megan's patient's chart.

Kyle. Fucking. LeBlanc.

31

Cats are bossy

Magnolia

My eyes were heavy, a dull ache forming at my temples as the streetlights strobed past the car windows. I was so freaking tired—physically, mentally, emotionally, all of it.

"Are you hungry?" Taylor asked softly, his hand tightening around mine where it rested on the center console.

He hadn't let go since he met me outside Aunt Evie's room at the end of his shift. He'd laced his fingers with mine, guiding me along as he said goodbye to his coworkers and walked me out of the emergency room. He'd held them tighter as we crossed the parking lot, the gentle pressure a comfort against the turmoil in my mind. But he never said a word. He didn't try to make small talk or convince me that everything was going to be okay. He didn't pepper me with questions about how I was doing or what I'd been up to.

He was just *there* for me, like an old, sturdy oak withstanding gale-force winds.

And, Mother above, I was grateful for that.

Grateful for *him.*

"Sunshine?" Taylor's voice pulled me from my thoughts as his thumb swept lightly over my knuckles.

I hummed in response.

"Are you hungry?" he asked again, a small chuckle in his voice.

"I could eat."

In all actuality, the answer was a resounding *no*. A migraine was coming—I could feel it creeping in at my temples—and that meant nausea, migraine's unwanted sidekick, wasn't far behind. But I knew if I didn't get something in my system, it would hit me harder and faster than it would on a semi-full stomach.

"Do you have a preference? Or do you just want me to find a drive-thru?"

"Anywhere that has hot, salty fries and Coke."

"As you wish," he murmured, still tracing soothing lines along my hand.

I smiled at his words, at the memories they invoked, and let my eyes drift closed. He'd turned on my seat warmer, and *sweet baby cheeses*, did it feel good. I melted into the leather, letting the heat soak into my tired body as the steady rumble of the engine became my sound machine, lulling me into the closest thing to peace I'd felt in over a week.

By the time I opened my eyes again, we were pulling into Taylor's driveway, the crunch of gravel beneath his tires grounding me. I hadn't meant to fall asleep, but even with a power nap, I was struggling to keep my eyes open.

Starbursts of light flared from his porch bulbs, cutting through the darkness. I knew they were practical, but at that particular moment, it felt like someone was driving an icepick straight into my skull. My stomach twisted violently in response.

Taylor said something, but his voice sounded distant, muffled, like he was talking underwater and *somehow* still too loud.

Not. Good.

I needed food. Needed the darkest corner possible so I could bury my head until this passed.

A loud noise cracked to my left, and I flinched, my jaw clenching as it reverberated in my skull. Pressing my fingers firmly into my temples, I concentrated on my breathing. *Long inhales through the nose, slow and even exhales through the mouth.* Over and over until the throbbing dulled enough that I could peel my eyes open without wanting to hurl.

"Come on, baby. I've got you," Taylor murmured, his arms wrapping around me as he pulled me from the car.

I clung to him like a koala as he walked us the ten measly feet to his front door. He set me down on the porch swing, the jingle of his keys sounding more like a gong as he undid the latch. Then, before I could even think about standing, he scooped me up again and carried me bridal style into the house.

A tiny flutter stirred in my chest. *Carried over the threshold.*

The thought sent a cascade of images through my mind—late-night porch swings, dancing in the kitchen, spending endless nights wrapped in his arms. Candlelit dinners, streaks of gray threading through our hair. Tiny, blonde-haired, blue-eyed—

Whoa.

I didn't even know I wanted kids.

Did I want kids?

I cracked an eye open, peering up at Taylor as he maneuvered through the house. *Blessed Mother, he was gorgeous.* But more than that, he was strong, steady, and kind. The kind of man women dreamed about bringing home to meet their families.

And through all the chaos, this *beautiful, wonderful* man still chose me. Again and again.

The last eight days without him had sucked. I hadn't realized just how much I leaned on him until he wasn't there to hold me. Cleaning *CharCutie* had been a decent distraction during the day, but at night?

At night, I drowned my dumbass decision to ask for space in canned whip cream and cookie dough ice cream.

But when I got the news about Aunt Evie, he was the first person I wanted to call.

Did I *need* him in my life? No. I'd survived thirty years just fine without him. Hell, I'd even thanked the Mother and did a little dance when he finally left town all those years ago.

But now?

Now I *wanted* him in my life. I wanted to wake up every day curled in his arms, to watch sunrises and sunsets together while the dogs he wanted so badly ran through the yard. I wanted him to hold me through the bad moments and celebrate the good ones.

Love was selfish like that, always looking for what the other person could do for you. But it was also selfless when reciprocated.

And Mother above, I wanted those things for *him* too. I wanted to be the person he leaned on, to be his safe harbor in the storm of life. To share his burdens. He deserved someone who would give that to him and so much more.

And I wanted to be that person for him.

Tears pricked my eyes as I *really, truly* looked at him. Not just at his face or his body, but at the *soul* inside.

The man who had once been the bane of my existence had somehow wormed his way into my heart.

And made himself at home there.

I was falling. Hard.

No—scratch that.

I'd already *fallen.*

Three words I never imagined saying blared to life in my brain, big and bright and fluorescent. My breath caught.

I love you.

Taylor glanced down at me, a smirk tugging at one corner of his lips. "You've gotta stop looking at me like that, sunshine. You're gonna give me a complex."

I love you.

It hovered on the tip of my tongue as he gently set me on the edge of his bed. It stayed there as I collapsed onto the soft down comforter, watching through half-lidded eyes as he moved around the room.

I flinched when he turned on the bathroom light, squeezing my eyes shut as I rolled over.

"You okay, Mags?" he asked softly, the bed dipping as he sat behind me, warm palm sweeping along my back in a soothing caress.

"Yeah, just a headache. I'll be better after I get some food in my system."

"Alright, I'm going to go grab everything from the car. I put a t-shirt and the sweatpants you keep trying to steal on the edge of the bed if you want to change."

"Thank you."

I sat up, reaching for the clothes, but even that small movement made my head swim. *Nope.*

I was still sitting there, clutching his shirt like a security blanket, when he walked back in, food in hand.

"Okay, so do you want... Mags?" His voice was wary, his gaze searching mine. When a single tear rolled down my cheek, his eyes widened. "Shit. No, no, no—don't cry."

He practically dropped the food and was in front of me in a heartbeat, hands running up and down my arms.

"It's more than just a headache, isn't it?"

"Maybe," I squeaked, pinching my eyes closed and pressing my fingers into my temples.

"Alright. Arms up, sunshine."

"What are you doing?"

"Helping. Scale of one to ten, how bad is it?" His fingers gripped the hem of my shirt, and I raised my arms.

"Are you really trying to play doctor right now?" I asked, aiming for humor and falling short when my voice cracked with the pain.

"Not playing, sunshine. Give me a number."

"Seven." Skeptical sapphire blues met mine as he discarded my shirt. "Seriously, it's a seven. Trust me, I've had worse."

"Okay, what usually helps?" he asked as he sat back on his heels and started unlacing my tennis shoes.

"When I don't have my meds?" He nodded and pushed to his feet. "Salty snacks, chocolate, Coke, and a dark room. Sometimes a shower, but I don't know if I could handle that right now."

"Do you think you can stand long enough for me to get your pants over your hips, or would laying down be better?"

"I can do it, Taylor."

"I know, but you don't *have* to. Let me help, Mags. When was the last time you let someone take care of you?"

I scrunched my nose.

"That's what I thought."

Taylor helped me out of my remaining clothes and into his, then helped me move up toward the pillows. Once he had me tucked in like a toasty little burrito, he brought over the food. As much as I *wanted* to eat, and knew that I needed to, the smell had bile rising in my throat, and that was a one-way ticket to the porcelain throne.

It must have been written all over my face because he placed it back on the dresser and asked, "Nauseated?"

"Very."

"Is there anything else I can get you? Tylenol? Excedrin?"

I shook my head against the pillow and hiked the covers higher. "When they're this bad all that helps are my meds and a cold cap. Sleep should help take the edge off, though." A yawn escaped with the final words.

"I could go get them for you, if you'd like."

"Really?"

Taylor sat down next to me and gently swept my hair behind my ear. "One of these days you'll get it."

"Get what?" I asked through a yawn so wide that my eyes watered.

"That you're it for me, Magnolia."

As he tucked me into bed, a whisper drifted through my mind once more.

I love you.

I wanted to say it. But my eyes were too heavy, my body already sinking into sleep.

"Get some rest, baby. I'll be back soon."

I love you.

Taylor

I stood frozen in the doorway to my room, my eyes locked on where Magnolia was curled into a ball on the bed. I wasn't sure if she'd meant to say it aloud or if she'd thought I was already gone, but *holy fuck.* I wanted to throw a damn parade, do a stupidly giddy dance in the hallway—hell, shout it from the rooftops.

But even from across the room, I could see her features contorting—pain wracking her body, even in sleep.

Focus, Taylor. It doesn't count.

Not yet.

And she needed me more than I needed to hear it again.

With a relieved smile on my lips, I hurried into the kitchen and stashed the food in the fridge before digging into no-man's land—a woman's purse. Thankfully, Magnolia's was at least somewhat organized, making it relatively easy to find her keys.

Her mumbled confession echoed in my ears, the sound growing sweeter with every repetition, as I drove toward her house. Suddenly, the stars were brighter, the crisp winter air more refreshing, and—to my unending surprise—Christmas music wasn't quite so obnoxious.

Amazing what hearing that the woman you loved, loved you back could do to a person's mood and general outlook on life.

Bellevue Manor was dark when I pulled into the drive, save for the icicle lights draping from the porch awning. I had to turn on my phone's flashlight to find my way up the steps. But as I slipped the key into the lock, it hit me—I had no clue where I was going.

I'd never been in Magnolia's room. Hell, I'd never been further into the house than the living room and kitchen. And yet, she trusted me enough to traipse through her house unaccompanied to find the things she needed.

A love confession and a new level of trust in one day? I needed to buy a lottery ticket.

The moment I pushed the door open, a strange warmth wrapped around me, trickling down my spine—seconds before something tapped against my shin, followed by a very angry-sounding yowl.

"Well, hello to you too, you angry cotton ball."

"Meow." The tone was unmistakable—*fuck off.*

"Well, that was rude. Can you show me where Magnolia's room is, please?"

Meowfoy narrowed his eyes before flopping onto the floor like a fluffy barricade.

"You know I can just step over you, right?"

"Rraaaarr... Hisss."

I sighed. "I have no idea what you're trying to say, but I'm pretty sure that was a threat. One I'd be inclined to heed, if it weren't for the fact that your mother sent me here to get her migraine medicine."

A smaller mewl came from the stairs. Shifting my gaze, I spotted an orange version of the marshmallow at my feet, tail flicking side to side as it studied me... curiously? *I don't know. I don't understand cats.*

"Hermeownie, I presume?" I asked as I stepped over my arch-nemesis.

Naturally, Meowfoy took offense—swatting at my shoe, trying to bite my pants, hissing like a damn snake.

"Would you stop it? I'm just trying to help."

A delicate *mrrow* sounded from the staircase before Hermeownie stood, arching into that signature feline stretch, before turning to head up the stairs.

Taking the cue, I hastened my steps away from her angry counterpart and followed.

The upstairs was bright and colorful, the walls adorned with countless frames—artwork, family photos, snapshots of life frozen in time. I wanted to take it all in, to see Magnolia at every stage, to glimpse the childhood that had shaped her. My gaze snagged on a blonde-haired Magnolia, head thrown back in laughter as she swung on a tire swing tied to an old oak tree—

An impatient yowl snapped me out of it.

"All right, all right, I'm coming." *Geez, these cats are bossy*, I thought as I made my way to where she seemed to be sitting sentinel outside a door.

Don't ask me why, but as I pushed the door open, I glanced down at her and asked, "Do you know where Mags keeps her meds?"

She gave me what looked like a curt nod before sashaying into the room.

Flicking the light on, I took a moment to take in Magnolia's space. Jewel tones mingled with bright colors, soft surfaces met hard edges, books and knickknacks and art covered the walls and tables. It was an amalgamation of everything *her,* and I just wanted to soak it in.

Hermeownie jumped onto the bed, padded to the nightstand, and pawed at the covers before spinning in a circle and sitting down. Her expression—shockingly expressive for a cat—seemed to scream *stop gawking and look over here, idiot.*

Sure enough, three orange bottles caught my eye.

Picking them up, I checked the labels—Propranolol, a preventative, and two pain relievers, the generic versions of Fioricet and Maxalt.

"Damn, baby. How do you live like that?" I muttered, searching for something to carry them in. Finding a bag, I tossed the bottles inside and turned back to the cat. "Wanna help me find her some clothes?"

I had officially lost my mind. Or maybe I was turning into a Disney princess. Either way, I went with it.

To my increasing amazement, Hermeownie led me around the room, meowing at drawers and pawing at closet doors, directing me to what she apparently deemed acceptable options. I packed a small overnight bag, then asked, "Do you know where her cold cap is?"

With an exasperated huff—*finally, you idiot*—Hermeownie strutted back to the nightstand and brushed against it.

My confusion vanished when I opened the door and a blast of cool air hit me.

She had a *mini fridge* built into her nightstand.

Genius.

Grabbing two caps, I tossed them into the bag. "Thank you," I said genuinely.

To my surprise, she brushed against my knee, nuzzling into my hand. Her purrs vibrated up my arm.

"I like you more than the other one," I whispered, scratching behind her ear.

"Brrrow."

+)>●((+

The trip had taken longer than I'd intended, but when Magnolia didn't respond to my text, I took it as a sign she was still asleep. With that in mind, I decided to take the long way home—swing by the supermarket.

She'd said chocolate and Coke helped her migraines, so I was going to get her some, dammit. Stock every nook and cranny with whatever she needed. Tampons, disks, liners? Just tell me the brand and size. Hell, if she had a condom preference, I'd switch in a heartbeat.

But as I turned down the street, my eyes locked onto a different destination.

Rage, which had dulled to a simmer while I took care of Magnolia, surged back, boiling over.

Kyle LeBlanc had stepped one toe too far out of line.

And it was about damn time someone put him in his goddamn place.

My knuckles turned white against the steering wheel as I took a sharp turn down the drive leading to the Mayor's house. I'd spent most of my senior year here—studying, partying, watching my so-called friends skate through life. But now, all I saw were white walls housing hatred and bigotry.

I was out of the car and banging on the front door before I could second-guess my actions.

"If you don't stop that racket—" The door flung open, and Cherie—their longtime housekeeper—went from annoyed to shock as she said, "Taylor. How good to see you."

"As much as I love a friendly face," I said, pushing past her, "where is he?"

"Who? Kyle?" She sighed, rolling her eyes. "What did that boy do *now*?"

"Does it matter?"

"Guess not. He's in there, probably making a mess I'll have to clean up later."

I waited until she turned down the hall before throwing the doors open.

Kyle jolted, amber liquid sloshing over his glass, cigarette nearly slipping from his lips. His face was flushed, eyes glassy—*three sheets to the wind* didn't even cover it.

His smirk widened as he staggered to his feet. He didn't have a single scratch on him from what I could tell, and that just pissed me off even more.

"Taylorr! Mymanss. Fin'ly come to your senses?" he asked, his words slurring together.

"What the fuck is wrong with you?" I seethed, closing the distance between us.

Was this a HIPAA violation? Oh, no question. Especially since Magnolia hadn't said who had been responsible for the accident. I wasn't even sure if she knew, but I was past the point of caring.

Knocking the glass out of his hand, I shoved him toward the wall. "Not only did you drive, drunk off your ass by the looks of it, but you could have *killed* someone, you jackass!"

"I don know what you're talkin' 'bout." His words were a little clearer than they had been, though they still muddled together. But it was that insufferable, cocky smirk that he always had when he knew he would get away with something that snapped the last thread of restraint I'd been clinging to.

Slamming him back into the sheetrock, I gripped his shirt in my fists. "Do you *know* who you ran your car into? Do you *know* the extent of the damage you caused?" His smirk widened. "Do you even fucking *care*?"

"Why should I?"

It was the clearest his words had been since I'd stormed through the door, and the fire in his eyes stoked my own. He didn't give two shits. Why would he when he always got away with everything? He had for as long as I'd known him.

Rage was a living force in my veins, growing stronger with every beat of my heart. I didn't care about the repercussions that beating the crap out of the Mayor's son would bring. All I knew was that I wanted to slam my fist into his face and wipe that fucking smirk off his lips. Before I could think twice about what I was about to do, I raised my fist, arm cocked and ready to pummel the piece of shit in front of me.

Red filled my vision.

I *wanted* to hit him.

But then—

A slow, Southern drawl grated against my nerves.

"I'd think twice about that if I were you."

The Mayor.

Fist still poised to strike, hand still fisted in Kyle's shirt, I gritted out, "Why's that?"

"Well, Dr. Hallows, we wouldn't want that license you worked so hard for to get taken away, now would we?"

Kyle's smirk deepened, smug and malicious.

My teeth ground together. "No."

"Good. Glad we could come to an understanding." He exhaled, feigning relief. "Surely, whatever my idiot son has done this time isn't worth all this mess."

I let my fist drop, shoving Kyle back as I straightened my own shirt. "He's not worth the breath in his own damn lungs."

Without another glance at either of them, I turned on my heel and stormed past his dad, out of the house, before I could change my mind.

Kyle wasn't worth losing my medical license over.

But that wasn't the only reason I stopped.

I wasn't about to risk losing Magnolia over that worthless piece of shit.

32

I'll turn him into a toad

Magnolia

"Mags, baby. I need you to wake up for me."

The soft, soothing cadence of Taylor's voice lured me from my subconscious, and I groaned. I had no idea what time it was or how long I'd been asleep, but with the persistent throbbing in my head, it couldn't have been long. Either that, or this migraine had every intention of lingering far past its welcome.

"What time is it?" I croaked, my throat and mouth feeling drier than the Sahara.

"It's about nine. You've been out for around an hour and a half."

Warm fingers traced along my face, gently sweeping sweat-slicked hair from my brow.

"Can you sit up for me?"

With a shaky nod, I cracked my eyes open—then immediately regretted it. It wasn't bright, but it also wasn't the pitch black I craved when it felt like my head was about to explode. A halo of buttery light cast one half of Taylor's face in shadow, highlighting his sharp features and the stubble along his jaw. *Mother above, the man was gorgeous.* But there was no way I was going to be able to sit up. The smallest movement sent pain pulsing through my temples.

"There you are," he whispered, a soft smile tugging at his lips. "How are you feeling?"

I crinkled my nose, closing one eye so half the tiny fireflies dancing in my vision disappeared.

"Like an elephant is sitting on my face and a vice grip is squeezing my brain."

"That was... vivid," he said with a light chuckle. "I brought you a Coke and your meds. Think you can sit up?"

"You found everything okay?" I asked, pinching the pressure point between my thumb and forefinger. Sometimes acupressure helped, sometimes it didn't. At the very least, it eased the nausea for a little while.

"I had some help." A bemused smile tugged at the corners of his lips as he shook his head. "Those cats are something else."

Seeming to realize I wasn't in any hurry to move, Taylor slipped a hand behind my shoulders and helped me upright. Even with his support, the room spun, and I dropped my head forward into my hands.

"Take it slow, baby. I'm right here."

"I don't deserve you," I groaned, pressing my fingers into my temples as I willed the fluorescent squiggles from my vision.

"I disagree, but we can argue about that later. Here."

Lifting my head, I rolled my neck in a weak attempt to relieve the tension that always built there when a migraine hit. With a deep breath, I finally allowed myself to fully open my eyes.

"Hey, beautiful."

Taylor held out a hand, a green capsule nestled in his palm, and passed me the drink he held in the other.

"Bottoms up."

The bubbles tickled my tongue as I took a long pull from the straw, then dropped the pill into my mouth. After a few more sips, I handed the cup back to Taylor with a sigh.

"Thank you."

"You don't need to thank me, Mags."

"Yes, I do. You didn't have to do that."

"Maybe, but I wanted to. I don't like seeing you in pain. Now come on, you need to eat."

I groaned, my stomach souring at the mere mention of food.

"You'll be more nauseous if you don't."

"I know." I scrubbed my hands down my face before letting my head fall back between my shoulders. "You're bossy as a doctor."

"Yeah, well. You're bossy in general, so it all balances out," he teased before pressing a kiss to my brow and slipping from the bed. "I have a Snickers or plain potato chips. Your fries from earlier are cold, but I can throw them in the oven if you want those instead."

"Chips, please... Wait, no. Snickers... Both? Yeah, let's go with both."

Taylor's chuckle mixed with the crinkle of the plastic bag on his dresser, and I couldn't help but smile. Adjusting in the bed, I scooted back against the pillows and crossed my legs beneath me as he brought over the food.

I'd spent so much of my life taking care of others—my sisters, my friends, people in our coven and the witch community—it was nice to have someone looking after *me* for once.

We fell into easy conversation while I ate. Taylor told me about what happened with Meowfoy, how Hermeownie had helped him find everything I needed. I explained what a familiar was, watching his eyes widen with each word. When I finished, he muttered something about how he *knew* they understood him, and how unfair it was that he couldn't understand them back.

And though it made my head throb worse, I couldn't help but laugh.

I swear, the more that man learned about witches and the craft, the more his mind got blown.

Once I was done, he tossed the trash and handed me the bag from my house. He dimmed the lights in his bathroom so I could brush my teeth, then helped me back into bed, bringing my cold cap along with him.

I sighed in relief as the bitter chill seeped into my skull, dulling the ache. The meds had kicked in, and eating had helped, but nothing worked quite like being enveloped in ice packs.

Once he'd gotten me tucked in—something that was quickly becoming my favorite little quirk of his—he pressed a kiss to my brow.

"Get some sleep, sunshine. I'll be on the couch if you need me."

Panic gripped my chest at the thought of being alone.

So much had happened.

And now that my mind was clearing from the pain, I could feel the ache in my chest. Cracks and fissures spread with every breath, the terror I felt when I got that phone call crashing back in.

I'd had flashbacks to my parents' accident. Memories of our nanny crying as she held Maddie and me, Meredith sleeping soundly down the hall, as she explained we were now orphans.

Black lace dresses and tights.

Tear-stained cheeks.

Countless condolences.

Saying goodbye to the only life I knew.

It all came slamming back into me with resounding clarity. I hadn't been able to breathe until I'd seen the rise and fall of my aunt's chest in that hospital bed.

I didn't know what I would have done if I'd lost Aunt Evie.

I didn't know what I would have done if Taylor hadn't shown up in that hallway when he had.

I'd never felt more alone in my life than I had in that moment. And just *seeing* him had saved me.

Slipping my hand from beneath the covers, I latched onto his before he could walk away.

I could feel the tears streaming down my cheeks.

Mother above, I'm so tired of crying.

"Stay. Please," I managed around a suppressed sob. "I... I know I haven't been the best girlfriend, and you deserve so much more, but could you just... hold me? Just for a little while, at least."

Taylor dropped to his knees beside the bed, lacing our fingers together with one hand while gently sweeping away my tears with the other.

And *sweet baby cheeses*, the way that man looked at me—like the sun rose and set with every beat of my heart—was intoxicating. It was *addicting* in the best way. He may not have *said* it, but he'd shown me love in every other way I could imagine.

"Baby, I'll stay as long as you need me to. I just didn't want to... overstep. You asked for space—"

"I don't want it. Not anymore. I didn't really want it in the first place, I just... I didn't know how to process everything. I'm sorry."

Taylor's lips were soft against mine, his touch grounding me in a way nothing else could.

I was *completely* gone for this man.

And there was no turning back.

Not that I wanted to.

It didn't take long for him to join me in bed, his strong arm draping across my middle and pulling me until I was nestled against his body. "Goodnight, sunshine."

"Goodnight, cowboy."

·)) ● ((·

"You're here early," Aunt Evie whispered, wincing as she adjusted in the hospital bed.

"I got a ride with Taylor this morning since he had to work." I grabbed her uninjured hand, giving it a gentle squeeze. "How are you feeling?"

"Like I got hit by a car," she joked, her lips tugging into a wry smile.

I glared at her.

She let out a small laugh. "Too soon?"

"You're unbelievable."

"Yeah, well, one of us has to have a sense of humor about this or we'd both be a mess. How're your sisters?"

"Maddie's on her flight home, and I'll call Meredith after her last final." I hesitated before adding, "How are you feeling about surgery? It's this afternoon, right?"

When we arrived at the hospital this morning, Taylor had gotten the rundown from Dr. Fredmont. Miraculously, Aunt Evie only had a mild concussion—not that I was surprised, given the amount of protective charms she wore on a daily basis. But she also had a displaced fracture in her left arm that needed surgery, meaning at least one more night in the hospital.

Aunt Evie shrugged. "I'm not worried about it. Did I hear you say that Taylor dropped you off this morning?"

"You did, but we're talking about you right now."

"No, we're talking about that hunky doctor who looks at you like you hung the moon and all the stars."

"Aunt Evie—"

"No, Magpie." Her voice softened. "I don't want to talk about me. And I need you to hear me when I say this, okay? I'm here. I'm safe. I'm... relatively unharmed. But, babygirl, I'm fine."

I swallowed hard, nodding as she squeezed my hand, blinking rapidly to keep the tears at bay.

"Now," she continued, her expression shifting back to something far too knowing, "tell me why Taylor brought you this morning. I thought y'all took a break—or whatever it is y'all call it?"

I sighed. "I maaay have stayed at his house last night."

"Uh-huh, go on."

I groaned and dropped my head onto the thin mattress. "I don't know, Aunt Evie."

"Yes, you do. You just need to have the courage to say it out loud."

"But what if—"

"Don't even let that thought finish forming in your mind, Magnolia Lynn." Her grip on my hand tightened. "You and I both know that man is in love with you. But after everything you've been through since y'all started seeing each other, and everything you've endured at the hands of that silly little town we call home, he's probably scared shitless to say it."

"But what if he doesn't?"

"Doesn't what? Love you?" She let out an exasperated sigh. "Magpie, there is a greater chance of twenty feet of snow in the middle of June than there is that he doesn't think the sun shines out your ass."

"But... there's still a chance."

"Well, if you wanna be a negative Nancy about it, then yes, there's still a chance. *And if*—and that's a big *if*—he doesn't, then I'll turn him into a toad."

I snorted, shaking my head. "So, you're saying I should tell him?"

If there was ever a picture in the dictionary next to the word *dead-pan*, it would be of the look my aunt gave me in response.

"Alright, alright. You win."

"Magpie, I didn't win anything. *You* did, when you decided to give that boy an actual chance." Her voice softened. "I couldn't imagine a better man for you to be with."

"You barely know him, Aunt Evie."

"I don't need to know him. I know *you*. And I have never seen you light up about anyone like you do for Taylor. I've seen you smile more in the last few months than I have in years—even when you claimed to hate him."

My cheeks burned, and tears pricked at my eyes, but she just held onto my hand tighter.

"You deserve to be happy, Magpie," she said. "You just have to let yourself."

I stayed at the hospital until the nurses came in to prep Aunt Evie for surgery. Before I left, I whispered a quiet prayer of protection and healing over her, then promised to come back when she was out of recovery—to which she promptly and emphatically told me *no*.

Feeling lighter as I made my way toward the elevator, I pulled out my phone and fired off a quick text.

Magnolia

> Aunt Evie is getting prepped for surgery, so I'm going to go home for a bit.

I must have caught him between patients, because almost immediately, three little dots appeared.

Taylor

Swing by the ER lobby and I'll give you the car keys.

MAGNOLIA

I can call ZydeGeaux and get a ride.

TAYLOR

You can also take the Bronco.

Where are you right now?

MAGNOLIA

Just stepped off the elevator in the lobby.

TAYLOR

Don't move.

I paused just outside the elevator, glancing around the main lobby before shifting toward the sitting area in the center.

"Mags!"

Taylor's voice rang through the space, and I turned just in time to see him jogging down the hall, his shoes squeaking against the polished linoleum.

"What are you doing?" I asked, laughing as he came to a stop in front of me.

His mouth quirked at the corners, and my heart flipped.

He was in green scrubs, his hair slightly mussed from his sprint down the hallway, and worst of all—he was wearing those godforsaken glasses today. Every single inch of him called to every cell in my body.

"Bringing you these." He pulled his keyring from his pocket and held it out. "You going to the house, or back to the manor?"

The house.

Never, *ever*, his house.

Was now the time to tell him?

Once again, it was on the tip of my tongue, but before I could get the words out, the overhead speaker crackled to life.

"Doctor Hallows, you're needed in the ER. Doctor Hallows to the ER."

"Shoot. Sorry, baby, I gotta run. Text me, okay?"

He pressed the keys into my hand, tugging me into his arms for a quick hug. Then, with a soft kiss to my cheek, he turned and jogged back down the hall.

But before he got too far, the words tumbled from my lips.

"The house."

He turned mid-step, his smile spreading slow and wide, and my knees damn near buckled.

Then, with a wave and a wink, he disappeared around the corner.

33
Will it keep?
Magnolia

I MUST HAVE SAT in the driveway for at least ten minutes, staring at the front door with the house key Taylor had given me dangling from my pointer finger.

I knew it worked—I'd used it when *CharCutie* had been destroyed. But something about using it now felt bigger. Weightier. Choosing to come here instead of going to the manor was huge for me. I'd spent more time in that house than I had out of it. And though this was what I wanted, making myself get out of the car was proving harder than I expected.

Drawing in as much air as my lungs could hold, I took the first step toward a future I could finally see. One brighter than any star in the night sky. With each step, the tightness in my chest eased, my breaths coming smoother—until they caught in my throat, freezing me in place at the entrance of the living room.

I hadn't noticed it the night before, what with the migraine and the turmoil in my heart. And this morning had been a blur of forcing myself to wake up early so I could ride with Taylor to the hospital. But I saw it now.

It was as if a veil had lifted, and I was finally seeing through clear lenses instead of frosted glass.

There, in the corner of the living room by the windows, sat *the* chair. The one I'd fallen in love with while furniture shopping. A rich peacock-blue blanket draped over the back, and beside it, a gold floor lamp.

I wasn't sure how I still had tears to shed, but they filled my eyes all the same as I moved deeper into the house on unsteady legs.

Pictures decorated the bookshelves in a hodgepodge of frames that, somehow, worked. There were candid shots of Taylor with his parents and sister, ones that made me smile. But the one that twisted my stomach into knots?

The framed photo of us at Addy's engagement party.

"Fucking hell. How do I turn off the waterworks?" I muttered, swiping at the tears that refused to stop falling.

Deciding my heart would burst if I looked at the photos any longer, I headed to the kitchen.

It wasn't much better.

Cabinet after cabinet, I found more and more things that *I* would have in a kitchen. An entire shelf filled with my favorite snacks. Baking supplies neatly stacked beside ingredients I often used. My favorite blend of coffee sat next to the pot, my creamer tucked in the fridge.

I couldn't stop the tears if I tried. So I didn't. I let them fall freely, let them drip onto my shirt as I turned toward the front door—love and determination guiding every step.

Taylor deserved more.

So, Mother dammit, he was going to get it.

+)) ● ((+

Taylor

"Thanks, Chelsea," I said, opening the passenger door of her car.

"No problem, doc. See you after the holidays."

Closing the door, I turned toward the house. I wasn't entirely sure what I expected to find when I got home, especially after Magnolia had asked me to get a ride. But it certainly wasn't darkened windows.

My brows furrowed as I approached the front door, scanning the property for anything amiss—nothing. But as soon as I stepped inside, a warm, savory scent wrapped around me, making my stomach tighten with hunger.

"Mags?" I called out, hanging my coat on the entryway tree and dropping my backpack beside it. No answer. But soft music trickled from the kitchen, guiding me forward. "Baby, are you in—"

My words stalled the moment I pushed the pocket doors open.

The lights were off, the only illumination coming from flickering candles scattered along the countertops and table, and the twinkle lights lining the banquette windows.

It was like something out of a romance movie.

"Hi."

Her voice was soft, a nervous smile tugging at her lips as she shifted from one bare foot to the other.

The glow of the candles danced across her face, and my heart gave a hard, fluttering kick to my ribs.

She was stunning.

More than that—she looked *comfortable*. At home. Dressed in simple leggings and a cropped sweater, her hair loose in waves down her back, not a stitch of makeup on her gorgeous face.

I closed the distance between us, pulling her into my arms without hesitation. Spice, floral, and that underlying sweetness that was *just* Magnolia enveloped me as I buried my face in her neck.

"What is all this?" I murmured after pressing a kiss to her skin.

She shrugged, pulling her bottom lip between her teeth as her gaze flicked between mine.

"What is it?" I asked, my stomach tightening with something more than hunger. "Is everything okay?"

"Yeah, I just... I wanted to do something special for you."

"I appreciate it, and it smells and looks wonderful. But why?"

Tears rimmed her eyes, making the blue take on an almost gray hue. She gave me a watery smile.

"Because I love you."

Time stopped. The world ceased spinning on its axis as her words sank in.

She'd said it. She'd *fucking* said it.

Out loud. To my face.

My heart pounded so violently it threatened to break free from my chest. But I had to ask. Had to make sure I wasn't hallucinating after a long, grueling shift.

"What... What did you just say?"

With a little more vibrato than she had moments ago, she straightened her spine and said it again.

I barely heard it over the rushing in my ears, my mind reeling, my hands shaking.

"What's for dinner?" I demanded in a rush.

Her brows furrowed, head tilting. "Pot roast?"

"Will it keep?"

"I mean, yeah. It's in the crockpot on the warm setting—"

Her words cut off with a sharp yelp as I scooped her up by the thighs and carried her out of the kitchen.

"Taylor! What are you doing?" she screeched, her arms looping around my neck.

"I'm going to make love to you."

"Mother above, that's such a cringey phrase."

"Cringe or not, I'm going to show you just how much I love you."

I stopped walking at her sharp intake of breath, holding her gaze.

"Because I do. I love you, Magnolia Bellevue. I have for a while. I was just waiting for you to catch up."

Her lips crashed against mine, fingers threading into my hair as I carried her to our bedroom.

Because if I had *anything* to say about it, she'd be moving in sooner rather than later.

Her feet had barely touched the floor before fumbling hands were reaching for buttons and hemlines. Our lips barely parted as each inch of skin was revealed, and by the time Magnolia kicked her leggings from her feet, she was back in my arms, legs wrapped around my waist as I carried her to the bed.

Time stilled, marked only by the rhythmic beating of our hearts as I laid her out across my covers. Moonlight streamed through the windows, bathing her in silvery light, accentuating the soft rise and fall of her chest. Her cheeks were flushed, her pastel hair a halo around her head. And fuck me—she was in goddamn lingerie.

A groan rumbled in my throat, my hands clenching at my sides, itching to trace every inch of her as I took in the sight before me. Teal lace covered her breasts, leaving very little to the imagination, the bronze of her nipples visible through the delicate fabric. But it was the coordinating panties—the ones with the slit down the center—that held my attention far longer than they should have.

She looked like a goddamn goddess, and I was the lucky bastard who got to worship her.

"Fuck, baby."

"See something you like?" she purred, her voice sliding down my spine, pooling low in my gut.

"I see a whole lot that I love, cher. But this?" Her legs widened, giving me the opening I needed to step between them. Another groan slipped free as I ran two fingers through the slit in her panties. She was already wet for me, her breath hitching as I added just enough pressure to tease her entrance. "This is an unexpected bonus."

Her head tilted back against the bed, her back arching with every slow, deliberate stroke of my fingers. Her moans, her sighs—they were the sweetest melody. She dug her nails into my arm, guiding me, silently pleading for more. Any other night, I might have let her take control. But tonight, I wanted to take my time. Wanted her to see what it looked like to be cherished—to be loved despite all the cruelty meant to drive a wedge between us.

She whined my name, dragging out each syllable as I worked her closer to the edge.

"Do you have any idea how beautiful you are?" I murmured, pressing a kiss to her sternum as I curled my fingers inside her. "How stunning you are when you fall apart for me?"

"Taylor, please. I need you."

"Say it." I slowed the plunge of my fingers but added pressure to her clit, watching her body tense in response. "Say it again for me, cher, and I'll let you come."

Bright blues locked onto mine, her palm cradling my cheek.

"I love you."

The words had barely left her lips before she shattered beneath me, her back bowing as her mouth fell open on a perfect, silent cry. I pressed my lips firmly against hers, working her through the waves of pleasure, refusing to let go until the last tremor faded from her body.

A contented hum vibrated in her chest as I pulled away, brushing sweat-dampened hair from her brow.

"I love you, too," I whispered.

Her hand drifted lazily down my torso, each featherlight touch making my muscles jump. But when she wrapped her fingers around my length, my head dropped forward, a low moan escaping my lips.

"Show me," she breathed, her grip firm, steady, stroking from root to tip. Every pass of her palm had me seeing stars, slicking her hand with precum as she worked me.

"Baby, if you keep that up, I'm going to come like a teenager who just figured out what his dick could do."

She chuckled but didn't stop. My jaw clenched, and I bit my cheek, desperate for control.

Pulling her hand away, I pressed a kiss to her palm before reaching for a condom from the nightstand. Her bottom lip disappeared between her teeth as she watched me roll it on, her eyes dark and hungry. I stroked myself twice before lining up with her entrance and pushing inside.

Home.

Her legs wrapped around my hips, fingers threading into my hair as I pressed my lips to hers. I rocked into her slow and deep, savoring every gasp, every moan, every shudder of pleasure. We moved together in a rhythm only we knew, our bodies in perfect sync, drawing each other higher.

I loved her like this—uninhibited, unburdened by the world outside. Just us. Just this.

She was always beautiful—sharp-witted, stubborn, unapologetically her—but watching her unravel beneath me was like witnessing a masterpiece in motion.

Every hitch in her breath painted colors across an unseen canvas. Bright contrasts with every flex of her muscles. Deep shadows with every arch of her body. And when she shattered, when she reached the peak, the final highlights were added—completing the picture, bringing it to life.

Wrapping my arms around her, I pulled her against me as I sat back, her thighs tightening around my hips as she settled into my lap.

"Yesss, Taylor," she moaned, her head falling back as she rocked against me, slow and deliberate. "Fuck, you feel so good."

"Eyes on me, Mags."

Time seemed to slow to a crawl when she met my gaze.

There was something to be said about fucking, about getting lost in raw need, letting go of everything else. But there was just as much to be said about this—slowing down, pouring every ounce of love into someone, letting them feel it.

And there was so much love in her eyes, it stole the breath from my lungs.

Her forehead rested against mine as I held her to me, quickening my pace, matching every roll of her hips with an upward thrust. Her breaths turned to broken little gasps, her fingers digging into my shoulders as we climbed this peak together.

"Come for me, baby," I pleaded when I felt her walls begin to flutter around me.

With a few more rocks of her hips, she shattered in my arms, my name a cry from her lips. Her body trembled against mine, and with a groan into her neck, I followed.

I'd follow that woman anywhere.

To the edge of pleasure. Out of this town. To the other side of the world.

It didn't matter.

Anywhere she went, I'd be right beside her.

34

Brace for impact

Magnolia

"I'M NOT AN INVALID," Aunt Evie sniped, swatting at me as I tried to help her out of the front seat of Taylor's Bronco.

"No, of course not. You only got hit by a car and are recovering from surgery, but what do I know?" I drawled, fixing her with an exasperated stare.

"Magpie, just because you're datin' a doctor doesn't mean you get to treat me like I'm your patient," she huffed.

"Oh, well, by all means. Let's consult a doctor. Taylor?"

"Don't drag me into this," he exclaimed, raising his hands in surrender.

"Smart man," Aunt Evie muttered—but the words barely left her lips before a wince stole across her face as she shifted.

"You gonna keep being difficult?" I deadpanned, crossing my arms over my chest.

She'd always been stubborn, always insisted on doing things her own way, in her own time—and she wonders where I got it from. But even I'd learned when to lean on people, that I couldn't do everything on my own. That it was okay to ask for help. Sure, it might have taken the man standing behind me to show me that I didn't have to shoulder every burden myself, but that wasn't the point.

She was being more stubborn than a mule.

Aunt Evie and I locked eyes, neither of us flinching, blinking, or damn near breathing as we silently willed the other to back down.

"Come on, ladies, it's Christmas," Taylor said brightly, clearly trying to defuse the standoff.

"Shush, you," we snapped in unison.

At least we were aligned there.

I raised my brows, barely hiding my smirk as my aunt's face twisted in pain when she attempted to turn in her seat. With a groan of frustration—and a scathing glare at Taylor when he chuckled—she finally caved and accepted my help.

"It's a Christmas miracle," I whispered, carefully holding her elbow and supporting her shoulder just as the physical therapist had instructed before her discharge.

I let her set the pace, only moving when she did, while Taylor hovered behind me just in case.

Mother above, if I didn't already love that man, I would now. He was always a strong, steady presence at my side—never overstepping, but always there when I needed him.

Aunt Evie sighed in relief, her head falling back as her feet finally settled on solid ground, shoulders dropping from her ears. But when she opened her eyes again, confusion flitted across her face. "What's with all the cars?"

"Jae and her parents are here. I asked them to bring some food over since I, uh, haven't really had time to cook for Christmas with everything else going on."

The sun dipped below the horizon, a velvety blanket of deep purple stretching across the sky as night settled in. In the fading light, I saw the shimmer of unshed tears brimming in my aunt's eyes.

"Aunt Evie? Are you okay? Are you in pain?"

Glassy green eyes—so much like my mother's—met mine. "I'm fine, Magpie. You just... you have so many good people in your life, and I am so very proud of you."

My breath caught. My mouth opened, but no words came out.

Silence stretched between us, my vision blurring as my own tears welled. How I had any left after the last few weeks, I wasn't sure. But I couldn't deny she was right.

I did have good people in my life.

Not many, maybe. Probably not even enough to count on both hands. But I'd rather have a few I could trust than a hundred I couldn't.

"Y'all ready to head in?" Taylor asked quietly, his hand a warm brace against my back as the winter wind sent a chill through me.

I nodded, offering my aunt my arm for support as we made our way toward the house, the sound of laughter filtering out onto the porch as we climbed the steps.

"Aunt Evie!" Meredith screeched when she saw us, her face lighting up as she practically skipped down the hall toward the door. "You're here! Guys, they're here!" she hollered back toward the kitchen.

"Where else would I be, Gator?" Aunt Evie asked with a laugh, stepping inside just as my sister pulled her into a careful but eager hug.

"Gator?" Taylor murmured as I stepped past him, his brow winging up so comically high I nearly choked.

I tried—and failed—to stifle my laughter, my hand flying to my mouth as a snort slipped free. "Oh, cowboy. My sister may look like sunshine and rainbows, but she is the definition of 'fuck around and find out.'"

"Elaborate," he demanded, eyes narrowed in amused disbelief as we lingered outside the kitchen, the clink of dishes and murmured conversation drifting toward us.

Keeping my voice low, I explained, "Mer has a temper. A bad one. When she was little, she'd go off like a bomb over the smallest things—throwing herself on the ground, rolling around—"

"Like an alligator," he guessed, lips twitching at the corners.

"Exactly. She's reined it in over the years, but there are certain things that make her fuse extra short."

"Such as?" he asked, palming my waist and pulling me into him.

"Such as her sisters being mistreated. Bigots. Idiots. Men being all of the above simultaneously."

Taylor hummed, leaning closer. "And should I be worried about your sister?"

His words were a whisper over my lips, sending goosebumps cascading over my skin. Would there ever be a time when he *didn't* affect me like this?

Mother above, I hoped not.

"No, of course not," I breathed, pressing myself against him and winding my arms around his neck as I pushed up onto my toes. Lips hovering a hair's breadth from his, I whispered, "You have to worry about *both* of them."

His arms tightened around me, our smiles mirroring each other's. "It's a good thing you love me, then."

"It's a good thing they know *you* love *me*."

His mouth had barely brushed mine when Jaelyn poked her head into the hall.

"Are y'all just gonna hover out here all night, or actually come in and help us get this holiday started?"

"Your timing is impeccable as always, Jae. Thank you," Taylor groaned, resting his forehead against mine.

Chuckling, I turned over my shoulder. "We'll be right there."

·)●((·

"Superhero!" Maddie shouted.

"Pretty sure he's a villain," Taylor responded, quirking a brow in my sister's direction.

"Watch it, doctor boy. That's my husband you're talking about."

"Loki," I said with a laugh, flipping the phone downward just as the timer dinged, signaling the end of the round. "Oh, cool. I got thirteen out of fifteen."

"I still don't understand how you missed Magneto," Maddie huffed, leaning back in her chair.

"You said 'magnet,' you can't do that," I retorted, passing the phone to Meredith before sinking onto the couch next to Taylor with a contented sigh.

He immediately wrapped an arm around my shoulders and pulled me into him, pressing a kiss to the top of my head.

"You sure you don't need to be at your parents' house?" I asked.

"I'm right where I want to be, sunshine. Plus, they went up to Baton Rouge with Addy to celebrate with Colin's family."

"If you're sure."

His response was another kiss—just a quick peck, nothing crazy—but it still made my toes curl.

"If you two are quite finished, I'd like to kick your ass now," Meredith scolded, bouncing on the balls of her feet in front of the fireplace like she was about to step into a boxing ring.

"By all means, do carry on," Taylor said in a mock English accent, waving his hand dramatically in her direction.

"Pretty sure you have a death wish, cowboy."

I chuckled when Meredith cut him a scathing glare, but before I could shout my first clue to my sister, the doorbell chimed through the house.

Pushing up from the cushion, I glanced at Meredith and said, "Bitten by an eight-legged creepy crawly."

"Spider-Man!"

"I've got the door. Y'all keep going."

"You want me to come with?" Taylor asked as I rounded the corner of the couch.

"No, it's okay. Should only be a minute."

I laughed to myself as the sound of clues being shouted at my sister followed me down the hall, each one more ridiculous than the last. But my steps slowed as I took in the person standing on the other side of the screen door.

"Magnolia, how ya doin', honey?"

Geraldine—one of the oldest gossips in town—stood there, her bright blue eyes flicking nervously over my face.

"I'm fine, Ms. Geraldine. What... what can I do for you?" I asked, pushing open the screen door and wrapping my cardigan tighter around my torso.

"I heard about your dear ol' auntie. Awful, just awful." She sighed, shifting the covered dish in her hands. "And, well, I got to thinkin', what with everything y'all have been dealin' with, and, well... Here. I made y'all some crawfish étouffée. Freezer and reheat instructions are taped to the top."

My limbs froze as I stared down at the dish she was trying to hand me. "Why?"

She heaved a heavy breath, a sorrowful smile barely lifting the corners of her mouth.

"We take care of our own down here. I know we haven't always been the most welcoming, and I know I've said some things I shouldn't've. But you ladies are just as much a part of this community as anyone else. And I'm sorry if we... if *I* ever made you feel differently."

"Everything okay, Mags?" Taylor's voice carried down the hall, his footsteps growing closer as I held the old woman's gaze.

"Yeah," I whispered before repeating the word louder. I hesitated before taking the dish from Geraldine with a soft, "Thank you."

It was still warm, the scent of spicy crawfish enveloping me, making my mouth water despite the fact that I was far too full.

"Hey there, Ms. Gerry," Taylor said smoothly as he wrapped his arms around my shoulders.

"Why, Taylor Hallows, good to see you, dear."

"You too."

"Well, I'm gonna skedaddle. Don't wanna take up too much of y'all's night. Y'all have a Merry Christmas."

"You too, Ms. Geraldine," Taylor and I responded in unison—his tone chipper while mine still carried the weight of confusion.

We watched as she made her way back to her car, and once she was safely inside, Taylor asked, "What was that about?"

"She brought us étouffée."

"That was nice."

"That was... confusing."

"Either way, it smells good, and it's cold out here. Let's go back in."

I nodded slowly, my eyes still glued to the taillights of her car as it disappeared down the driveway. Never in a million years did I think someone from town would willingly show up at our house, let alone bring us food—despite that being a deep-rooted Southern tradition when someone in the community was sick or struggling.

And yet, here we were.

As I stood there, something warm settled in my stomach.

Maybe there was hope for this town yet.

The rest of the night was full of laughter and games, and a lot more people showing up at the house with dish after dish until our fridge and freezer looked like we were stockpiling casseroles for the apocalypse.

I was floored.

Flabbers completely *gasted* each time the door swung open to reveal another neighbor bearing food.

Pies and cakes littered the counters. Jambalaya, gumbo, and breakfast casseroles had been packed into every available cold space, and what didn't fit got divided up between the Jacksons and Taylor.

Needless to say, no one needed to cook for a while.

As midnight rolled around, we all huddled by the front door, slipping on coats and contributing to the Southern goodbyes that always took thirty minutes longer than they should.

They started somewhere in the house then transitioned out the door, where another ten to fifteen minute conversation would commence. Then they moved to the porch.

Then someone insisted on walking you to your car, and the process would repeat until someone finally caved and left.

So far, we'd only made it to the foyer, and we'd been there for about fifteen minutes.

"Well, Evie, I think you're set on food for a while," Josie—Jaelyn's mom—laughed as she slipped her arms into her coat and stepped through the door that Mr. Bill was holding open with an impatient look on his face.

"Too much food. You and Bill sure you don't want to take anything else home?" my aunt asked, her voice taking on a pleading tone as we all followed them out onto the porch.

"Honey, our ice chest is already full, and so is the icebox at home. But I'm sure Doctor Hallows over there would love to take more."

Josie arched her brows at Taylor.

I watched as he fumbled over how to respond—we'd already filled an entire ice chest with food for his place, and I wasn't sure his fridge could hold much more.

Taylor palmed the back of his neck, his face flushing. "Uhh... of course... sure. I'd love to take some more off your hands."

The women erupted into laughter, my aunt clutching her slinged arm closer to her chest as she shook with mirth.

When they finally calmed, Josie kissed Aunt Evie's cheek, embraced each of my sisters, then turned to me.

She wrapped me in a warm hug before grinning up at Taylor. "You're a sweetheart," she cooed, patting his cheek as she passed on her way to the front door.

We all stood on the porch, watching as the Jacksons loaded into their car, then waved as they drove away—until their taillights became nothing but a blip in the darkness.

I was *dog tired*. Bone weary.

All I wanted was to crawl into bed and sleep for ten-plus hours.

And now that everyone had gone, I could finally do just that.

But as I turned toward the door, Taylor caught my wrist and tugged me into his arms. Perched on the railing, he kissed me long and slow.

"Hi, sunshine."

"Hiya, cowboy."

"A lot of people showed up for y'all tonight."

"They did. It was a little weird, but also... nice? I've never really felt like I belonged here. Let alone that people cared."

"And now?"

"Now... I don't know. It's hard to process when you've basically been a pariah all your life. But I guess it's nice to know that there are people in this town who actually have my family's back."

"Aren't you glad you didn't curse the whole town?" he asked, a cheeky smile tugging at his lips.

"Taylor!"

"What? Too soon?" He laughed.

"Hardy har har," I groaned, letting my head fall against his shaking chest as I blew out a heavy breath. Taylor pressed a kiss to my crown, then nudged my chin up so I had no choice but to look into his eyes.

My lanta. It was like willingly getting lost at sea when I stared into those sapphire blues.

"I love you, sunshine."

"I love you, too."

I don't think I'd ever tire of seeing his face light up like a Fourth of July fireworks show when I said those three little words. It happened every single time, and every single time, my heart flipped.

"Come home with me. *Stay* with me."

"You... you want me to move in?"

"If you want just a drawer and a toothbrush first, we can do that. But I want you in that house, Magnolia. I want it to really, truly be *our* home. I may have bought it because you liked it, but it doesn't feel right when you're not there. I want to wake up to you every morning and fall asleep with you every night. But we go at your pace, baby. I don't want to push you into—"

"Yes," I said swiftly, cutting him off.

"Yes? You're... you're sure?"

His eyes widened with excitement, and as I nodded, tears welled in my own. I pressed my lips to his—hard, insistent—before pulling back just enough to whisper, "Never been more sure of anything in my life. I love you. I just need to say bye to everyone first."

"Bye!" my sisters and aunt hollered in unison from inside the house.

"I will not miss the lack of privacy!" I yelled back, though I couldn't help but laugh when they answered with a chorus of, "Love you!" before the front door clicked shut.

A smile permanently affixed to my face, I turned back to the man I loved more than I ever could have fathomed. "Take me home, cowboy."

+)●((+

One month later...

I stood behind the counter, absently fingering the necklace Taylor had surprised me with for Christmas, a goofy smile on my face. It was beautiful, and when he'd explained the meaning behind it, I'd cried... *again.*

Mother above, I was tired of crying.

But how could I not, when the man I loved had told me, *"It's called a sunset pendant, so now you can carry our sunsets with you wherever you go."*

Needless to say, I'd swooned—hard. Then I'd fussed at him when I realized exactly how much he'd spent on it.

I let my mind drift as I watched customers chatter in the booths and browse the display cases. The grand reopening of *CharCutie* was going off without a hitch. I'd arrived to a line at the front door, and cheers erupted as I flipped the sign to *open*. We'd been slammed since, and I'd never been more grateful for this small town.

I'd never been the one they rallied behind, and finally being on the receiving end of that kind of support? It was a feeling like no other.

"We're out of mini king cakes, Mags," Jaelyn said, rounding the counter with a fresh tray of pastries.

"Already? It's only one o'clock."

"They sell like hot cakes… Pun intended."

We both laughed, but mine died off as the bell chimed over the door.

Sophie Larson had only set foot in my shop once in the three years I'd been open. And yet, there she was, looking no happier than I was to have her there.

"Sophie," I greeted in my cherriest customer service voice.

She rolled her eyes, scoffing, but took another step forward as the bell chimed again behind her.

"Sophie Marie Larson," a woman scolded as she stepped inside, and that's when I realized exactly who she was—her *mother*.

And the way she was glaring at her daughter made me want to burst into laughter.

Sophie was Taylor's age—thirty-four—so seeing her get reprimanded like a misbehaving teenager was *comical*, to say the least. I risked a glance down at Jaelyn, who was crouched behind the pastry case, eyes wide, lips curled inward to keep from laughing.

"What's happening?" she whispered.

"I don't know—"

"Go. Now." Mrs. Larson shoved her daughter forward.

"Shit, she's coming this way."

"Brace for impact," Jae joked, ducking lower and busying herself with the pastry case.

Sophie huffed as she approached the counter, and I prayed to the triple goddesses that I could keep from cracking up. I had no idea what was happening, but I had a distinct feeling I needed a bucket of popcorn to fully enjoy it.

"Sophie. Mrs. Larson. How can I help you ladies today?"

"Hi, sweetie. I'll grab some pastries in a bit, but first..." She nudged her daughter again, and I could *feel* the way Sophie's skin must have been crawling under her mother's scorching glare.

"My daughter has something she'd like to say to you."

Sophie took a deep breath, glaring at me as she ground out, "I'm. Sorry."

"Oh, I don't think so. I raised you better than that, missy. You do it right, and you do it right now."

Sophie's eyes widened, jaw tightening, but when she spoke again, her voice was less strained. "Magnolia, I'd like to *apologize* for my part in making you feel *unwelcome* in this town. I was raised better than that, and bullying is wrong."

There was no way in *hell* I believed a single word. But watching her squirm? *That* was repentance enough.

Apparently not for her mother, though.

"Sophie," Mrs. Larson ground out, her face turning a mottled shade of red.

Jaelyn snickered behind the counter, and I shot her a quick glare before either woman could catch it. They were locked in some silent argument, and it was clear Sophie was losing.

"Mrs. Larson, it's quite alright. We're both adults, and I believe we can move on from this and be cordial."

"You're such a sweetie."

"Thank you, ma'am. Now, what can I get you today? We just put out some fresh croissants."

Oh, this day just keeps getting better and better, I thought as I helped Mrs. Larson with her selections.

Not only was my business thriving again, but I'd gotten an—albeit *forced*—apology from Sophie, and I'd seen Kyle picking up litter on the side of the road in a bright orange vest on my way in this morning.

After *a lot* of convincing, Aunt Evie had pressed charges once she got the police report after the holidays. Kyle was now under house arrest and serving an ungodly amount of community service hours.

A lesser sentence than he *should* have received, but at least for once, he wasn't getting off scot-free.

I waggled my fingers at Sophie as she and her mother left. As soon as the door shut behind them, Jaelyn and I burst into laughter.

"I thought her head was going to explode," she wheezed, tears leaking down her cheeks.

"Highlight of my *life*. Never in my wildest dreams did I imagine that happening."

"I still don't understand why you didn't just curse her ass. She deserves at least that after all the bullshit she's put you through."

I shouldn't have been surprised that she *wasn't* surprised when I finally told her I was a witch. But now that the proverbial cat was out of the bag, I was thrilled that I didn't have to hide that part of myself anymore. It was like I could finally breathe now that all of the people closest to me knew... *all* of me.

Ever since I'd told her, she'd asked me time and time again why I didn't use my magic more. She'd gaped at me when I told her that magic was a gift, not a shortcut, when she'd asked why I did things the 'normal' way and not what she considered the 'fun' way. But the question she asked repeatedly was why I hadn't sought revenge on the people who'd wronged me in town.

"Vengeful magic comes with a price, Jae. And it's much too high for my blood."

She huffed but grabbed her tray and headed toward the kitchen.

"Don't forget we're closing early today! I have to go—"

"I know," she drawled. "Geez, mom."

"Not yet," I joked, smiling as I turned to greet the next customer.

Taylor

Smoke billowed from the chimney as I pulled into the driveway, and a smile formed instantly. Coming home to Magnolia was the highlight of my day. Getting to relax, to just *be* in a shared space without watchful eyes, felt like a weight off my shoulders.

She'd been gradually moving in over the last month, adding personal touches to every room in the house. Her sister's books had their own dedicated shelf in the living room. Her clothes were slowly encroaching on my side of the walk-in closet. She'd rearranged the kitchen at least three times before deciding the original layout was best. We'd even hosted a few family dinners.

Every day with her was a new adventure, and I couldn't wait to see what else was in store.

"Mags," I called when I walked through the door.

Instead of her voice, I was met with excited yips and laughter.

"Shhh, you have to be quiet," she whispered, amusement lacing her tone.

Thoroughly intrigued, I dropped my bag by the door and made my way toward the living room. But I didn't see her.

"Sunshine?"

"Arf, arf, arf!"

"Hush, you're going to get us in trouble," she giggled.

Rounding the couch, I spotted a pair of slippered feet poking out from the other side. Chuckling, I closed the distance.

"Baby, what are you—" The words stalled in my throat as I took her in. Magnolia was sprawled on the floor, holding onto a very wiggly—*was that a puppy?*

"What do you think?" she asked nervously, struggling to contain the spotted creature in her arms as it whined and scrambled to get free.

"It's a Catahoula," she added quickly, as if I might protest. "Is that okay? You never mentioned a specific breed, so I just went with the cutest one I could find, and—"

"It's *mine*?" I asked, awed, crouching down beside her.

"He's yours, yes."

She loosened her grip, and the little fur ball immediately bolted toward me, jumping up and pawing at my chest, desperate to lick my face. I laughed until my stomach ached. He was mostly gray, with black spots along his back, a sable-colored snout and paws, and sky-blue eyes.

He was perfect.

"You got me a dog," I breathed through my laughter, trying—and failing—to calm the puppy. "Does he have a name?"

She shook her head. "I thought you'd want to name him."

Grabbing his face between my hands, I rubbed his head and watched as his velvety ears flopped around.

"Gumbo."

"You want gumbo?" she asked, already turning toward the kitchen. "I think we still have some in the freezer."

"No, baby." I grinned. "The dog. His name is Gumbo."

"Whatever you say, babe," she laughed. But as her smile faded, something flickered in her eyes.

Suspicion tightened my chest. "What is it?" I asked, drawing out the words.

"Do you like your puppy?"

"Of course I do... Why?"

"Because that's not the only surprise I have."

Something about the way she said it—*hesitant, nervous*—made the hairs on my neck stand on end.

She took a step back.

Memories of New Year's Eve flashed through my mind. We'd both been drunk, a little careless... *Surely not*—

She *could* be.

I was a doctor, for fuck's sake. How had I not noticed?

"Magnolia, are you..." My gaze flicked to her abdomen. I swallowed—hard.

"What? *No!*" Her eyes widened. "Oh my lanta. *Hold, please.*"

She bolted from the room, disappearing down the hall toward our bedroom.

My heart thundered as I tried to recall when her last period had been—just in case. But when she reappeared, peeking into the living room from behind the wall, my anxiety over an unplanned pregnancy shifted to... curiosity?

"You ready?" she asked.

"As I'll ever be, I guess."

Blowing out a slow breath, she stepped into view. Nestled in her arms was a tiny, striped *kitten*.

"Meet... I don't know her name yet. She just showed up today."

"A *cat?*"

"Technically, it's a *familiar* in cat form, but yes."

"What about the cats at the manor?"

She padded over to where I still sat on the floor, Gumbo curled up in my lap, snoring.

"Meowfoy and Hermeownie are *family* familiars. They stay at the manor." She glanced down at the kitten. "And this little girl found me. *Here.* And since I'm moving in, I guess the Mother decided to gift me with my own."

"You haven't named her yet?" I carefully stretched out a hand, stroking a gentle path down the kitten's back. She was tiny, gray and black with faint tiger stripes and a pink nose. I might not have been a cat person, but even I melted a little over the tiny fluff ball.

"I haven't, but since you named the puppy Gumbo, I think I'll name her... Filé."

"Filé and Gumbo." I huffed a laugh. "If those aren't the most Southern pet names I've ever heard, I don't know what is."

"You're *sure* you're okay with this? Pets are a big responsibility."

"They're perfect, Magnolia. *Thank you.*"

"Okay, good." She let out a relieved breath. "Because I've already set up their food bowls and bedding... and spent way too much on toys."

"Of *course* you did." I chuckled, gently shifting Gumbo onto the floor before leaning in to press my lips to hers.

She sighed against my mouth, then whispered, "Hold that thought." Pulling back, she stepped toward the window and placed the kitten in her chair.

I stood as well, wrapping my arms around her the moment she turned back to me.

"You have me completely charmed, Magnolia Bellevue."

"The feeling is mutual, Taylor Hallows." She slid her hand into mine, backing toward the hallway. "Now, why don't we take advantage of the kids being asleep *before* they keep us up all night?"

I grinned. "I thought you'd never ask."

Epilogue
Magnolia

"Thank you," I said with a bemused smile as someone handed me a beautiful blush-colored peony. I quirked a confused brow at Taylor, but he just shrugged in response, looping his arm around my shoulders as we continued walking through town square.

The sun was setting, painting the sky in vivid shades of orange and pink, turning the clouds a stunning lavender that had me seriously contemplating a hair color change.

"That was odd," I murmured once we were far enough away.

"Yeah?" There was an edge of nervousness to his tone.

"Taylor," I drawled, stopping abruptly on the sidewalk and turning toward him. "What's going on?"

"What? Nothing." His hand tightened on mine. "Come on, we're going to be late for our dinner reservation."

Narrowing my gaze, I let him guide me forward, suspicion prickling at the edges of my mind.

The day had been absolutely amazing—full of fun little surprises, from my favorite breakfast to a trip to the *Audubon Zoo* in New Orleans—but there had been an undercurrent of *something* I couldn't quite put my finger on. At first, I chalked it up to exhaustion; Taylor had been working a string of graveyard shifts, our hours completely opposite to the point that we barely saw each other in passing. I'd been *thrilled* to learn he had a few days off before switching back to days. Even more so when he told me he had planned *an entire day* for us.

We could have stayed home, snuggled up with our two little fur babies, wrapped in each other and ignoring the world, and it still would have been a perfect day. But the fact that he'd planned every detail—apparently down to the *minute*—had my heart skittering in my chest, my knees weak, and the need to climb the man like a tree nearly impossible to ignore.

A cool breeze kissed my cheeks, sneaking past the collar of my coat, and a shiver wracked my body. Wrapping my arms around Taylor's waist, I huddled in close to absorb his warmth. Was this the best way to walk with someone? No, probably not—I had to make a conscious effort not to trip over either of our feet. But the heat radiating off him, the security I felt when he tightened his hold on me? Well worth the tripping hazard.

"Oh, look at you two," Mrs. Dorothy cooed as she stepped out of the flower shop.

"Hey, Mrs. Dotty," we responded in unison.

Even a year later, it was still a smidge surreal to be on the receiving end of friendly smiles and warm welcomes from people who once seemed to abhor my presence.

"Those are pretty," I gestured toward her bouquet with a tilt of my chin, refusing to release Taylor and lose his warmth for even a second. January was always cold, but *Mother above,* this was ridiculous. I couldn't feel my nose anymore.

"Aren't they?" She brought the bundle to her nose, inhaling deeply before beaming at me. "Here, cher. You take one."

"What? No, Mrs. Dotty, that's okay. I don't—"

My words fell on deaf ears. She had already plucked a stem from her arrangement and was holding it out to me.

"It complements your other one quite nicely, don't you think?" she asked, something flickering in her brown eyes that I couldn't quite place.

"It does," I responded softly, taking the dark pink peony she offered and adding it to the other in my opposite hand.

What the hell is going on?

We said our goodbyes, and as Dorothy walked away, I turned my glare on Taylor. "You're up to something."

"Why would you think that?" he asked, a mischievous smile tugging at his lips as he pulled me closer and started walking again.

"Gee, cowboy. I don't know." I waved the flowers in front of his face.

"Maybe they're just being nice."

"Not likely."

"Never know, sunshine. Maybe they just wanted to share a pretty flower with a pretty lady."

"Maybe you're full of shit," I said with a laugh. His lips curled upward at the corners, amusement dancing in his eyes.

"I'm on to you, Hallows."

"Whatever you say, sunshine."

By the time we reached the restaurant, I had accumulated a grand total of *six* peonies, and every time Taylor looked at me, he burst into laughter. Not that I could blame him. I was pretty sure I had been stuck in a perpetual state of shock.

"What am I supposed to do with these?" I balked as I stepped through the doors of *Cypress on the Bayou*, awe swallowing the rest of my words.

I'd walked past the restaurant countless times but never stepped inside. Never had a reason to, since it was the *fanciest* place in town, and their prices were a tad out of my range for a casual dinner.

Which, apparently, this was *not.*

Rich, polished mahogany with gold and cream accents filled the space. Etched glass panels lined the area around the center bar, depicting the moss-draped trees our state was known for. The lights were dimmed—bright enough to see but low enough to create a warm, intimate ambiance. It was *gorgeous*, and the aromas wafting through the air had my mouth watering instantly.

Taylor merely shrugged in response to my question, letting the door swing shut behind him as he led me toward the hostess stand.

"Ah, Mr. Hallows. We have your table all set for you. If you'd both follow me."

Taylor laced his fingers through mine, tugging me along as we wove through the restaurant toward the back.

"Where are we going?" I asked in a hushed whisper.

Taylor stopped in front of the double doors leading to the kitchen. He pulled me out of the way as they swung shut behind the hostess, then cupped my face in his hands.

"Mags, baby. I need you to trust me." His thumbs brushed along my jaw. "Stop trying to figure out what's going on and just enjoy it. *Please.* You're making me nervous."

I bobbed my head and took a steadying breath.

"Good."

Taylor pressed his lips to mine, soft yet demanding in a way that turned my insides to liquid.

Was I hungry? Absolutely. My stomach felt like it would claw its way out of my body if I didn't feed it soon.

But as his mouth moved over mine, slow and languid, as his hands slid into the hair at the nape of my neck…

I was *famished* for him.

Taylor broke the kiss—far too soon, if you asked me—and grasped both my hands in his before backing through the swinging doors.

The kitchen noise engulfed me instantly. The symphony of orders being called, the rhythmic clatter of pans, the chorus of *yes, chef* warmed my heart. White-coated chefs moved with the effortless coordination of a dance, and the scent of sautéed garlic and fresh herbs filled my lungs.

"What do you think?" Taylor asked, allowing me a moment to take it all in before leading me to where the hostess stood waiting.

"This is amazing, Taylor."

The delicate scrape of wood against tile caught my attention as he pulled out my chair. I finally tore my gaze from the flurry of kitchen staff, only to freeze in place.

A vase of peonies—exactly like the ones in my hand—sat at the far edge of the table. Tea lights flickered along the crisp white linen, gold chargers and matching silverware marking our places.

"Holy shit, cowboy," I breathed, tears burning the backs of my eyes as I lifted a trembling hand to my mouth.

"Do you like it?" There was a nervous wobble to his words that made my heart clench.

I turned to meet his gaze, finding those sapphire blues shining with unshed tears of their own.

"I love it. Thank you."

+‧)❍((‧+

"I feel like a whale," I groaned dramatically as Taylor helped me out of the car when we got back home.

Dinner had been delicious... divine... honestly, I wasn't even sure. At some point, I was pretty sure I blacked out from the sheer explosion of flavors dancing over my taste buds. But now that we were home, all I wanted to do was curl up on the couch and pass the fuck out. I'd make it to bed eventually, I was sure—but the couch was closer, and the food coma was calling my name.

"Cutest whale I've ever seen," he chuckled, pulling me from the car and into his arms. "Did you have a good day?" he asked, pressing a kiss to my crown.

"It was the best day. Thank you, for everything." I pushed onto my toes, capturing his lips in a slow, lingering kiss. "I think I'm going to go die now, though. Death by food overload."

His chest vibrated against mine as he laughed, his hand trailing soothing lines up and down my spine.

"Do you think you could hold off on your coma for a little bit?" He released me and reached into the car for my vase of flowers. "I have one more surprise for you."

"Another one?" I squawked, in a very unladylike manner.

"Come on, I'll show you." Taylor held the vase in one arm and linked his opposite hand with mine. Interest thoroughly piqued, I followed—not that I wouldn't have anyway, considering I lived there and all.

"I don't think I'll ever get used to that," he mused as he stepped through the front door.

The enchantments I'd woven into the house tickled over my skin the second I crossed the threshold. It was the same welcoming sensation I felt every time I walked into the manor—like a warm embrace wrapping around me. The fact that Taylor could feel it, too, had me wondering if perhaps he had a witch somewhere in his bloodline.

"You will," I said with a shrug as I hung my coat on the rack beside the door. But when I turned back toward Taylor, all the nervousness I'd sensed from him earlier had magnified tenfold, radiating from every tense line of his body.

"Are you okay?" I asked, concern edging my words as I stepped forward and took his fidgeting hands.

"Yeah, yeah. Just, uh... close your eyes."

"Taylor, what's going—"

Pulling his hands free, he cradled my face between his palms and slanted his mouth over mine.

My stomach flipped, heart hammering as his lips brushed against mine, slow and teasing. Each kiss sent heat curling low in my belly, embers stoked to life with every press, every pull, every soft exhale of his breath.

Food coma be damned, I wanted him to devour me.

I gripped his shirt at his waist, tugging him closer, deepening the kiss. But just as quickly as he started, he pulled away, resting his forehead against mine. His breath mingled with mine, warm and ragged in our shared space.

"Why'd you stop?" I panted, running my hands up his chest, twisting my fingers into the fabric there.

"Later, baby. I promise." He was just as breathless as I was, his voice rough as he slid his hands down my arms, encircling my wrists as he gently pried my grip from his shirt. "One more surprise, and then I'm all yours."

"Promise?"

"Promise. Now, close your eyes, sunshine."

I searched his face once, twice, before finally sliding my eyes shut. My heart raced as every other sense sharpened in anticipation.

Step by step, I let him guide me forward, focusing on the steady cadence of his breath and the soft murmur of his voice as he navigated me around what I assumed was the living room furniture.

"Okay, stop here."

"Can I open my eyes?" I asked tentatively.

"Not yet."

Taylor exhaled slowly, then dropped my hands and breathed, "Illuminare."

Wait. Illuminare?

Latin? Why was he speaking Latin... *Wait. Why is he...?*

Before I could ask, light flickered beyond my closed eyelids, and I sucked in a sharp breath at the same time Taylor let out a stunned exhale.

"Holy shit, it worked," he muttered.

"Taylor, what the hell is going on?" My nerves spiked. Every second with my eyes shut felt like an eternity, and without his hands grounding me, anxiety clawed at my stomach.

The swirling kaleidoscope of butterflies settled as he clasped my hands again. Releasing a breath, he whispered, "Open your eyes, baby."

It took a moment for my vision to adjust, but when it did...

The gasp that tore from my throat echoed in the quiet.

Holy. Shit.

My hands flew to my mouth, smothering the hiccupping breaths as my gaze swept over the room in a daze.

White candles littered the floor, side tables, and mantle, their flames flickering delicately, casting the room in a warm, golden glow. Twinkling lights draped behind the window sheers, soft and ethereal. Pink rose petals blanketed the floor.

Tears burned my eyes, slipping down my cheeks as I finally met Taylor's gaze.

Sapphire blues shone with unshed emotion, tracking my every movement. He barely seemed to be breathing, waiting—watching—for my reaction.

I didn't know how he expected me to say anything.

Taylor had rendered me speechless more times than I could count. Turned my insides to goo with just a flick of his gaze.

But this?

Mother above...

There were no words for the love, the awe, the sheer overwhelming emotion coursing through my body. I wanted to jump up and down with excitement while simultaneously melting into a puddle of tears at the outpouring of love he constantly and *consistently* showed me in both words and actions.

His eyes held a silent plea, and I forced a breath through my trembling lips, dropping my hands as I willed my brain to form words.

"How... how did you do all this?"

Not exactly what I'd been aiming for, but okay then.

"How do you think?" He chuckled, though the nervous edge remained. "Magic."

"Ah... okay. Umm... You gotta help me out here, cowboy." My voice quivered, matching the shaking of my hands. My damn knees felt moments away from giving out.

"Right." Taylor exhaled, stepping closer, grasping my hands between his. "Magnolia—"

A hiccupping sob slipped free, cutting him off. I tipped my head back, staring at the ceiling to get some sort of grip on my emotions.

But when I met his gaze again, the love shining so brightly in his eyes nearly undid me.

"You are by far the most incredible woman I have ever had the privilege of knowing. You're strong, fierce, kind, and beautiful, inside and out. Not a second goes by that you're not on my mind. Not a single thing that doesn't remind me of you in some way. You're in the air I breathe. You're in every thought. You fill every dream."

"Taylor," I sighed, another sob wracking my chest.

Switching to hold both my hands in one of his, he used the other to swipe away the tears streaming down my cheeks.

"Let me get this out, baby. Please."

I nodded, watching as his own tears slipped free. His lower lip trembled as he took a steadying breath.

"Being with you is like seeing the world in color for the first time after a lifetime of black and white. You've flipped my world upside down. And it would be the greatest joy of my life to spend the rest of it with you."

Oh, shit. It's happening.

I gasped as Taylor slowly sank to one knee. It was as if my brain hadn't fully registered what *exactly* was happening. Like it was in denial—even with all the flowers, candles, lights, and gloriously beautiful profession of love—until I saw him kneeling before me.

Breathing felt impossible.

It all but stopped when he pulled a ring box from his suit jacket pocket.

In. Out. Repeat.

My heart slammed against my ribs as he flipped the lid open. But I didn't bother looking. It could have been a damn Ring Pop and I would have said yes.

"You're shaking," I whispered.

"So are you," he murmured, voice cracking.

"Magnolia—"

"Yes. A thousand times yes!" I shouted, tears blurring my vision before free-falling down.

He blinked. "You didn't even let me ask," he said with a chuckle.

"Shit. Sorry."

"Magnolia Lynn Bellevue, will you—"

"Yes."

Laughing, he shook his head. "Would you let me ask the damn question, woman?"

I bit my cheek and watched as Taylor visibly relaxed. Curling my lips inward, I nodded my head to signal that he could continue, and I wouldn't interrupt again... hopefully.

Let's be honest, my brain and mouth tended to do what they wanted when I was overwhelmed.

"Magnolia Lynn Bellevue..." he paused, raising his eyebrows at me in expectation, but I managed to keep my mouth closed. "Love of my life... would you do me the honor of becoming my wife?"

"Yes!" I screeched, launching myself into his arms and slamming my lips to his as we tumbled backward onto the floor.

"I love you, so much," I breathed when we came up for air.

"I love you, too, *Mrs.* Bellevue."

"Hallows," I amended, brushing the tip of my nose against his.

"Yeah?"

"Yeah."

The End

Also by Jessica Hoffa

Gems of Ixora Duet

Complete Series:
Of Storm and Emerald
Of Blood and Garnet

Witches of Bellevue

Charmed, I'm sure
Book two (Spring 2026)
Book Three (Summer 2026)

Acknowledgements

Sweet baby cheeses, here we go again.

To my READERS, whether you just found me or you've been here since Of Storm and Emerald, thank you for reading Magnolia and Taylor's story. This book, and series as a whole means so much to me, and wouldn't have happened if it weren't for each and every one of you. I am eternally grateful for that. Every time you open a book, you breathe life into the characters and give the story the wings it needs to fly. So thank you. Thank you for choosing my book. For being the air in my characters' lungs, and for making it soar.

To my ARC team, thank you so much for everything!

DELYNDA, my favorite trash panda bestie. I would not be where I am without you. You've been with me since before I even started writing OSAE, and have helped me learn and grow as an author. Thank you for being there for me through every up and down of this process, especially during this book. You truly are one of the best, and I am so lucky to have you in my corner. Thank you for talking through scenes with me—and caring about Magnolia's groceries when I was too excited to get through the picnic. For telling me to 'slow my roll' when I panic spiraled over timelines for books I hadn't even started yet, and for just being you. I love you, sunshine!

SYDNE, my favorite chaos gremlin and recipient of the most narrow chicken eyes. Thank you for everything you do. Whether it's commiserating mom life, or characters going off script, you've been there for me through it all. You've helped me grow as an author, been there for me every step of the way, and have talked me off more than one cliff—while simultaneously shoving me off another in your own books. You are my sister at heart, and I am so very grateful to have you in my life.

To CHRISTINE, KIRSTEN, and ALEXIS. My G.R.I.T.S. girls. You ladies have been with me for so long, I don't remember what my life was like without you. Y'all are the inspiration behind so much in not only this book, but in every female friendship I write. Thank you for being there for me through everything, regardless of the time or distance. I love all of you to the moon and back.

MOM, where would I be without you? I certainly would not have "ZydeGeaux" if it weren't for you. You have always been my hero, a giant inspiration, and one of the strongest people I know. Not only do you tell me that I can do anything that I put my mind to, but you show me that it's possible. That it doesn't matter how late you start, just as long as you start. Thank you for being one of the biggest hype people for my books, for recommending it to anyone you think will read it, and for being excited to see what I write next. Your support means more than you know, and I am so grateful that you're in my corner. I love you.

MAKENZIE and LORELAI. My two beautiful girls. Thank you for being patient while mommy followed her long time dream. You won't know it, but you two are all throughout this book. In name, in sass, and stubborn attitudes. It's because of you that I finally had the courage to pursue this dream, and I hope that I will make you proud...just never read it. I don't think I'd survive that. I love you both more than anything, and remember that you can do anything that you set your mind to.

KEGAN. Love of my life and piece of my soul. I would not, COULD not, have done this without you. Thank you for your unwavering support in everything that I do, and for making sure that I follow every dream and crazy idea that I have. Thank you for letting me fangirl at you over my own characters. For letting me become a hermit when I needed to work out chapters or edit my manuscript. Thank you for hyping up my book to guys who would probably never read it, but you have somehow convinced them that they need to. Thank you for letting me spue quotes at you that were completely out of context, and for nodding along like you knew exactly what I was talking about, or laughing purely because I couldn't stop. You are more than I could have every hoped for, and I will never be able to thank you enough.

Thank you for plying me with dried mango, coffee, and Dr. Pepper.

Thank you for everything. I love you so very much. ALWAYS. I pinky promise.

To my wonderful editor, SAMANTHA. Lord have mercy. Thank you for turning my ramblings into cohesive sentences. I am beyond lucky to have had you in my corner since Of Storm and Emerald, and I can't imagine working with anyone else. You are Queen of the chaos gremlins, and I am but one of your humble gremlins of chaos. Thank you for all that you do, and for being such a fun person to work with.

My books would not be what they are without you. And as always, In Sam We Trust.

A huge thank you to my amazing artists:

CHELSEA CHIRA, with Sterling Dawn Art & Design (@chelzd_art). Thank you for the beautiful cover and art you created for this book. You were a dream to work with, and I can't wait to create with you again.

STEFANY (@suusliks), thank you again for the amazing work you do. Thank you for bringing so many of my characters to life and for being a dream to work with.

About the author

As a lover of life and art, Jessica is constantly looking for the beauty in the world around her. She grew up in Louisiana, where Mardi Gras had its own season, good food and music were paramount, and there was beauty wherever you looked.

Since marrying her husband—a United States Navy sailor—she's lived in South Carolina, immersed herself in the cultures of Hawai'i, and embraced the cold of Washington. She and her husband have two beautiful daughters, a dog, and have recently added a cat to the mix. Though her life is uniformed chaos, a mix of highs and lows between deployments and homecomings, she wouldn't have it any other way.

Throughout Jessica's life, books have always been her safe haven, using the written word to escape to lands of mythical creatures and happily ever afters. It's what sparked her love of writing, what drove her to journal and craft short stories, and what eventually led her to publish her own.

When she's not reading, writing, or spending time with her family, she can usually be found crafting in one way or another. Whether it's painting, sewing, messing with clay, or trying something new, she's always looking for a creative outlet.

The beach and the bookstore are her happy places, tattoos are her therapy, and though she loves coffee, she could live off of Dr. Pepper. As a Louisiana native, she's a lover of spice...both in food and in her books.

For more information about the author and the books she writes, make sure you follow her on social media.

www.ingramcontent.com/pod-product-compliance
Lightning Source LLC
Chambersburg PA
CBHW020325010826
48973CB00005B/1124